STRONG VENGEANCE

A CAITLIN STRONG NOVEL

Jon Land

FORGE®

A TOM DOHERTY ASSOCIATES BOOK • NEW YORK

This is a work of fiction. All of the characters, organizations, and events portrayed in this novel are either products of the author's imagination or are used fictitiously.

STRONG VENGEANCE

Copyright © 2012 by Jon Land

All rights reserved.

A Forge Book
Published by Tom Doherty Associates, LLC
175 Fifth Avenue
New York, NY 10010

www.tor-forge.com

Forge® is a registered trademark of Tom Doherty Associates, LLC.

ISBN 978-0-7653-6838-6

Forge books may be purchased for educational, business, or promotional use. For information on bulk purchases, please contact Macmillan Corporate and Premium Sales Department at 1-800-221-7945 extension 5442 or write specialmarkets@macmillan.com.

First Edition: July 2012
First Mass Market Edition: July 2013

Printed in the United States of America

0 9 8 7 6 5 4 3 2 1

For Brown University Football
Then, now, forever
Ever true

ACKNOWLEDGMENTS

Welcome back to those who've been with me before and welcome to those visiting the world of Caitlin Strong for the first time.

I know I sound like a broken record with all those I need and want to thank but, hey, some names bear repeating, starting at the top with my publisher, Tom Doherty, and Forge's associate publisher, Linda Quinton, dear friends who publish books "the way they should be published," to quote my late agent, the legendary Toni Mendez. Paul Stevens, Justin Golenbock, Patty Garcia, and especially Natalia Aponte are there for me at every turn. Natalia's a brilliant editor and friend who never ceases to amaze me with her sensitivity and genius. Editing may be a lost art, but not here, and I think you'll enjoy all of my books, including this one, much more as a result.

Some new names to thank this time out, including Mireya Starkenberg, a loyal reader who, starting with this book, has offered her services to make sure I don't keep butchering the Spanish language. Booke Bovo, meanwhile, provided key insights into the design and function of offshore oil rigs that, as you're about to see and probably noticed from the cover, play a big role in the book you're about to read. My friend Mike

Blakely, a terrific writer and musician in his own right, taught me Texas first-hand and helped me think like a native of that great state. I've been writing about Special Forces operatives for years, but getting to know Doren "The Stranger" Ingram for a possible nonfiction book has given me fresh respect and insight into that world you will see front and center in these pages.

Check back at www.jonlandbooks.com for updates or to drop me a line. I'd be remiss if I didn't thank all of you who've already written or e-mailed me about how much you enjoyed the first three tales in the Caitlin Strong series. Rest assured this fourth one does not disappoint. That's a promise and to watch me keep it, turn the page and let's get started.

P.S. For those interested in more information about the history of the Texas Rangers, and to see where a lot of my info comes from, I recommend *The Texas Rangers* and *Time of the Rangers,* a pair of superb books by a great writer named Mike Cox, also published by Forge.

The strongest man in the world is he
who stands alone.

—HENRIK IBSEN,
An Enemy of the People, 1882

PROLOGUE

When Sam Houston was reelected to the presidency in December 1841, he saw the effectiveness of the Rangers and on January 29, 1842, approved a law that officially provided for a company of mounted men to "act as Rangers." As a result, 150 Rangers under Captain John Coffee "Jack" Hays were assigned to protect the southern and western portions of the Texas frontier. Houston's foresight in this decision proved successful in helping to repel the Mexican invasions of 1842, as well as shielding the white settlers against Indian attacks over the next three years.

—Legends of America:
Texas Legends: The Texas Rangers—Order Out of Chaos

"Give me our bearings, Mr. Jeffreys," Alfred Neal, captain of the *Mother Mary*, asked his first officer.

Jeffreys met Neal's gaze with his hooded eyes, then once more consulted his map in the light shed by a lantern hanging from a pole. "The fog's waylaid my direction, but we're steering on course, Captain."

The massive four-masted schooner creaked through the murky night, clumsily negotiating the Texas coast's swampy channels. Low-hanging cypress branches scraped at the multidecked galleon's sails, as gators darted back up on sodden land to avoid her lumbering menace. The fetid heat and stagnant air left the sweat to soak through the woolen jackets and cotton breeches of the men standing on the bridge, further attracting hungry mosquitoes fat with blood. The buzzing, blood-crazed swarms hung over the deck, thickening as the night wore on, perhaps having summoned more of their hungry brethren from the nearby shores.

"We'd best hope so," Captain Neal grunted and rotated his spyglass again. But the night yielded nothing through the dense fog other than stagnant water the color of tea from fallen leaves both clinging to the surface and lining the bottom. Besides the gators, packs of swimming nutria, and an occasional Night-Heron, the only signs of life the *Mother Mary* had encountered since nearing the Texas shores was an

Indian paddling an old pirogue carved out of a tree trunk. And that was precisely the point, given the nature of the cargo now contained in the hold below. That much Neal had fully expected; it was the passenger who had boarded at the same port that had taken the ship's captain by surprise.

"This is the right channel, sir," Jeffreys resumed, returning his map to his belt pouch. "I'm sure of it."

"You'd better be," came the voice of that passenger from the other side of the bridge. Both Neal and Jeffreys watched the squat bulbous form of the man who said his name was Quentin Cusp step into the thin light cast by the lantern. "It'll mark the end of your days on the seas if you're wrong. Both of you."

"I know I'm right by the smell, sir," First Officer Jeffreys told him.

"And a foul odor it is. Musty and sour."

Captain Neal almost told the man to smell himself. "I hate these damn waters," he groused, "and I hate whatever it is you're carrying there in your belt."

Cusp jerked both hands down to his waist, as if to protect whatever his belt was concealing.

"I've seen you checking the hidden pouch or whatever you've got sewn in there ever since we picked you up. A man of your standing wearing the same trousers these many weeks leaves anyone of sane mind wondering as well."

"Wondering isn't what I paid you so handsomely for, Captain," Cusp snapped, clearly offended.

Neal squared his shoulders and held his gaze on Cusp's belt. "Maybe you're a spy for the British. Maybe whatever secrets you're carrying brands me a traitor by association. I don't intend to hang for your crimes against the country, Mr. Cusp."

"I'm no spy, sir, and you were hired for your reputation for discretion as much as anything, Captain, apparently not well earned."

"You mean like those gunmen who cordoned off the dock while you waited for our skiff?"

Cusp looked surprised.

"My men are trained to be observant," Neal continued, "especially in dangerous waters."

Cusp started to turn away. "Then I hope they serve you just as well as sailors, Captain, so we might make port before the light gives us up. Because if we don't—"

Cusp's words halted when the ship shook violently. A scraping sound rose through the night, and the sailors on the bridge were jostled about as the *Mother Mary*'s hull shuddered and quaked before grinding to a halt that pushed tremors through the black water.

"You've run us aground, Mr. Jeffreys!" Neal said, swinging around. "Helmsman, bring us hard to port to catch the currents!"

"Aye-aye, Captain!" yelled back the helmsman, already fighting with the wheel.

"They'll be hell to pay for this, Captain," an enraged Cusp hissed, cutting off Neal's path to the wheel.

Neal pushed him aside, studying the utter blackness of the night. "Hell might be just where we are."

He continued moving to take the wheel himself, when a steel baling hook soared over the aft portion of the deck and jammed itself into the gunwale.

"My Lord," Cusp uttered, "what in the name of the Almighty is—"

"Sound the general alarm!" Neal ordered the mate nearest the bridge bell.

Even as the mate reached for the bell pull and began ringing, Neal glimpsed more baling hooks being hurled through the fog over the *Mother Mary*'s sides fore and aft, snaring on the gunwales. The ship's mate continued to work the bell, rousing the sleeping sailors from their berths as a succession of dark shapes climbed on board and dispersed in eerily synchronized fashion.

Pirates, Neal realized, wheeling about in search of some form of weapon to find only a handheld ax used to cut lines in a storm-wrought emergency. He twisted past the lumbering Cusp and dropped down to the main deck just as the fog parted to reveal a tall man with a thick, well-groomed mustache that hung over his upper lip standing ten feet before him.

"Best of the evening to you, Captain."

"I'll be damned," Neal managed.

"I see you recognize me," the pirate grinned.

"Jean Lafitte . . ."

Lafitte stepped further into the thin light shed by the bridge lantern. His black eyes twinkled. "At your service, Captain."

He was tall and sinewy thin with keen black eyes peering out from beneath a battered black felt hat angled low over his forehead. He wore a tight red jacket that clung to his bony shoulders and stopped just short of the baggy trousers wedged into his well-worn black leather boots.

His neck seemed too long for the rest of his body, almost birdlike, Neal thought, also noticing bands of stringy muscle lining that neck and extending all the way to a frayed bandanna neatly tied just over the collar of his low-hanging shirt.

"You dare mock me, Captain?"

Neal showed his ax. "Have at it then."

Ignoring the challenge, the pirate brushed back his coat to reveal both musket and sword at the ready.

Neal continued to brandish his blade. "You'll not have my ship!"

Lafitte glanced back through the fog at his well-armed pirates taking the first sailors to emerge from below prisoner. "It would seem it's already mine, so drop your weapon, Captain."

But Neal held fast, feeling the now moist ax handle quivering in his grasp.

"Your weapon, Captain."

"Never!"

"Then I'll save you for last, so you can watch all of your men die."

Neal felt his breath seize up, the pressure building in his chest. He'd let his ship be taken when at its most vulnerable, the pirates' measured assault too much to overcome. He released the ax and listened to it clamor to the deck.

"There'll be hell to pay this time, Lafitte."

"Why, Captain, didn't anyone tell you the import of slaves into any United States port is illegal? But rest easy, sir, my partner and I will be glad to take them off your hands," Lafitte said, turning at the sound of another man's approach.

In that moment, Neal noticed a shorter man draw even with Lafitte, a man who held a musket in hand and a knife sheathed to his belt instead of a sword.

"I know you," Neal said, squinting to better see through the night.

"I should think so," the man followed. "Our paths crossed when we beat down the bastards from England a few years back."

Neal's arms stiffened by his sides. "Jim Bowie?"

Bowie bowed slightly. "At your service, Captain. And you should be aware that Mr. Lafitte fought on our side as well."

"Until the governor of Louisiana put a five-hundred-dollar bounty on my head."

"Good thing you had an answer for him," Bowie said to the pirate.

"Indeed," Lafitte acknowledged, addressing Captain Neal. "I offered fifteen hundred for the governor's."

Neal knew that story, just as he knew Lafitte had been born to a poor family in France in 1780. A sharp-witted, quick study of a man when he accompanied his brother Pierre to the United States. There he set up shop in New Orleans to warehouse and disperse goods smuggled by his brother before turning to the pirate's life himself. By 1810 he was presiding over his initial band of outlaws on Grande Terre Island in Barataria Bay in the Gulf of Mexico. In 1814 the British offered the pirate a pardon, a captaincy in their navy, and $30,000 if he would aid them in an attack on New Orleans.

Lafitte refused and proceeded to inform the United States of the British plans, offering the services of the Barataria smugglers to the U.S. instead. He fought with General Andrew Jackson in the Battle of New Orleans and received a pardon by President James Madison for his efforts. When the end of war came, he moved his headquarters to Galveston Island off the Texas coast, where he established a colony called Campeche and went back to the pirate's life, partnering with Jim Bowie in running slaves through the newly established Texas territory.

"You might even call my friend Jean here a hero,"

Bowie quipped to Captain Neal, drawing broad laughter from Lafitte's assembled pirates, now holding the whole of the *Mother Mary*'s crew on their knees hostage, most still stripped down to their skivvies. "But we've little time to spare for such pleasantries," he cautioned. "We need to get the slaves loaded onto the *Goelette la Dilidente* before first light."

"Then bring me the first mate," Lafitte ordered.

Mr. Jeffreys, now with arms tied behind his back, rose to his feet and was dragged to Lafitte by one of his pirates.

"You'll do no harm to any of my crew, sir!" said Captain Neal, shoulders stiffening and chest protruding outward.

"Turn around," Lafitte ordered Jeffreys, ignoring him.

As the first mate of the *Mother Mary* swung around, Jim Bowie whipped out the knife that would one day bear his name. Before anyone could so much as breathe, the blade came down in a blur and sliced neatly through Jeffreys's bonds.

"Good work, cousin," Bowie said, as Jeffreys swung around to face him.

"Running the ship aground was nothing, cousin," Jeffreys said back, stretching his arms. "I still know these waters like the back of my hand."

"Traitor!" Neal shouted, launching himself into a feeble lunge Jean Lafitte effortlessly intercepted.

The pirate kicked Neal's legs out from under him, dropping the captain hard to the deck, and placed a booted foot atop his chest. "Don't tempt my graces further or next you'll feel the tip of my sword." Then Lafitte spotted Quentin Cusp hanging back in the darkness of the bridge, his bulbous form squeezed behind a thin abutment that left his stomach protruding. "And what have we here?"

"A passenger, nothing more," Neal gasped from the deck. "Paid for passage to our next port of call."

"Was access to the bridge part of his ticket?"

Lafitte gestured to a pair of his pirates who rousted Cusp and dragged him down from the bridge. "State your business, sir."

"I don't answer to you or any pirate," Cusp insisted dryly.

"Would you rather answer to the gators snoozing on the shoreline?"

Cusp swallowed hard, his bravado vanishing as quickly as that.

"I didn't think so." Lafitte noticed the thick belt enclosing Cusp's considerable waist. "And what have we here? Allow me to relieve you of your burden, sir."

And with that Lafitte stripped the belt free to reveal a thick, narrow pouch sewn into the back of its leather lining. "Now, let's see what the captain's good passenger has been hiding, shall we, Jim?"

Cusp feebly tried to pull free of his captors. "You'll live to regret this, I swear it! Know that I have powerful friends, pirate!"

"Do you now? Then I'm sure I've crossed paths with them before. And each time they emerged on the wrong side of the battle, as they will again," he said confidently, eyes twinkling and flashing a smile in the thin spray of lantern light.

Lafitte tore the pouch open at the seam and pulled the material apart to better inspect its contents.

"Mother of tears . . ."

Jim Bowie's mouth dropped at the sight, his eyes

bulging. He blinked several times, as if to reassure himself the sight was real.

"Are those what I think—"

"They are indeed," Lafitte answered before Bowie could finish, then looked back toward Cusp. "It would seem we're in the company of a man who stows his riches with his brains—just over his ass."

"I'm only a messenger," Cusp railed, remaining strident. "And if you don't leave them in my possession, my employers will kill you for sure."

Lafitte wrapped the pouch back up, careful not to disturb its contents. "They'll have to catch me first, won't they?"

"And catch you they will. You can rest assured of that, pirate."

Lafitte moved his gaze to Captain Neal before returning it to Cusp. "Captain."

"Mr. Lafitte?"

"Prepare your crew to evacuate your ship."

"But . . ."

Lafitte held Cusp's stare with his black eyes. "I'm going to sink her, Captain. Punishment for the rudeness of your guest."

Neal's face reddened with rage. He pulled futilely against Lafitte's pirates still holding fast to him. "I beg you to reconsider, captain to captain."

"Too late for that, I'm afraid. Your fate is sealed."

"And yours too now, pirate," Quentin Cusp said, quivering in the cool of the night. "Yours too."

PART ONE

Texas officially became part of the United States in 1846, which also started the Mexican War when the U.S. attempted to establish the boundary at the Rio Grande River. During the two-year affair, the Texas Rangers were called on to assist the American Army and soon achieved worldwide fame as a fighting force. Superbly mounted with a large assortment of weapons, the Rangers were found to be so successful against Mexican guerillas that they soon earned the name *"los diablos Tejanos"* or the "Texas Devils."

—*Legends of America:*
Texas Legends: The Texas Rangers—Order Out of Chaos

I

SAN ANTONIO, THE PRESENT

"This isn't your play, Ranger Strong," Captain Consuelo Alonzo of the San Antonio police said to Caitlin Strong beneath an overhang outside the Thomas C. Clark High School. Her hands were planted on her hips, one of them squeezing a pair of sunglasses hard enough to crush the frame.

Caitlin took off her Stetson and let the warm spring sunlight drench her face and raven-black hair that swam past her shoulders. Her cheeks felt flushed and she could feel the heat building behind them. She'd left her own sunglasses back in her SUV, forcing her to keep her view shielded from the sun, which left the focused intensity in her dark eyes clear enough for anyone to see. Her cheekbones were ridged and angular, meshed so perfectly with her jawline that her face had the appearance of one drawn to life by an artist.

Caitlin met Alonzo's stare with her own, neither of them budging. "Then I guess I heard wrong about a boy with a gun holding hostages in the school library."

"No, you heard right about that. But this isn't a Ranger matter. I didn't call you in and my SWAT team's already deployed."

Caitlin gazed at the modern two-story, L-shaped mauve building shaded by thick elm and oak trees.

The main entrance was located at the point of the school where the L broke directly before a nest of rhododendron bushes, from which rose the school marquee listing upcoming events, including graduation and senior prom. A barricade had been erected in haphazard fashion halfway to the street to hold anxious and frantic parents behind a combination of sawhorses, traffic cones, and strung-together rope.

"SWAT team for one boy with a gun?" Caitlin raised.

A news helicopter circled above, adding to Alonzo's discomfort. "You have a problem with that? Or maybe you've never heard of Columbine?"

"Any shots fired yet?"

"No, and that's the way we want to keep it."

"Then I do have a problem, Captain. I do indeed."

Alonzo's face reddened so fast it looked as if she were holding her breath. She'd lost considerable weight since the day Caitlin had met her inside San Antonio's Central Police Substation a couple years back. They had maintained a loose correspondence mostly via e-mail ever since, both appreciating the trials and tribulations of women trying to make it in the predominantly male world of law enforcement. Plenty accused Caitlin of riding her legendary father and grandfather's coattails straight into the Rangers. But Alonzo's parents were Mexican immigrants who barely spoke English and lacked any coattails to ride whatsoever. She was still muscular and had given up wearing her hair in a bun, opting instead for a shorter cut matted down by her cap.

"This is the Masters boy's school, isn't it?" Alonzo asked Caitlin.

"Yes, ma'am. And he still uses his mother's last name—Torres."

"Well, I can tell you the son of that outlaw boyfriend of yours is in one of the classrooms ordered into lockdown while we determine if there are any other perpetrators involved."

Caitlin glanced at the black-clad commandos squatting tensely on either side of the entrance. "When was the last time your SWAT team deployed?"

"That's none of your goddamn business."

"Any shots fired, innocents wounded?"

The veins over Alonzo's temples began to throb. "You're wasting my time, Ranger."

"And you're missing the point. You're going in with SWAT without exhausting any of the easier options."

"Like what?"

"Me," Caitlin told her.

2

SAN ANTONIO, THE DAY BEFORE

It had been four months now since Cort Wesley Masters had turned himself in to the Texas authorities on an extradition request from the Mexican government. The first two of those months had been spent in a federal lockup and the next two in the infamous Mexican Cereso prison just over the border in Nuevo Laredo across the Rio Grande. With no other adult in the lives of his two teenage sons besides an aunt who lived in Arizona they didn't remember meeting, Caitlin had taken it upon herself to step in and fill the void.

She'd moved into their home in the San Antonio suburb of Shavano Park, never imagining Cort Wesley's freedom wouldn't be secured in a timely manner, much less him being imprisoned south of the border. Having the responsibility for his boys, Dylan and Luke, thrust upon her for what was now an indefinite stretch of time left her feeling trapped and claustrophobic. On edge like a tightrope walker negotiating a typically precarious balance, while blindfolded to boot since she'd never been responsible for anyone but herself. Given her already close relationship with the boys, Caitlin had assumed the transition would be easy and the duration relatively short, neither of which had proven true. Rangering and childrearing, even in modern times, just didn't seem to mix well. Although she'd cut back on her duties as much as possible, raising a pair of teenagers was without question a full-time job that had hit her with the brunt force of a glass door you didn't know was there.

"Mexican authorities haven't given in at all on the visitation rights," Caitlin had told her captain, D. W. Tepper, just yesterday in the smaller, shaded office he'd moved into because it was cooler in the hot summer months. The office already smelled of Brut aftershave and stale cigarette smoke with stray wisps clinging to the shadowy corners well after Tepper had finished sneaking a Marlboro.

"What happened that one time they let you in?"

"I made a few comments about the conditions."

"Imagine that didn't go over too well."

"Apparently not."

"State Department help some?"

"Well, since they got involved even the e-mails stopped. He could be dead for all we know."

"This is Cort Wesley Masters we're talking about,

Ranger," Tepper said matter-of-factly, as if that were something Caitlin didn't already know.

"So?"

"He ain't dead." Tepper pulled his finger from a furrow that looked like a valley on his face and checked the nail as if expecting he'd pulled something out with it. "How's this mothering thing going?"

"How do you think? I figured it would last a few weeks tops. That was four months ago now."

"No choice I can see. And they're good boys anyway, 'less Dylan gets it in his head to mix it up with stone killers again."

"I think he's had his fill of that. Caught him with a joint, though."

"You arrest him?"

"Thought about it."

"Shoot him?"

"Thought about that too."

"I caught my oldest smoking a Winston when he was twelve. Made him put it out and eat the damn thing."

"Now that," Caitlin told Tepper, "I didn't think about. I don't believe it's a regular thing."

"Course it's not," Tepper said with a smirk. "Never is for a high school boy."

"Dylan's got himself in the Honors program now. Starting to get his mind set on college, even talking about a college prep year. And Luke's so smart it's downright scary."

Tepper leaned back in his desk chair far enough to make Caitlin think he was going to topple over. "So how's it feel?"

"How's what feel?"

"Hanging up your guns."

"When you start doing stand-up comedy?"

"When was the last time you drew your pistol?"

"Been awhile."

"Patriot Sun shoot-out, right?"

"What's your point, Captain?"

"That in a crazy way this experience has been good for you. Something to bring you into the current century instead of fancying yourself the last of the old-time gunfighters."

"It was never me doing the fancying."

"You embrace it or not?"

"What's that matter?"

Tepper tightened his gaze on her, the spider veins seeming to lengthen across his cheeks. "It's bound to catch up with you, that's all I'm saying."

"You ever been known to be wrong?"

"I was going to ask you the same question."

"Nobody's perfect, D.W."

Tepper's eyes didn't seem to blink, looking tired and drawn. "'Cept when you draw your gun, Ranger, you'd better be."

3

SAN ANTONIO, THE PRESENT

Captain Consuelo Alonzo closed the gap between them in a single quick step, close enough for Caitlin to smell sweet perfume and stale spearmint gum. Alonzo's neck was sunburned as if she was religious about slathering sunscreen on her face while neglecting pretty much everywhere else.

"Listen to me and listen good, Ranger," she said, shoulders stiff and squared, to Caitlin. "You got a reputation that precedes you by about a mile, and the last thing we need is your trigger finger making the call in there."

"Save it, Captain," Caitlin returned dismissively. "I had six weeks training with the FBI in Quantico and I've diffused more hostage situations without gunplay than your SWAT team has even dreamed of."

"And this has nothing to do with Cort Wesley Masters's son being inside the building?"

"You told me he was in a locked-down classroom, not a hostage. School of fifteen hundred, nice to see you've got your thumb so centered on the situation."

Alonzo's cheeks puckered, her eyes suddenly having trouble meeting Caitlin's. "Truth is we haven't got a firm fix on who the gunman's holding in the library."

"I thought so. What about the suspect?"

"Near as we can tell it's a junior named William Langdon, age sixteen. Honor student with no previous criminal record. Principal says he's been bullied."

Caitlin turned her gaze again on two SWAT officers poised on either side of the school entrance, armed to the teeth and wearing black gear and body armor. "Yeah, men like that oughtta be able to talk him down for sure."

"Why don't you just button it up?"

"Because your actions are about to get people killed, Captain."

"I'm well aware of the risk, Ranger."

"I don't believe you are. In rescue situations most hostages are actually shot by SWAT team commandos acting like they're playing paintball. Once the bullets start flying, they tend to do strange things, like hit people they weren't necessarily aimed at who have a tendency to start running in all directions."

Alonzo looked Caitlin in the eye again. "You know your problem? You take this 'One Riot, One Ranger' crap too much to heart. That might have been the case a hundred fifty years ago, but the simple truth is it's not any more. You're a dinosaur, Ranger Strong, a goddamn anachronism."

"You finished, Captain?"

"Yes, I am, and so are you. You just haven't figured it out yet."

Spine stiffened, Captain Alonzo walked off to confer with a San Antonio deputy police chief who'd just arrived to provide political cover once the press showed up in full force. Caitlin waited until Alonzo's back was turned before approaching the school entrance as if she was doing exactly what she was supposed to, pausing at the entrance to eye the SWAT commandos posted on either side.

"I'm glad to be in the background on this one, boys," she said, reaching for the glass door. "Don't bother moving. I'll let myself in."

4

SAN ANTONIO, THE PRESENT

The only sound she heard from that point was the soft echo of her boots clacking against the tile floor. Caitlin knew the layout of Thomas C. Clark High School pretty much by heart, but this was the first time she'd ever walked these halls when they were so empty and quiet. Her only company as she drew closer to the library were members of Captain Alonzo's SWAT team at various strategic positions in sight of the school library entrance. All of the commandos tensed further at her approach, their flak jackets seeming to grow as if pumped with air. But not a single one made a move to approach and signal her back. Even with her own experience and legacy to uphold, it never ceased to amaze Caitlin the degree of respect Rangers commanded. No one, law enforcement or otherwise, ever questioned their presence or involvement.

Still, there was no doubt several members of the SWAT team were currently reporting her presence in the building over the microphones built into their helmets. Those reports would throw Alonzo into a rage, though there was nothing either she or her commandos could do about it at this point.

Caitlin felt her focus seem to tighten, every one of her senses sharpening as the library came into clear view, endless shelves of books visible through clerestory windows mounted high on the wall. She felt her heart continuing to race before suddenly slowing to a heavy rhythmic throb in her chest. Her legendary grandfather, Earl Strong, had told her countless stories about the many gunfights he'd managed to survive, always stressing those moments before the inevitable transcended. The feeling was surreal, almost dreamlike, close to feeling detached from your own body. Once a gunfight began, instinct took over to the point where it felt like someone else was pulling the trigger. Earl had told her that the anticipation was worse because it was so hard to keep the mind focused on the task at hand with so many other thoughts clamoring to be heard.

Caitlin slid past the six SWAT commandos positioned to stage their attack through the library's two separate entry doors. All the window blinds were drawn, denying view in but view out as well, which would keep William Langdon from seeing more commandos prepared to storm the room.

As she neared the door, Caitlin spotted the SWAT team leader and pointed to her eyes. He responded by pointing out the sixteen-year-old captor's position inside. Then, without hesitation, she was through the door and immediately awash in the scent of books, glue bindings, and paper. The deserted hallways had maintained the smell of AXE body spray and flowery shampoo or perfume, mixed with denim and leather. But inside the library the smell of fear quickly rose above that of books and everything else.

Her own hands in the air, Caitlin's eyes instinctively swept across the terrified faces of the hostages seated on chairs at large rectangular tables or on the floor. Her first thought was how young they looked, all the teenage bravado lost to the terror of having their lives threatened by an indiscriminate gunman. Their eyes pleaded with her for help, rescue, solace—anything. And, with that in mind, Caitlin turned her gaze to an overweight boy with a full, round face muddied by red patches of acne growing beneath hair tangled in grease. He stood with his back against a shelf support holding a collection of the old Encyclopedia Britannica. His shoulders and back were stiff, the Glock 19 with extended thirty-shot magazine quivering slightly in his grasp.

"I imagine this isn't the way you thought this day was gonna go when it started," Caitlin said, heart strangely steadied. She stood so straight she might have been about to reach up for something, shifting her weight forward onto her toes to facilitate the quick motion she might need.

"I could've shot you when you came through that door," the boy said to her.

Caitlin swallowed hard, her mouth dry and tongue pasty. She now bore the awesome responsibility for the fate of the hostages. However this turned out, it was all on her. For a brief moment she began to re-think the steps that had brought her this far, then refocused herself on the overweight boy before her, seeing only his gun.

"But you didn't," she said, "because that's not what you are or who you are, son."

"I'm not your son."

"True, but you're a son of Texas, that's for sure, and as a Texas Ranger, that places you in my regard and makes you my concern."

"That's a load of crap and you know it."

"William, you hand me that gun and walk out of here by my side and I promise you that's where you'll stay until all this gets sorted out. That's a promise from me and the Rangers. You made a mistake, but so far no one's been hurt and there's still time to get out of this with that remaining the case."

"I'm scared," William Langdon said, his entire body starting to tremble, the pistol in his hand shaking as if attached to a paint mixer. Caitlin began to fear, along with everything else, he might open fire accidentally.

"I know."

"No, you don't. You don't understand!"

"I'm willing to try. Just lay that gun down and give me a chance."

"I . . . can't."

His eyes shifted to the right, subtly but enough to make Caitlin wonder why he was looking that way. The gun looked all wrong in William Langdon's hand, hardly strong or firm enough to hold it up with the extended magazine, which meant, which meant . . .

Which meant *what*?

Caitlin felt a flutter ripple up her spine. Something was wrong here, something beyond the thinking of Captain Alonzo and her commandos.

I . . . can't.

Why can't you, William? Caitlin asked in her mind, seeing in the boy's eyes not just resignation but fear that mirrored what she'd seen on the faces of the roughly thirty hostages seated at tables or clinging to the floor. The same eyes that had just managed a side-long glance.

What was she missing?

"We're gonna get out of this together, William," Caitlin said, finding his eyes with hers, stalling for time to make sense of what felt wrong about this. "You're no killer, son. You never hurt anybody in your life no matter how much they hurt you. You think I don't know how you feel?"

"You don't!"

"Think again. When most girls were gossiping and playing sports in high school, I was out shooting guns. I smelled of gun oil instead of perfume and I never had a boyfriend. But I knew who I was and that made it all right."

"You don't know *me*, you don't!" the boy sputtered.

"I know this isn't you. I know somebody put you up to it." The words coming now ahead of Caitlin's thinking, as everything fell into place. What William

Langdon had been looking at, what she had missed. "And I know he's in this room right now."

With that, she snapped her right hand downward and in a flash of motion whipped her SIG from its holster. Already twisting, searching for the motion she knew would come.

And it did.

A rangy, stringy-haired boy whipped a cheap, semi-auto submachine gun from under his leather jacket. Even from forty feet away to her left, she could see his eyes bursting with rage, the thirst for violence frozen on his expression. He almost grinned as he turned the MAC-10 not on her, but on a boy wearing a Letterman's jacket seated at a nearby table.

In her mind Caitlin saw herself shooting for his wrist, blowing the MAC-10 out of his grasp. But at this point instinct was in command, conscious thought banished to the background.

Caitlin put three bullets into the tall boy, spinning him around as muzzle flashes burst from the MAC-10's barrel and nine-millimeter bullets stitched across the library to a torrent of screams and cries. But then he managed to steady himself, grabbing the boy wearing the Letterman's jacket by the collar and jerking him from his chair for cover. His face froze in terror, bulging eyes seeking Caitlin out and latching upon her.

Body armor! How had she missed that?

Caitlin opened fire again before the young shooter had gotten his hostage all the way up. Her first bullet caught the boy in the Letterman's jacket high in the shoulder, jamming him back against the shooter and opening up a fresh sightline for her. Caitlin fired three more shots in rapid succession, all aimed for the head with two of them finding the mark.

She watched the shooter splay backward against a freestanding magazine rack that tumbled under the force of the impact, spilling the latest issues to the floor, the tall boy crumpling atop them.

Caitlin was immediately conscious of a flood of sound and motion, as Captain Alonzo's SWAT team burst into the library from all angles, gun smoke wafting toward the shattered windows through which several of them had just crashed. She tried to process all that had happened, but her focus was gone, the world turned very small and centered on the SIG-Sauer suddenly hot and heavy in her grasp. But she held it steady in the next sweep of her eyes that caught the boy in the Letterman's jacket holding his shoulder, his face twisted in agony and blood dribbling between his fingers. Directly before her, William Langdon had slumped all the way to the floor, the Glock 19 resting by his side with his hands cupped on his stomach to stanch the blood flow. His face was milk pale and his lips were trembling so hard Caitlin could hear the clacking of his teeth from across the room.

The SWAT commandos split and spread, the young hostages beginning to stir amid the cries and whimpers. Sirens wailed.

"Nice work, Ranger," the SWAT team leader, a man named Esteppa, told her. But she couldn't tell whether he meant it or not.

5

"I messed things up good, D.W.," Caitlin said, holding her head in her hands. "I messed things up for sure and a lot more blood got spilled than should have on account of that."

Tepper sat down next to her on the curb set before the NO PARKING, SCHOOL BUS ZONE yellow grid. "I didn't hear anything in advance about a second shooter."

"The other boy's eyes glanced that way a few times. I should have noticed, I should have noticed before I finally did. I should have made that boy as the real shooter in my first scan of the room. But I was too busy looking for Dylan and his friends."

"So you're criticizing yourself for being human."

Caitlin finally looked up at Tepper. "My grandfather was human, my dad too. Neither of them would've messed up this bad. They would've figured on the fact the real shooter might've been wearing body armor."

"Hell, Ranger, in Earl Strong's heyday the closest thing they had to body armor was a truck to hide behind. And if it means anything that boy you got in the shoulder is gonna be just fine." Tepper's expression wrinkled. "The second perpetrator, well, it don't look as good for him but those aren't your shells inside him either."

"William Langdon was no perp, Captain."

"That Glock and those thirty bullets said otherwise, Ranger, and don't you forget it." Tepper stuck a cigarette in his mouth, but didn't light it. "Ask yourself what if Dylan had been in that library in the line of fire. Ask yourself that."

Caitlin spotted Captain Alonzo firing off some choice words at a Department of Public Safety official who'd taken charge of the investigation. "Guess she's not too happy."

"Too bad. Her trigger-happy SWAT team did the deed instead of you, we'd have lots more than two rescues leaving the scene right now."

Tepper said that just as medical examiner Frank Dean Whatley followed a pair of paramedics wheeling a dolly toting a black body bag through the door.

"Dean Sturgess."

"What?" Caitlin asked him.

"The name of the kid with the MAC-10. Posted something on his Faceblog account that he was gonna take a bunch of kids with him today."

"Facebook," Caitlin corrected.

"Huh?"

"It's called Facebook." She cocked her gaze back toward Captain Alonzo, their stares locking just long enough for her to catch Alonzo's hateful sneer cast her way. "Gonna be hell to pay for this, D.W."

"We should talk about that," Tepper said, finally lighting his Marlboro.

"Did either my dad or granddad ever shoot a kid?"

"Can't say. Neither one of them ever asked for an ID before firing."

"I figure things out when I should have, maybe this ends different, Captain."

Tepper yanked the cigarette from his mouth and glared at her. "And maybe it doesn't, Caitlin. Even God screws up; how else could a human mess like Dean

Sturgess find his way into the world? If you had another choice inside that school, I can't see it."

"Maybe I could have . . ."

"What? Shot some books to come tumbling down on Dean Sturgess? Blow off a fire sprinkler head and douse him into submission? You been watching too much television since you went mom on me. Things don't end as such anywhere outside TV land. And I lied to you before."

"Captain?"

"When you asked me whether Jim or Earl had ever killed a kid. Truth is you know plenty about old Earl's exploits in cleaning up Sweetwater back in the oil boom days, but you don't know all."

"I know what he told me."

"And he likely left out the part about the teenager shooting up the local saloon trying to get the man who left his father for dead in a field. Winged two ladies of the night and gut-shot the piano player. Earl had no more of a choice back then than you did today. And he saved a bunch of lives, just like you did."

Caitlin felt like reaching out and touching his shoulder warmly, but didn't. "What else is on your mind, Captain?"

Tepper looked around him, as if to gauge exactly where he was. "Remember the last time you and me sat on a curb outside a building?"

Caitlin nodded. "The Survivor Center after Cort Wesley and I gunned down that Special Ops team three years ago now."

"I gave you back your badge that night. Talked you into returning to the Rangers."

"You did at that, sir."

Tepper tossed his Marlboro aside and slid closer to

her. "Now I want to do something different. I want to talk you into taking some time off."

Caitlin just looked at him.

"I promised myself that was the way it had to be the next time you got in a gunfight."

"But you just said—"

"I know what I said, just like I know what I'm saying. I think it's coming too easy for you, almost like it's what you want. Today was a lesson for both of us, Ranger. I'm doing this before Austin forces my hand based on what Captain Alonzo over there is sure to tell them. You can come in and work a desk while Luke and Dylan are in school, but I want you home by the afternoon to keep your focus on them for a time. Get your priorities straight."

"My priorities?" Caitlin repeated, feeling the back of her neck go fiery hot.

"Anybody else, this would be routine procedure. I can't give you cover anymore. There've just been too many bullets and too many bodies. You've become a poster child for excess and a rationale in Austin for cutting back our budget."

"That what you believe, D.W.? Why don't you just tell me straight?"

Tepper cocked his head to the side, the sunlight diving deep into the furrows lining that cheek. "I believe what you just told me about Dylan maybe having an effect on your thinking when you walked into that library. I believe this mothering thing has changed your thinking and altered your focus to the point where you've become a liability for the Ranger force."

"You want me to quit, why don't you just say so?"

"Because I don't. Because I want to believe all this will settle itself out."

"But you're not sure."

"Are you?"

She watched Tepper push himself back to his feet, knees creaking and cracking. "How long exactly, Captain?"

"How long it take Samson to topple that temple with his bare hands?"

"I have no idea."

"Well, Ranger, neither do I."

As he said that, Captain Alonzo slowed near Caitlin on her way to the school entrance.

"Any shots fired, Ranger, innocents wounded?" she asked, shaking her head.

PART TWO

Their role changed once again in May 1874, when the state Democrats returned to power and Governor Richard Coke, along with the Legislature, appropriated $75,000 to organize six companies of 75 Rangers each. By this time, Texas was overrun with outlaws, Indians ravaging the western frontier, and Mexican bandits pillaging and murdering along the Rio Grande River. The new troops were stationed at strategic points over the state and were known as the Frontier Battalion. During this era, the Ranger Service held a place somewhere between that of an army and a police force.

—*Legends of America:*
Texas Legends: The Texas Rangers—Order Out of Chaos

6

South Texas, seven months later

Saud Harrabi watched the desert come alive before him in the night, dust swirling and rising in the truck's wake. Normally darkness would have obscured its approach, but the glow of wildfires burning out of control fifty miles to the east lit the sky with an amber glow that gave up the night's secrets.

Harrabi watched the truck's lights flash and flashed his in return, his heart hammering with excitement. He hand-combed his thinning hair into place and wet his fingers with his tongue to further mat the stubborn strands down. His cotton button-down shirt was moist with sweat and the seat of his khaki trousers stuck to the seat's upholstery.

Before him, the truck's lights burned brighter as it continued its approach. The great man's arrival signaled that the final stage of the plan was about to begin, bringing all of Harrabi's labor, and the holy purpose behind it, full circle.

Listen to me, he thought, *I sound like one of them.*

Specifically, one of those he had resented and even loathed since his youth growing up as an American and detesting those from the Arab culture who did not see this as their country. As a child, his parents had registered him as "Sam" Harrabi in elementary school, and during those years he never had call or reason to believe himself to be any different from the other children. He was an American, just like them. His parents were well-educated, successful, and his house was just as big as everyone else's and bigger than plenty. He never identified himself as an Arab, or Muslim, and demonstrated his priorities perfectly by marrying a white Christian woman, thus turning his back on his heritage in favor of embracing the culture he far more saw himself a part of.

But that was all gone now. Everything had changed.

The truck slid to a halt thirty feet before Harrabi, its high beams blinding him as he stepped out into the cool desert night. The sweet smells of mesquite and chaparral were tinged by the harsh scent carried by the wildfires to the east, something like leaves burning in autumn. That thought made Harrabi think of his family and he felt his stomach muscles knot, recharging his resolve.

A man emerged from the truck and walked out of the harsh spill of the high beams toward him. Average height, even slightly below average with narrow, stooped shoulders. Against the most ardent teachings of his fundamentalist beliefs he'd actually shaved his beard. The great man had also cropped his hair so close to the skull it made for little more than a dark outline of his receding hairline. He wore thin glasses that made him look somehow dull and bookish in stark comparison to the hero Harrabi had never met but nonetheless had come to idolize.

"I'm blessed by God to see you, *sayyid.*"

"We are all blessed in the eyes of God, my brother," the cleric said, touching his head.

Harrabi looked closer at the great man. He'd never

seen him pictured in anything but the robes of a cleric
and the civilian clothes hung shapelessly over his
frame, his shirt billowing in the desert winds.

"We have much to attend to," the cleric continued
abruptly, his voice stiff with a concern Harrabi first
passed off to the long journey and difficult final stretch
coming up along this back route from Mexico.

"All is ready, *sayyid*, everything prepared to the precise specifications we discussed."

"Later," the cleric said. "First you must take the
oath of jihad. Kneel before me, my brother."

As Harrabi knelt on the hard desert gravel, a pair of
SUVs with lights flashing tore onto the scene. He recognized them as Border Patrol vehicles, fearing all the
precautions taken had not been enough.

But the cleric seemed unmoved as the twin SUVs
screeched to a halt, laying his hands firmly upon Harrabi's shoulders. "This oath," he explained, as if unaware
of the armed men leaping down from the vehicles
with assault rifles leveled, "is called *Hilf al-mutayyabin*,
an oath of allegiance taken in pre-Islamic times by several clans of the Quraysh tribe, in which they under-
took to protect the oppressed and the wronged. Do
you make such a commitment here before me today?"

Harrabi was too distracted by the border patrol
agents to respond, one coming straight for him and the
cleric, the other toward the cleric's truck. "But *sayyid*—"

"Swear your allegiance, my brother."

"I swear."

"Then hear my words and obey them."

"*You two, hands in the air and turn around slowly!*"
the approaching border patrol agent shouted.

"You swear by Allah that you will strive to free the
prisoners of their shackles, to end the oppression to

which our people are being subjected, to assist the oppressed and restore their rights even at the price of our own lives, to make Allah's word supreme in the world, and to restore the glory of Islam. Do you so swear?"

"Hands in the air or I'll shoot you as you stand!" threatened the border patrol agent who'd stopped twenty feet away with assault rifle steadied, as the other agent reached the truck.

"*Sayyid,*" Harrabi started.

"Do you swear?"

"I . . . swear."

With that, a series of soft spits sounded, their echoes sounding like coughs in the wind. Harrabi flinched, watching the border patrol agent closest to them fall, the one near the truck already lying still beside the truck's passenger-side front tire.

The cleric never turned to look, never reacted, never acknowledged the approach of his bodyguards who appeared out of the night. He left his hands on Harrabi's shoulders, continuing.

"Then know that you now stand with God to join us in this battle to vanquish our greatest of enemies. May you and all who follow be blessed in that pursuit. May you join me and more of your brothers in bringing about the death of the Great Satan, deceiver to the world and destroyer of all that is holy." The cleric eased his hands away and backed off. "Now rise, my brother."

Harrabi pushed himself back to his feet, the gravel sticking to his pants at the knees as the cleric's bodyguards dragged the bodies of the border patrol agents back toward their SUVs. He realized he was trembling and canted his body so the great man wouldn't notice.

The cleric followed his gaze. "This is just the beginning, my brother. In a week's time, many more thousands, *hundreds* of thousands, will join them at our hands."

"*Āmin*," said Harrabi.

7

GULF WATERS OFF THE COAST OF TEXAS,
THE PRESENT

"What the hell's that, Caitlin?" Dylan Torres asked from the stern of their charter boat.

The orange raft was drifting straight for the fishing boat she'd chartered earlier that morning out of Baffin Bay. There was no passenger in view, which did nothing to ease the odd feeling that had raised her neck hackles and left her reaching for the pistol she'd been trying to discipline herself not to carry all the time.

Caitlin Strong felt something scratch at her spine, the sweat pasting the cotton shirt to her back going cold in an instant. Around her the Gulf waters looked like ridged blue glass, the bright sunlight starting to bake the air against the sea breeze's concerted effort to temper the heat. With the sun free of clouds right now, she had to cup her hand at her brow to better follow the approaching raft.

"Caitlin?" Dylan, son of the imprisoned Cort Wesley Masters, prodded. He was seventeen, dark wavy hair still worn long enough to make him look like some kind of brooding rock star. Except he had what Caitlin's dad and granddad had called "gunman's eyes"—eyes that didn't always jibe well with the rest of him.

"Must've broke loose from that jack-up oil rig off to the east there," said Captain Bob, baling hook already in hand. "We'd best reel her in."

"Emergency rafts and life pods can't break loose," said Cort Wesley's now thirteen-year-old son, Luke. "They gotta be launched."

"Well, maybe it got launched by accident," Dylan snickered.

"No way," Luke insisted

"The boy's right," added Captain Bob, making Caitlin's heart flutter a bit.

Caitlin didn't know Captain Bob's last name, but he had a prison tattoo inked during a stretch in Huntsville and had let his stare linger in recognition on her signature scrawled at the bottom of the registration form a few hours earlier. Caitlin's own father, Jim Strong, had taken her to fish Baffin Bay many times, sometimes with her grandfather Earl before the great man's passing in 1990. They'd roomed at the very same Cast 'n Stay Lodge and eaten at the King's Inn, just as she, Dylan, and Luke had the night before.

"You don't remember me, do you?" Captain Bob asked, as he readied the baling hook to reach out for the runaway raft.

"Can't say I do, sir."

"Your father used to hire me every time he came down here. You were just a little girl back then. Believe I remember your granddad too. Texas Ranger legends for sure, but out here they were just men, holding a rod and reel instead of a gun. Believe they liked it that way."

Caitlin looked at Captain Bob, searching her memory to no avail.

"Your dad once caught a speckled trout that weighed damn near twenty-five pounds. You remember that?"

"I'm the one who hooked it. Wore me out trying to reel the damn thing in," she said, smiling nostalgically at the memory.

Caitlin had hoped the fishing trip would at least distract Dylan and Luke from the fact that no amount of cajoling or influence with the Mexican authorities had gained them visitation rights to see their father. Leaving her gun behind, if nothing else, gave her reason for insisting the boys do the same with their cell phones. Nothing to spoil their trip together.

Until now.

"That rig's called the *Mariah*," Luke said from the gunwale, staring off toward the oil rig that wasn't much more than a speck on the water from this distance.

"Say what?" Dylan snapped.

"The rig. It's called the *Mariah*. I looked it up before we came down here."

"You looked it up?"

"Yeah. What's wrong with that?"

Dylan snickered and blew air through his pursed lips, scowling as if he'd suddenly realized how far away he was from the teenage world he'd constructed for himself.

"Jack-up rigs like the *Mariah* operate in shallow

water, up to seven hundred feet or so," Luke continued. "They're cool."

"Cool?"

"Yeah."

Dylan just shook his head and turned away.

A thin cloud formation slid over the sun, a narrow enough gap created to cast a spotlight-like shimmer downward that captured the raft in its glow. Captain Bob leaned over the deck rail, baling hook extending forward until the shaft of light caught a shape flattened out on the raft floor amid a thin pool of bobbing water.

"Oh my Lord," he uttered, as Caitlin again felt for the pistol she wasn't carrying.

8

NORTHERN GULF STREAM, THE PRESENT

The man's body lay twisted at an odd angle on the floor of the raft, arms and legs splayed in opposite directions and shoulders propped up against its starboard sill alongside the tiny outboard engine. One of his hands seemed to still cling to a plastic hold not far from the outboard's control arm he had likely held fast to until his strength had given out. The pooling water Caitlin had first taken for muck-strewn she now saw was actually streaked with thickening ribbons of blood. MARIAH was emblazoned in phosphorescent letters on both sides of the raft.

"Shit," said Dylan, as the escape raft plopped up against the charter boat. "Man's dead for sure."

"Back up a bit," Caitlin told him.

"Huh?"

"And take your brother," she added with Luke pushing his torso over the gunwale to better see the body. Caitlin turned to Captain Bob. "Call the Coast Guard."

"Gonna be a while before we see them show in these parts."

"How about the local sheriff?"

"These waters are outside his jurisdiction, Rangers' too."

"Don't think he cares too much about jurisdiction right now," Caitlin said, eyeing the corpse.

A blue jumpsuit, zippered high to the neck and stained with grease, fit the man snugly. Caitlin figured him for six-foot-two or -three with thick arms and hands marred by chapped skin and callus. One eye hung open, the other a mere slit encased by purplish bruising. The raft bobbed in the currents, making it seem as though he were trying to lift himself from the rust-colored pool of water lapping over his legs.

Caitlin's gaze rose from the corpse and drifted a good mile out to the shape of the *Mariah*, nothing more than a husk of steel from this distance.

"Coast Guard's en route," Captain Bob reported, back at her side. "But it's gonna be awhile on account, it turns out, a couple of drunk college kids fell off a party boat last night. Bodies could be all the way to Florida by now."

Caitlin's eyes gestured toward the *Mariah*. "Can you radio the rig?"

"I'll sure try but I got no clue as to the frequency."

"Call the Coast Guard again. They'll have it. You inform them you had a Texas Ranger on board?"

"No, ma'am."

"Now be a good time to do that too." Caitlin held her gaze on the jack-up, as Captain Bob slid back to the bridge. "Luke, how many men you say work a rig like that?"

"A couple dozen," the boy said, "give or take a few."

"Uh-uh," from Dylan.

"Uh-huh."

"The rig that spilled all that oil into the Gulf had over a hundred."

"The *Horizon* was a deepwater rig that can drill down as much as five miles or so," Luke elaborated. "This one's smaller and is made for shallow water, like I said before if you bothered to listen."

"Think you're smart, don't you?"

"'Cause I am," Luke shot back.

"Jeez," Dylan said, drawing close to Caitlin again. "I know what you're thinking, Caitlin."

"What am I thinking?"

"What about the other twenty-three."

"Pretty much, son, yeah."

She'd been on the bigger deepwater rigs twice, representing the Rangers on tours conducted for the Texas Department of Public Safety. The purpose of the tours was always to show off how safe the rigs were with all their redundant safety features. They reminded Caitlin of giant erector sets built on the sea, heavy with steel atop decks so crammed with equipment and rigging it was difficult to move. The rigs she'd been on had fully equipped gyms, movie theaters, recreation rooms, and prefabricated housing units all watched over by sentinel-like oil derricks that towered toward the sky. She remembered being brought onto the rig from a Coast Guard cutter in a basket swaying in the wind beneath a massive crane. Coming from law enforcement, what interested her most was the absence of alcohol, the greatest cause of violence among hardscrabble men she'd had to face down in bars on more occasions than she cared to remember. Made her realize how far away from all that she'd felt these last few months. Like she was a different person altogether and not one she knew very well.

Caitlin also recalled how the oil companies' PR people had stressed the evacuation procedures in the event of a catastrophic emergency, showcasing the array of rafts and what they called the life pods Luke had just referenced. Releasing them from their moorings in the event of such an emergency required a series of steps that made for a complex task in itself and one not to be taken lightly, much less by a single man.

"You're gonna check the rig out, aren't you?" Dylan asked her.

Instead of responding, Caitlin slipped out of her boots and rolled the cuffs up on her jeans as far as they would go. Captain Bob had wedged the baling hook between the deck rail and gunwale to keep the raft in place against the fishing boat's hull.

"Hold her steady now," Caitlin told Dylan, as she eased herself over the rail and dropped down into the pooling, blood-rich water.

9

Caitlin landed with a plop, the raft's floor spongy beneath her feet as she moved toward the rear where the body lay near the outboard engine. The raft listed from side to side with each step, driven by a sea that appeared dark and menacing around the craft but crystal blue just beyond with the sun's rays making the chop look like giant snakes massing below the surface.

"I can't raise anybody on the rig," Captain Bob called down to her. "Nobody's answering my calls."

She was conscious of him, Luke, and Dylan all watching her as she reached the body and did a cursory inspection, careful not to disturb anything that might compromise the potential crime scene. Bruising was evident across the man's hands, fingers, and knuckles, evidence of an altercation that must have occurred in the moments prior to him fleeing the rig. Up close, the area around his closed eye had swelled to a level that suggested blunt force trauma. Impossible to tell at this stage what exactly had caused it, but such a blow wouldn't have been enough to kill a man of his size and strength.

Caitlin ran her eyes down from his face along his torso, stopping at a darker spot near his thorax where his blue jumpsuit seemed to bunch up, turning in on itself. Gazing closer she saw the material had peeled away in a roughly circular pattern consistent with a gunshot wound. Caitlin pushed the lapping water away, then watched it pool back in a slight vortex over the spot she'd detected.

A bullet hole for sure, located not far from several blotchy orange stains.

She wasn't about to disturb the body further by easing it over to check for more wounds. This was enough for now, though it suggested nothing about what had led to a gunfight on board a jack-up oil rig that wasn't responding to calls. Depending on exactly how long the raft had been drifting in the Gulf's currents, the man could have been shot over an hour ago or even significantly longer. Plenty of time for the Coast Guard to respond with crash boats and choppers, no matter how many college kids had gone missing from a booze charter. That seemed to indicate the rig hadn't issued a distress call.

And now nobody on the *Mariah* was answering the radio.

"How long the Coast Guard say they'd be?" Caitlin called up to Captain Bob.

"They didn't."

She considered calling Captain Tepper but wasn't exactly sure what to tell him or what he could empower her to do. "Help me up," she said, wading back toward the charter boat and taking both Captain Bob's and Dylan's extended hands to help hoist her back on board.

"You want me to call the sheriff now?" Captain Bob asked her.

"He got a boat?"

"Couple of skiffs and a whaler."

"So nothing that can get out here anytime soon."

"No, ma'am."

Caitlin looked out toward the *Mariah,* shielding her eyes from the sun. "Then I guess it's up to us." She caught Captain Bob shaking his head and resumed, "Something wrong, sir?"

"Nope, nothing," he said, a smile dropping from his face as quickly as it had appeared. "You're just like your dad and granddad, that's all."

"How's that?"

Captain Bob's eyes aimed past her back toward the body bobbing in rhythm with the raft atop the sea's surface. "We got a dead body and can't raise another living soul on that rig out there."

"So?"

"So what if whoever's responsible is still on board?"

10

NORTHERN GULF STREAM, THE PRESENT

Caitlin's nerves started jangling when they drew close enough to the *Mariah* for its shadows to catch their charter boat in their grasp. Up close, the rig looked like some kind of alien robot that had just raised itself out of the sea on three legs to take over the world.

"Know why they call it a jack-up?" Luke asked, hand clenched warmly on her shoulder.

"No, son, I don't."

"I do," Luke beamed, while nearby Dylan chortled and rolled his eyes. "Rig like this isn't much more than a floating barge. Some have to be towed while others, like the *Mariah*, are self-propelled. Either way, once they get to their chosen location, the legs are jacked down onto the seafloor. Then the weight of the barge and additional ballast water are used to drive the legs securely into the bottom to keep the rig steady. Then a jacking system raises the entire barge and drilling structure above the water, creating what's called an air gap. That way the waves and currents pass under the actual structure, and that's why they call it a jack-up rig."

Caitlin felt Captain Bob slow the charter boat to a crawl as it neared a support leg outfitted with a steel ladder that climbed all the way to the rig's deck. The big deepwater rigs she'd been on had no such ladders, but she thought she recalled their installation being mandated for emergency use in the wake of the *Deepwater Horizon* disaster. The shadows cast by the *Mariah* had swallowed all of their fishing boat by then. The currents felt stronger this much farther out, as if angry over having this iron interloper invade their world. Caitlin had seen no trace of movement on the rig as they drew nearer and could see no trace of it now.

"You finished?" Dylan chided his brother.

"Matter of fact, I am."

"Good thing."

Caitlin regarded the boys, both of them looking more like their father each day in different ways. Or maybe the resemblance was more an illusion she cast upon herself to ease the pain over missing Cort Wesley Masters. She never thought she could miss anyone so much, and being with his boys, looking after them like she was, was the only thing that soothed the sense of emptiness she felt.

The house she'd grown up in outside San Antonio had recently been put up for sale, and for reasons she didn't fully grasp Caitlin had offered the asking price. Why do that if Cort Wesley and his sons represented home to her? It was as if she had a foot in two worlds that could only exist side by side and not independent of each other.

"Now let's get the two of you below," Caitlin said to Luke and Dylan, as their fishing boat nuzzled up against the *Mariah*.

11

NORTHERN GULF WATERS, THE PRESENT

"You going up alone?" Dylan asked, after Caitlin had practically dragged him down into the cabin. "I'll go with you if you want."

"I appreciate the offer but, no," she said, tightening her gaze on him. "But I will take that pistol you got stowed in your backpack."

Dylan stiffened, his expression freezing in place. "How'd you know?"

"I didn't, not for sure anyway. Now hand it over."

Dylan frowned and blew the air from his face. He tanned easily and a few days in the sun brought out the Latino features he got from his mother. Caitlin watched muscles not unlike his father's, only smaller, ripple under his sleeveless shirt as he fished through his backpack and emerged with his father's .40 caliber Glock.

"Last thing I promised my dad was that I'd protect you and Luke," he said, handing it to her.

"Then I suppose we'll let this go," Caitlin told him, racking the slide and clipping the holster to her belt. "This time."

She closed the cabin door behind the boys, ignoring

the last of their protestations and not bothering to explain how vulnerable they all were to a gunman firing from the deck sixty feet above. They'd towed the emergency raft the whole way with them, speed kept slow to keep its contents as undisturbed as possible.

Caitlin reluctantly pulled out her cell phone and called D. W. Tepper at Ranger Company D headquarters, while Captain Bob worked to tie down their boat against the support leg.

"I thought you said you were going fishing," he said, after she'd filled him in.

"I did. Caught something I wasn't expecting."

"Bodies just seem to keep finding you," he said after what seemed like a longer pause than it really was, "don't they?"

"At least this is one I didn't kill myself, D.W."

"Clang-clang, Caitlin. That's the sound of the desk I chained you to. And I gotta tell you I'm of a mind to have you wait for the Coast Guard. You wanna tell me why I shouldn't?"

"Because there's bad trouble sixty feet away and maybe more people dying. You want to explain to them or their families why you waited for the Coast Guard?"

"Why do I think you planned this whole damn thing?" She heard him retch and cough up some phlegm, thanks to the pack-a-day habit he'd quit a hundred times only to resume just as fast. "What would you do if I ordered you to wait for the Coast Guard?"

"Probably climb on board that rig anyway."

"I see all that desk duty has really mellowed you, hasn't it? You got your gun?"

"No, sir," Caitlin said, not bothering to elaborate.

"Just stay put, and that's an order."

"I could take Captain Bob along."

"He tell you how he first became acquainted with your daddy?"

"Nope. I assumed it was being hired for a charter."

"Not quite. Man was captain of a boat known for ferrying bales of marijuana, not people. Jim Strong and I busted him on the back of a shrimp trawler the Rangers raided after learning it was picking up more than shellfish at sea. Believe Captain Bob did himself a stretch in Huntsville as a result."

"His tattoos bear that out."

Caitlin heard Tepper clear his throat and cough up some more mucus. "Damnest thing is that was the last time I was ever on a boat. I got so damn seasick, I puked on my boots. Your daddy was still laughing when we dropped our badges on the poor bastard."

"That why he became the Strongs' choice for charter?"

"That and the fact that we found the biggest trout and striped bass you ever saw on the same ice that was hiding the drugs."

"I'm heading up to the rig, Captain," Caitlin said, starting for the ladder.

"No, you're not. Ranger, you listen up here and listen good. . . ."

But she hit End before Tepper could continue.

12

Save for the hot steel of the rungs burning her flesh, the climb passed easily with no sightings of any threats above and the stiff winds posing only a minor inconvenience. As soon as she crested the ladder and climbed aboard the *Mariah*, Caitlin noticed the scorching heat first, the vast assemblages of steel holding the sun's blistering rays like a blast furnace. A jack-up rig like the *Mariah* might be only half the size of its massive deepwater brethren, but Caitlin could otherwise see little difference on deck. Baffles and mounts rose from the surface everywhere, fighting for space amid what looked to be a random assortment of multileveled clutter when she knew quite the opposite was true.

Everything aboard an offshore rig came with a purpose, and the *Mariah* was no exception. She smelled grease and paint where the deck rails had been given a fresh coat. The pungent odor of a strong industrial solvent laced the air as well, evidence that the decks had recently been swabbed down. She caught the sour stench of drilling mud stored in an endless array of fifty-five-gallon black drums stacked on shelves reachable only by cranes that hovered over the deck like silent sentinels. She didn't recall seeing this many of them even on board the larger deepwater rigs that were so self-contained they even mixed their own drilling cement.

It was the lack of sound on the rig that bothered Caitlin the most, her hand straying close to Cort Wesley's holstered Glock on her belt. Other than the rhythmic whirring coming from the louvered engine room, there was nothing. No deafening clatter emanating from the driller shack or heavy *thunk-thunk* of the derricks driving steel downward. No boisterous yells or calls from the deckhands and roustabouts who should have been everywhere but instead weren't anywhere to be seen.

The *Mariah* looked to be a newer rig or had perhaps been retrofitted to be more efficient and economical. Caitlin's tour of one of its larger deepwater brethren had stressed the fact that rig owners and operators received regular reports of the pumping operation itself twenty-four/seven. They'd also be constantly in contact with personnel on board the *Mariah* via phone or computer. With that in mind, she figured somebody at headquarters was likely already panicking and she'd be surprised if other calls hadn't been put into the Coast Guard in addition to the one Captain Bob had made.

The wind picked up, carrying a rusty odor on the air with it, and Caitlin thought she could feel the platform wobble ever so slightly beneath her feet.

Wait . . .

The smell of rust that lingered briefly increased her unease for the most part because she could see none in evidence. So maybe it wasn't rust at all, but something else, and only one other thing applied there:

Blood—the odor faint enough to be missed by any but someone both trained to know it and, like Caitlin, having experienced the distinctive smell firsthand all too often.

Caitlin drew the Glock, which made her feel no better at all. She slid past the exhaust manifolds and ventilation ducts. The platform was rectangular with several abutments jutting outward over the sea. One held a helipad that was currently empty, twin drilling derricks resting atop two more.

She moved toward the two-story stack of prefabricated housing units. The elevated drill shack containing the bridge and office of the operations installation manager, or OIM, together with the derricks combined to throw shadows across the deck, slicing it into splotchy grids and making Caitlin further feel as if she had entered some world ruled by a robotic race. Emergency alarm pulls were stationed everywhere it seemed, adding even more to her deep sense of foreboding. It seemed impossible to even conceive of something catastrophic occurring on the rig without a single of those alarms being pulled. But clearly none had been triggered, which meant that whatever had befallen the crew had happened so fast none of the two dozen or so could reach a station.

She bypassed the housing units in favor of the engine room. The steel entry door, more like the hatch variety normally associated with a submarine, was cracked open and Caitlin entered to the clatter of piston-driven machinery loud enough to make her ears bubble. Everything must have been functioning on autopilot since not a single worker was in evidence.

Caitlin did a cursory check of the claustrophobic chamber, smelling no blood amid the grease, oil, and superheated steel. But the sudden tinny blare of sound left her slightly disoriented and discomfited that her ears could no longer provide advance warning of a potential attacker's approach. She emerged from the engine room even more wary and certain that whatever had sent the gunshot victim fleeing the *Mariah* aboard the emergency raft was long done.

Fresh paint . . .

She recalled the orange stains on the dead man's jumpsuit and followed the line of WET PAINT signs stuck to the drying handrails. She came to a point not far from where a flotilla of emergency escape craft, including the oblong life pods and more rafts like the one currently tied to Captain Bob's charter boat, were located on the furthermost edge of the deck. Sure enough, she found a spot on the handrail that was marred by grease and smudged to reveal the dull old paint beneath the new. Still palming the Glock, Caitlin crouched and studied the grated deck floor, catching what could have been dried blood.

Though shot, the dead man had managed to get this far and then used one of the inflatable rafts to escape. Caitlin pictured him at work inside the engine room when gunmen burst in firing. He'd been hit but managed somehow to delay death at least long enough to take flight. But he wouldn't have been alone in the engine room, so where were his workmates? Where was the rest of the *Mariah*'s crew?

Both Caitlin's father and grandfather preached that they'd never been scared of anything they could see or stood before them. It was the unknown—a drunk laying in ambush, a punk wanting the criminal glory of taking down a Texas Ranger, a meth head poised behind a door in a darkened room—that cost them sleep and became fodder for nightmares. But Caitlin couldn't recall a single one of even Earl Strong's many tales where he'd come up against anything like this, where a couple dozen or so men had simply vanished into thin air.

Caitlin edged onward, trusting her nose now. She could remember her granddad's tales of hunting down escaped cons literally by catching wind of their stench. It got so word spread through the penal system not to run before taking a shower. So she sniffed the air for the coppery rust scent she'd caught on the wind earlier.

Trouble was the wind was whipping everywhere now and likely spreading the blood scent with it. Caitlin continued her inspection more traditionally instead, finding the mess hall, media center, and recreation room all empty and undisturbed. Whatever had happened here, whatever had befallen the crew, had gone down too fast to get out a Mayday call. The normal condition and working order of the rig itself seemed to eliminate some form of attack, sabotage, or violent spree by a wayward roustabout or deckhand. That left something premeditated and thought out to the last move, and that didn't bode well at all for the fate of the crew. She wondered if this might have been a kidnapping, the force behind it with an ax to grind against whatever oil company owned the *Mariah*. Or maybe it was terrorism.

Caitlin had started to carve a serpentine path through the endless machinery, baffling and venting toward the cabins when a door marked GYM caught her eye. She'd missed it in her initial survey of the deck, recalling only now Luke's mention of such a facility as a mainstay of even the smaller jack-up rigs like this.

Caitlin holstered the Glock long enough to turn the hatch wheel until the door snapped open. She eased it inward and started inside, gun in hand again. A few stray rays of the sun illuminated her path just before something struck her hard and fast, a gunshot exploding in her eardrums.

I3

Cort Wesley Masters faced the giant from the center of the makeshift ring atop the dirt, gravel, and stones of the prison yard. He could feel the heat from the relentless sunlight earlier in the day steaming his feet through his shoes. His prison-issue trousers bagged on him like a burlap sack and the matching shirt was dry and scratchy against his skin. That sunlight was intermittent now, coming and going between clouds that had grown darker and more ominous as the day wore on.

The prison yard came complete with two cracked asphalt basketball courts featuring steel nets and dinged flat walls to play a paddle game Cort Wesley hadn't quite figured out yet. If not for the white stone walls topped by barbed wire and three guard towers, only one of which was manned, he supposed this could have been a schoolyard instead. But he doubted that schoolyards came with dust so thick it coated the occupants' mouths and airways to a degree no amount of coughing could relieve, almost as if they'd swallowed chalk. It clung to everything here in Cereso prison, its residue lingering on flesh and hair long after the sun and heat had given up their holds on the day.

The man before Cort Wesley, today's opponent, was well over six feet tall, all of it ugly right up to his rotting teeth held in something trapped between a sneer and a smile. He circled left and then back right, in and out of the sun-dappled grounds darkened by encroaching storm clouds, eager for the fight to start.

Fellow inmates of Cereso prison formed a circle around them, the lowlifes who called themselves guards keeping the choicest spots for themselves. Cort Wesley tightened his fingers into the thick callus pads at their base, squeezing the air from his fists to maximize the efficiency of the blows he was about to unleash. Had to land them fast and sure while keeping his distance. In close the giant, who reeked of something between body odor and dried feces, would gain an advantage he'd never be able to overcome. But keep him moving and parrying, and he would tire fast enough for Cort Wesley's hammer-like fists to finish the job.

The giant was Cort Wesley's twelfth opponent, or maybe his thirteenth. He was the sole American here at Cereso, allowed to live only because his reputation and skills preceded him. He'd bested the reigning champion his first week in and every challenger since, aware each time that losing bore its own terrible price. His myth destroyed and purpose lost, his fellow prisoners would descend upon him with clubs, rocks, and blades the way they would've already had he not provided such great entertainment and discussion. And now the very skills and proclivity for violence that had landed Cort Wesley here in the first place were the only things keeping him alive.

Cereso, like many Mexican prisons, was essentially run by inmates. There were guards about, even what passed weakly for an administration with a warden housed in a white office building enclosed by a separate fence and protected by the single operational guard tower stocked with machine guns that looked vintage World War II. But the inmates kept order themselves, their own hierarchy and pecking order determining virtually every perk and privilege, or the lack thereof.

That protocol had unofficially taken effect in the wake of a series of violent outbreaks that included a 2007 riot staged with rocks, bullets, and blades while three hundred women and children there for visitor's day cowered in fear for their lives. The violence continued for nearly three days before five hundred state and municipal police officers finally managed to quell it. The riot had not been an organized revolt for prisoner's rights or against the awful overcrowding of a facility designed for fifteen hundred inmates, but bursting at the seams with twice that number squeezed in. It had erupted instead out of a power struggle between rival gangs, most notably the Aztecas and the Mexicles.

The state's solution was to create a governing board run by leaders of those and three more gangs. Order was kept, and violence restrained, by the open staging of bare-knuckle fights that made the days of the ancient Roman coliseum seem civilized by comparison. Men chosen for their prowess like Cort Wesley, or others selected as sacrificial lambs served up to the jeering crowd, fought for their lives on the dried gravel and dust of the prison yard. The very prison guards occupying best viewing points also operated lucrative side businesses smuggling all manner of contraband onto the grounds with the acquiescence of the prison administration.

Cort Wesley had been recruited by the Mexicles gang his first day in. They'd made sure he was placed in their cellblock and didn't offer up much negotiation as to terms. The four years of his life he'd spent in the brutal Huntsville, Texas, prison known as The Walls were nothing compared to his first four days in Cereso. And it was abundantly clear that the only way he could survive his stay was to remain in the Mexicles' good graces by keeping the unofficial championship in their block. The giant with the rotting teeth standing across from him now represented the Aztecas, who were committed to ending Cort Wesley's reign here today.

He had never seen the prison yard so full; thousands had assembled today to watch a battle between the champions of two rival gangs for prison supremacy. His ribs ached from the pounding they'd been taking over the course of so many fights. His knees swelled from the sudden twists and slips on the prison's gravel yard where the fights were staged.

Killing a piece of shit Mexican drug dealer had been what landed Cort Wesley in Cereso. Turned out the dealer was the cousin of the local governor who didn't take kindly to Americans blowing away his family members in a cantina. The extradition request to Austin, forwarded from the U.S. State Department, had made for quite the diplomatic crisis until Cort Wesley turned himself in on advice of a counsel who proved no match for the corruption on both sides of the border. His imprisonment here was a kind of compromise while he awaited trial in Mexico. In the interim, corrupt officials on both sides of that same border tried to work out a compromise that would grant his freedom. It was supposed to take a month tops.

Cort Wesley was beginning his tenth month inside Cereso today.

The anger, the frustration, fueled his rage. He stored and bottled it inside him until he needed it the most, then let it go. Each punch he threw, each blow he struck, had that unrestrained fury behind it, and each time one landed he saw the face of Dylan, Luke, or

Caitlin Strong and knew he was that much closer to getting home to them.

If he was ever going to see them again, though, he had to get past the giant whose rancid smell flooded his nostrils from ten feet away. Thunder crackled in the darkening sky, sounding like the thunk of a fist mashing flesh, jawbone, and teeth. Then drizzle began to pepper the air, the storm clouds still somehow leaving thin gaps for the sun to sneak in and out of.

"*Man's a beast, bubba,*" he heard old Leroy Epps say from his side, the way a trainer might.

"He is at that, champ," Cort Wesley said soft enough so no one else would hear.

Leroy Epps had been a lifer in The Walls, busted for killing a white man in self-defense, whose friendship and guidance had gotten Cort Wesley through his years in captivity. The diabetes that would ultimately kill him had turned Leroy's eyes bloodshot and numbed his limbs years before the sores and infections set in. As a boxer, he'd fought for the middleweight crown on three different occasions, knocked out once and had the belt stolen from him on paid-off judges' scorecards on two other occasions. He'd died three years into Cort Wesley's incarceration, but ever since always seemed to show up when needed the most. Whether a ghostly specter or a figment of his imagination, Cort Wesley had given up trying to figure out. Either way, here in Cereso Epps was his only friend and the only person, or whatever, he could talk to.

"*You know what they say about the bigger they are,*" Epps continued.

"The harder they fall?"

"*Nope, the more likely they are to kick the shit out*

of you if you don't take the fight to them first. You know what I'm saying here?"

"I've got a pretty good idea."

"You gotta take this sumbitch quick, bubba. We'll celebrate afterwards with a root beer." Old Leroy shook his head and sucked in some breath. Cort Wesley imagined the thickening rain running rivulets down his dried skin and beading up on his close-cropped graying afro haircut. *"Man, I miss the ring, yes I do."*

"All that's missing here, champ, is the bell."

"Ding-ding," Epps said, the crowd erupting into crazed cheers when a guard captain brought a hand down between the two combatants to start the fight.

14

NUEVO LAREDO, MEXICO; THE PRESENT

The giant came in fast and hard, used to ending fights quickly on brute strength and power. He'd transferred in a month before and beaten two men to bloody pulps in his previous forays into the yard. Cort Wesley had watched the final fight in which the giant had hammered his opponent's face so hard and so often that nothing even recognizable as human was left when he was done, the man looking as if someone had driven a pickup truck over him. The giant was massive, the giant was strong, but he wasn't particularly quick or skilled, relying on his size and ability to absorb pain to win him his first two bouts. All he need do was land one punch in a bare-knuckled brawl like this and the fight would be effectively over, and that's the way it had been in his first two fights.

But not today.

The giant was quicker than he looked from a spectator's viewpoint and much lighter on his feet than Cort Wesley expected. Looked as if he'd been holding plenty back in those initial fights, perhaps to goad Cort Wesley into a false confidence that would lead him to take the bait the giant was now offering. Cort Wesley sidestepped his way into a circle, the giant matching his motions like a mirror. The crowd's cheers quickly gave way to jeers, thirsting for the action and blood they were expecting.

"He's giving you his whole right side," Leroy Epps warned in his ear. *"That means you don't take it."*

Cort Wesley flicked the rain from his face and slid in and out of the irregular shafts of sunlight that brightened the otherwise blackening ground. He could have opted to try tiring the poorly conditioned giant out, except for the fact he was too much the worse for wear to trust his own conditioning. The crowd might have loved a long, bloody fight staged between prodigious rivals. But the truth was ending the fight as early as possible was the key to staying alive long enough to see his boys and Caitlin again with his brains intact as opposed to mush.

"Got a bum knee on the left," said Leroy Epps. *"Can tell by the way he's keeping his weight forward on the right even when it's against the grain."*

"Gotcha, champ."

"Miss your chance and he'll tear your face off, bubba."

The giant wheeled in toward him with a sudden lurch, uncorking a wild roundhouse blow Cort Wesley ducked under and then hammered the giant's ribs with a right-left combination on the way by. It was like hitting concrete. Didn't even draw a flinch or wince. The giant simply sneered and loped in sideways, more cocky than confident.

He looked confused when Cort Wesley didn't take the bait, choosing instead to backpedal and test the giant's maneuverability by launching a quick flurry of blows that smashed his jaw with no measurable effect at all. The giant spit blood and saliva onto the hard-packed gravel, his booted feet kicking a storm of debris into the air.

"You see that, bubba?"

"See what?"

"I was wrong before 'bout why the monster's favoring his left so. Ain't no trick, no. On account of that right eye instead. It's watering like Niagara friggin' Falls."

Leroy Epps was suddenly standing right there for no one else to see, aglow in a ribbon of sunburst that looked like a tunnel carved from sky to ground. Cort Wesley swung from the illusion, ghost, specter, or whatever it was just as the giant wheeled in on him, slamming a fist that felt like a steam iron into his torso. Cort Wesley turned at the last, taking the brunt of the blow on his ribs and feeling them bend inward on impact, nearly cracking.

A vast whoosh of air blew out of him and he staggered backward. He ducked under the giant's next blow, slipped on the now soaked gravel, and felt the giant's massive hands grabbing for him. One closed on his shirt collar, going for his throat, but Cort Wesley twisted, leaving his shirt instead of his skin in the man's deadly grasp.

He turned fast, nearly slipping on the drenched earth again as the giant whirled toward him. Cort Wesley backed out of range of the next blow, then launched a kick that the giant intercepted before it found his groin. Next thing Cort Wesley knew he was airborne, pitched through the drenching rain and slapping the ground hard upon landing to deflect the impact.

A thin beam of sunlight peeked out, then vanished behind the giant's massive bulk. The giant raised a booted foot over Cort Wesley's face and brought it down like a pistol-driven anvil. Cort Wesley rolled free of that blow and another, jerking back to his feet and feeling his damaged ribs press up against the flesh and cartilage containing them.

"*Ugly mother's mashing your juice to shit,*" Leroy Epps was saying.

"Tell me something I don't know," Cort Wesley thought, or maybe said out loud.

"*How 'bout this, bubba: sun's coming.*"

"So?"

"*Take a good look.*"

Before Cort Wesley could do that, the giant rushed him in an old-fashioned graceless charge. He twisted aside like a matador facing a bull, tripping the big man up and sending him sprawling into a pool of water collected in a depression in the yard. Cort Wesley pounced on his back and shoved his face into the fetid pool of rain, gravel, and stones, but the giant used his great strength to wrench himself free.

Cort Wesley tumbled off to the side and spun away from another wild attack. The giant was gasping for air now, his breaths turned to rancid whistling wheezes that sounded bizarrely like a baby's whine. A fresh shaft of sunlight appeared like a beam from the sky, as Cort Wesley fought to keep his own breath.

What was it Leroy Epps had just said? . . . *Sun's coming.* . . .

And there it was, bright and blinding amid the torrents of rain that bled in and out of its ribbon trailed by rainbow colors flitting about the strange tunnel carved from the sky.

"*Now, bubba, now!*"

Cort Wesley feinted. Launched a purposefully wild flurry of blows meant only to drive the giant into the sun.

"*I was wrong before 'bout why the monster's favoring his left so,*" Leroy Epps had told him. "*Ain't no trick, no. On account of that right eye instead.*"

So Cort Wesley sidestepped to make the giant use his right eye to follow him, then positioned himself to push that right eye's sightline straight into the sun in the last moment before the storm clouds swallowed it once more.

Cort Wesley attacked, the move born of instinct and bred of his training in the Special Forces. Before he could record his own action, he'd scissor-kicked the giant's left knee, buckling it. The giant sank at the waist, and Cort Wesley hammered his groin with a knee and thorax with an elbow. The breath flooding from him sounded like a balloon popping, the man's head in his hands now, a single twist to snap the neck.

But Cort Wesley didn't twist, jamming thumbs into both the giant's eyes and then slamming a fist into his throat with enough force to drop him without crushing his windpipe. The giant crumpled to his knees, flailing for his face and neck, then keeled over facefirst into the rainwater lapping across the gravel surface.

Thunder rumbled. No, not thunder at all, but the wild applause and hoots of the Mexicles gang members celebrating his, and thus their, victory over their dreaded rivals, the Aztecas.

Cort Wesley looked to the sky, eyes open to the rain, letting it wash him clean under the certainty the filth wouldn't stay off for long.

"*Winner and still champion, bubba,*" said Leroy Epps.

15

NUEVO LAREDO, MEXICO; THE PRESENT

Cort Wesley stood in the shower, the steaming hot water feeling like needles against his skin that was angry with pain. He got to take a shower inside in a stall normally reserved for the guards every time he won a fight. His ribs throbbed, his face hurt, and the back of his skull felt cottony numb. He listened to the thunder booming outside and the torrents of rain hammering the roof over his head. The stench of spoiled milk drifted down from the cellblock, courtesy of many Mexican prisoners' penchant to leave it to curdle so they could make their own cottage cheese.

His hair had grown out, longest it had been in years, the near total lack of mirrors sparing him the sight of the gray tinting the black in thickening patches. He shaved blindly, often with cold water and bar soap for cream. Normally, showers were taken outside under heads dribbling cold water that stopped when he let go of the chain over his head. The stench of the place was awful, his as bad as anyone else's. But in the Gulf War he'd once gone seventy days without a shower and only one change of clothes. He'd gotten used to stinking like a goat there just as he had here.

"*Why didn't you kill that sumbitch, bubba?*" Leroy Epps asked him, drawing not even a flinch from Cort Wesley, whose neck muscles had finally loosened from the hot water cascading against them.

"I didn't want Caitlin and the boys to see me do it."

"*Only one watching of any regard was me.*"

"Not in my mind, champ. Caitlin and the boys were there too. They're always there."

"*Keeps you going, I reckon.*"

"For ten months now."

"*Wish I could see the end to all this. But even from where I stand, it's not exactly clear.*"

"I think you're holding out on me, champ."

"*When have I ever done that, bubba? I can't see it, 'cause it's not there, not all of it anyway. All kinds of roads ahead and they all lead someplace different. Ultimately, choice is gonna be yours.*"

"That's comforting."

"*Didn't mean it to sound that way.*"

"No?"

"*Trouble's coming.*"

"How's that?"

"*You'll see. Don't wanna go breaking any more rules than I have already. But there's a doorway about to open out.*"

Cort Wesley turned off the water and swung to find old Leroy standing before him, bloodshot eyes drooping and sad.

"*Where it leads ain't where you wanna go precisely being the problem. Trouble for sure, bubba, of a different kind.*"

Cort Wesley had started to respond when the door to the staff changing room opened and the captain of the guards poked his head through. He seemed to look in Leroy Epps's direction briefly before finding Cort Wesley in his gaze.

"You got a visitor, amigo."

16

NORTHERN GULF STREAM, THE PRESENT

Whatever had slammed against her felt stiff and flaccid at the same time, formless somehow. Caitlin had spun, whipping the Glock around and forgetting its infamous hair trigger in the process. The reverberation of the gunshot in the blast oven confines of the *Mariah*'s gym deafened her while the muzzle flash freeze-framed the sight she'd just started to register:

Bodies, two dozen of them maybe, piled askew atop the equipment and floor, their limbs hanging every which way and the stink of death permeating the air.

She shoved the corpse that must have been perched behind the door from her, ears still ringing but eyes using the light sifting through from the platform beyond to begin to discern what had transpired. The coppery stench of blood was thick and strong, this windowless room clearly the source of the smell she'd caught on the wind shortly after she'd first mounted the platform.

Judging by the amount of blood soaking into the rubber flooring laid in place to cushion the sounds of clanking steel coming from the gym, the *Mariah*'s crew had been gathered in here and killed execution style. The first four victims she was close enough to study clearly had fallen to perfectly placed headshots, two for each by the look of things.

Caitlin saw it all in her mind, picturing three or four shooters spread in front of the door firing away at men utterly baffled by what had befallen them, the reasons for their murders lost somewhere in the roar of bullets and gun smoke. The engine room worker must have avoided the initial roundup and then fought off the attackers long enough to reach an emergency escape raft with at least one bullet in him.

She didn't have a flashlight, nor did she want to disturb the crime scene any more than she already had, allowing herself only a cursory inspection of the gym. But that was enough to reveal not a single bullet hole in the walls, either from a miss or a through-and-through. And that could only mean that the three or four killers she'd pictured in her mind earlier were top professionals. Cort Wesley Masters level even.

So, near as she could tell, a team of professional gunmen had found their way on board a jack-up oil rig and murdered two dozen workers. If there was any conceivable sense in that, Caitlin couldn't see, find, or imagine it.

She emerged back into the light of the platform, never gladder to smell fresh sea air. The Coast Guard was still nowhere in sight and didn't have the proper investigative apparatus to handle a mass murder of this scope anyway. Neither did the local sheriff's department, so Caitlin decided to save some time and slice through a bit of red tape.

"You better not be calling me from up on that rig, Ranger," Tepper said angrily, as soon as she got him on the line.

"We got a code word for the kind of emergency we don't want broadcast for anyone to hear?" Caitlin asked him.

"Nope. Why?"

"Because I believe we're gonna need one."

17

NORTHERN GULF STREAM, THE PRESENT

Tepper arrived with a Ranger forensics team via helicopter three hours later, ninety minutes after the Coast Guard finally pulled up in a pair of crash boats fresh from finding the bodies of two of the missing college kids. He climbed out from the chopper onto the helipad and clambored down the steel steps to the deck, his face ashen and eyes looking as if he'd taken the trip with the angel of death seated next to him.

"You don't look so good, Captain," Caitlin greeted at the bottom of the stairs.

"Neither do you, Ranger."

"Finding a couple dozen men and women gunned down as they stood will do that to you."

"Women?"

Caitlin nodded. "Two. I didn't even know they pulled duty on a rig like this."

Tepper gave her a longer look. "Yeah, women are

making progress in all kinds of previously male-dominated worlds." He started to take off his Stetson, then fit it back into place. "Man, I hate the water, especially when I gotta go someplace I don't want to go to meet someone who doesn't belong there in the first place."

Caitlin gazed about the expanse of open sea around them. "You see any other law enforcement body in the area?"

Tepper held his eyes on her instead, sternly. "What I see is someone prone to ignore whatever I tell her. You're still riding a desk, as far as I'm concerned."

"Tell that to the bodies I found."

Tepper wrinkled his nose. "Well, at least I'm not seasick."

"You've hated boats ever since . . . What was it again?"

"Galveston Island, with your dad and granddad. Was your granddad's last case and don't ever ask me about it again."

It might have been the light or a product of Caitlin's imagination, but Tepper's face looked even more ashen. He took a pack of Marlboros from his jacket and stuck one in his mouth.

"We're on an oil rig, Captain."

"So?"

"I'd imagine they have a strict no-smoking policy here."

Tepper frowned deeply enough to send the deep furrows branching across both cheeks. "I don't see anyone here of a mind to protest."

And he fired up a match.

* * *

"You shot up plenty in your time, Ranger," Tepper said after completing his own initial survey of the scene inside the cramped gymnasium in the company of the Ranger crime scene team, "but this is the first time you shot up a corpse."

"I'm not used to a Glock."

"I suppose I shouldn't ask where it came from."

"Good idea."

Tepper cast his gaze over Caitlin's shoulder. "Speaking of which, I think you got company, 'mom.' "

The platform's cross-breeze tossed Dylan's hair across one side of his face and then the other. He ended up holding a hand in the thick black waves to keep it still.

"Coast Guard told us to go back to Baffin Bay."

"This is a crime scene now, son."

"And I gotta watch Luke while you go back to being a Ranger."

"When did I stop?"

He pulled his hand from his hair and blew his breath through it. "Last couple of days just felt nice, that's all."

"And you saying you missed your friends, your girls."

The boy kicked at the deck with his sneaker. "Why you have to put it that way?"

"What way?"

"Like it's a joke."

"You see me laughing, Dyl?"

"I'm seventeen," the boy said, squeezing his features taut and stopping just short of a scowl. "I've got a life."

"I don't think you need to tell me that."

"I mean a *real* life, with *real* friends and *real* girls."

"I have absolutely no idea what you're talking about."

Dylan flashed a smile at her that quickly slid from his face as if the wind had brushed it off. "That's what my father always said."

"Past tense?"

"For now."

Caitlin smiled too. "Well, he was fond of saying the same thing to me. I guess that's where I picked it up."

"Can I have my gun back?"

"No."

"Can I get yours out of the truck?"

"No."

Dylan grinned again and shook his head, his face disappearing in a mask of hair. "I feel you, Caitlin," he said through the strands.

"Boy misses his dad," Tepper said, as Captain Bob's charter boat motored away from the *Mariah*.

Caitlin watched it shrinking toward the horizon, no longer able to make out the shapes of Dylan and Luke looking back at her. "Some days I get it in my mind to bust their father out of that damn place."

"You miss Masters too, just as much. He plugged a big hole in your life, but that's not all."

"What else is there?"

"He lets you be. Not many men out there are willing to play second fiddle to that gun of yours."

"Not a problem lately."

"You blaming me for that, Ranger?"

When Caitlin failed to respond, Tepper swirled his tongue about his parched lips. They looked pale and chapped, the late spring heat taking its toll.

"I had a dream about your friend Guillermo Paz last night," Tepper said, referring to the former Venezuelan assassin who always seemed to surface when Caitlin needed him most. "He was on top of the Empire State Building, swatting away biplanes."

"I haven't seen him since the shoot-out at the Patriot Sun, Captain."

"Nobody has. That's what worries me."

"I'd likely be dead if it wasn't for Paz. You should keep that in mind.

Tepper stared up into the sun until his eyes watered. "Had a friend once worked at a game preserve tending the crocodiles, one of which was a twenty-five-footer named Oscar that might've been a thousand years old for all he knew. Used to boast about how he'd bonded with the thing 'cause he fed it. Could pet Oscar like he was a goddamn dog. This went on for years until one day, just like any other, he was walking through its paddock and Oscar ate him whole."

"What's this have to do with Paz?"

"I think you know what I'm getting at."

Caitlin looked at Tepper but didn't respond. Eager to change the subject, she swept her eyes about the deck, focusing on the Rangers supervising evidence collection on the part of Coast Guard personnel. With a storm brewing and whatever evidence there was soon to be compromised by the elements, they had to work fast as well as thoroughly.

"We're looking at the biggest mass murder in modern Texas history," Tepper said, sparing Caitlin the need to talk further about Cort Wesley.

"You forgetting Waco?"

Tepper looked as if he'd just swallowed something that disagreed with him. "I was one of the first inside after they put the fire out. You bet I'm trying to forget that."

18

"Okay," Tepper told Caitlin, the two of them in the shadow cast by one of the drilling derricks as the last of the afternoon sun bled from the sky, "this is what we got. This jack-up crew hasn't done any oil drilling in ten days."

"Come again?"

"You heard me."

"One of those new offshore ordinances shut the rig down?"

"Nope, they only apply to the deepwater rigs, not the shallow. According to the logs, the crew stopped of their own volition. Some big shots from GSEP are en route now. Hopefully, they'll be able to shed more light on the situation."

"GSEP?"

"Gulf Strategic Energy Partners. A consortium of smaller companies operating jack-up shallow-water rigs like the *Mariah*. Not nearly as much profit potential as their deepwater brothers but not nearly the same risks either. Thing is they're held to the same monitoring and safety requirements Shell, Chevron, BP, Exxon are."

"Tell that to the crew," said Caitlin.

The Department of Public Safety in Austin gave the Rangers formal charge of the investigation a few minutes later, Caitlin and Tepper waiting for the GSEP execs to arrive by running through everything they knew so far.

"You want me to stay on this or not, D.W.?"

"Well, you've come this far, and I don't have anyone else available right now."

"Does this qualify as an official reinstatement?"

"Let me put it this way, Ranger. I'm not clearing your desk out at Company headquarters yet. Long as we're talking, what do you make for the timeline?"

"Started not long after dawn," Caitlin told him.

Tepper took off his Stetson and smoothed his thin hair slathered with Brylcreem back into place. "Explain."

"Raft outboard was cold to the touch by the time the man who escaped reached the *Mariah*. I don't know if he ever even got it started and if so he didn't hold on to it long. Thing has a dead man's switch . . ."

"Literally, in this case."

"Right. His hand drops off the control, the engine shuts down. Now, judging by the sunburn on his face I figure he was drifting on the currents for ninety minutes, maybe two hours at the outside. Almost nine o'clock on the button when Captain Bob reeled the raft in. Backtrack the time the killers showed up and it brings you to around dawn."

"Not much activity. Perfect time to strike."

"That was my thought too."

"We found plenty of half-eaten meals in the mess hall, like the killers interrupted their breakfast." Tepper paused, started to reach for a fresh Marlboro but changed his mind. "So why not kill them there? Why drag them all the way to the gym to do the deed?"

"Haven't gotten that far in my thinking yet, Captain."

Tepper turned and gazed into the sun dropping for the horizon, the late-afternoon rays exaggerating the length and depth of the furrows he wore like fade spots on a favorite leather jacket. He held a cupped hand upon his brow, as a helicopter grew in the narrowing distance, soaring straight for the *Mariah*.

"Looks like we got company, Ranger."

19

NORTHERN GULF STREAM, THE PRESENT

The Gulf Strategic Energy Partners executives numbered three, a pair of vice presidents and Robert Killibrew, who introduced himself as the operations manager. Killibrew wore his grief in bloodshot, weary eyes. Caitlin had given too many family members bad news in her time, and the shell-shocked look on his face most resembled theirs, genuine in the pain and helplessness it portrayed.

"The bodies need to be positively identified," he said before Caitlin or Captain Tepper could. "I'm going to inform the families personally."

"I'm sure they'll appreciate that, sir," Tepper told him. "But if you'd rather wait until—"

"No, Captain. I think it would be more prudent to do it here." He shook his head, stuffed his hands in his pockets to still their trembling. "As OM, I spent ten or so days a month on the rig. I rotated off just two days ago, so I could just as easily have been . . ."

Killibrew let his voice trail off. The stiff wind blowing across the *Mariah*'s deck billowed his windbreaker outfitted with a fancy GSEP logo. He wore glasses and had thinning blond hair that was blowing every which way. Except for the knot, his tie was concealed by the windbreaker and he wore khakis that looked too tight on him.

Coast Guard personnel had just finished moving the bodies from inside the gymnasium, a Ranger having demonstrated how to use bedsheets to wrap them tightly enough to be impervious to the stiff wind. The plan was then to use one of the rig's cranes to off-load them onto the two crash boats for transport back to the mainland where rescue wagons would be waiting to take them to the nearest medical examiner's office. Even though the sun still burned strong enough in the sky, someone had switched on the rig's bright night lighting or maybe it had gone on automatically by itself.

"I appreciate and respect your concern for your employees, sir," Caitlin told Killibrew, "but right now the best thing you can do for them is help us figure out what exactly happened here."

"Mr. Leon and Mr. Golding can handle the IDs," Killibrew said, clearing his throat when his voice wouldn't stop cracking. "That leaves me at your disposal, Ranger."

Caitlin, Tepper, and Killibrew reconvened inside the media room where a DVD of the latest movie directed by Clint Eastwood had been the last one to play. The room was cool and dimly lit, welcome respite from the sun's heat and rays that had dominated the day. The three of them took seats on faux leather chairs complete with cup holders, but Killibrew bounced up quickly, unable to remain still. He started pacing, the clack of his shoes the only sound in the room other than a ceiling fan with a loose bolt whirling noisily overhead.

"You should sit down, sir," Caitlin advised finally.

He stopped pacing, then resumed just as fast. "I should be back on deck, with my crew."

Whether he meant Leon and Golding or the twenty-five who had perished on the *Mariah,* Caitlin wasn't sure. She glanced at D. W. Tepper whose nod told her to take the lead.

"Your crew are the reason you need to talk to us, Mr. Killibrew. You're the only one who may have some notion of why this happened and who may have been behind it."

Killibrew stopped pacing. His thin blond hair had formed itself into a forelock that drooped toward his eyebrows, grazing the top of the one on the right. The ceiling fan pushed dark shadows across his face, covering one eye and then the other.

"Just tell me what you need to know," he said.

Caitlin crossed her arms. "Well, one odd thing springs immediately to mind, that being why the rig's work logs show they shut down the drilling operation ten days ago."

"That was on my orders," Killibrew said, unmoved by the revelation.

"Was there something wrong with the equipment? Did you have any reason to fear a blowout, something like that?"

"No, not at all. We just find the oil, we don't bring it up—that's a drilling platform's job. Before this rig had a chance to find anything, though, the camera on our ROV, remote operated vehicle, caught something that looked strange and my foreman had the sense to put a hold on things," Killibrew told her. "Turns out he is, I mean was, an amateur historian, enough to know something potentially important when he sees it, a shipwreck in this case."

Tepper leaned as far sideways as his chair would let him. "Shipwreck?"

"Maybe the most famous ever in these waters. The *Mother Mary*."

Caitlin watched Tepper nearly slide all the way out of his chair, the furrows on his face straightening to the point where his expression took on the texture of glass a stiff breeze might shatter. He lifted his Marlboros from his jacket but struggled to open the pack with his knobby, arthritic fingers that were now trembling.

"No smoking allowed on this rig," Killibrew warned. "A spark settling in the wrong place could blow us all to hell."

"We may already be there," Tepper said, heading for the door.

"What's got you so spooked, D.W.?" Caitlin asked Tepper outside the media room.

Tepper finally got his pack opened and cigarette lit. "You believe in ghosts, Ranger?"

Caitlin thought of catching Cort Wesley having conversations with his dead cellmate from The Walls, and her own visions of spotting her dad or granddad from time to time. She felt a sudden chill amid the heat still roasting the rig around her, gooseflesh prickling her arms. "Never thought about it much," she lied.

"Well, I feel like I just saw one."

"That shipwreck Killebrew mentioned, the *Mother Mary*?"

Tepper took a deep drag on his Marlboro, then flicked it aside and stamped it out with his boot. "I hate the goddamn water, Caitlin. I hate the water, I hate islands, and most of all I hate boats."

Tepper stopped, his thoughts hanging in the air the way the trail of his cigarette smoke lingered.

"I'm still listening, D.W.," Caitlin told him.

"Galveston Island, Ranger. It's time you finally heard the story."

20

GALVESTON ISLAND, 1979

"You don't look too good, D.W.," Jim Strong said in the back of the launch ferrying them out to Galveston Island. A recent tropical storm has washed out both the Interstate 45 causeway to the north and the San Luis Pass-Vacek Toll Bridge to the south, necessitating the Rangers make this trip to the island via boat. "Last time I saw a man that yellow, he was an alcoholic with a shot liver who died of jaundice inside of a week."

"Nah," Earl Strong said from his perch by the gunwale, lowering a boot back to the deck, "smoking'll be the death of D. W. Tepper long before drink will."

"You boys just keep having your fun at my expense," Tepper managed in between retches. "But there's nothing in the Ranger code says a man can't get seasick. How long we been doing this and I ain't never had to ride the waters before."

The Strongs, father and son, exchanged a smile, as Tepper leaned further over the launch's stern on the chance his breakfast might make a return trip up his throat. Earl had just celebrated his seventy-ninth birthday. Other than his sun-weathered skin that had taken on the look of cracked leather, though, he showed few signs of age. His still thick hair had equal patches of gray and white. He kept the same weight he had from twenty years ago and, with Stetson fastened tight and Springfield model 1911 .45 holstered on his hip, he looked every bit the part of the Texas Ranger legend he was.

This was the man, after all, who'd pretty much cleaned up Sweetwater, the dirtiest of the oil boomtowns of the 1930s. He'd faced down Al Capone's boys when they made a run at returning Texas to the Old West, sending more of them to the grave than back to Chicago. Not surprisingly, Capone's outfit never returned to the Lone Star State. Earl had also laid waste to the Mexican drug cartels in the legendary Battle of Juárez in 1934, after waging his own personal war with them north of the border. Earl Strong defined the Texas Ranger of the twentieth century, an example to be held high for others to emulate while never quite reaching.

Earl's son Jim had been born into a different age, one filled with more rules, regulations, and paperwork for legendary lawmen whose founding dated back to a time in the 1800s when many of them couldn't read or write. But that didn't stop Jim Strong from making his own mark as a Ranger, albeit without the spectacular gunslinging exploits of his legendary father.

He'd been dispatched to the Rio Grande valley in 1966, four years after becoming a Ranger at the age of thirty, when the United Farm Workers struck for higher wages, setting off a firestorm of violence. He'd been on the front lines when a criminal named Fred Gomez Carrasco led inmates in an armed takeover of the Walls Unit in Huntsville State Prison in 1974. But he'd curtailed his efforts as of late following the brutal murder of his wife at the hands of the very drug cartels his father had laid waste to four decades before. There was the raising of his daughter, Caitlin, to focus on now, his number one priority.

"Been meaning to talk to you about something," his father said, sliding up next to him as D. W. Tepper vomited over the stern again. "Figured it's time I pulled back a ways, stop tempting fate to come chase me down."

"Dad," Jim Strong started, "if fate was gonna catch you, it would've done so already. You got it running scared, just like everything else ever stood in your way."

"Point being that I'd hoped to be ranging 'til I was eighty, and a year advance of that at this stage don't hold a lot of weight."

"Never figured you for the retiring type."

"Didn't say I was or had any intention of being. But we got ourselves a little girl to raise and spending the rest of my days educating her in the ways of the Rangers is an attractive prospect from where I'm standing."

"Caitlin's three years old, Dad."

"You put a toy pistol and a doll out for her and you know which one she'd pick every time, son, so I won't have age used as a factor here. She's gonna be a Ranger; you know it, I know it, so let's get started early to give her the advantages a woman in our ranks will sorely need."

"That what you really want for her?"

"Four generations have come and gone before her. Wasn't a question for them and it won't be for her. Fact that she's a woman means a lighter gun, that's all. But her bullets'll be the same weight and travel at the same speed."

Jim Strong could only shake his head as D. W. Tepper heaved up the rest of his breakfast behind him. "Earl Strong, babysitter."

"Kind of has a nice ring, don't it?"

The Rangers had been called to Galveston Island by Sheriff Mumford Plantaine, better known as Mugsy, to investigate a murder. Details were sketchy at this point. All Jim and Earl Strong knew was that it was bad. And since Austin had dispatched the two of them along with Tepper, it must have been *really* bad. Strangely enough, Jim and Earl had never actually worked a case together. Sure, there were occasions when prison or labor riots, jailhouse takeovers, and outlaw groups had called them out among a whole assemblage of Rangers. But Galveston was the first criminal investigation on which they'd ever been paired.

Galveston had long occupied a distinct place in the history of Texas, as well as a distinct character. It was a beautiful, sun-swept island rich with the vibrant colors of oleander trees that towered over its pristine beaches and shorelines, as well as dotting the main residential streets and commercial thoroughfares. In 1528, when the first Europeans landed, Galveston Island was home to Akokisa and Karankawa Indians who camped, fished, and hunted the swampy land. The Spanish explorer Cabeza de Vaca was shipwrecked on the island and lived among the Karankawa for several years as a medicine man and slave. In the late 1600s, French explorer Robert Cavelier de La Salle claimed the island for King Louis and named it St. Louis.

But later Galveston would be formally named for Bernardo de Gálvez, a Spanish colonial governor and general. Gálvez sent José de Evia to chart the Gulf of Mexico from the Texas coast to New Orleans, and on

July 23, 1786, de Evia charted an area near the mouth of a river and named it Galveston Bay. Later, the island and city took the same name. Bernardo de Gálvez died the same year, never once setting foot on his namesake island.

But history hadn't always treated the beautiful island so well. In September of 1900, Galveston was struck hard and fast by what became known as the Great Storm. At the time the island had a population of 37,000 and was the fourth largest city in Texas following Houston, Dallas, and San Antonio. One-third of the city was completely destroyed, including over 3,600 buildings. More than 6,000 people were killed, far too many for conventional burials. At first, they were weighted and buried at sea. When the corpses started washing ashore, they were instead burned on funeral pyres all over the city.

The Great Storm might have sounded the final death knell for the island were it not for Prohibition. Thanks in large part to that era's bootlegging, Galveston evolved into a gambling and drinking mecca, giving it a second life and bringing back enough commerce to keep its residents afloat. But that era came to a sudden end on June 10, 1957, when Texas Rangers under Earl Strong's command raided the city to serve injunctions against the gambling joints and took axes to the slot machines, sending Galveston into yet another economic and social tailspin.

The once sparkling island languished for years but a revival had been undertaken when investors saw a potential gold mine in Galveston's sun-drenched shoreline and pristine landscape. Their goal was nothing less than to turn it into an island resort that would become the envy of the Northern Gulf. Earl hadn't kept much track of things there since his own raid, although Jim had told him the island elders, some of whose Galveston bloodlines dated back centuries, were planning to enact a New Orleans–like Mardi Gras to kick the process off. Besides that, and tourists perusing the remnants of the famed pirate Jean Lafitte's Campeche base camp, for all Earl knew he'd been returning to a world of slot parlors and strip joints.

"Should I bring my ax?" he'd asked Jim with a smile when the younger Strong picked him up.

Sheriff Mugsy Plantaine met their launch at the main pier. Plantaine, who neither Earl nor Jim could remember not showing dark splotches of sweat through his uniform top, looked about as bad as D. W. Tepper; even more pale, in fact, while not quite as yellow.

"What's got you looking like a raccoon staring down a semi, Mugsy?" Jim Strong asked him.

"And why all the secrecy about what got us called here?" Earl added, as D. W. Tepper coughed up some stray spittle and joined them on the pier.

"We don't want or need any press on this, boys, and by the way it's good to see you too."

"You don't look like it's good to see us," said Jim.

"Let me correct that impression: it's great to see you on the island; it's the circumstances that'll make you puke."

Earl took off his hat and looked up at the sky as if to study the sun. "Only need one Ranger for a riot, Mugs. Seems a lot to have three of us for a killing."

"*Killing*, Ranger? I only wish."

* * *

Sheriff Plantaine drove the three Rangers along a road that rimmed the coast of Galveston Island, showing off the beauty of a shoreline dominated by winglets, gulls, and terns buzzing the sky in search of their next meal. The island didn't boast many residents in comparison to modern-day standards, but the sand was alive with strollers and joggers who almost surely didn't appreciate the pristine beauty that would soon be violated by all manner of tourist and vacationer. All three Rangers found themselves smirking at the wild hairstyles worn by men and women, the shorts and bathing suits of the men so tight they seemed to be crushing the private parts contained within.

"What's that music?" Earl Strong asked, hearing hammering riffs drifting with the wind.

"Disco," Jim Strong told him.

"What the hell's disco?"

"You know," said Jim, "I really can't say. I guess you'd call it dance music."

"People *dance* to that these days?" Earl could only shake his head. "Well, I'll be glad to be back somewheres the words got some sense to them and you can actually hear what's being sung."

A similar song came on the radio in Plantaine's truck.

"Believe that's the Bee Gees," said Tepper. "My daughter's got all their records."

"Now I think *I'm* gonna be sick," moaned Earl.

Plantaine shut the radio off. "Strange thing about Galveston," he began. "Only part of the island the Great Storm didn't beat to hell was the remaining wild part, last remnants of Jean Lafitte's Campeche colony where his pirates made camp and kept their stolen slaves prior to sale. Jim Bowie was a Ranger when he ran those slaves into Texas for him, wasn't he?"

"Nope," said Earl. "Rangers didn't exist yet back then. Bowie was a prime Texas landowner who took a Mexican wife. He was at the Alamo to protect his own acres as much as anything."

"Doesn't seem to be any way to talk about a Texas legend."

"You heard some of the stuff that's been said about me?" Earl asked him.

"Anyway," Plantaine started again, his cheeks flushed red and his eyes too small and narrow for the rest of his round face, "the crime scene is located smack dab in the middle of Campeche country. Fraternity brothers from the University of Texas at Austin."

"Plural?"

The sheriff of Galveston Island simply nodded, swallowing hard.

His deputies had secured the crime scene located at the mouth of a cave camouflaged by moss and weeds, the entrance nearly invisible. The ravaged bodies of the five fraternity brothers remained undisturbed or touched, exactly as they'd been found lying amid streams of their own entrails on ground darkened by blood.

D. W. Tepper inspected the bodies more closely while Jim and Earl Strong walked the perimeter of a clearing where Jean Lafitte himself had likely bedded down before he'd fled to South America around 1820.

"Tracks are every which way," Earl noted.

"Got no expended shells or blood trail," Jim added, crouching to better study the overgrown ground as he moved. "I don't see a lot of signs of a struggle. When this happen exactly?"

"Last night sometime, as near as we can figure. Couple of locals found them. Think they may be ready to put their homes on the market after seeing all this."

"Got a couple head wounds here that make me think these boys got taken by surprise, likely from the rear," Tepper reported. "But I got no idea what did all the rest of this damage. Looks like they've been gutted. I can see some wounds that are multiple, shallow, and jagged, like the blades were old and fit more for skinning game than killing. Seems to me the gut spilling came afterwards, maybe even postmortem, for effect as much as anything it could be."

"Toward what end?" asked Sheriff Plantaine.

"Divert attention from a brutal murder by making it seem it's something it's not."

"Like what?"

"Can't say yet."

"Look," Plantaine said, his shirt considerably more sweat-soaked than it had been when they set out from the dock, "Galveston is about to burst onto the scene in a big way. We don't get this resolved pretty quick, there's gonna be some serious hell to pay from the money behind those new hotels, resorts, and marina we passed on the way out here."

"Not to mention all them golf courses," Earl Strong added.

"Glad you understand the stakes here."

"Only steaks I know are the kind you grill over charcoal, Sheriff, and I don't give a hoot about the political pressure you're under here. What me, Jim, and D.W. over there care about is finding whoever sliced up these boys for no apparent reason. And the only ones behind anything we care about are these boys' folks. We're going to do right by them. No ifs, ands, or buts about it."

"Did I suggest anything otherwise?" Plantaine asked.

"It seemed you were fixing to. Might be the way local law enforcement works but there's nothing local about Rangers."

"Well, it's hard for me to envision anyone local to the island doing something like this. Hell, I know practically everyone by sight."

"That include all the workmen it takes to build this resort community of yours?" Jim Strong asked him.

Plantaine gulped down some air in response.

"Yeah," Jim added, "that's what I figured."

"The point being," Earl picked up, "that we got suspects coming out the wazoo and who knows what these dead boys might've walked in on them doing."

Earl and Jim both moved to the cave mouth, gazing inside in tandem before turning back toward Plantaine. "Tell us about this," Jim said.

"Not much to tell."

"Ever been inside?"

"Far enough to tell you it doesn't lead anywhere."

"What about Jean Lafitte's lost treasure?" Earl picked up. "What exactly is it supposed to be?"

"Don't know. Nobody does. Legend's got all kinds of things to say on the subject, but the one that's got the most gumption to us locals was that Lafitte stole it off some dandy passenger on a slave ship called the *Mother Mary* in the company of Jim Bowie himself. Same legend claims that was the last ship Lafitte ever raided and that he sunk it for good measure."

"Nothing about what the treasure was exactly?"

"Lots of things, from a chest full of gold doubloons to riches that were supposed to be transported back to some queen, maybe in Spain or maybe in England. I don't know what to believe. Could all be bullshit."

"These five boys didn't die for bullshit," said Tepper, joining them near the cave.

"We're gonna need a list of all the workers on these construction crews," Jim added.

Plantaine's eyes suddenly grew evasive. "Could be a problem there."

"How's that?" Jim Strong asked him.

"Well, the construction contracts for the buildup of Galveston came down the pipe of some of the biggest names in all of Texas."

"Meaning?"

"I'm talking about oil men, politicians, industrialists, bankers—you name it."

"Any Texas Rangers on that list?" Earl wondered.

"I expect not."

"Well, there are now and we take precedence over all others."

"Companies may not see it that way."

Jim Strong took a step forward. "And how do you see it, Sheriff?"

Plantaine hitched up his gun belt, which had slid gradually down his hips. "I've been mediating these kind of situations since the first boat unloaded their John Deeres."

"Then you've had multiple murders before?"

"No, sir, we haven't."

"Well, you do now," reminded Earl. "So if there's any question about your loyalties in the matter, just tell me who they're to so I can shoot them."

"Disco music's not the only thing to hate these days," Plantaine said, face wrinkled as if he'd bitten down on a lemon.

"This is our case now, Sheriff," D. W. Tepper told him. "Any assistance you can provide would be much appreciated and duly noted. Any assistance you can't, we'll handle on our own."

"What the Ranger means," followed Earl Strong, "is that we'd be glad to talk with whoever we need to ourselves if you don't believe yourself to be up to the task."

"Did I say that?"

"Close enough from where I'm standing."

"You don't wanna take these folks on, Ranger."

"Yeah," Earl nodded, taking off his hat. "That's what all those drug dealers, organized criminals, and Mexican bandits kept telling me. And I didn't listen to them either, did I, son?"

"No, sir," Jim Strong replied.

Earl swung toward Plantaine, hands planted on his hips. "Guess that means I'm not gonna start now, Sheriff. I learned a long time ago how to get people out of my way who weren't of the same mind on such things. Tends to be a lot easier, and less painful, to stand by my side than end up under my boot. Anyway, it's a free country, so the choice is yours."

Plantaine rotated his mouth, as if chewing on the insides of his own cheeks. "What chance we got of keeping a lid on this?"

"Damn good one," Earl said, throwing him a wink. "Until we solve it."

21

"But you, Earl, and Jim never did solve it," Caitlin said to D. W. Tepper after he stopped.

"I'm starting to feel sick," Tepper said, instead of responding.

"How about the rest of the story? What else happened that day on Galveston Island?"

"Don't make me regret loosening that chain hitching you to a desk, Ranger."

"Not ready to cut it yet?"

"You keep bothering me about Galveston Island, I might just lose the key for good."

Before Caitlin could respond, a Coast Guard captain named Lauderdale approached looking dour and unsettled.

"We'd like permission to start off-loading the bodies, Captain," he said to Tepper. "They've all been positively identified now."

"Make sure we cover the victim on the escape raft."

"Already done."

"In that case, permission granted."

Lauderdale took his leave, Tepper still reluctant to meet Caitlin's gaze, but she spoke anyway.

"You think the *Mother Mary*'s why these men were killed, don't you, sir?"

Tepper sighed. "I think I wanna get back to San Antonio and have a look at that video footage," He said, finally looking at her again. "See exactly what it was they found."

PART THREE

Over the next three decades the Rangers' prominence and prestige waned, although they continued to occasionally intercept cattle rustlers, contended with Mexican and Indian marauders along the Rio Grande River, and at times protected blacks from white lynch mobs. By the turn of the century, critics began to urge the curtailment or abandonment of the Texas Rangers. As a result the Frontier Battalion was abolished in 1901 and the Ranger force was cut to four law enforcement companies of twenty men each.

—Legends of America:
Texas Legends: The Texas Rangers—Order Out of Chaos

22

After Cort Wesley pulled his prison jumpsuit back on, two guards escorted him outside and across the yard to the administrative building housing the visitor's center. They bypassed the large open space lined with wooden tables and a children's play area, where families came on Sundays, in favor of the windowless holding rooms where inmates met either with their lawyers or mules from the outside in need of orders. The rooms all stank of dried sweat mixed uneasily with stale perfume. They were hot and poorly ventilated with heavy grates over the windows that also left the light exclusively to a single dome fixture hanging loose from the ceiling in more cases than not.

Only his attorney had been able to see him, since Caitlin Strong had mixed it up with some guards who tried to cut their time short by five minutes just when she was showing Cort Wesley a story Luke had written for school. It was science fiction, about a boy who wakes up one morning to find everyone else in the world has turned to something like ash and he begins a journey to find others still alive.

"It's me," Cort Wesley had said.

"Huh?"

"The boy in the story, like a projection or something. Alone, all by himself in the world trying to find his way."

"I had a different interpretation."

"What's that?"

"The way Luke feels about things from his own perspective since you've been gone."

"Kid's fine in your hands. Dylan too."

"I'm not their father."

Cort Wesley folded his hands before him on the chipped wood. Nearby a Mexican toddler kicked a ball that settled under their table. He retrieved it, casting them a smile.

"Dylan still talking about taking a year off after high school?"

"It's not a year off, it's a prep year."

"What's that mean exactly?"

"He'd be going to school to better ready himself for college."

Cort Wesley frowned, as the toddler's ball slid past their table this time. "Kid doesn't even know what he wants to study yet."

"He's talking about some facet of law enforcement."

"You put that in his head, Ranger?"

"Nobody puts anything in Dylan's head. You know that as well as I do."

Cort Wesley leaned forward and started to take Caitlin's hands in his when a guard slid over.

"*Se acabó tu tiempo.*"

"No," Caitlin told him, tapping her watch, "I still have five minutes left."

"*Se acabó tu tiempo,*" the guard repeated, his tone a bit firmer.

Caitlin tapped her watch again. The guard reached for her chair to pull it back and Caitlin swept his legs out, dropping him to the ground.

That was the last time the prison had let her visit, Cort Wesley wishing she had another chance to swap those five minutes for all the visits they'd lost as a result. But he knew he would've done exactly the same thing, the two of them so used to living in the moment that sometimes long-term concerns and rational thinking got left in the cold.

So Cort Wesley figured it must be his aged lawyer, R. Lee Shine, come to pay him a visit, hopefully with good news about his continuing efforts to have the U.S. authorities extradite him back to Texas. Something he was working on. A long shot, but better than nothing.

The guard opened the door and bid Cort Wesley to enter the holding room. But it didn't smell of sweat or stale perfume today, but hair oil and musty clothes.

"*Buenos días,* outlaw," said Guillermo Paz from behind the single small table.

23

NUEVO LAREDO, MEXICO; THE PRESENT

Paz rose from his chair, wearing the blue uniform of a Mexican *federal* policeman that fit his massive frame much too tightly, the seams stretched to the point of tearing.

"You switch sides, Colonel?"

Paz looked down at the uniform as if to remind

himself he was wearing it. "What do you think? How does it look on me?"

"Bad fit, in more ways than one."

"But required today, along with the badge and identification that came with it."

Paz retook his chair and Cort Wesley sat down across from him. "Caitlin send you to check up on me?"

"The Ranger has no idea I'm here. A good thing too."

"Why's that?"

"The purpose of my visit."

"Which is?"

"To get you out of here, outlaw."

The giant Cort Wesley had bested earlier that day was big, but Guillermo Paz was bigger. Flirting with seven feet tall in his boots, every bit of the frame squeezed into the blue uniform of the infamous *federales* composed of rock-hard muscle. He had wild black hair that shone with grease and hung to his shoulders in twisted ringlets. His ancestors were Mayan warriors and he himself had grown up in a Venezuelan slum en route to becoming a colonel in Venezuelan president Hugo Chavez's secret police and one of the most feared killers in the world. Cort Wesley's and Paz's paths had crossed first tragically and then out of necessity that left them fighting together alongside Caitlin Strong. She was all they had in common, but it was enough.

"Your exploits here have reached the outside world. They call you *el gringo campeón*."

"So you come to take me on?"

Paz grinned, his white teeth glowing even in the

holding room's dull lighting. The overhead fixture was outfitted for three bulbs but Cort Wesley could only see one was screwed in.

"You're being released on orders of the Mexican government. Two of my men are waiting outside."

"*Your* men," Cort Wesley echoed.

"We have a meeting across the border in Laredo. I brought a change of clothes for you." Paz hesitated, studying Cort Wesley closer. "I see you've already showered."

"What's this about, Colonel?"

"Your freedom."

"There must be a catch somewhere."

Paz grinned again. "Interesting how fate continues to throw us together. Einstein wrote that coincidence is God's way of remaining anonymous."

"Like you being hired to kill the mother of my two boys, what, three years ago?"

Paz laid his massive arms on the table before him, his shirt darkened by sweat spreading out from the underarms. "And because of the tragic indiscretion on my part, those boys ended up a part of your life."

"I don't like where this is going."

"Where would you be without them, outlaw?"

"Not here, for one thing."

"With the Ranger?"

"What's she have to do with this?"

"That day she saved your boys linked you to her forever."

"She saved them from you, Colonel, as I recall."

Cort Wesley's head felt fuzzy, as if cotton was wedged up between his ears. Maybe it was the lingering effects of today's fight, maybe it was trying to make sense of a man determined to speak in riddles, denying him the clarity he craved after months in a place where others did his thinking for him.

"Precisely my point," Paz told him. "I was the instrument that brought the two of you together. And since then it's been my responsibility to keep you that way."

"So that's what this is about?"

"Ultimately, you mean?"

"Can you just give me a straight answer?"

Paz rose, coming up just a half foot short of the light fixture. "Your release papers are being processed," he said and lifted a plastic bag from the floor, laying it on the table.

Cort Wesley took the bag, found clothes inside; civilian clothes, welcome beyond measure after wearing prison uniforms that were washed once a month.

"What's waiting in Laredo, Colonel?"

"Get changed, outlaw."

24

SAN ANTONIO, THE PRESENT

"Take this," D. W. Tepper said to Caitlin, pulling something old and rusty from his desk's top drawer.

"What is it?"

"Key to that chain holding you to a desk," Tepper told her, laying the key down between them. "I'm giving it to you on a provisional basis."

"What are the provisions?"

"You don't piss me or anybody else off."

"Two dozen oil rig workers are dead, Captain. I'm bound to piss somebody off."

Tepper stuck a Marlboro in his mouth. "I switched to Lights. Aren't you proud of me?"

"I suppose you are adding a few hours to your time clock," Caitlin told him.

"To hopefully replace the ones you took away. You weren't the best I've got, that key would remain in the drawer for sure. But I figure this case requires the best."

"I visited that boy I shot in the shoulder," Caitlin said abruptly.

"I know."

"Somebody else told you?"

"Nope. I just knew. I hear he's doing just fine."

"If you call losing his dream of playing quarterback all the way to the pros fine. Not easy losing your dream."

"We talking about him or you, Ranger?"

Tepper took in a deep drag and the smoke raced out his nostrils in competing streams that dissipated in his office's dull lighting. He liked to tell Caitlin it was because he didn't want to add any more heat to the sun-baked confines. But she had begun to suspect it was more about wanting to keep views of his own reflection as blunted as possible.

"Tell you what, Ranger. You solve me this case and I'll quit for good and that's a promise."

"One you've made before, D.W."

"But never before with a mass murder of epic proportions on the line. You don't believe yourself to be up to the task, just say so and I'll keep enjoying my smokes. Thing you can't get past, Caitlin, is how much better I feel since I went back to stuffing my body with nicotine. Anyway, our tech guy Young Roger is poring over the underwater recordings the *Mariah*'s ROV made of that shipwreck right now. Every time I pass his office, I mistake him for a college kid."

"That how he got the name 'Young Roger'?"

"Nope, that was on account of we used to have another Ranger named Roger who retired five years back."

Caitlin didn't bother pressing the issue further. "That would seem to give us time for you to finish the story about those murders on Galveston Island."

Tepper shook his head and stifled a cough. "You know what you sound like? The little girl old Earl used to tell stories to while seated on his lap."

"He never told me the one about Galveston."

Tepper's nose wrinkled like he'd just smelled something rotten. "That's 'cause it didn't have a happy ending."

He might have been about to say more, but his phone buzzed sparing him the effort.

"This is gonna have to wait," Tepper said, hanging it back up. "I need you down at the Medical Examiner's Office. We got a body there they pulled from a wreck on I-35 a couple days back."

Caitlin's expression tensed in displeasure. "This more important than the murder of two dozen oil rig workers?"

"Thing is, Ranger, the dead man had already died once before. Fifteen years ago."

25

"Challenges are merely Allah's way of testing us," the cleric said to Sam Harrabi, as they made their way down the dark hall in the mosque's basement. Morning prayers had just ended, the crackle of departing footsteps above sounding like the rattle of old-fashioned typewriter keys. "To see if we are truly worthy of His divine mission."

"You believe the car accident was part of His plan?"

"This man had completed his part in the mission, had he not?"

"He had, *sayyid*."

"Then I believe choosing him to test us was hardly random." The great man paused, his tone taking on more of an edge when he resumed. "There's nothing that can possibly connect this man to us, of course."

"Nothing. I made sure of that. And the others are all accounted for."

The cleric smiled reassuringly as he pressed a code into the keypad alongside the heavy steel door at the end of the dark hall. "Then let us greet them."

The door opened with a loud *click* and the cleric entered ahead of Harrabi. At the sight of him, the dozen men working inside the secret room dropped to their knees, heads bowed reverently. They were plainly dressed in casual Western clothes, wearing mostly khakis or dress pants and fitted shirts. Beardless with hair neatly groomed. Nondescript in all respects with nothing to suggest their part in the operation, no different from the neighbors whose lives they would soon be party to taking.

"Rise, my brothers," the cleric said, scanning the room's contents and holding his stare on a huge, computer-generated map of Texas projected on a wall-sized screen. A series of black lines crisscrossed the state, shaded thicker and darker through the cities of Dallas, Houston, and San Antonio. Those cities were colored a deep red in circular grids closest to those lines, changing to blue slightly further out, and then, finally, to yellow.

The cleric turned back to the men who had been working behind computers, studying topographical maps, or were involved in phone conversations his appearance had interrupted. They were all on their feet now, standing rigid and reverent before him. Harrabi noticed the angry sneers that had replaced reverently placid expressions on four of the men's faces. These four were breathing harder than the others, the ones he recognized as paying the heaviest price for their faith just as he had. Rage may have festered below the surface of all the men, but the others had managed to supplant it beneath the great purpose before them while these wore it like a scar. Harrabi preferred to keep his terrible scars within, even though his pain was just as great as any of theirs.

"We have not met before," the cleric greeted, comfortable to have Harrabi by his side, "but I and all of Islam are blessed by your presence and your commitment. You have sacrificed much for the great victory soon to be visited upon us. You have channeled your own personal pain and tragedy into this holy mission blessed by God Himself, and I am made prouder by your acquaintance."

"Tell our leader the good news there is to report," Harrabi said, nodding toward a thin, bespectacled man with coarse thinning hair.

The man looked back toward the wall-sized map of Texas. "We believe there will be upwards of ten million people inside the areas shaded in red when the blessed moment arrives. Of these we can reasonably expect a five percent mortality rate. Five hundred thousand victims," he continued after a pause, "with an expected quarter million to follow in the blue and yellow zones. That is phase one."

"And phase two?"

Another of the men pressed a button on his computer and the wall-sized map switched to one of the entire eastern seaboard. It was shaded in similar fashion, only with thick swatches of the coastline colored red, the blue and yellow areas extending further inland.

"The major cities and population centers are designated by the grids you see in black," this man explained. "We are operating on theoretical grounds here, but it is safe to assume that given the right conditions the effects will be nothing short of catastrophic, just as your vision dictated."

"Not my vision," the cleric corrected, "*God's* vision. What are these right conditions?"

"A storm when the blessed hour comes."

"Then Allah will make one for us, rest assured. But I have another question for you, for all of you," the cleric said, widening his gaze. "Was it not worth it? Is not all your pain and suffering now justified by the blessed mission you all find yourselves party to?"

To a man, they nodded resolutely.

"God has a plan for us all and divine happiness comes only when we embrace that plan. All of you have done that and I can only express my most profound gratitude and appreciation for your efforts. I speak for Allah when I say many men pass through history; you all share the distinction of making it."

The men continued to regard him reverently, the cleric reveling in running his eyes over each of them one at a time.

"I understand better now the necessary sacrifice of one of our brothers, since it left us with twelve of you standing before me. The perfect number since in Shi'a Islam there are said to be twelve imams who stand as legitimate successors to the prophet Mohammed. But the Christian Bible has something to say about that as well, does it not, Brother Harrabi?"

Harrabi nodded, a bit stung by the cleric referring such a question to him, referencing a part of his life that seemed so far in the past now. "A woman, thought to be the Virgin Mary, wears a crown of twelve stars, each representing one of the twelve tribes of Israel. And each of the twelve tribes has twelve thousand people."

"Yes," the cleric acknowledged, "as covered in Chapter Twelve, Part One. Of which part of their Bible, my brother."

"The Book of Revelation," Harrabi told them all.

26

"Man was identified at the scene as Alejandro Pena," said Frank Dean Whatley, a small, thin man who'd been the Bexar County Medical Examiner since the time Caitlin had been in diapers. He'd grown a belly in recent years that hung out over his thin belt, seeming to force his spine to angle inward at the torso. "Highway Patrol recovered his wallet and the car registration matched perfectly. Routine as they come."

"So what changed?"

"Fingerprint check. Also routine."

"No, it's not," Caitlin told Whatley.

The Bexar County Medical Examiner's Office and Morgue was located just off the Loop 410 not far from the Babcock Road exit on Merton Minter. It was a three-story beige building that also housed the county health department and city offices for Medicaid. Caitlin had been coming here for over twenty years and what struck her was how it always smelled exactly the same, of cleaning solvent with a faint scent of menthol clinging to the walls like paint. The lighting was overly dull in the hallways and overly bright in offices like Whatley's.

"Okay," Whatley said, "you got me."

"Keep talking, Doc."

"Alejandro Pena, what was left of him after a semi tore his car apart anyway, didn't look Hispanic to me."

Whatley stopped to suck in some air and Caitlin let his remark settle between them. His teenage son had been killed by a Latino gang when Caitlin was a mere kid herself. Ever since then, Whatley had harbored a virulent hatred for that particular race, from the bag boys at the local H.E.B. to the politicians who professed to be peacemakers. With his wife first lost in life and then death to alcoholism, he'd probably stayed in the job too long. But he had nothing to go home to, no real life outside the office, and remained exceptionally good at performing the rigors of his job.

"How's that?" Caitlin asked him.

"Skin tones were wrong. Next step was to run his ID and social, usual check that came back anything but usual since the real Alejandro Pena died fifteen years ago of a cerebral hemorrhage while watching his son play a high school football game. I printed out the obituary for you," Whatley said, handing it across the desk.

"So what else can you tell me about the real victim?" Caitlin asked, taking it.

"He was in lousy health, Ranger. There was blood in his intestinal track and rectum. Skin tone and temperature indicated a recent infection, source of which could have been some unhealed cuts on his legs not consistent with trauma from the accident."

"Any idea what exactly you're describing here?"

"None at all, or even if any of this is particularly relevant. People steal identities all the time."

"Rangers don't get called out to most of them, Doc." Caitlin was ready to leave it at that but something stopped her from standing up. "When was the victim's driver's license issued in Pena's name?" she asked instead.

Whatley consulted one of a dozen clipboards hanging on the wall behind him, Caitlin realizing for the first time that he hadn't even switched his computer on.

"Six months ago, it looks like here."

Now Caitlin did rise. "I'll check it out." She started to move for the door, then stopped. "One other thing, Doc. Mexican druggers murdered my mother. But neither one of us has a right to hold an entire ethnic group responsible for the tragedies that chew us up inside. Otherwise we'd spend our entire lives hating everything."

"I thought you weren't working cases anymore, Ranger," Whatley said, his eyes deep and sad.

"Things changed."

Caitlin felt the sweat soaking through her shirt by the time she approached her SUV parked in a corner of the building garage. She'd found a spot in the relative cool of a lower level but exhaust from the upper decks blew shafts of superheated air down against her at regular intervals, making the walk feel as if she were slogging in and out of a steam room. To save money, much of the garage's lighting was turned off during the day, the sun's rays streaming in through the open walls leaving checkerboard patterns across the garage floor.

Caitlin wondered if she'd been too hard on Frank Dean Whatley, a man without companionship or purpose outside of his job. The mere thought made her value the presence of Luke and Dylan Torres in her life all the more, the price extracted in becoming their surrogate mother well worth it if they kept her from becoming as sad and bitter as Whatley. Still, his findings about the man who had assumed the identity of Alejandro Pena left Caitlin with a burning against her spine, not unlike a nagging sunburn. She'd stop off at the impound lot next to see what, if anything, had been gleaned from an inspection of the wreckage of his vehicle. Probably nothing, since there was no reason to suspect any crime behind the accident. But now she needed to request a full tech workup on the vehicle, starting with any and all fingerprints, fibers, any evidence whatsoever that might tell her who the victim was and why six months ago he'd adopted another man's identity.

She used the remote to click open the SUV's doors, wondering what life might be like if it was possible to just start over again. What would you do different? Which mistakes would you rectify first? Caitlin imagined just about everybody would make different mistakes in trying to correct their previous ones. Life was more like a gunfight, she supposed, than most realized: often times, you only got one shot.

Caitlin yanked open her door, freezing at the sight of a man in the passenger seat all but lost to darkness.

27

LAREDO, THE DAY BEFORE

"Your passports, please."

The two men in the front seat of Guillermo Paz's massive Chevy Suburban slipped theirs out the open window, as Paz handed his and the one he'd had made for Cort Wesley up as well. All four men had the badges and IDs of Mexican *federales* and were crossing the International Bridge into Laredo on the pretext of a cooperative law enforcement meeting. They were cleared through moments later, only Cort Wesley breathing a sigh of relief it had been so easy.

"Your men look familiar," he said to Paz, eyes angling for the two in the front seat.

"They were the ones who found your son's kidnappers last year."

Both men cocked their gazes briefly backward and regarded Cort Wesley with a slight nod.

"So who's this friend we're meeting, Colonel? What's this about?"

"I should think you'd just be happy with your freedom."

"Temporary as it may be."

"You read Spanish?" Paz asked him, handing over a tri-folded letter.

"Not very well."

"Then let me save you the trouble. That's a pardon signed by the president of Mexico himself."

Cort Wesley regarded the letter, recognizing the president's name but not much else. "Okay, you've got my attention. This have something to do with that friend we're meeting?"

"Everything, outlaw."

"So I know him."

"He's a friend of a friend."

"You like confusing me, don't you?"

"I'm not at liberty to say any more."

"You forget how well I know you, Colonel. You're at liberty to do whatever the hell you please."

"Not this time," Paz said as they slid off the International Bridge and continued into Laredo, approaching San Agustin Plaza in the center of the old section of the city.

Cort Wesley saw the spire of San Agustin Church rising over the plaza rich with tourists strolling past sidewalk kiosks and open storefronts, snapping pictures with their cell phones and fishing cash from their wallets. The Suburban snailed past the famed Rio Grande museum contained in an L-shaped adobe building that reminded him of one of the five buildings housing rival gangs at Cereso prison. He knew he should've felt more a sense of relief, especially with a pardon in hand from the Mexican president. But he couldn't get past the foreboding sense of unease over what the terms of his miraculous release might be exactly. If Guillermo Paz was involved, they promised not to be pleasant.

But the driver had left the window open after the Customs stop, the air smelling dry, dusty, and laced with the scents of grilled food sifting out from restaurants featuring open fronts. Cort Wesley caught whiffs of spices and women's perfume in stark contrast to the stench of sweat and urine that had dominated his world in prisons on both sides of the border for nearly a year now. He started thinking of Caitlin Strong's lilac-scented shampoo. He might as well have been a million miles away from her while in Cereso; they were still several hundred apart now, but it felt like around the corner by comparison.

Paz's driver parked the Suburban illegally in front of a Mexican restaurant called Los Jacales, and Cort Wesley trailed the colonel out of the vehicle and inside while the other two men dressed as *federales* remained in the car. Paz saying nothing was Paz saying just enough, Cort Wesley content to follow him into the sparsely occupied restaurant. They moved toward a back alcove separated by a bead curtain Paz parted to reveal a single muscular figure, who rose from his chair at their approach.

"Name's Jones, Mr. Masters," the man greeted, extending his hand. "Take a seat."

28

LAREDO, THE DAY BEFORE

Cort Wesley took the man's extended hand and didn't let go until he did. "Jones as in Smith?" he asked. They sat down together, while Paz remained standing.

"I guess my reputation precedes me," Jones smiled. He wore his hair close-cropped in a military style that exaggerated the square shape of his head and angular cheekbones as well as stiff jaw. He looked like a life-sized cardboard cutout of every CIA "wet" operative Cort Wesley had ever met in his past life that had ended nearly two decades before. Amazing how the profile hadn't changed. Then again the times, for men like Jones here, pretty much hadn't either.

Caitlin had met him on several occasions, a combination of fate and the pots she kept stirring up thrusting them together, first in Bahrain when Jones was still Smith and the Middle East was his domain. He officially became "Jones" once transferred back stateside, where he was put in charge of a division of Homeland Security dedicated to security threats to the country coming from the inside instead of the out. One of those had been a militia group called the Patriot Sun, taken down by Caitlin, Cort Wesley, and Guillermo Paz who, it turned out, had been building a private army in Mexico on Jones's behalf.

"I recognize your voice too," Cort Wesley told him. "You speak to Caitlin lately?"

"No more than you."

"That's a relief, since I don't believe you've got a mind to stop until you get her killed."

Jones frowned, then smirked. "That woman's a true gunfighter of the highest regard. Shame what they did to her."

"What they'd do to her?" Cort Wesley asked, his heart skipping a beat.

"That's right, you haven't heard. Our favorite gunfighter's been behind a desk since she shot a kid."

"Bullshit."

"She went Rambo in a hostage situation inside your son's high school."

"My son . . ."

"He's fine. Three other boys, not so much, especially the shooter she took out. I reached out to express my regrets but she never returned my calls."

"She's been busy."

"Right. Babysitting your kids. Great job for a person with her skill set," Jones added, shaking his head.

"You bust me out of prison to bring me up to speed on current events?"

"Feel like you know me, don't you, cowboy?"

"I'd imagine the feeling's mutual, Jones."

"I've committed parts of your file few have ever seen to memory."

Cort Wesley leaned back, stealing a glance at Paz blocking nearly the entire bead curtain with his bulk.

"And I imagine those parts are the real reason why I'm here."

Jones leaned forward into a bright swatch of light shed from a dangling fixture adorned with a colorful shade. "Do I look scared to you, Masters?"

"Nope."

"I should, because I am. Terrified, in fact."

"You shaking in your boots beneath the table?"

"Why don't you take a look?"

"I'm afraid I might see a gun pointing at me too."

"We're on the same side here, Masters."

"So I'm supposed to be scared too?"

"Yes, you are." Jones used his napkin to dab the sweat from his brow. The alcove was outfitted with a ceiling fan that wasn't currently spinning. "But if you're not, I'll be glad to tear up that letter from the Mexican president and have Colonel Paz drive you back to Cereso."

Cort Wesley could feel Paz stiffen at the alcove entrance, a burst of breath blowing from his mouth that sounded like something between a grunt and a growl. Jones's gaze angled toward him, then returned to Cort Wesley.

"You're here because he insisted. Wouldn't do the job without you."

"What kind of job?"

"Kind you do best, Masters, kind guys like you and me were born to do. Tell me you didn't have the time of your life over in the Gulf War. Tell me."

"Okay, I didn't."

"You're lying, friend. I can see it in your eyes and already saw it in your file. The three men in this alcove belong to a fraternity where membership is rare indeed. Not just because we're as good as we are at what we do, but also because we're survivors. Even kryptonite can't kill us and we don't have to wear a red cape either."

Cort Wesley locked his gaze on Jones. "I'm gonna ask you to stop lumping yourself in with me."

"Don't think I'm up to the task anymore, cowboy?"

"I don't know whether you are or not. I just don't trust you, not one goddamn bit."

"This coming from a man on the verge of spending the rest of his life behind bars until someone stronger and faster puts him down for good."

"If you're saying I don't have a choice, I'm not arguing. Just don't expect me to take whatever it is you're talking about at face value."

"I'm talking about a war, the one we're gonna be fighting for the next century or so unless we do something about it now. I'm talking about the enemy blossoming right under our goddamn noses."

"Could you be any more cryptic?"

"Who do I work for, cowboy?"

"What is this, a quiz now?"

"Just answer the question."

"Homeland Security, last time I checked."

"Called such because we defend the homeland. And right now the primary terrorist threat to the homeland's coming from right inside our borders."

"Homegrown terrorists . . ."

Jones slapped the table hard enough to rattle the water glasses and stole a quick glance at Paz. "Give the man a cigar, Colonel, he's right as rain."

"I don't smoke, Jones."

"Know what?" Jones asked, grinning. "I can see why you and the Ranger get along so well. Goddamn match made in heaven. The two of you figure you can take down Godzilla fighting side by side. But this solitary gunman act's wearing a bit thin, on both of you. It's like you're still living in the nineteenth century before there were airplanes flying into buildings. You crack wise because you figure there's no problem you can't shoot or fight your way out of. But I'm here to tell you that's not the case this time and that's why you're here."

Jones stopped, awaiting a response from Cort Wesley that didn't come.

He folded his arms back on the table. "Let me lay it out for you, cowboy. The biggest cell in the homegrown terrorist world is right here in Texas. How do I know this? Because one of my men managed to infiltrate it until he disappeared. Pieces of him started showing up last week." Jones's cocksure sneer had turned to a grimace and his eyes took on a level of sadness consistent with what you'd see at a graveside funeral for a loved one. "You don't believe me, I'll show you the pictures."

"Just keep talking."

"We're going to hit them at the mosque in Houston where they've been gathering. We're talking a commando raid into hostile territory that would make SEAL Team 6 proud. Explains what you and the colonel are doing here. I can't use my own men; even as deep as my department is buried, we still have accountability, and going to war in Texas doesn't fit the job description. Like I said, other than me there's only three people I trust to get that job done and two of them are in the room right now." Jones rotated his gaze from Paz to Cort Wesley and back again. "I think we all know who the third is."

Cort Wesley looked at him across the table, opting for silence to keep Jones on the defensive.

"Look," Jones continued, "the one hard bit of intelligence my man relayed before they sliced and diced him was that we're looking at a coming attack that will make nine/eleven and Oklahoma City look like amateur hour. It's going down in Texas and we're talking casualties into the six figures within the state and plenty more outside of it. That's hundreds of thousands of people, Masters."

Cort Wesley pretended to count numbers out on his fingers. "I believe you're right there, Jones."

Jones shoved his chair backward, as if to better size him up. "And am I right about you?"

"Which part?"

"The part about how good you are at this sort of shit."

"I wouldn't be here if you didn't already know the answer to that." Cort Wesley leaned forward, close enough to Jones to make him pull back a bit. "Now tell me if I'm right about *you*."

"What's that?"

"That you're an unreliable, untrustworthy son of a bitch only interested in serving his own ends."

"If you mean the country's by my own ends, I suppose you've got me nailed dead solid perfect."

"So what is it you're not telling me here, Jones, what are you leaving out of the picture?"

Jones smacked his lips together and doused them with his tongue. He rocked backward in his chair, stealing the light from his face.

"Time to show your cards, Masters," he said, instead of answering the question. "You in or not?"

Cort Wesley nodded. "On one condition."

29

SAN ANTONIO, THE PRESENT

Caitlin hadn't even realized her hand had dropped to her SIG, thoughts jumbled and breath bottlenecked in her throat until she recognized Cort Wesley seated in the darkness.

"Tell me you're not a ghost."

"I'm the one who sees them, remember?"

Caitlin glanced into the backseat to see if Cort Wesley's old prison pal Leroy Epps might be sitting there too. "Should I ask?"

"Not unless you want to know."

"Don't tell me: Paz."

"Paz."

"He didn't break you out, right? Please tell me that much."

"Might've been cleaner if he had; your old friend Jones is holding his leash now."

"Nobody holds Paz's leash, except Paz himself."

Caitlin climbed into the cab and closed the door behind her, twisting a knob to leave the dome light on to better see Cort Wesley. His hair was the longest she'd ever seen it, his frame leaner and not as muscled as nine months before when they'd last seen each other. It was his face that looked the most different, and not in a figurative sense either. It was typically prison pale, yes, but also marred by pockets of healed-over tissue and bruises that dotted his skin. One of his eyelids drooped downward as if it had forgotten how to open all the way.

"You've looked better," she managed.

"That the best you can do?"

Caitlin didn't remember leaning over the bucket seat to kiss him. She held her eyes closed, smelling a combination of stale soap and the musky odor of nervous perspiration over that of stiff clothes fresh out of the box.

She didn't remember the kiss ending any more than it starting. One moment their faces were pressed together and the next they weren't. She felt Cort Wesley cringe when she hugged him tighter.

"Ouch."

"Was it something I said?" Caitlin asked him, easing away.

Cort Wesley cupped her cheek in a hand that felt like sandpaper. "I like your hair."

"It's too long."

"Looks good that way. Something else is different too."

"Not that I'm aware."

"Your eyes look tired."

"Maybe it's the bad light."

"More likely the stress that comes with raising two boys."

"Watching, Cort Wesley, not raising."

Cort Wesley looked away, then back again. "Jones told me about your reassignment."

"It's been rescinded, on a provisional basis according to Captain Tepper."

"How'd you manage that?"

"Happened to find a couple dozen murdered oil rig workers off Baffin Bay."

"Lucky you, Ranger."

Caitlin smiled. "I am now."

Cort Wesley leaned closer to her again. "So you got

time to hit a motel room?" he asked with a wink, his old self for that moment at least.

"You don't want to see the boys?"

"Want, yes, more than anything. But I don't want them getting the wrong idea."

"What idea is that?"

"That I'm back."

"You're sitting right here."

Cort Wesley scolded her with his stare. "This is your friend Jones we're talking about."

"He had you sprung to do a job for him, that it?"

He nodded. "In return for an official pardon letter signed by the president of Mexico."

"Must be a big job."

"It is. Right here in Texas too."

"You want to be a bit more specific?"

"Nope."

"Just tell me you don't trust Jones."

"I don't trust Jones."

"Then you mind explaining why you don't want to tell me what he's up to?"

Cort Wesley shifted about in the passenger seat until he faced her with shoulders squared. "Because I don't want you inviting yourself along."

"You're starting to piss me off, Cort Wesley. If something's going down in Texas, don't you think the Rangers should know about it?"

"That's Jones's call, not mine."

"Since when did something like that stop you?"

"Since I promised not to tell you any more than I already have. I owe him for getting me out of jail and that's a hell of a debt. The Mexicans can keep me stashed at Cereso forever or until I'm dead, whichever comes first." A smile flirted with his lips, then lingered there. "When they told me I had a visitor, I figured it had to be either you or my lawyer. Then I got one look at Paz wearing a *federal* uniform and I knew he was my ticket back to you and the boys."

Caitlin squeezed the wheel, accidentally blaring the horn in the process, which made her jump in her seat. "You haven't even asked about them yet."

"'Cause I know they're fine, better than fine. It's you I'm worried about."

"Jones filled you in about the school?"

Cort Wesley nodded. "Sounds like you got the shaft."

"I got what I deserved, Cort Wesley. I messed up, plain and simple."

"You?"

"Sucks being human, doesn't it?"

"Raising teenagers'll do that to you." Cort Wesley paused. "You can tell me whatever bad thing Dylan's done lately if you want."

"Well, I caught him with a joint."

"What else?"

"He brought a gun with him on a fishing trip we were just on. Told me you charged him with protecting me and his brother."

"I did at that," Cort Wesley nodded. "And you only would've found he had a gun with him if you needed it. That oil rig?"

Now it was Caitlin who nodded. "Your turn."

"I got something else I'd rather do instead."

This time it was Cort Wesley who leaned across the seat, their arms wrapping around each other, Caitlin feeling his rough, hard hands swimming through her hair. She started wondering what he'd done with those hands, where the bruises had come from, how he'd managed to survive in a prison run by human excrement whose worth was less than the shirts on their tattooed backs. She felt him touching her, not wanting it to stop, the thought of poor Frank Dean Whatley entering her mind for some reason when her cell phone buzzed.

It took six rings before Caitlin managed to extract herself from the embrace, her head leaning against Cort Wesley's chest when she saw D. W. Tepper's number flash in her caller ID.

"Where are you?" he asked her, the phone screen's dim glare cast across Cort Wesley's face, making his bruises look like ink blotches.

"Still at the ME's office," she said, clearing her throat, enjoying the feel of Cort Wesley's heart thumping against her.

"Well, get on back here. Young Roger says he found something on those tapes we need to see."

30

SAN ANTONIO, THE PRESENT

Teofilo Reyes Braga sat by himself in the bleachers, apart from his wife and family, his son Jorge stepping into the batter's box in the bottom of the sixth inning with the score tied. Two outs and two men—well, boys—on. Base hit from Jorge would win the game and propel the El Diablos into the playoffs.

His company, Braga Waste Management, was the team's sponsor and Braga himself had personally designed the company "devil" logo embroidered on the front of each uniform top. The nicest the San Antonio Little League had ever seen.

"Strike one!" the umpire bellowed, even though the pitch looked clearly down and in to Braga, so much so it had backed ten-year-old Jorge off the plate out of fear of getting hit.

Braga cringed and gnashed his teeth, glared at the rotund umpire who wouldn't be able to see him through his mask even if he looked. He pressed his hands into his linen slacks, feeling perspiration leaking through a matching light cotton shirt. He fought the urge to undo more of the buttons, or strip the shirt off altogether as he would've done while working in the fields as a boy Jorge's age. He never wore jeans or shorts, nothing too casual, so as to present only his best possible face at all times—residue, he imagined, of spending his youth as a migrant worker inevitably shunned and disparaged. Braga imagined the fat umpire having never done any kind of real labor in his life. For him cheating young boys with a lousy strike zone in the midday heat was probably as rough as it ever got.

Jorge stepped out of the batter's box, wiped some dirt onto his hands, and stepped back in.

The sight made Braga think of himself at that age, growing up on a series of farms concentrated mostly in Texas. He'd actually been born on one of them in the fetid heat of a summer night in the back room of a barn. No celebration, or birth announcement in the local paper, and his mother was back to work the next day with him stowed in an old wooden drawer his father had found amid the garbage. But being born in Texas made him an American citizen, the significance of that never lost on him, even as a boy.

"Strike two!" the fat umpire barked, and Braga

seethed as he watched his son look back at the man as if to question where the pitch was. It looked outside this time and high enough to make the catcher come out of his crouch to snare it.

Braga sat in the sun no matter how hot it was. The experience reminded him of the fields, his roots, how far he'd come. He had just turned fifty but looked ten years younger with a full head of thick black hair, matching mustache, and body still toned thanks to regular weight-lifting workouts in a solarium gym he'd added to the Alamo Heights mansion he'd purchased a couple years back. Braga had tried a personal trainer for a time, dismissing him after five workouts when it became clear he wasn't comfortable having someone tell him what to do and how to do it. His skin showed few ill effects from so many years of overexposure; dark, yes, but not creased and leathery the way his father's had been.

The umpire took off his mask and wiped a hand through his greasy, sweat-soaked hair. Then Braga saw him look ever so subtly toward the opposing team's bench where the coach stood on the top step of the dugout. It wasn't much and could have been innocent, if not for the way the coach looked back. Braga watched their stares meet, however briefly, but long enough for more than a casual connection to be made.

Braga had been ten years old when his interest in the waste management industry effectively began the night he'd accompanied his dad and two other men to a construction site for a local housing development outside of El Paso. Any number of large Dumpsters had been set there to handle the day-to-day refuse. The farm owner had lent the men a truck they'd packed with all manner of garbage collected from

cans outside the tiny shacks the migrant workers
called home. The black bags filled out the truck's rear
and Teo Braga had ridden atop them, balancing himself in the stiff wind.

Once at the construction site, his job was to drop
the bags from the truck's rear to be retrieved by his
dad and the two other men for deposit in the Dumpsters. Everything was going fine until Braga saw four
men wielding two-by-fours coming around the truck.
He started to shout out a warning to his dad, but fear
swallowed his words. He burrowed down and hid amid
the garbage while the thunks of wood against bone
and the screams of the men split the cool, quiet night.

Lost amid the darkness and the stench, Braga tried
to cover his ears, but it did no good. The screams and
thunks continued until he heard the rattle of the boards
being discarded, then the footsteps of the men moving
away followed by the roar of a car engine and screech
of tires.

One of the three men was dead by the time Braga
got to him, his father and the other man both alive but
barely. His father woke up long enough to climb into
the cab on his own, but Braga had to drag the other
man to the truck and then find a way to get him settled in the cab as well. Even then, with both his father
and the other survivor unconscious, it was left for him
to drive the truck all the way back to the farm.

Braga let instinct guide him the whole trip, the ride
pretty much a straight shot until he got to a series of
local winding roads that all looked the same in the
darkness. But he made it back somehow and another
of the workers who'd been trained as a medic in the
Mexican army got his father's wounds stitched and
his broken limbs splinted.

Braga quickly realized his father had lost an eye and the use of much of his right arm because trash was expensive to dump. Landfills charged by the pound for dumping and even in the huge sprawl of Texas, there weren't enough of them to go around. Farmers like the ones the Braga family worked for couldn't spare the expense and were thus forced to find illegal dumping grounds like rivers, roadsides, or conveniently placed construction sites.

Braga couldn't let go of the memory of cowering within the trash while the sounds of his father's screams and bones breaking reverberated in the air. So one day a few weeks later he rode a stolen bicycle back to the housing development site where his father had almost been beaten to death. It took awhile, but he picked out the four men, construction workers, who'd wielded the two-by-fours that awful night. He lingered about until he could identify the trucks belonging to all of them.

He came back another week later on the same bicycle. While the four men who'd beaten his father and killed another man worked their way through the day, Braga slashed the tires and sugared the gas tanks of their trucks.

All told, he'd never felt better, filled with a sense of satisfaction and fulfillment like none he'd ever felt before. That night, he slept soundly and without fear for the first time since his father's beating.

"Strike three!" the fat ump yelled. "You're out!"

His son Jorge dropped his bat, unable to believe another ball had been called a strike. That was it, game and season over for the El Diablos. And as the ump walked off the field he crossed paths with the opposing coach and Braga again saw them hold gazes, each smiling ever so slightly.

Braga lingered in the new wooden stands seething, peeling the fresh blue paint from the row before him off with his fingernails. The crowd filed out, Braga paying none of the greetings and commiserations passed his way any heed whatsoever. A breeze had blown in from the south, squeezing the heat from the air and turning the afternoon surprisingly cool. Braga could feel the heart thudding in his chest, so angry he was trembling.

"Can you believe that?" a parent of another kid on the team said, as he stormed down the aisle. Braga didn't know his name or his son's. *Number 16*, he thought.

Braga didn't respond.

"We should file an appeal, a protest, a complaint. *Something*."

"Yes," Braga heard himself saying, "something."

31

SAN ANTONIO, THE PRESENT

"So here's the thing," Young Roger said from behind his computer, "everything that happened in the waters beneath the *Mariah* was recorded by their ROV, remote operated vehicle."

"Anything in these recordings gonna explain why they suspended their drilling operations on account of that shipwreck?" Caitlin asked him.

"You bet. See that?" Young Roger asked, clicking his mouse over a section of his computer monitor to enlarge it.

"No," Captain Tepper said, before Caitlin had a chance to. "What exactly are we looking at?"

Caitlin and Tepper were squeezed into Young Roger's cramped cubicle in the basement of the Ranger Company D headquarters on the outskirts of San Antonio. The young man was a Ranger himself, but the title was mostly honorary, given after his technological expertise as a computer whiz helped the Rangers solve a number of Internet-based crimes ranging from identity theft, to credit card fraud, to the busting of a major pedophile and kiddie porn ring. Caitlin had never seen anyone so mad as Tepper when they raided the ringleader's home, his face going so red that the color filled out the furrows and creases to the point where his skin looked baby smooth. In that moment Caitlin saw the younger Ranger who'd spent years ranging the same modern trails as her father and grandfather, often in the company of one or the other. Young Roger had accompanied the team on the raid, there to preserve whatever the ringleader's hard drive yielded.

He worked out of all six Ranger Company offices on a rotating basis as needed by the current investigative caseload. Young Roger wore his hair too long and played guitar for a rock band called The Rats. Caitlin had never seen them play but she'd listened to the CD. Not the kind of music she preferred, but Dylan told her it was pretty good.

"This is footage captured by the ROV of the *Mother Mary*'s wreckage," he explained. "They reported the findings and that's when the rig's owners followed protocol and ordered drilling operations suspended. You can see the ship's remains here, here, and here,"

Young Roger said, clicking to enlarge on the spots in question with his mouse in sequence.

"You call us down here to explain something we already know?" Tepper asked him, sounding annoyed.

"No, sir. Turns out the ROV captured something else along with the wreckage," Young Roger said, enlarging a section of the screen yet more. "Here, check this out."

Caitlin leaned in over Tepper's shoulder. "Those look like barrels, oil drums maybe."

"Something else I need to show you," Young Roger said, working his keyboard until the screen changed, or seemed to. "Here's the same area the day before the killings."

"So what are we supposed to be seeing this time?" Tepper asked.

"It's more a matter of *not* seeing, Captain."

"The barrels are gone," Caitlin realized.

"Yes, ma'am," Young Roger affirmed.

"Maybe the currents took them away."

"Not with that kind of barrel weight, especially the way they were dug in. Almost like somebody had put them in that spot on purpose, Captain, and nobody would've ever noticed if the *Mariah*'s ROV hadn't uncovered the remains of that shipwreck first."

"Then wouldn't the ROV have recorded whoever came for those barrels?" Caitlin asked.

"Except it either malfunctioned or was tampered with."

"So you're saying somebody showed up and picked the barrels up," Tepper concluded. "Just how in all that's holy could they manage that?"

"First off, this footage recorded by the ROV was sent in compressed form over the Internet to Gulf Strategic Energy Partners. And when you think of the Internet I want you to picture a bank that leaves its doors opened and vault unlocked for anybody who wants to steal money. That's about as secure as the Web is."

"So you're saying . . ."

Young Roger clicked the mouse, returning the enlarged shot of the barrels to the screen, and then wheeled his desk chair backward. "That anybody who pulled this feed off the Web could have been responsible for getting the barrels out of there."

"And if that happened to be the same party that put them there in the first place," Caitlin said, leaving her thought at that.

Tepper started to reach for his Marlboro Lights, then changed his mind. "Next question being who might that be exactly?"

"Don't have an answer for you there yet, Captain," Young Roger told him.

"Hold on a sec, what's this?" Caitlin asked, pointing to a section of the screen highlighting the enlarged barrels with her finger.

"What's what?"

"There's a mark, an impression, on this barrel."

"Probably just a smudge or a scratch."

"I can't see anything," Tepper said, squinting again.

"No, it's there," Caitlin insisted. "Looks like a symbol, maybe a drawing or something."

Young Roger maneuvered the mouse to the area beneath Caitlin's finger and clicked three times. "You're right, Ranger."

"What the hell is that?" Captain Tepper asked, whatever Caitlin had spotted went fuzzy under the enlargement.

"I can't say for sure," she told him, "but it looks like a devil's head."

32

Teofilo Braga thought he might calm down as the day went on. By nightfall, though, his anger over the umpire calling his son out on balls out of the strike zone only intensified. So with that umpire's cell phone number in hand, Braga used the tracking software his company used to keep tabs on its trucks to pin his location down to a bar beyond the edge of San Antonio's tourist district, well past the River Walk.

He sat innocuously at a back table, nursing a trio of Coronas with limes squeezed down their necks, fidgeting at the sight of the bulbous umpire chomping down chicken wings and ribs, chased with shots of Jack Daniel's and Budweiser. The spices brought a shimmer of sweat to his skin that made his basketball-shaped head look as if it were glowing under the bar's dim lights.

But Braga still hadn't decided what to do, and was actually thinking about making himself go home, when the opposing coach from that afternoon's game entered and took a seat next to the ump. The coach stayed only long enough to pick up the umpire's tab, after which the two of them exchanged a ridiculous high school half hug before the coach took his leave.

Braga rose and headed for the door, leaving his final Corona only half finished.

He watched the umpire waddle out of the bar twenty minutes later, stumbling back to his car illegally parked in a nearby alley. He'd backed his Mercury Marquis in, blocking access to a Dumpster that was serviced by Braga Waste Management. Steam rose off pools of water collected near drainage gates in the humid night, the silence of which was broken by a stubborn car alarm wailing from several blocks away.

In those brief moments, Braga felt again like the young boy hidden amid the trash bags while his father was beaten with two-by-fours. He felt the same nervous flutter in his stomach knotting his muscles. Even the stench rising out of the overflowing Dumpster smelled the same. The umpire brought back every painful memory of a youth dominated by weakness and subservience, memories that no amount of power and wealth he'd accumulated as an adult could vanquish. The difference tonight was that he held a baseball bat in his right hand, adding his left as he approached the umpire now fumbling drunkenly for the car keys in his pocket.

Before Braga could mentally record his actions, the bat was coming up and around, impacting against the side of the umpire's knee with a crunching thud.

"Strike one," Braga said, as the overweight man who stank of garlic and beer dropped screaming to the ground.

Braga brought the bat down on the front of his other leg, landing just over the knee this time and leaving the umpire clawing for that spot instead as he wailed in agony.

"Strike two."

Braga raised the bat a third time, focusing on the umpire's ribs. But at the last moment his rage bubbled over and he altered his aim for the man's head, bringing the bat straight down and striking the umpire's skull with a sickening crunching sound. Blood and brain matter burst from the man's ears and oozed out of the crack carved down the center of his scalp.

"You're out," Braga said, walking off back toward his Cadillac with bat still in hand.

PART FOUR

Organization of the Ranger Force, 1901, House Bill No. 52

An Act to provide for the organization of a "Ranger Force" for the protection of the frontier against marauding and thieving parties, and for the suppression of lawlessness and crime throughout the State; to prescribe the duties and powers of members of such force, and to regulate their compensation.

Section 1. Be it enacted by the Legislature of the State of Texas: That the Governor be and is hereby authorized to organize a force to be known as the "Ranger Force," for the purpose of protecting the frontier against marauding or thieving parties, and for the suppression of lawlessness and crime throughout the State.

Section 2. The "Ranger Force" shall consist of, not to exceed, four separate companies of mounted men, each company to consist of, not to exceed, one captain, one first sergeant and twenty privates, and one quartermaster for the entire force. The captains of companies and the quartermaster shall be appointed by the Governor, and shall be removed at his pleasure; unless sooner so removed by the Governor, they shall serve for two years and until their successors are appointed and qualified.

33

Guillermo Paz stood outside the San Fernando Cathedral on West Main Plaza in San Antonio, studying the plaque that proclaimed it to be the oldest cathedral sanctuary in the United States. Jim Bowie was married here before dying at the Alamo at the hands of Santa Anna, who used the building as an observation post. The cathedral claimed that Bowie, along with Colonel Travis and Davy Crockett himself, had been ceremonially buried in the church's graveyard as their official resting places. But Paz knew of other locations that had made the same claim. Since the heroes' bodies had all been burned after the famous battle, he supposed anybody could claim anything they wanted to.

Paz mounted the stone steps and entered the chapel to the smell of something like lacquer. He looked down to see the old wood floors he recalled as being faded and worn had been refinished with a fresh coat, and the wooden pews looked reconditioned as well. The church smelled of candles and light incense, relaxing him instantly. It was the same smell he recalled from his youth growing up in the slums of Venezuela where the local church was the only refuge from the gang-riddled streets, making him feel truly at home as he made his way to the confessional perched in the church's rear.

Paz squeezed himself into the confessional and eased the door closed behind him. He noticed the armrest just below the confessional window had been refinished as well, obliterating the P-A-Z he'd carved into it with a twelve-inch commando blade during his last visit.

He'd barely gotten himself settled when the window opened, leaving only the screen between him and the priest.

"Bless me, Father, for I have sinned. It's been, oh, about a year since my last confession."

"Your voice is familiar, my son."

"I've visited you before, padre, a few years ago when I was a different man altogether. I think you'd be proud of me, since I really did take your advice. And it's nice to see you put the money I left you to good use."

"Oh, no," Paz heard the priest mumble under his breath.

"Don't worry, I'm not going to do any more carving. Those days are behind me. Care to hear why?"

There was a pause, then, "Please, my son."

"I think I used to carve my name in places like this to remind God I'd been there, so He wouldn't forget. That on account of the fact that I hadn't done much good for Him to remember. That's all changed now."

Paz waited for the priest to comment, continued when he didn't.

"Last priest to hear my confession did so in a church of my own making. Well, a tented plank floor with folding chairs anyway, set in the middle of the Mexican desert. Didn't get much use other than me, unfortunately. Grand opening was set for last Easter but I ended up being elsewhere at the time."

Paz could see the priest fidgeting on the other side of the confessional screen. "Do you have something to confess, my son?"

"I'm getting to that. See, it's been a long process for me, padre. I didn't go wrong overnight and going right has taken me some time. It's not like I woke up one morning determined to change; it just sort of happened, starting down in Juárez, Mexico, where I got tired of innocent people being chewed up by the drug cartels."

"Ángel de la Guarda," the priest muttered. "The Guardian Angel . . ."

"So you've heard of my work down there."

"I . . . I didn't think it was real, *could be* real. One man against . . ." The priest's voice tailed off, as if he'd lost his breath along with the rest of the words.

"Know what I've realized, padre?"

"Tell me."

"That my confessions always correspond to these battles that have helped redefine me. I guess I feel them coming. That kind of foresight kind of runs in the family. Does that make any sense?"

"Are you suggesting achieving purity through violence?"

"No, but that has a nice ring to it. I don't have a lot to confess right now but I do need some advice, counsel."

"I'm listening, my son."

Paz shifted his vast bulk in the cramped confessional. On the other side, he could see the priest finally stop fidgeting and settle into place.

"You read Aristotle, padre?"

"Some," the priest told him.

"For a long time, Greek philosophers had the way the world works all wrong. Take Plato. He figured the world as an unchanging place of intelligible forms and ideas. But then Aristotle shows up and changes everything. Comes out and insists the world's all about change. Matter of fact, I believe he said it was the only constant. But he also said the reason something changes is because something makes it change. You see my point?"

"I must say I don't."

"It's confirmation of what I've always suspected, that my Texas Ranger is my catalyst. She's what has moved and changed me. Makes perfect sense since Aristotle also believed that change is bred by a greater aim, goal, or purpose."

"I believe, my son, he was saying that change isn't an end in itself, but a means to a greater end. Like salvation."

"Or peace?"

"They could be interpreted as much the same thing."

Paz leaned back against the confessional wall and felt the boards creak under the strain. "You sure know your Aristotle, padre."

"I remember the profound effect this Texas Ranger had on you the first time you met her."

"Trying to kill each other will do that for you."

"And does your return here have something to do with . . ." Again the priest's voice trailed off, as if he didn't want to finish a question for which he feared the answer.

"That's the other reason why I came to see you. It shouldn't, but I'm starting to think it does. See, I've got that feeling again. We're up against a bad enemy this time, and I just needed someone to bounce this stuff off of, help me get my thoughts straight on the subject. You're a good listener."

"This . . . new enemy. Should I be afraid, my son?"

Paz pushed himself up off the seat, suddenly missing the fact he wasn't leaving his mark behind. "We'll see, padre."

34

ALAMO HEIGHTS, THE PRESENT

Teo Braga liked to water his lawn manually with a hose, even though the yard was equipped with underground sprinklers. He enjoyed the feeling of doing it himself, not trusting the sprinklers to manage the same coverage. He'd never stopped being hands-on, no stranger to getting those hands dirty even as the most successful waste management baron in the country. No, it wasn't glamorous, nor did it hold the seeds of some greater ambition. But it was work he remained proud of with a genuine belief of the good he was doing and the pride he held in a job done well. He treated his employees as his first boss, Alvin Jackson, had treated him and, as for his rivals, well, Braga had come to the conclusion there were times when a pen was called for and other times when a baseball bat was more fitting.

His first job outside of the farms and ranches through the desert southwest had been hauling trash because he'd never lost his fascination with the reason behind his father having nearly been beaten to death. He was only fifteen at the time, but Alvin Jackson, the first black man he'd ever known and as close to a mentor as Braga had, wasn't concerned with formalities like age or a birth certificate. Many of the workers were Mexican just like him, though none he met were actually born in the United States as he was. And that seemed to make Braga see the experience in an entirely different light.

When he walked from the bus stop to the truck depot every morning, he'd pass a long line of trucks pulling out for their morning runs, so many he always lost count. Braga would come up with a rough estimate of the number and multiply it by the amount of tonnage they hauled away on a daily basis. The sum was staggering, city and municipal contracts being garbage gold.

The company for which Alvin Jackson served as foreman had the El Paso contract until a rival bidder with better political connections stole it away.

"I gotta let you go," Alvin Jackson told him, his voice cracking.

"I understand, sir."

"You're a good kid and I want to do right by you, but we just lost half our business." Alvin Jackson seemed finished, but then quickly resumed. "Why'd you call me that?"

"What?"

"Sir."

"Because you've treated me well and I respect you, Mr. Jackson."

The rival company made its workers, many of them itinerant, pay for their own gloves and work clothes. The price, Braga heard, was deducted from their first paycheck, maybe three times what the same stuff would cost at the local department store. Not content with the municipal contracts, the rival company began going after private contracts as well. Alvin Jackson called Braga back to work when a crew of Mexican illegals from his company was ambushed, beaten, and found in the back of their own truck amid the refuse.

The day after his sixteenth birthday, Braga accompanied Alvin Jackson to visit the men in the hospital and listened to them tell their story in Spanish, closing his eyes so he could picture his father being beaten by construction thugs just for using the site's Dumpster.

"Something's gotta be done about this," he told Alvin Jackson, realizing too late he'd actually spoken the words in Spanish.

A week later a spark in the rival company's garage set off a gas-line leak that took out half their fleet and the company Braga worked for got the city contract back. Braga's next paycheck had a nice raise in it and the one after that came with one even nicer. Alvin Jackson had handed him both checks personally.

"I got big plans for you, son," he promised. "Big plans."

Jackson was a beefy ex-football player with a warm smile and hearty laugh. He'd been born and raised in Louisiana, the great-grandson of slaves who claimed his grandfather practiced voodoo and could set grisgris spells on anyone for a price. He claimed he'd inherited a portion of his grandfather's powers and had set a spell using a special amulet the night before that fire had ravaged the rival company's depot.

"You think it was magic that got us the business back?" Braga asked him.

Jackson looked him right in the eye. "Something like that."

But magic had nothing to do with the meteoric rise Teo Braga had made since then. Two years back he'd purchased an eight-thousand-square-foot red-stone mansion that sat on four and a half lush acres in Alamo Heights. The property, originally owned by a drug dealer, had been confiscated by the Texas Rangers, who had used it as a safe house of all things. It featured a pool, tennis court, tree house, and two-stall covered barn, and had originally been on the market for $2.5 million. That, though, was before a shoot-out there claimed the lives of two Texas Rangers protecting a couple of kids who'd supposedly gotten themselves involved somehow with a mythical Mexican criminal. A neighbor who was a Vietnam veteran compared the gun battle to the Tet Offensive, which dropped the asking price by another half million and Braga ended up buying it for half the asking price.

Braga had just started to water a different section of the lawn when his cell phone rang, the office calling. "I'll be there in twenty minutes," he said.

But his assistant wasn't calling to inquire about his pending presence; someone had called to request a meeting.

"Texas Ranger?" Braga said, stiffening a bit, afraid maybe someone had witnessed him bashing in the umpire's brains the previous night. "Alright, call him back and tell him I'm on my way in. . . . What do you mean it's a 'her'?"

35

"Thanks for seeing me so quickly, Mr. Braga," Caitlin greeted, finding the man's handshake just firm enough to let her know how strong he was. She had come here straight from the impound lot where, to her dismay, the remains of the car belonging to Alejandro Pena had yielded no further clues as to his true identity or motivation for changing it. Accidents involving eighteen-wheelers don't tend to leave much behind, and in this case the unrecognizable carcass of the car was little more than a mangled husk of scorched steel.

"My pleasure. Just never figured the Rangers would have much interest in the waste management industry."

"Something came up in the course of one of our investigations."

"You mind elaborating further while I make my rounds?" Braga asked, moving casually toward an open Jeep outfitted with the devil's head logo familiar to her from the barrel she'd spotted on the tape in Young Roger's office cubicle. "I like to do that every day just to make sure all the pieces are running the way they're supposed to. Amazing how much you can accomplish by just staying on top of things."

Teofilo Reyes Braga spoke like a man with nothing to hide or fear. He tried to appear genuine but came off as if he were reading from a script, the authenticity he was striving for lost in his glib grin and gleam forced on his eyes like a sweater that didn't fit. He wore his confidence like a badge, smiling so easily and

often the gesture seemed more part of an illusion he
was casting than a glimpse into his true nature. Some
men, and criminals especially, Caitlin knew, disguised
their true natures by disarming their foes with fake
shows of deference and respect. Her father and grandfather had always told her they could spot a guilty
man a hundred feet away in the dark because they
seemed to shine. Well, Caitlin was looking at Braga in
the light and he seemed to be shining too.

Young Roger had finally managed to identify the
devil's head symbol imprinted on the otherwise unidentified barrels in the waters beneath the *Mariah* as
the corporate logo of Braga Waste Management. Two
phone calls later Caitlin was headed for the Covel
Gardens facility Braga owned and operated on Covel
Road fifteen minutes from Company D headquarters.

"I'd love to join you, sir," Caitlin said, climbing into
the Jeep's passenger seat and studying Braga closer as
he moved around to the driver's side.

He was of average height or so, but the way he carried himself made him look taller. He wore a dress
shirt with the same logo that adorned the Jeep affixed
to his lapel, definitely not a suit and tie guy, as his impressive bio indicated. A true self-made, first-generation
American who had gone from migrant worker to the
biggest name in waste management in the state, if not
the entire country. Braga's dark skin indeed had a glow
to it, thanks to a light sheen of sweat brought to the
surface by the sun and the heat. She could see tiny
pockets of perspiration growing on his underarms,
wondering if he was a man who didn't use antiperspi-
rant or one on whom its effects were negligible. His
hair was full and black, so neatly styled that it looked
chiseled into place.

The open Jeep's gray interior was hot to the touch and Caitlin leaned forward to keep it from roasting her back. The steel roll bar overhead seemed to radiate more heat than an oven.

"This facility's eight hundred acres in total," Braga said, slamming the door behind him. "We use five hundred of those for waste disposal and the remaining three hundred for recreational facilities, support buildings, and buffer zones."

"I noticed the courts and ball fields on the way in," Caitlin told him.

"Braga Waste Management, BWM, sponsors my youngest son's Little League team, the El Diablos. They play their home games here. We lost our last game of the season just yesterday. You have any children, Ranger?"

"No, sir, I don't. Not really, anyway," Caitlin then added, thinking of Dylan and Luke.

"I'd imagine it would be hard for you, being a Texas Ranger and all."

"I'd imagine it would be just as hard for a man of your standing in such a big industry."

He cocked his gaze toward her as he eased the Jeep onto the road that swirled through the entire complex. "I think we have something in common. Your grandfather, Earl Strong, ran Al Capone's boys out of Sweetwater during the oil boom of the thirties."

"Yes, sir, he did at that. One of those rare occurrences where legend and fact are the very same."

"I had a similar experience with what some people call the Dixie Mafia here in Texas."

"Did you now?"

"They pretty much owned the waste management business in the state when I got started in it as a boy."

"I imagine that presented its share of problems," Caitlin said, grateful that the breeze had at least somewhat cooled the scorched upholstery superheating her skin.

"My first boss was a man named Alvin Jackson. We were a union shop in those days, but Jackson didn't appreciate having to pay tribute to those without the best interests of his men in mind. That's putting it mildly."

"What did Mr. Jackson do?" Caitlin asked, genuinely interested.

"You're going to laugh," Braga said, suddenly relaxed. "But he set a spell."

"A spell?"

"That's what he claimed. See, Jackson was from Louisiana. Said his grandfather was a Cajun witch who taught him something called gris-gris voodoo."

"Did the spell work?"

"Well, the Dixie Mafia never came back to collect their tribute. You can make up your own mind, Ranger."

Caitlin let him see her staring at him, his eyes wide and unblinking.

"Exactly what I intend to do, Mr. Braga."

"And what Texas Ranger business has brought you out here today?"

Caitlin tried to get a firmer fix on Braga but couldn't. His face reminded her of a museum statue's texture, open to differing interpretations depending on the angle from which it was viewed.

"Well, sir, barrels bearing the logo of your company were recently spotted in the Gulf waters off Baffin Bay."

"You don't say."

"I'm afraid I do."

"Let me show you the grounds, Ranger. We can talk as we drive."

36

"Covel Gardens was built to be developed in phases," Braga said, driving the Jeep slowly along the complex's private road. "We've got fifteen phases planned and have gotten through seven so far with each representing an individual disposal cell. I'll show you what I mean as we get further out into the complex."

Braga started Caitlin's tour at something he called the Scale House.

"This is where we weigh the incoming dump loads," he explained, directing her eyes toward a line of trucks three deep waiting to take their place on one of four scales. "Necessary for billing and to make sure we don't exceed our limit for any of the disposal cells."

"I don't see any of those big trash mounds," Caitlin noted, gazing out into the distance with hand cupped over her eyes like a visor.

Braga smiled. "That's because the cells are contained belowground, which is more sophisticated, environmentally friendly, and far less unsightly."

He drove on again.

"Okay, this is the Customer Convenience area," he picked up when they reached a covered concrete off-loading area. "We use it during inclement weather. Customers drop their loads onto an elevated platform beneath which lie eight large roll-off containers. Once the containers are full, we shuttle them to the current active disposal unit where the loads are dumped."

Caitlin's eyes fixed on a covered building open on three sides. "Looks like a picnic area there."

"Close. It's the Helper Hut. From this point, only drivers are permitted to continue on to the disposal units. Anyone else they may have brought along waits here."

Braga proceeded to point out to Caitlin a plant that collected landfill gases and processed them into energy that was then distributed to the local community to reduce their energy costs. He slipped quickly by the facility's simple office buildings contained in what looked like shotgun-style ranch houses. He breezed past the maintenance yard, beaming at what he called the Solidification Area.

"Let me explain," Braga said, when Caitlin professed ignorance on the subject. "Direct disposal of bulk liquid waste is prohibited, which means liquid loads must be solidified before disposal in the landfill. We manage this by off-loading the liquids into what we call mixing basins. Once in the basins soil from the site is added and a backhoe mixes the two until we have solid material. Then the same backhoe loads the contents of a mixing basin into a large dump truck and the waste is transferred to the disposal area."

"Very impressive, Mr. Braga."

"I was hoping you'd see my point."

"What point is that?"

"We take our commitment to the environment seriously here, Ranger. Everything that comes in or goes out of here is measured and accounted for. That includes every truck, every drum, every barrel, and every gum wrapper. Am I making myself clear?"

"I believe you're telling me you had nothing to do with those barrels we found in the Gulf bearing your logo."

"That's exactly what I'm telling you," Braga said, as if he'd been somehow offended.

"The problem, sir, is we have your drums down there on tape, Mr. Braga."

"Did you bring them up?"

"They disappeared before we could manage that."

"Disappeared?"

Caitlin held his stare briefly. "Somebody removed them after they'd been spotted," she said, leaving things at that.

"So we really can't be sure of anything, can we?" Braga's lip started to curl upward in a sneer, but quickly stopped. "Look, Ranger, you can find my logo on maybe a million barrels that fit your description, and I can't be responsible for what becomes of them once in the hands of our hundreds of jobbers and subcontractors. And I suppose at least a few of my subsidiaries statewide still drop drums into the ocean. I don't support the practice, but the truth is it happens."

"Can you get me a list of those subsidiaries so I can check them out?" Caitlin asked him.

"When did the Texas Rangers become the environmental police?"

"After an entire jack-up oil rig crew got murdered directly over the spot where your barrels were found."

Braga's expression wavered but his rigid, angular features didn't so much as crack. Maybe the sheen of perspiration coating his flesh had deepened a bit, but maybe not. "Like I said, they're not—"

"I understand you're claiming they're not your barrels directly," Caitlin interrupted. "But they had your logo on them, which makes you the only place we've got to start our investigation."

She watched Braga fight to keep his frown from dissolving back into a snicker or sneer. But the sneer prevailed anyway. "Maybe I should ask for a warrant."

Caitlin pulled a multifolded set of pages from the back pocket of her jeans and handed it to him. "I thought you might just do that, Mr. Braga."

37

SAN ANTONIO, THE PRESENT

Caitlin expected any number of reactions from Braga, cracking a smile being the last of them. He left the warrant in her hand, suspended between them as if he were enjoying the challenge she provided. "You think you know me, Ranger?"

"I know when a man's hiding something, sir."

Braga finally took the warrant. "I'll have my lawyers review this, if you don't mind."

"Suit yourself. And in the meantime, maybe I'll look into that labor dispute you mentioned earlier."

Something changed in Braga's expression, the facade suddenly broken like mirror glass, so his very features briefly looked disproportionate and exaggerated. "Excuse me?"

"Mr. Braga, you made Alvin Jackson out to be a hero in the company's battle with the Dixie Mafia. Truth is my father was involved in the resulting investigation after four Dixie mob enforcers were found with their throats cut and testicles jammed into their mouths. He had two witnesses who claimed the killers spoke Spanish but neither could identify the suspects further." Caitlin studied Braga for a reaction, continued when he showed none at all. "One of those witnesses is still alive. Any pictures you can recommend me showing him from back then?"

Braga's expression became statue-like again, the restored facade forced back over his features. The wind picked up but didn't budge his thick crop of hair in the slightest. Caitlin could see the perspiration stains spreading on his underarms.

"How many bad men did your grandfather gun down in Sweetwater?"

"Being a Texas Ranger afforded him the luxury of doing whatever the hell he wanted."

"I'd ask that you not take that tone with me, Ranger."

"And what tone is that, sir?"

"Just answer me this: exactly how many men have *you* killed?"

Caitlin took a few breaths to steady her breathing. "In my first year as a Ranger I worked a case in Lubbock where three bodies were found in a Dumpster serviced by one of your competitors. I believe I interviewed the foreman who ran your facility there."

Braga grinned, his ivory teeth sparkling in the sunlight. He pulled the Jeep to a halt in clear view of a series of fenced-in fields adorned with thick Arkansas blue star that was actually the darkest shade of green Caitlin had ever seen in a grass.

"Toward what purpose, Ranger?"

"The bodies belonged to three drivers from that rival company. I believe Braga Waste Management was involved in some bidding disputes with it at the time."

"Ever catch the men responsible?" Braga wondered, holding Caitlin's stare.

"No, sir. The state's attorney took the case over.

You may remember him, a man named Durfee. You gave ten thousand dollars to his campaign."

Braga's brow grew even shinier with sweat as he looked away. The air seemed to thicken between them, Caitlin listening to Braga breathe noisily through his mouth as she looked back toward the fields layered with thick Arkansas blue star.

"All your disposal units are located under those fields, aren't they? The first seven phases anyway."

"What makes you ask?"

Caitlin held his gaze. "Just the fact that it doesn't look at all like that's the case from what you can see on the surface."

Braga smiled thinly, something else lurking behind the gesture. "How about I have the information you're requesting about those subsidiaries of my company hand delivered later today?"

"E-mail or fax would be fine, sir."

The smile lingered. "I prefer this means. To avoid any further misunderstandings between us, Ranger."

Caitlin fitted her hat back into place, the inside of its brim wet with sweat from her brow. Her cell phone rang and she stepped outside the vehicle to answer it, never taking her eyes from Braga.

"Ranger Strong, this is Annabel Horbst, principal of Harris Middle School. I'm afraid we need you to come down here right away. It's about Luke Torres."

38

Sam Harrabi led the cleric down the center row of the massive facility lined top to bottom with black fifty-five-gallon drums.

"Phase one, *sayyid*," he pronounced.

The cleric gazed about, not bothering to hide his amazement. "This was the accident victim's task."

"It was."

"A shame he will not be able to celebrate our victory with us, but he will witness the fruits of his labors from heaven where he celebrates with those in his family who departed before their time."

Harrabi stiffened at that, noticeably enough to draw the cleric's attention.

"My apologies for my indiscretion, my brother."

"It's alright, *sayyid*."

"Is that because you regret the indiscretions of your past?"

"I do, *sayyid*."

"Relax, my brother. I do not wish you to be punished any further for them; you have been punished enough. I'm only glad I was able to provide you a release from the terrible pain you have suffered at the hands of those in whom you once placed your trust."

Harrabi lowered his head. "I was wrong."

"Say it again."

"I was wrong."

"And now you must use the pain your indiscretions have wrought. You must channel that pain to keep your focus on the holy nature of our mission as your opportunity to redeem yourself before God and your people." The cavernous confines left a lingering echo in the air, giving the cleric's words a tinny, hollow twang. "You were chosen for a reason and while we may question the plan of God, we must also accept it. We do not always ask for the lots life gives us, but we must embrace them all the same."

"May I speak plainly, *sayyid*?"

"Of course."

"You seem in pain yourself, at least bothered."

The cleric nodded. "You are wondering why now, why would we risk all our resources on this one mission that will leave us hunted men forever."

Harrabi nodded, shrugged.

"We had the ingredients and instructions for bomb assembly up on our private, secure Website. One day last year an intruder replaced it with a cupcake recipe. You see my point?"

"A single hacking incident doesn't mean they've penetrated our defenses, *sayyid*."

The cleric's eyes narrowed. "We traced the intrusion to British intelligence sources."

Harrabi felt his breath seize up.

"The point, my brother, is that the Western forces have pierced our network and are closing on us just as they closed on bin Laden. His death allowed them to turn their focus elsewhere. You ask why now, why put all our resources behind a single mission? The answer is because we may not have another chance. It *must* be now, since we don't know how many tomorrows we have left."

The two men stopped in the center of two rows. They stood lost in the shadows cast by the mountains of barrels stacked around them, the echoes of their clacking footsteps fading out.

"It is hard for me too sometimes, *sayyid*," Harrabi said.

"Because you miss your sons, my brother."

"I miss them terribly."

"And who took their lives?"

"The Americans," Harrabi managed through the lump that had formed in his throat.

"Then their deaths at the hands of those you once embraced is what you should be focusing on now. The point, my brother, is that we are all serving a higher cause here. Our own lives are inconsequential with respect to that greater purpose we will soon see realized."

With that, the cleric stretched a hand out toward Harrabi's head. Harrabi bowed it slightly again, believing he was about to be blessed. Instead, though, the cleric eased a finger over the ridged and callused depression on the right side of his forehead just before it met his skull.

"I know of the night you came by this, my brother, the night that changed your place in the world forever and returned you to us. It was your fate, a blessed moment which I know makes the pain no more easy to bear."

The cleric might have been about to say more but Harrabi's phone buzzed once, halting his train of thought.

"Only e-mails pertaining to the mission come to this phone," Harrabi said apologetically. "If you don't mind, *sayyid* . . ."

"Please," the cleric nodded.

Harrabi checked the e-mail, which must have been

short judging by the brief time it took to review the contents. "It's the American. He wants to talk."

"Then call him."

"He says he wants to meet in person."

Harrabi tried not to show any trepidation but his tone must have betrayed his efforts.

"Then perhaps I should come along," the cleric offered.

39

SAN ANTONIO, THE PRESENT

"You wanna tell me what's going on?" Caitlin said to Luke in the front seat of her SUV after she'd picked him up at school.

"How much trouble am I in?"

She let him see her turn off her cell phone. "How'd the fight start?"

"Kid tried to cut me in the lunch line. Thought he was tough. Happens a lot on account of things."

"What things?"

"You, my dad. People figure I'm tough because of all the stories they hear about the two of you."

Caitlin swallowed hard, unable to push much air past the lump that had formed in her throat. She'd never imagined her own choices and lifestyle infringing on Luke's or Dylan's. It confronted her hard and fast with the fact that until Cort Wesley's incarceration, she could come and go as she pleased in and out of their lives. Now, instead, she had to worry about meals, homework, college applications, report cards, and, now, fighting in school. That made for a lot of walls that felt like they were closing in on her.

"So they say things they know will push my buttons," Luke continued.

"Like what?"

"Like who's killed more people, you or my dad. Like you're both murderers who hate Mexicans and Latinos and shoot innocent people."

Caitlin weighed the boy's words in conjunction with the hurt look on his face. Like his older brother, he'd begun to show his discontent by blowing his breath through the hair dangling over his face. He'd grown it out recently, making him look older, and she'd also noticed he was spending more time listening to his iPod and on Facebook than playing video games.

"How about we get ourselves some ice cream?"

They went to Ben & Jerry's Scoop Shop on the River Walk, claiming a shaded wrought iron table close enough to the water to hear the tour guides' standard spiel as their boats cruised past. Luke got a cone of Cherry Garcia, Caitlin a dish of Chocolate Chunk.

"The kid I got into the fight with today . . . his brother was the football player you shot in the shoulder at Dylan's school."

Caitlin had just pushed a big spoonful into her mouth and forced herself to swallow it. "That was a bad mistake on my part."

"It's why you almost lost your job."

"It's why I got reassigned, yeah."

"Kid said his brother's never gonna play quarterback again on account of you."

"And I'm sorry about that. But I'm more sorry about

it being my fault you have to go through all this in school."

Luke plopped his ice cream cone down back in the cup it had been served in. "I hear you on the porch sometimes at night. Is that why you're crying?"

Caitlin felt herself cringe. "I still have nightmares about that day, I still wake up running it through my head to see if there was something I could've done different to avoid gunplay. Thing is, if I hadn't done what I did, how many kids would the real shooter have killed? The boys in school sure know how to push your buttons, but put them in the same situation in the school library and they'd be begging for someone like me to do exactly what I did. I know that may not make it any easier for you, but it's the truth for sure. I'm sorry I shot that boy's brother. I'm sorry he won't be playing quarterback anymore. But I got the rest of those kids out safe and alive, including him." Spoken as if she were really trying to convince herself. "And if I had it to do all over again, I'd likely do exactly the same thing, hopefully with better aim."

Luke's eyes told Caitlin he got what she was saying. But then he pursed his lips and blew out some more breath, not aiming for the hair that had flopped over his face this time.

"How 'bout we head out to the range next week?" Caitlin proposed without thinking.

"You mean it?" the boy said, perking up.

"Wouldn't have said it if I didn't."

He grinned at her, looking more like his brother—and father—every day. "You don't want me to shoot the kids instead of punch back, do you?"

"Nope. I want you to have something you can do that they can't. Nothing gives you more confidence to walk away from a fight than knowing that if it ever comes down to it you're not gonna miss."

Luke's gaze deepened again, his smile fading away. "You missed at Dylan's school, Caitlin."

40

HOUSTON, THE PRESENT

Cort Wesley Masters, wearing the uniform of a worker for the Houston Department of Public Works, sat in the back of the van in clear view of the Bear Creek Islamic Center in Coventry Park on the outskirts of Houston. Paz was somewhere close by with the six former Mexican Zeta commandos he'd brought along for the job.

"Counting down to zero hour, cowboy," Jones told him. "How are the nerves?"

Cort Wesley didn't respond, just kept his focus on the mosque on one of the surveillance screens built into the van's rear.

"That's what I thought," Jones said, and Cort Wesley could visualize him smiling.

"The problem, Jones, is you *don't* think, not nearly enough."

"That a fact, cowboy?"

"You've been out of the game too long. Something doesn't add up here and your vision's too narrow to notice."

"My intelligence is solid."

"But the man you had inside the cell is gone and presumed dead. I got that right?"

"Not entirely," Jones said, sweat beading up over his upper lip. "I'm gonna turn up the air-conditioning."

Cort Wesley reached out and latched a hand onto his forearm. "Wait a sec. What is it you're not telling me?"

Jones looked down at the hand restraining him. "I got you out of prison, secured you an official pardon, cowboy. That buys me the courtesy to tell you whatever the hell I want to and nothing more."

"Why do I think there's a lie in there someplace?"

The Bear Creek Islamic Center was a sprawling structure boasting a fully equipped community hall that included a stage and state-of-the-art sound system. It was laid out with an elongated V-shaped design equally fit for a church or synagogue. It boasted a membership of nearly a thousand and was generally considered to be a positive contributor to the community.

"You want to tell me more about these homegrown terrorists," Cort Wesley said, when Jones remained silent.

Jones angled himself so he could look at the window and Cort Wesley at the same time. "Since nine/eleven fourteen Americans have been killed in jihadist terrorist attacks on U.S. soil. Thirteen of those were gunned down at Fort Hood right here in Texas, and the fourteenth was a young military recruiter who was shot outside a recruitment center in Little Rock, Arkansas. In both cases, the suspects were Americans—Major Nidal Hasan and Carlos Bledsoe—who appeared to have some connection with al-Qaeda's arm in Yemen.

"The Times Square bomber, Faisal Shahzad, was a young American of Pakistani descent with an MBA. Shirwa Ahmed, a young Somali-American from Minneapolis, was a college student who went to Somalia and now owns the dubious distinction of being America's first suicide bomber. He drove a truck full of explosives into a U.N. building in Puntland. The FBI matched his prints to the remains of a finger found at the scene.

"So we're no longer looking for some poor kid from Pakistan who's come to the U.S. to find his path to the afterlife and however the fuck many virgins are waiting for him. Radicalized Americans who spent time overseas in Crazy World stand out on our radar like jumbo jets. But the new model is the mountain coming to Muhammad instead of vice versa. Planners out of Yemen mostly making the trip to the dreaded West to oversee the whack jobs who've sworn allegiance to jihad. Signed themselves up as willing recruits whose psychological profiles are then vetted and the courtship process begins. The bottom line being that, as is the case with whatever's going down across the street here, the al-Qaedas of the world are building an army under our very eyes we can't see."

Jones hesitated, Cort Wesley having trouble seeing his eyes in the van's dull lighting.

"And here's the other thing, cowboy," he continued. "Osama bin Laden's dead and Ayman al-Zawahiri's a dinosaur, yesterday's news. But that doesn't mean we're out of the woods, far from it, and that's my point. The plot to bomb New York City subways, which was described as the worst plot leveled against the U.S. since September 11, would have killed dozens had Najibullah Zazi succeeded in mixing the chemicals and getting them on the trains. Had the bombing of Northwest Flight 253 on Christmas Day succeeded, it would've killed hundreds."

Jones swung all the way toward Cort Wesley, the light hitting him in a way that made his eyes look all black, no whites at all. "Now we've got a basement lair inside this mosque for these American Muslims who've gone to the dark side. We don't know what's going on down there or what they're up to exactly. But they all dropped off the face of the earth right after my man filed his final report, into identities we imagine they'd been ghosting all along. We've got confirmation that the men we've been watching entered that mosque yesterday and have yet to emerge, so we're gonna hit it hard and fast, take no prisoners in the process, and learn what we can learn before Texas goes boom. How's that?"

"Not bad for starters."

"Starters?"

"Time to fill in the blanks, Jones," Cort Wesley said to him, "like what was in your agent's final report about how big this really is."

Jones looked at him across a compartment that reeked of stale coffee and gasoline fumes. "Try this on for size. All those attacks on American soil I just mentioned were the work of one man: Anwar al-Awlaki, an American-born cleric living in Yemen."

"Then I guess it's a good thing a Predator drone took him out last year."

"Try again, cowboy. Al-Awlaki played us. There was no body to recover or DNA to test, so we're relying strictly on intelligence that turned out to be manufactured." Jones hesitated, as if to collect his thoughts. "Man needed some freedom to operate, to plan something that will make nine/eleven look like a fire drill. The piece of shit's fingerprints are all over this Texas plot and all our information indicates it's going to be a game changer of epic proportions. And that's not all."

"What else could there be?"

"Al-Awlaki himself. We're convinced he's running things from Ground Zero, cowboy, right here in the Lone Star State."

41

SHAVANO PARK, THE PRESENT

"Who's that?"

Dylan Torres was teaching Luke how to skateboard in the half-pipe he'd reconstructed in the front yard when a pickup with an extended cab and double rear tires slid to a halt at the curb.

"I have no idea," Dylan told his younger brother as a man who wore his cowboy hat tilted so low his eyes were lost to the shading climbed out.

Dylan moved between Luke and the street as the man spread his black suit jacket just enough to reveal the shoulder holster contained beneath it. He walked listing slightly to that side as if his gun was weighing him down. His clothes looked too big for his gaunt frame, which made Dylan think of sick people he'd met who had trouble keeping food down. The man was stringy thin, his boots outfitted with spurs as if his pickup was actually a horse he needed to prod into motion. The parts of his face that weren't shaded by his hat were red and blotchy.

The man stopped five feet from Dylan, the hooded nature of his gaze making the boy backpedal involuntarily, measuring off the distance to retrieve his dad's Glock from inside the house. The man's skin didn't seem to fit him, Dylan thought, looked to have been fastened around his bones with tape and glue.

"I'm looking for Caitlin Strong," the man said. "Might she be home?"

"She doesn't live here."

"But she's staying with you while your father's in jail, isn't she?"

"That's none of your business."

The man started to reach under his jacket, making Dylan flinch and then stiffen until his hand emerged with a regular-sized envelope. "Well, I've got something here my boss asked me to deliver to her personally."

He extended the envelope toward Dylan, hitching up his cowboy hat to reveal eyes that leered at him in a way that made the boy's stomach flutter. He felt queasy all of a sudden, maybe a little unsteady on his feet. He made no move to take the extended envelope, nothing that would bring him any closer to this human freak show.

The man grinned, his ill-fitting skin rising on one side while lowering on the other. "Ranger Strong is expecting this," he continued when Dylan remained frozen. Then his narrowed, leering eyes widened in apparent recognition. "Say, you're that boy got himself kidnapped in Mexico last year by those slavers. Tell me, son, any of them have their way with you?"

Dylan cocked his gaze back toward his brother. "Get inside and do your homework."

But the man in the black suit took a few casual steps that planted him between Luke and the front door. "You experience that feeling like a hot poker being jammed up your innards?" His eyes seemed to twinkle as he said that. "Or maybe they just made you use your mouth on them. That can change the way a pretty-looking boy like you sees the world forever."

Dylan took his phone from his pocket. "Think I'll let Caitlin know you're here. You can give her the envelope yourself."

"Good idea, boy," he said pocketing it. "Tell her Jalbert Thoms came a calling. If she wants to pick up this here envelope later, you tell her I'll be at the Red Stripe bar off Vance Jackson Road."

Dylan touched CAITLIN on his favorites list, never taking his eyes off Jalbert Thoms, willing the call to go through quick.

"Those Mexicans got swizzle sticks for private parts. But a good American hot poker make you long for more. You walk around looking pretty as you do, you're asking for it, challenging the very inhibitions of good folk like me."

"Hey, Caitlin," Dylan said when the call went straight to voice mail. "There's somebody here looking for you."

Thoms tipped his hat and slid sideways back toward his truck. "Next time I'll show you my gun, boy. I'm a damn good shot once I got something fixed in my sights."

42

SAN ANTONIO, THE PRESENT

"When's it stop, Ranger?" D. W. Tepper asked when Caitlin finally made it back to Company headquarters.

"Excuse me?"

"My phone's been lit up all afternoon. Guess

Hurricane Caitlin has blown back into town in all her glory. Maybe I should have tossed you off that oil rig into the ocean instead of giving you charge of the investigation. Did I warn you not to make me regret that decision, or has my memory shit the goddamn bed?"

"This have something to do with Teofilo Braga?"

"Only everything. I'll say one thing for you, Hurricane, at least you pick on the high and the mighty."

"I didn't pick on him."

"Oh no? What do you call accusing a man of being party to a multiple homicide?"

"Was he talking about the *Mariah,* the four Dixie mobsters from a decade back, or the bodies found in a Lubbock Dumpster?"

"I really couldn't say. But this is what happens when you rattle the cages of powerful men who aren't used to explaining themselves or their actions."

"So did I do something wrong?"

Tepper just shook his head, scowling as he jammed a Marlboro into his mouth and fired up a match. "You're fixing to kill me for sure, Caitlin Strong. You realize my return to smoking coincided with your return to the Rangers?"

"I never asked you to explain yourself or your actions, D.W."

Tepper jabbed his cigarette at her. "That's not funny, Ranger. Every time you shake somebody's tree, I get mine shaken. Jesus Christ, Braga was on the cover of *Texas Monthly* a few months back as the ultimate immigrant success story."

"He's not Jesus Christ."

"No, but he's a millionaire lots of times over who started out as a migrant farm worker."

"And how'd that happen exactly?"

"Oh jeez . . ."

"I read the magazine article too, Captain. One day Braga is working for a waste management company and then practically overnight he owns it. Unless my issue was missing a page, something must be missing from his bio."

Tepper nodded the way a man does when a point's about to follow. "And how exactly might that be connected to the *Mariah*?"

"No way I can see."

"Then stick with what you can."

"Like you did with Earl and Jim on Galveston Island?"

Tepper looked like a man stifling an acid-laced belch. "Don't go there again, Ranger."

"Then tell me the rest of the story so I don't have to, D.W."

43

GALVESTON ISLAND, 1979

"So, Mugsy," Earl Strong said to Sheriff Plantaine, "we have us an understanding?"

"In other words," Jim Strong picked up, "you feel yourself up to the task of staring down all the money people with their own agendas or not?"

"There are plenty of good lawmen in Texas who ain't Rangers," he told them.

"Difference being that Rangers don't have to stand for reelection," Jim reminded. "And I imagine you gotta keep that fact in sight."

Plantaine ran his eyes over the mangled bodies of the dead frat boys lying in the clearing. "These victims are the only thing I got in my sight right now."

"Okay, then. What would've brought them out to this here spot?"

"We get our share of tourists and explorers in search of Jean Lafitte's Campeche grounds. But not on their own and certainly not on a night where you can't see squat even when the moon is as bright as it gets."

"They have these things called flashlights today," Earl reminded him with a wink and a nod.

"You'd need more than a flashlight to find your way in these parts. There's no actual remnants of Lafitte's camp and, besides our own tours, no one much advertises he made one of his homes here, the other of course being in the Louisiana bayou, which reminds me . . ."

"What?" Earl spurred.

"The Cajuns there talk of a legend they call the Rougarou. Mythical figure kind of like Bigfoot. Not quite as big, but twice as mean."

"This is Texas, last time I checked."

"I'm only raising that on account of Lafitte's roots elsewhere."

"So," Jim Strong said from over his inspection of one of the bodies, "you figure this Rougarou may have been hanging around all these years looking for some frat boys to kill."

"Disemboweling the bodies this way has got Cajun practices written all over it."

"You talking voodoo, spells, sticking needles in dolls—all that sort of shit?"

"I'm just thinking out loud here," Plantaine told

them. "Maybe there's something ritualistic about all this, like these boys were sacrifices or something."

"Looks more like they surprised somebody," noted D. W. Tepper. "And I don't see any evidence of voodoo dolls on the scene."

"My granddaughter Caitlin's got three dolls herself," Earl Strong chimed in. "Stuffing's all falling out of each."

"On account of you teaching her to shoot the poor things with a BB gun," Jim said.

"Well, I didn't think she was old enough at three to try my Colt, son."

"I believe," started D. W. Tepper, "we can now see why the famous Rangers Strong, father and son, have never been paired up on a case before."

"First time for everything," said Jim.

"And I'd say the bodies of five mutilated frat boys from the University of Texas certainly calls for it," Earl added.

That was enough to plunge the three men back into the horrible reality of what was before them. Scavenger birds neither Earl nor Jim even knew were native to Galveston Island buzzed the skies overhead. They looked sleeker and less imposing than buzzards, but their aims were the same and the stench of human remains and entrails had likely sent their primal instincts spinning into overdrive. Back on the ground, the Rangers knew the encroaching swarm of insects and maggots made their investigation of the crime scene a race against time and decay. It would probably be best to chopper the remains back to medical examiner Frank Dean Whatley's office, but they might have to settle for Sheriff Plantaine's men bagging the bodies for transport back via their launch. Either way they were dealing with a finite amount of time to continue their inspection of the crime scene.

"Come have a look at this," D. W. Tepper called to the others.

Plantaine hovered just behind the Strongs as they knelt even with one of the dead frat boy's feet.

"Check out this boy's boots," Tepper continued, pointing to the pasty contents of the deepest grooves with the tip of his pen. "I make this as some sort of red soil or clay."

"Like nothing I've ever seen on the island," Plantaine remarked.

"Nor in the area of the University of Texas at Austin either."

Tepper wiped his pen on his pants and slid it back into his pocket. "I'd say a tennis court, 'cept who plays tennis in his boots?"

"Guess Doc Whatley's gonna have his hands full with this one," from Earl.

A stiff wind came up and Sheriff Plantaine backed off, suddenly clenching his hand over his nose, the stench slamming into him hard. "What exactly you boys figure did this?"

"You mean as in weapon?" Earl asked him.

"If it wasn't this Rougarou thing, of course," said Jim.

"As in weapon," Plantaine affirmed.

Earl took a quick glance at the nearest body, then turned back grimacing, as if he'd had enough of the sight. "I'm thinking something like the fork hoe I use to cultivate my seed beds."

"A garden tool?"

"'Nother possibility would be a hand cultivator.

Reason I say one of those is because the cuts and tears are jagged. So whatever did this to these boys was sharp enough, but not in the razor or weapons sense of the word."

"Goes along perfectly with what I was figuring, Dad."

"And what's that, son?"

Tepper watched his mentor on the left and best friend in the Texas Rangers on the right standing face-to-face, two true legends who along with him likely made up the last of a breed.

"That whoever killed these boys didn't plan it. That the victims just happened to be in the wrong place at the wrong time."

"Random as opposed to premeditated."

"From where I'm standing."

Earl Strong took off his Stetson and mopped his brow, the smell of his own sweat infinitely preferable over that of the bodies sprawled in the clearing. "They surprised somebody who'd come here for the same purpose."

"Maybe Jean Lafitte's treasure," added Jim.

"Rangers," said Sheriff Plantaine, "I've had my fill of Cajun monsters and treasure talk for the day. What say I call in my team to get these poor boys ready to travel?"

Plantaine did just that, a deputy assisting a nervous paramedic calling out to him when they got one of the bodies straightened out.

"What is it, Tyrell?"

"There's something over here on the ground. I think it fell out of the dead kid's hand when we turned him."

Plantaine joined the Strongs and D. W. Tepper in crouching over the body.

"Looks like a crucifix," the sheriff noted. "Not regular like, but a cross all the same. Poor kid must have been the religious type, holding fast to it as he was dying."

"Everything else suggests they were taken by surprise, remember?" said Jim Strong, using a gloved hand to slide the crosslike pendant into a small evidence bag. "Can't have it both ways."

"So if he wasn't clutching it as he went to meet his maker, what then?"

"Don't know," Jim answered. "Guess we'll have to wait to find out what exactly."

Frank Dean Whatley's initial examination of the bodies well after dark that night confirmed pretty much all of the initial conclusions reached in the field.

"So you agree with me it was either a fork hoe or hand cultivator?" Earl raised.

"Which of them has three prongs again?"

"Fork hoe."

"That'd be the one."

"Tool used on raised beds and flower gardens," said Jim Strong.

"Or, in this case, maybe hoeing the ground for missing treasure."

"Except according to legend," interjected Earl, "Lafitte's legendary treasure's somewhere in the Louisiana bayou, not Galveston Island."

"What about that cross?" Jim asked Frank Whatley.

"Haven't gotten to it yet."

"You're too young to start slowing down like me, Doc," Earl told him.

"Except for that one quick coffee run, you boys have been shadowing me since you brought the bodies in. You see me wasting any time along the way?"

"Take all you need," Earl said, starting for the door with his eyes on his son. "Three of us are gonna trace this back to where it all started while you putter around."

"Oh, there is one other thing," Whatley remembered. "That substance on the soles of their boots, what you called clay."

"What about it?"

"Wasn't clay at all, but fill. The kind used in swamp lands to shore up levies and shorelines."

"Like in the Louisiana bayou?" Jim Strong asked him.

"It's a swamp, the last time I checked."

"And now it looks like our frat boys made a stop there as well."

44

SAN ANTONIO, THE PRESENT

"So we all went up to the University of Texas at Austin," Tepper finished.

He sucked in as deep a breath as his ragged lungs allowed. Caitlin had to admit his color and energy were better when he smoked than when he didn't, though she couldn't even begin to explain why.

"It won't work, you know, Ranger."

"What?"

"Trying to distract me from the matter at hand, you being a political Claymore mine blowing up anyone who gets close to you. When you gonna learn to dial it down with people who carry power in their pocket like it's a wallet?"

"I don't recall either Jim or Earl providing much counseling on that subject."

"Politics are everywhere now, and Hurricane Caitlin seems determined to blow through every last bit of them."

"Braga is dirty, Captain. There's something all wrong about him. And I don't buy this migrant worker, American Dream, self-made man crap for a minute."

"Even though all those descriptions seem to fit him to a T."

"I'm gonna follow the trail of those missing barrels, see where it takes me."

"Teofilo Braga's trail, you mean."

"Did I say that?"

"I'd say choose your steps wisely and be discreet for once, if I thought it would do any good."

Caitlin stood up. "How much you know on the subject of waste management, D.W.?"

"Nothing."

"Neither do I. Very few do, and that's the point. Braga can get away with anything he wants because there's a general ignorance of what he's doing in the first place. Other than the EPA, I don't think there's a single law enforcement body that gives one hoot about what might be inside those barrels spotted underneath the *Mariah*."

Tepper weighed her words in between puffs. "My

question is what's so important about them that they'd make Braga risk alienating the army of officials, elected and otherwise, he's got watching his back?"

"I'm thinking more along the lines of how those barrels connect with two dozen oil rig workers murdered directly overhead," Caitlin said, flipping her cell phone back on and freezing as her latest voice mail started to play.

"Ranger?"

"Oh, shit," she said, listening to Dylan's message.

PART FIVE

In 1914, during the early days of World War I, the Rangers had the daunting task of identifying and rounding up numerous spies, conspirators, saboteurs, and draft dodgers. In 1916, Pancho Villa's raid on Columbus, New Mexico, intensified already harsh feelings between the United States and Mexico. As a result, the regular Rangers, along with hundreds of special Rangers appointed by Texas governors, killed approximately 5,000 Hispanics between 1914 and 1919, which soon became a source of scandal and embarrassment.

—*Legends of America:*
Texas Legends: The Texas Rangers—Order Out of Chaos

45

"No sign of Paz," Cort Wesley said, manning the binoculars now.

Jones smirked. "That's why he's here. You too."

"I'm not like him. Nobody is. Wouldn't surprise me if he opened his coat one day and wings sprouted out. Maybe those Mexican peasants had it right when they called him Ángel de la Guarda."

"Then I guess it's a good thing he's on our side."

Cort Wesley thought he might have glimpsed old Leroy Epps seated up in the van's cab, as he often did when worry and overthinking threatened to consume him. He didn't fancy the notion of going into an enclosed space to face a potential firefight without any idea of the precise logistics, much less having not fired or even held a gun for a year now.

"Not a bad deal, eh?" Jones raised suddenly. "Get your life back in exchange for one night's work."

"It's never that simple."

"You still don't trust me?"

"Not for one goddamn minute."

Jones looked at Cort Wesley with the same intensity he'd been focusing on the mosque. "Problem is you've got something to lose."

"You don't?"

"Nope. Not a thing. Not a steady woman, not a close relative. And you wanna talk about friends? The Ranger's as close as it gets."

"She's not your friend, Jones."

"My point exactly."

With evening prayers having ended, and the long line of mosque members gone, the plan was for Paz and his men to secure the main floor of the building, after which he'd make the call that he was ready for them.

"Why now?" Cort Wesley posed. "What brings someone as big as al-Awlaki back to his hated homeland after faking his death."

"Because we've cracked his armor; his, al-Qaeda's, and its various offshoots. You know why they're moving today? Because they might not be able to move the day after or the day after that. Because we're *winning*. We've got them on the run and they're desperate."

"You know what they say about wounded animals, Jones."

"You just made my point for me, cowboy."

"Because I'm wondering if this plant who supplied your intel was playing you, Jones. It's happened before."

They both heard Paz's voice at the same time in their earpieces.

"We're ready for you" was all he said.

46

Caitlin spotted Jalbert Thoms the moment she entered the Red Stripe bar on the edge of East San Antonio. She moved across the warped, knotty pine floor, bumping into two customers on her way. She had no idea really what she was going to do when she reached Thoms, until she got to his table and fastened a hand on his throat.

"You wanted to see me, Mr. Thoms?"

She felt the cartilage contract under the force of her grasp, Thoms's hands fluttering in the air before finally locking on her wrist as if prepared to pry her fingers from his throat.

"Well, here I am, sir."

He tried to smile at her through the gurgling sounds his mouth was making, failed there, but managed to tip his hat in the last moment before Caitlin released him.

"I heard you had something for me."

Thoms hocked up some spittle and let it fall to the bar floor, strings of saliva left dangling from both sides of his mouth he wiped clean with a cocktail napkin. His spurs clanged as he uncrossed his legs and left both of them under the table. He removed the envelope from the pocket of his suit jacket, his other hand remaining in his lap.

"Why don't you sit down, Ranger?" he said, still trying to clear his throat. "I'll order you something from the bar. My treat."

Caitlin took the envelope but didn't open it. "You're delivering this on behalf of Teofilo Braga."

"That's right."

"You think he understands the leash law in San Antonio?"

"Don't think I quite follow you, ma'am."

Caitlin held his stare, feeling her eyes tear up slightly from the rage building inside her. Dylan's description of Jalbert Thoms didn't do the man justice. He was like a human stick figure, his dark suit swimming on him, his spurs making him look like a reject from a past century. Even that, though, was nothing compared to the way his skin fit his body, as if somebody had poured too much on him in the mold.

"Law says all animals have to be leashed and that the owner is responsible for their actions if they're set loose, Mr. Thoms. That means everything you said to Dylan Torres might as well have come up out of Mr. Braga's mouth."

"I'll be sure to tell him that."

"I'm surprised he doesn't run background checks on all the people who work for him."

"'Cept I don't work for him, Ranger. I'm more the freelance type, kind of like a hired gun," Thoms said, his eyes twinkling.

Caitlin brushed back her jacket, revealing her SIG-Sauer. "Is that a fact?"

Dylan had still been shaking when Caitlin screeched to a halt in the driveway.

"I swear that man was more liquid than solid," the boy said once they got inside. He tried to drink some water, then changed his mind and laid the plastic bottle back on the table. "I thought he was going to melt right into the grass. A hundred degrees in the sun and he wasn't even sweating. I don't even think he was breathing."

"You protected your brother, Dylan. You did good, real good."

"The way he looked at me was like . . ."

"I know."

"What do you know?"

"I think we should leave it for now."

Dylan's shaking stilled. He leaned forward. "I don't."

Caitlin sat down on the couch next to him. "Among other things, Jalbert Thoms is a pedophile. He did seven years in Huntsville for raping a fifteen-year-old boy."

Dylan looked down. "Kid should've defended himself."

Caitlin slid closer to Dylan on the couch. "It's not always easy with men like Thoms. He's a human monster who knows how to use words as a weapon."

Dylan finally looked at her again. "What other things?"

"Excuse me?"

"You said 'among other things.' What else has Thoms done, kill boys as well as rape them?"

"Not boys," Caitlin said, leaving it at that. "He's a strongman for hire who specializes in intimidation. Since getting out of Huntsville, we believe he's connected to as many as three murders."

"Do I have to start carrying my dad's Glock in the front yard?"

Caitlin eased her arm around the boy's shoulder. "You let me handle this."

"I wanna tell him, my dad I mean."

"You know what he'd do if you did."

Dylan looked at her, his gaze wide and fearful.

A vulnerable teenage boy again, however briefly. "That's why I want to tell him."

Caitlin stood up. "What was the name of that bar again?"

It was a seedy place with sticky floors coated in cigarette ash and beer stains painting the walls. The air-conditioning was either broken or left off, and of the three ceiling fans, only one was spinning in wobbly fashion with a slight creak every second or so. The bar itself was chipped and discolored, and several veinlike cracks adorned a mirror before which bottles both house and higher-end brands were stacked.

Jalbert Thoms slid his chair backward a bit. "Why don't you take a load off, Ranger? Open up that envelope and peruse its contents. What can I get you from the bar?"

Caitlin sat down in the chair directly across from him. "You holding a gun on me under the table, Mr. Thoms?"

"Now, Ranger, you know as well as I that threatening a law enforcement official that way would surely get me sent back to Huntsville."

"All the same, the boy you assaulted earlier today says he saw a gun under your jacket."

Thoms grinned. "I didn't assault anyone."

"Words can be a powerful weapon too, sir."

"You gonna arrest me for what I said?"

"Felons aren't allowed to carry guns, even in Texas." Caitlin let him see the harshness building in her eyes. "Then again, I suppose it was the use of a different weapon that got you jammed up in the first place.

Pretty low caliber without much stopping power would be my guess."

Jalbert Thoms grinned broadly. "You wanna find out for sure?"

"I'm the wrong age. And gender." She held her eyes on him until his grin disappeared. "So how long you been sick?"

"Come again?"

"What is it, a case of AIDS you picked up in prison? Hepatitis? Maybe some of the younger meat there came already contaminated. Now that would be ironic. See, I worked at Brooke Memorial for a time, long enough to recognize what a man looks like when his muscles shrivel up but his skin stays the same. I saw what happened to those patients as they degraded. It wasn't pretty. Hope you can handle a high degree of pain and suffering, Mr. Thoms."

Some of the excess skin along Thoms's jowls puckered. He leaned forward, leaving that same hand beneath the table. "Know how I survived Huntsville, Ranger?"

"You mean when most child molesters leave with their bodies in a box or missing their private parts?"

Thoms flashed his toothy grin again, bright even in the bar's dull lighting. The air itself inside the Red Stripe stank to high heaven; Caitlin had never known air itself to smell so bad before, wondered if it wasn't the odor of old sweat and urine from the prison's halls clinging to Jalbert Thoms's gaunt frame like talcum powder. His grin might have been radiant white, but his skin color was milk-pale. With his sunken cheekbones and eyes set too far back in his skull, he looked like a corpse complete with a pasty, made-up face and formaldehyde for blood. Maybe that was what she smelled.

"Just take the envelope and leave, Ranger," Thoms said, the grin sliding off his face.

"We've come too far for that."

Thoms looked only slightly surprised. "You realize you're playing right into my hands."

"Mistake I've been known to make in the past. And I don't believe you're a match for me, gun under the table or not."

Thoms's grin returned. "Explains why I didn't come alone."

Something scratched at Caitlin's spine.

"Yup," Thoms continued, "what we got here is a genuine ambush. My advice is to take that there letter and be gone, leaving me to my whiskey. Your choice, Ranger, whether to walk out of here or be carried."

47

SAN ANTONIO, THE PRESENT

Caitlin let her stare linger on him, resisting the urge to sweep the bar to see if his claim was true. "So who was it, Mr. Thoms?"

"Who was what?"

"Your father, uncle, scoutmaster, priest, milkman. Almost all pedophiles were molested themselves at one point. I'm just wondering who's to blame for making you get off humping little boys."

Thoms's expression remained flat. "You got your gun on me now, don't you?"

"Why don't you try firing yours and find out?"

"You get me, men who accompanied me here'll get you."

"Chance I'm willing to take."

Now Thoms's face did change, flashing doubt for the first time. Caitlin never took her eyes off him, waiting for the slightest flinch or shift that would tell her he was about to fire. His eyes would tell her first, though, one of Earl Strong's first lessons.

"Then what do you say we have at it, Ranger? Gotta warn you, though. It's not gonna be like gunning down some loser in a high school."

"No, it's not," Caitlin said, lurching upward and up-ending the table over atop Thoms in the same motion.

A gunshot rang out from his pistol, smacking into one of the still ceiling fans overhead. But Caitlin had already swung from Thoms by then, foot on the table to hold him in place while she spotted one of his partners hitting the floor with gun steadying.

She fired four times, one of her bullets drawing a guttural grunt in the same moment a flicker of motion in the bar mirror gave up the second man lunging out in line directly behind her. Now it was Caitlin who dove, hitting the floor hard as his first bullets blew out the mirror and took a hefty complement of bottles for good measure. She got her gun sighted up on him before he could re-angle his down on her. Five shots fired in rapid succession that blew the gunman backward and spilled him over a table to the floor.

But the first man she'd hit was stirring in the same instant Jalbert Thoms lurched to his feet. No way Caitlin could hit two men with one gun, instinct directing her to Thoms while she pulled herself across the floor, struggling not to let her jeans get stuck to the wood.

Bullets whizzed by her as she fired at Thoms, in motion now toward the back exit and continuing to shoot a cannon-sized semiauto that blew divots of wood in all directions. Looked like a Brin-10 or Desert Eagle, packing the force of a shotgun shell.

Caitlin heard the wispy clatter of his spurs and felt the spray of splinters shower her as the other man made it back to his knees. He was shaking too much from a chest wound to get his pistol righted, and Caitlin put a bullet from her SIG dead center in his forehead before he could get off another shot. Even then she was twisting toward the back exit, Thoms in her sights in his rush to the door. She had him, squeezing off a final shot that would blow him out of his shoes.

Click.

Her hammer fell on an empty chamber, magazine expended, the only other sound that of the back door slamming closed behind Jalbert Thoms.

48

HOUSTON, THE PRESENT

Cort Wesley and Jones padded through the moonless night. The ground fog made for an added blessing, further disguising their approach from the street to the mosque entrance from anyone who might have been watching. They were dressed in black camo gear that included masks forming a tight fit over their faces. Their belts held flash grenades and Browning pistols, extra magazines, and additional sets of plastic cuffs. Their Kevlar vests were outfitted with slots for three refill magazines for the Special Forces model M4-A1 submachine guns slung from their shoulders.

The door was already cracked open when they reached it with the M4-A1s steadied before them, courtesy of Paz no doubt since Jones's intelligence indicated the entrance would normally be locked at this hour. Cort Wesley closed it behind him and turned the deadbolt into place. Then he and Jones moved out of the alcove into a hallway to find three of Paz's Zeta commandos standing over ten men wearing traditional Muslim robes and skull caps, now bound and gagged but clearly unharmed. The Zetas wore no masks and the only one who acknowledged Cort Wesley and Jones pointed toward the door leading into the chapel itself.

They entered to find Paz standing over the kneeling figure of the mosque's imam while his remaining three Zetas stood watch over what Cort Wesley could only assume was the man's family, four children and a wife, all lying prone with their faces pressed into the thin carpeting. The chapel was dark other than the spill of lights directly over the altar that rained down in a V-pattern, suggesting a descent from heaven. Paz had positioned the imam so he was kneeling in the very center of the light spill, his head bowed and eyes terrified when he peered upward.

"Imam Mustafa and I have been getting acquainted," Paz said. "Isn't that right, padre?"

The imam didn't respond. Paz held no weapon, just his massive hands upon the holy man's shoulders, the gesture tender and menacing at the same time.

"We've been discussing the Koran's view on fate," Paz continued. "Most interesting but in conflict with my own experience. Tell them, padre."

"*Insha Allah,*" the imam managed hoarsely.

"If Allah wills," Paz translated.

"Colonel," Jones started.

"According to the Koran," Paz continued instead of letting him speak, "everything happens by the will of Allah or, as it is written, 'Nothing will happen to us except what Allah has decreed for us. He is our protector.' Have I got that right?"

Imam Mustafa nodded, keeping his head bowed.

"Nice lessons in that book of yours," Paz said, patting him now on the shoulders instead of squeezing. "I especially like the one about peace. Goes something like, 'If anyone slays a person, unless it be for murder or for spreading mischief in the land, it would be as if he slew all people. And if anyone saves a life, it would be as if he saved the life of all people.' How's that, padre?"

The imam nodded again.

"Good. Then you won't mind answering our questions, since they're all about saving lives, will you?"

A third nod, the most demonstrative yet.

"That's what I thought," Paz said, hands like meat hooks clamped in place on the imam's shoulders as he looked toward Jones.

"Is there a secret basement under this building?" Jones asked the imam.

A nod.

"Are there men down there now?"

A pause before the nod came, less surely this time.

"Did anyone have time to alert them?"

The imam shook his head.

"Are they armed?"

A strangely noncommittal nod that left Cort Wesley feeling something was off here, wrong and out of balance, but he couldn't put his finger on what.

"Do you know a cleric named Anwar al-Awlaki?"

Imam Mustafa shook his head vigorously.

"But you've heard of him."

A single nod.

"Has he been here?"

"No," the imam uttered, speaking toward the floor.

"Have you seen him in the area?"

"No."

"How many men downstairs?"

No response.

"How many men are—"

"Twelve," the imam answered finally.

"Take us to them," Jones finished.

49

HOUSTON, THE PRESENT

The stairs leading to the basement were contained beneath a false door built into the floor in the mosque library that smelled of old paper, mildew, and paste. Imam Mustafa pulled back a small but elegant rust-dominant rug, revealing a section of the wood flooring unmarred except for what looked like a black imperfection in the center. The imam fit a wooden arrow-shaped key into that apparent imperfection, twisted, and then hoisted the hatchlike entrance.

"Down there," he directed.

"Lead the way," said Jones.

At the foot of the stairs, the walkway branched only to the right, lit by small overhead fixtures shedding dull luminescence. It was cool down here in stark contrast to the steamy night air outside.

Imam Mustafa did as he was told, seeming far more scared of the four Zetas who had accompanied them down here, two remaining posted above, than the prospects of what was to come. The four Zetas fanned out forward, taking lead, with Paz immediately behind them and Cort Wesley bringing up the rear with Jones and the imam. For his part Cort Wesley remained leery each step of the way, expecting an ambush at every juncture of the corridor they were in. He'd taken his M4-A1 assault rifle from his shoulder as soon as he stepped off the ladder and hadn't taken his grip off it since.

He'd been expecting the firefight to begin well before they reached the heavy steel door that had come into view in the murky light ahead of them. But as of yet no gunman had appeared and Cort Wesley saw no sign of any now.

"You don't need your weapons," Imam Mustafa said, and Cort Wesley felt again that something was out of place here, too many pieces that didn't feel like they fit right.

The imam continued on slowly, making no effort to flee or warn whoever might have been hiding in the unguarded room. A keypad was hidden in the wall on the right side of the door. The imam popped open the cover and keyed in an access code, Paz now pushing the elongated barrel of his submachine gun with sound suppressor affixed into Mustafa's back, studying his every move.

The door opened slowly, not with a whoosh but a grind.

And the smell and feel of death flooded outward.

Cort Wesley knew what awaited them before crossing the threshold: a dozen bodies, to be exact, lying on the floor. Neatly placed with their legs pressed together and hands cupped over their stomachs, the blood pools spread on the floor of the stench-filled room the only thing disturbing the otherwise placid scene.

"Fuck me," Jones muttered, surprise trumping his dismay for the moment.

"You laid them out like this," Cort Wesley said to the imam, realizing the dead men's folded hands were smeared with blood, their fingertips having been sliced off to eliminate prints.

Mustafa nodded. "Out of respect until they are removed."

"News flash, holy man," Jones snapped at him, shining his flashlight over a series of divots and scratches on the cheap tile flooring. "Nobody's coming back to clean up this mess. They're gone for good, and they took their computers and whatever else with them."

"Their hands aren't callused or rough," Cort Wesley said after checking the mangled hands on a number of the bodies. "Their hair's neatly cut and most are wearing wedding rings."

"Grunts," concluded Jones. "Techies doing our real bad boy's dirty work, until they outlived their usefulness." He looked toward Paz. "It would seem your friend the imam knows more than he's been telling."

Imam Mustafa shrank back toward the wall until a pair of Zetas blocked his path. "I provided them sanctuary, that's all!"

"It's enough," said Jones. "Makes you an accessory to whatever's about to go down, Holy Man, and if I can't stop it, I'm coming back for you."

"Come back, if you wish, but that does not change the fact I know nothing of what they were doing down here."

"But you knew the access code to enter the room," Paz interjected, his shadow nearly swallowing the imam. "Three-one-eight-five." He held his gaze on Mustafa as he continued, reciting. "'Every soul will taste of death. And ye will be paid on the Day of Resurrection only that which ye have fairly earned. Whoso is removed from the Fire and is made to enter Paradise, he indeed is triumphant. The life of this world is but comfort of illusion.'"

Cort Wesley and Jones looked at each other, then back at Paz.

"A prophecy foretelling the End of Days," Paz told them. "Section 3:185 from Surah in the Koran."

50

SAN ANTONIO, THE PRESENT

By the time she got home hours later, after filling out the paperwork with Captain Tepper hovering grimly over her desk, both Luke and Dylan were asleep. Luke had drifted off with a book in his grasp that she pried free and laid on his night table. As usual, Dylan had his iPod plugged into his ears and Caitlin eased the earbuds out to the soft din of the rap music she'd come to loathe and didn't understand for a minute.

She resisted the urge to smooth Dylan's hair, as she laid his iPod atop his spare pillow so he could plug it back in as soon as he woke up. She'd been through so much with these boys, especially him, but moments like this made them shrink by comparison, a fullness rising from her chest into her throat that was unfamiliar and pleasant at the same time.

She padded back downstairs to the sound of the rocker creaking on the front porch and felt for her gun as she eased the door open.

"We need to talk," Cort Wesley said, holding the swing steady with his boot.

"We got ourselves a problem," he continued, after she had sat down next to him, the swing still in the warm night.

"We," Caitlin repeated.

"You, me, the whole damn country."

"What happened?"

"Nothing. That's the problem. Let me tell you now what I couldn't before, why Jones sprung me from that Mexican prison. There's a homegrown terrorist cell plotting a major attack here in Texas, led by the radical cleric Anwar al-Awlaki."

"I thought he was dead."

"You and me both. But it turns out he's here, in the United States."

"You mean *back* in the U.S., since he's American-born. His parents were from Yemen, but his father was a Fulbright Scholar who earned his doctorate here before taking his family back to Yemen. Al-Awlaki himself remained there for a dozen years before returning to the U.S. for college on a foreign student visa and a government scholarship since he claimed he was actually born in Yemen."

"So we paid for his education, that's what you're saying."

"And his public defender when he was arrested twice for soliciting a prostitute in the late nineties in San Diego."

"A true hypocrite." Cort Wesley paused. "You pick this stuff up at Quantico?"

Caitlin nodded. "We spent a whole week on al-Awlaki and the ideology he represents, not long before his convoy got barbecued in Yemen. Supposedly."

"Jones claims this plot of his could kill a million people."

Caitlin felt a chill in the night air. For some reason she thought of Dylan and Luke, sleeping peacefully upstairs. The swing started rocking back and forth, slowly, as if propelled either by the breeze or the nervous tapping of Cort Wesley's feet on the porch floor.

"We were supposed to take the cell out, with the help of Paz and the Zetas he brought along for the ride," Cort Wesley continued. "Problem was we missed the party. By the time we crashed, al-Awlaki's terrorists were already dead. Grunts, we figure, their service done and fingerprints sliced off for their effort."

"How many?"

"A dozen. The attack's coming real soon, that's all we know. The homegrown Muslim radicals we found dead dropped off the face of the earth six months ago."

"People don't drop off the face of the earth, Cort Wesley. They become somebody else so whoever's looking for them won't be able to catch . . ." Caitlin felt something clench inside her. "Uh-oh."

51

She told Cort Wesley about the car accident victim who had assumed the identity of Alejandro Pena about six months ago according to his driver's license.

"Fits the timeline perfectly," he acknowledged. "He dies in this accident and the rest of al-Awlaki's grunts get murdered in a mosque basement. Question being what does it all mean?" He studied Caitlin's expression. "Next question being what else you're not telling me?"

"You really want to hear it?"

"What do you think?" Cort Wesley asked her.

Caitlin told him all of it, going back to the hostage situation in Dylan's school, to manning a desk during school hours, to the fishing trip in Baffin Bay that had ended abruptly aboard the *Mariah*. Cort Wesley looked at her in disbelief, shaking his head when she got to the part about the black barrels that had disappeared from the drilling site and Teofilo Braga's potential part in it all.

"So this pervert was working for Braga," Cort Wesley said at the end, calmer than Caitlin had expected. But sometimes men like Cort Wesley Masters held their violence just below the surface where it could simmer until it boiled over.

"I believe Braga's intention was to warn me off."

"Maybe take advantage of the fact that you just got your gun back."

"Officially anyway."

"Guess he doesn't know you too well."

"Doesn't matter. I'm just another obstacle in his life and he's gotten all the other ones shoved aside."

"First time for everything, I guess." Cort Wesley leaned back and cupped his hands behind his head, staring out into the night. "Know what? I think I'm gonna go check in on my boys."

He stood in Luke's doorway first, the boy looking so much older than last year, his hair the longest Cort Wesley had ever seen it. He was starting to look like Dylan and the boys' mother, Maura Torres, more and more.

"*Fine boy, bubba,*" Leroy Epps said, suddenly by his side. "*And that Ranger gal's doing a fine job raising him.*"

"There a point in there somewhere, champ?"

"*How's it feel to be free?*"

"I'll let you know when that's truly the case."

"*One of my true regrets is I never saw the outside again 'fore I passed. Didn't think it mattered much, but in retrospect it sure does. That's why I come around you from time to time. Get the feel of what I missed.*"

"Your children never came to visit you at The Walls, did they?"

"*I didn't want them to, bubba. Not for their sakes so much as my own.*"

"Why do I think there's a lesson in there someplace?" Cort Wesley said, Leroy Epps accompanying him to Dylan's room where they stood in the doorway and didn't enter.

"*What exactly would you have done without the Ranger gal?*"

"A question I'm glad I never had to answer."

"*I saw the two of you outside on the porch. Looked like a couple teenagers, you no different than your boy over there.*"

Cort Wesley gazed closer at Dylan, his eyes adjusted to the darkness now giving up the way the boy's long black hair splayed across the pillow like some kind of impressionist painting. "Forgot to ask Caitlin if he had a girlfriend."

"*She's got her own problems right now.*"

"On account of that school shooting you mean."

"*Remember what I told you was the key to living inside The Walls?*"

"Laying low."

"*I'm starting to believe the same thing goes for life, least it does when a person's no stranger to guns and violence. Problem with the Ranger is that's all any-body sees anymore when they look at her.*"

"I see plenty more than that, champ."

"*You don't get a vote on this one, bubba.*"

Cort Wesley glanced back at Dylan. "I don't want to see my boys hurt."

"*Pain's a part of life, bubba. Thing is to hope the source of it heals before it eats you alive.*"

"Once this is over, things are gonna be different."

Leroy Epps started to laugh and then silenced him-self, as if afraid of waking Dylan. "*I checked the fridge downstairs. Remind the Ranger gal to have some root beer on hand, will ya?*"

"Why you changing the subject?"

"*'Cause your comment don't deserve a response and you know full well what I mean.*"

"Who were you talking to up there?" Caitlin asked when Cort Wesley stepped back out on the porch.

He closed the door behind him. "Nobody. Myself."

"Thought I heard somebody talking back this time."

Cort Wesley grasped the porch rail, gazing out into the night as he squeezed it hard. "It follows us around, doesn't it, Ranger? We seem to attract this shit. No matter how much we try to avoid it, it trails us into our lives. You down in Baffin Bay, me in Cereso prison."

"Maybe that's a good thing. In this case anyway."

He turned toward her, his eyes wide and strangely vulnerable. "I'll never be able to thank you enough for what you've done."

"You don't need to say that."

"Yes, I do. If that wasn't Dylan's school, maybe you don't go in guns blazing. Same thing goes for what you did in that bar tonight. I know it came from what that piece of human excrement said to Dylan and what he dragged into both my boys' lives."

"I understand now," Caitlin said, almost too softly for him to hear.

"Huh?"

"I said I—"

"I heard what you said; I just don't read you."

"What you did when you killed that drug dealer in Juárez who killed Dylan's girlfriend running from the cops down in the hellhole they call Mexico. You did it because you knew how much it hurt Dylan and you had to do something, anything. And I imagine it was still worth it, in spite of the year you ended up losing."

"In many ways, I suppose it was. You comparing that to letting your career go down the shitter?"

"We're not gonna let anyone hurt those boys, Cort Wesley," Caitlin said, instead of answering, "not Jalbert Thoms and certainly not the terrorists who've got all of Texas in their sights."

"And how we gonna stop them, Ranger?"

"Just give me a chance."

52

SAN ANTONIO, THE PRESENT

"How the hell you figure this out?" medical examiner Frank Dean Whatley asked Caitlin the next morning, as they stood over the corpse of the man who'd taken the identity of Alejandro Pena.

"Just lucky I guess. Now tell me what you got, Doc."

She had called Whatley the night before, after learning of the dead homegrown terrorists Jones's team had uncovered in a mosque basement.

"Sorry to wake you, Doc."

"No, you're not," Whatley groused, voice dry and cracking with fatigue. "What is it you want?"

"To let you know you were right about that man identified as Alejandro Pena," she told him.

And now Alejandro Pena's body was laid out, covered by a sheet up to the neck, on a steel table in Whatley's lab. In Caitlin's experience, few actual settings lived up to the way they were portrayed on television and in movies, but the typical coroner's lab was the exception. They were all the same: cold, overly bright, and reeking of harsh chemicals that masked the scent of decaying skin and recently excised organs that would have otherwise clung to the air like glue.

"Oh, I got plenty," Whatley said, his cheeks bulging

like balloons filling with air. He held a Styrofoam cup of coffee that was shedding driblets down onto the white sheet covering Alejandro Pena's corpse. "And it all suggests your theory hit the bull's-eye dead center. Alejandro Pena's about as Hispanic as me."

"But is he . . ."

"Of Arab descent?" Whatley returned his attention to the body. "Let me show you what my examination earlier this morning—well, late last night—uncovered and you can draw your own conclusions."

He eased the sheet back, gently laying it down so the corpse was covered from the waist up. Whatley was nothing if not thorough, and his meticulous attention to those who ended up on one of his slabs knew no bounds, as if having lost so much of his own life made him respect those who had lost theirs entirely all the more. He switched off the bright exam lamp immediately overhead and picked up a rectangular UV light in its place.

"As I shine this over our friend here, I want you to tell me what you see."

Caitlin followed the light, studying the corpse's flesh. "Nothing but skin."

"Gold star, Ranger. If this man were Caucasian or Hispanic, the adipose tissue layer located directly beneath the surface epidermis would appear either pinkish or yellowed depending on the level of carotenes producing pigment. But in darker-skinned people, of Semitic or Arab descent, the epidermis is filled with melanosomes that obscure the underlying layers."

"Where the hell you learn that?"

Whatley switched off the UV light. "I did go to medical school, you know."

"Which class covered carotenes and melanosomes?"

"You finished?"

"I'm all ears, Doc."

Whatley resumed as if he were reading from a textbook. "Skin color is a quantitative trait that varies continuously on a gradient from dark to light, as it is a polygenic trait, under the influence of several genes. KITLG and ASIP have been found responsible for skin color variation between sub-Saharan Africans and non-African populations. SLC45A2, TYR, and SLC24A5 have been positively shown to account for a substantial fraction of the difference in melanin units between Europeans and Africans, while DCT, MC1R, and ATRN have been statistically indicated as possible sources for skin tone differences in East Asian populations."

"In English please."

"This man's genetic markers clearly indicate a North African DNA makeup consistent typically with men of Middle Eastern descent."

"Arab."

"Isn't that what I just said?"

Caitlin looked Whatley in the eye, hoping to see something there she wasn't catching otherwise. "Must've been some med school you attended, Doc."

"You want to hear more, Ranger, or check out my diplomas?" When she didn't respond, he continued. "Let me try to make this as simple as I can for you. Studies have shown that a lack of biochemical hypogonadism in elderly Arab men is directly associated with low bone density disease. In other words, they suffer from osteoporosis in far greater percentages than any other nationality, somewhere around thirty percent.

A bone density scan of this gentleman clearly showed early indications of the disease."

"Now I'm impressed," Caitlin said.

"You're about to be even more so," Whatley said, moving both his hands to either side of the corpse's face as if to frame it. "Studies have shown that Arabs have wider inter-inner canthal distance in their facial anthropometry than Caucasians, African-Americans, or Hispanics. And this man's face is totally consistent with those ratios."

Whatley cupped the man's head in his palms, as if to illustrate his point, then lifted them away.

"I also took a sampling of his lung tissue and found ample traces of shisha, which is basically tobacco soaked in fruit shavings. Ring any bells with you?"

"Sure. It's the kind of tobacco smoked in a hookah."

Whatley clapped his hands three times. "Why you must've gone to the same school I did, Ranger."

"No, but I did learn plenty during a six-week stretch at the FBI Training Academy at Quantico, Doc. And I seem to recall a few hours spent on that facial anthro-whatever stuff. So I've got to figure either you stole my notes or came by the info from a similar source."

Whatley wrinkled his nose, as if suddenly distressed by the room's smell. "Hey, you're the one who sent me down this path with that crazy phone call last night."

"Guess it wasn't so crazy, after all. What I don't get is how you knew exactly what to look for?"

"You questioning my skills?"

"Nope. Just how you came by these particular ones."

"I pay attention to the alerts that cross my desk, Ranger."

"Alerts . . ."

"It's called doing my job."

"Similar alerts cross your desk for any other nationality besides Arab?"

"I'm not aware of any other nationality committed to this country's ultimate destruction."

Caitlin's gaze drifted past Whatley to a picture on the lab wall directly over his right shoulder, dating back maybe twenty-five years, showing him as a much younger man standing amid a group of Rangers that included her father and grandfather.

"You're just like the two of them, you know," he charged, following her eyes. "Petulant, insistent, always so goddamn sure you're right."

"You worked with the Strongs in their investigation into the murder of those college boys on Galveston Island in '79, didn't you?"

Whatley pushed the air back into his cheeks, the balloons ready to pop again. "I did indeed, except we never solved it. I imagine that haunted Earl and Jim till the day they died."

"I was hoping you could tell me why that was, Doc, given that the Strongs were never much for walking away from something until it was finished."

"They didn't have much choice this time," Whatley told her. "The part I know about goes like this. . . ."

53

Jim and Earl Strong, along with D. W. Tepper drove up to the University of Texas at Austin, but went their separate ways as soon as they reached the campus. Earl and D.W. headed off to interview the fraternity brothers of the five boys murdered on Galveston Island, while Jim had a meeting scheduled with a member of the school's history department on another facet of the investigation.

Tepper and Earl Strong were making their way across campus when Earl stopped before what was known as The Tower, which housed twenty-eight floors of offices in the university's main administrative building. Earl took off his Stetson and swiped a sleeve across his brow, then used the hat to shield his eyes as he gazed up to the cupola at the Tower's top.

"What's wrong?" Tepper asked.

Earl held his gaze on the tower. His spine had stiffened, his expression drawn and deep-set eyes drooping. "Just thinking how I would've given anything to have been here August 1, 1966," he said, referring to the day a former marine named Charles Whitman had killed sixteen people and wounded thirty-two more with a sniper rifle from three hundred feet off the ground.

"Nothing you or anybody else could've done, Earl."

"But we'll never know that, will we?"

On the Rangers' instructions, all nineteen current members of the Pi Alpha Phi fraternity were gathered in a living room lounge lined with shelve[...] books and the smell of stale beer riding th[...] were a permanent fixture.

"They were pledges actually," said the fraternity president, Jimmy Roy. He wore tan khakis, had thick sandy hair, and claimed to be both a legacy of Pi Alpha Phi and a descendant of a man who'd died at the Alamo.

"What the hell's that mean?"

"Not quite brothers. There's stuff they gotta do before they can be initiated."

"Well," Earl followed, "I believe it's safe to say that's no longer much of a concern."

Jim Strong, meanwhile, was seated in history professor Al Dahlberg's office surrounded by more books than he'd ever seen in his life.

"Word is you are a leading authority on pirates, Professor," Jim said, "specifically Jean Lafitte."

"Well, my real specialty is the Barbary pirates along with their forebears the Cilicians from ancient Rome. I teach courses on both. Lafitte is more a hobby of mine."

"Does that hobby include any thoughts on his legendary lost treasure?"

"One, in particular, for starters, Ranger: it's not legendary at all."

"I almost just fell off my chair, Professor," Jim told him.

"You're not the first," Dahlberg said, lighting his pipe. "Tell me, have you ever heard of a slave ship called the *Mother Mary*?"

* * *

he Pi Alpha Phi fraternity house was located on the outskirts of the campus in an enclave of off-campus apartment housing reserved for upperclass students. Pi Alpha Phi was one of eighteen fraternities at the school, all scattered in the same general area. But it boasted the finest house, thanks to several alumni brothers who'd gone on to make millions, if not billions, in the oil industry. Accordingly, "Pi-Phi" brothers lived in a sprawling custom-constructed building modeled after an antebellum mansion complete with pillars and a wraparound sunporch. Besides the beer stench, it was well kept and outfitted with leather furniture discolored in patches from the sun's rays pouring through the ample lounge windows.

"What we'd like to know," D. W. Tepper picked up, "is exactly what kind of stuff brought them to Galveston Island?"

"Are you offering us immunity?" Jimmy Roy asked.

Earl moved closer to him, hands hitched up on his hips, drawing all eyes to the Springfield Model 1911 .45 holstered on the right one. "You the only one who talks here?"

"As president of the fraternity, I'm representing the house."

"And that's what you're doing in asking for immunity?"

"It is, sir."

"You figure you need it?"

"From the university maybe. See, hazing of any kind is prohibited by the Campus Life department."

"That what this is all about, hazing?"

"You haven't answered my question about immunity, Ranger."

"Okay, then let me now. Nope, I can't give you immunity, but if you help us out by answering all our questions fully and truthfully, I won't arrest the lot of you as accessories to murder."

That got the brothers of Pi Alpha Phi exchanging nervous glances, and a few, Earl was certain, squeezing their legs tight to avoid peeing their pants.

"So what do you say, Mr. President?" he continued.

"You didn't know Jim Bowie was a slave trader and Lafitte's business partner, did you, Ranger?" Professor Dahlberg asked behind a mist of sweet-smelling pipe tobacco.

"I think I've heard some on the subject, but chose not to believe it. Thought it was another legend."

"That's the thing about legends. Most, if not all, have some basis in fact."

"Some of the native folk on Galveston believe those frat boys were killed by something called a Rougarou."

"Legendary Cajun shape-shifter."

"That one of the true ones, Professor?"

"It's a myth, Ranger, not a legend and thus not my specialty."

Jim Strong leaned forward in the wood chair, feeling it creak beneath him. "So get back to your specialty and the *Mother Mary*."

"To begin with, it wasn't an ordinary slave ship."

"How's that?" Jim asked him, the cloud of pipe tobacco smoke enveloping him now as well.

"From what I've been able to piece together, the slaves on board spoke a language altogether different from the African dialects with which the traders were more familiar."

Jim found himself a bit anxious, as if something

very important were about to be revealed. "What else, Professor?"

"Somewhere along the way, the *Mother Mary* also picked up a passenger, an American traveling on some secret mission. I can't tell you what the mission was but the man said his name was Quentin Cusp. Except there's no record of such a man anywhere else either before the *Mother Mary* picked him up or after Lafitte sunk the ship. And, according to the legend, Cusp, or whoever he really was, brought something with him on board of incredible value."

Jim Strong leaned forward in his chair. "We talking treasure here?"

"We are indeed, Ranger. When Lafitte and Bowie seized that ship to steal its slaves for sale, they found themselves with an unexpected bonus. While there's no historical proof, there's plenty to suggest the partners made off with whatever riches Mr. Cusp had brought with him."

Dahlberg stopped there and resumed puffing his pipe, as if waiting for Jim to spur him along.

"I imagine we are getting to the climax here."

"We are indeed, Ranger."

Jimmy Roy nodded rapidly. "They went to the Louisiana bayou on a scavenger hunt. It's tradition."

"What, this scavenger hunt or the bayou?" Tepper asked him.

"Both, Rangers. Come back with the lost treasure of Jean Lafitte and they become brothers instantly."

"How old are you, son?" Earl wondered.

"Twenty-one, sir."

"All this crap you're spitting makes you sound like a twelve-year-old."

"It's a tradition, Ranger."

"You said that already. And I'm guessing you went to the bayou when you were a pledge, only you came back alive."

"I also never ended up on Galveston Island. Plenty of years the pledges don't actually ever get their hands on the treasure map. They've got to find this old man in the bayou who'll draw one for them for five hundred bucks. But the map never took anyone to Galveston Island before."

"And I'm guessing nobody ever did come back with the treasure, did they?"

"Of course not," said Jimmy Roy. "How could they if it doesn't exist? That's the whole point."

Earl and D. W. Tepper exchanged a glance, both of them looking as if they'd tasted something sour.

"So you sent these boys into the bayou for something you know isn't real."

"It's a bonding exercise, Ranger Strong, to bring the class together."

Earl nodded, pretending to get Jimmy Roy's point. "Well, it accomplished that much anyway, given that's the way they died."

"Ranger?" Jimmy Roy raised after swallowing hard.

"Yeah, son?"

Roy swallowed hard. "One of them was my first cousin."

Earl moved closer still to Jimmy Roy, his back taking the brunt of the sunlight streaming in through the windows and keeping it off the fraternity president's face. "Then tell me how to find this old man in the bayou."

* * *

Dahlberg repacked his pipe before resuming. "Lafitte and Bowie split whatever spoils they took from Quentin Cusp in half. Bowie used his half to buy up as much land in Texas as he could get his hands on, not long before he took a Mexican wife to further smooth the political way for his business interests. Then the revolution came and he ended up fighting not for Texas, but his own wealth, because if Santa Anna retook the colony, all the land Bowie had accumulated would be forfeit. I know all this flies in the face of Jim Bowie's reputation as a true hero of Texas, but that doesn't change the truth."

"It also doesn't change Bowie's heroism, Professor. Deeds he did still belong to him and heroism is a variable term—believe me when I tell you any Texas Ranger knows that firsthand. Now, sir, what about Lafitte's half of this treasure?"

Dahlberg grinned. "You ever study history, Ranger?"

"I guess you might say I'm a true product of it."

"Because you ask all the right questions. The truth is I don't know for sure what Lafitte did with his half of the treasure. But around seven months later, on May 7, 1821, Lafitte and the remainder of his men sailed from Galveston aboard three ships. He was also accompanied by his mulatto mistress and an infant son. Before leaving, the group burned their Campeche camp, eliminating all trace of their existence."

Jim Strong considered Dahlberg's explanation for why there was nothing left of Lafitte's former base where the five fraternity boys had been murdered. "But you don't believe it was that simple, Professor, do you?"

Dahlberg beamed. "Not at all and not for one minute, Ranger. I think Lafitte fled because someone was after him. Somebody was always after him, of course, but he'd never run before, and one theory says Quentin Cusp's employers hired professional gunmen to track the pirate down and get back what he'd stolen."

"What's the other theory?"

"That Lafitte went to South America in search of more of the treasure he'd pilfered from Cusp. He pirated the waters around Cuba en route to Honduras on a forty ton armed schooner named the *General Santander*. On the night of February 4, 1823, Lafitte attempted to take what appeared to be two Spanish merchant vessels. It was cloudy and visibility was low that night. Maybe that's why he didn't realize the Spanish ships were actually heavily armed warships. Their guns pummeled the *General Santander*. Lafitte was wounded in the battle and died just after dawn on February 5, buried at sea that same day."

"So he never found the source of Quentin Cusp's treasure."

"No, Ranger," Dahlberg said, sighing almost sadly, "he never did. End of story."

Jim Strong grinned. "I doubt it, Professor."

Dahlberg nodded, grinning back. "Lafitte allowed the crew of the *Mother Mary* to abandon ship before he sank her. Her crew members told their story to anyone who'd listen and the story kept getting passed along, some of it in writing in the form of journals, including entries from the captain of the ship himself leaving out mention of where they'd sailed from to reach Texas. As for Quentin Cusp, there's no record of him anywhere after that night. Like he flat out vanished. I don't know if he was a spy or some sort of pirate in his own right. But I do know that whatever he brought with him on board the *Mother Mary* changed a lot of lives forever. And I've believed for a long time that those Spanish warships were sent after Lafitte by Cusp's employers with orders to kill the pirate at all costs."

Jim Strong shrugged. "Professor, I'm just trying to figure out how a man who never existed and a lost treasure nobody's ever seen connects with the murder of five fraternity boys on Galveston Island."

"They're not the first to die because of that treasure, Ranger," Dahlberg said with a strange sense of assurance, his gaze narrowing in intensity. "And they won't be the last."

54

SAN ANTONIO, THE PRESENT

"That's how they told it when they got back from Louisiana," medical examiner Frank Dean Whatley finished.

His words shocked Caitlin back to the present. For a time she'd felt like a little girl again seated on her grandfather's lap as he spun one of his many yarns about the exploits that had made him one of the most famous Texas Rangers ever.

"And was it?" Caitlin asked. "Was the treasure real?"

"They never found out for sure," Whatley told her. "You wanna tell me what all this has to do with a car accident victim named Pena who turns out to be Arab?"

"Nothing, Doc. But it may be connected to something else I'm following up," she said, starting for the door and realizing how stiff and chilled she'd gotten from not moving an inch through the whole of Whatley's tale.

"Then I guess I can expect some more bodies on my slab soon," he said under his breath.

Caitlin stopped as she reached for the door. "What was that, Doc?"

"Nothing, Ranger."

"Thought so." She started to open the door, then swung back toward him. "Wait a sec, you said when my dad and granddad got back from *Louisiana*."

"That's right. Whole other part of the tale I've never heard in its entirety. All I seem to recall is your father getting himself in a tizzy over some trinket they found at the murder scene."

"Like a cross, crucifix, something like that?"

"I believe so. You'll have to ask Captain Tepper about the rest."

"Oh, I will," Caitlin assured him. "But right now there's someone else I need to see."

PART SIX

During the Great Depression, the Ranger force was reduced to just forty-five men. Adding fuel to the fire, the Rangers openly supported Governor Ross Sterling against Miriam A. "Ma" Ferguson in the Democratic primary in the fall of 1932. As a result, when Ferguson took office in January 1933, she fired every Ranger for his partisanship, salaries were slashed, and the budget further reduced the force to thirty-two men. Without the protection of the Rangers, Texas soon became a haven for outlaws such as Raymond Hamilton, George "Machine Gun" Kelly, and Clyde Barrow and Bonnie Parker.

—*Legends of America:*
Texas Legends: The Texas Rangers—Order Out of Chaos

55

Cort Wesley hadn't wanted to leave Caitlin or his sons the night before. The thought of a genuine psychopath like Jalbert Thoms standing on his property, leering at his boys with a soul that defined the very pit of hell, turned his blood cold while the thought of Thoms returning flushed heat through his entire system. He was sweating and chilled at the same time, a rage welling up inside him like none he'd ever felt before. But the rage came coupled with frustration, since Cort Wesley knew he couldn't focus his efforts on finding Thoms right now.

"I don't wanna tell you what I'm going to do to this man once I get my hands on him," he'd told Caitlin.

"I think you should leave, Cort Wesley," she said, stiffening.

"Why?"

"Because if you don't leave now, I'm not gonna let you leave at all."

Cort Wesley finally left around three A.M. when an approaching storm turned the air breezy and cold, the smell of ozone seeming to spill out of the shifting tree branches. But he parked the vehicle he'd appropriated from Jones down the street and around the corner, still in view of the house he had bought in the middle of suburbia so the mother of his kids could raise them safely.

And look at how things turned out.

Cort Wesley half expected Jalbert Thoms to return and half wanted him to. In moments like this, that part of him which had a thirst for violence he could neither explain nor fully control inevitably got the better of him and he couldn't get out of his head the image of the pederast Thoms leering at Dylan in a way that made his flesh crawl.

He lingered until dawn, greeting the sunrise with the false relief that somehow the light would make everything safe. In this case it brought with it the crackle of thunder and first drum of raindrops on his windshield. To Cort Wesley it sounded like gunfire, the storm's power shrinking the world to the confines of the car and nothing more. He felt claustrophobic, memories of his cramped cell in Cereso prison stoked enough for his mind to conjure up the rancid smells to the point where he cracked the window open. The storm rushed in, drenching him through the mere slit between frame and window like a tepid shower. Enough to cleanse the car of the stench, imagined or otherwise, and leaving Cort Wesley to compare the storm's pounding rattle to the staccato burst of machine-gun fire during his stretch in Iraq. He tried telling himself this was just another battle, but Caitlin Strong and his boys hadn't been part of his life back then, and he squeezed the now sodden steering wheel hard enough to make his knuckles crack.

When the storm abated, Cort Wesley drove back to the motel where Jones had set him up, thinking of Jalbert Thoms the whole way. He almost took out his cell phone and called Caitlin to tell her that the man brought all his inadequacies front and center, all the years he'd been absent from Dylan's life magnified by Thoms's sudden immersion of himself into it.

As Cort Wesley lay atop the motel room bedcovers, he tried to focus on where the makeshift team Jones had assembled would go from here. What exactly the homegrown terrorists murdered in a mosque base-ment had been up to on behalf of Anwar al-Awlaki. Even though their fingertips had been sliced off, Cort Wesley expected Jones would have IDs and full back-grounds on the victims within a day, maybe telling them more but almost certainly not enough. He tried to sleep, but quickly gave up. Instead he sat with arms cupped behind his head and eyes wide open to the light struggling to brighten amid a typical late-spring thunderstorm that pounded the roof and windows with a fury that would be gone as quickly as it had come.

He wanted Caitlin Strong to be lying here next to him. He wanted to be home in Shavano Park ready to take a Gatling gun to the likes of Jalbert Thoms. He wanted the ghost of Leroy Epps to show up to provide the counsel he'd come to rely on.

Cort Wesley wanted a lot of things, but mostly he wanted to yank Jalbert Thoms's sternum up his throat. Lying here this way was akin to letting the leering psy-chopath turn into a festering, sucking wound in his consciousness that finally led him to place a call to the cell phone of a young guard at The Walls prison in Huntsville.

"Yeah?" a groggy voice answered.

"Guess who, Frankie?"

"Oh, shit."

"Glad you remember my voice," Cort Wesley said.

Frankie came to Huntsville straight from a stretch

in Iraq and Afghanistan. Not much more than a kid who'd seen the worst of things and had finally let it get to him. He received an honorable discharge that could have helped secure him a better job than prison guard in general and The Walls in particular. The cons called him Frankie Cakes because of his fondness for sweets, especially store-bought cupcakes, leaving him with jowls that looked like a birth defect atop his otherwise chiseled frame. Cort Wesley hadn't talked to him in a long time, but the kind of relationships formed in prison aren't soon forgotten. That was especially true here since a Latino gang inside The Walls had threatened to kill even the most distant of Frankie's relatives if he didn't agree to move dope for them inside. Cort Wesley intervened on his behalf as a fellow war vet and the problem went away.

"What's this about, Masters? I'm due at work in twenty."

"Tell me what you know about Jalbert Thoms."

Silence save for Frankie's suddenly rapid breathing filled the dead air.

"You don't want to get mixed up with him in any way, shape, or form."

"Too late, Frankie."

"How so?"

"He paid a visit to my oldest son. Seventeen, looks like a rock star. How much more of this picture do I have to draw for you?"

"Thoms has been out just over a year now and I was never more glad to see a con go."

"Keep talking."

"Child molesters are supposed to be the lowest form of life in the prison food chain, Cort Wesley, but this man turned the tables from his first day in. A black

man who was all-Conference playing defensive line-
man looked at him crossways and Thoms shoved a
broom stick so far up his ass they had to snake out
most of his intestines. You know we get the toughest
of any in here, but this man scared me more than any
of them ever did. Took special pleasure in breaking in
the newest and youngest cons whether they be black,
Latino, white, or polka-dotted. Call him an equal opportunity rapist."

Cort Wesley's skin felt like it was trying to turn inside out.

"He fancied himself a gunslinger, a real cowboy. He
was in the Corps for a while and tried his hand at Recon until his fingers got the better of him on some
twenty-year-old fresh meat and they dishonorabled
him out. The man's a human stain, Cort Wesley, and if
he's got eyes for your boy, my advice is to cancel his
ticket before he comes within a hundred feet of the
kid again."

"Thanks, Frankie," Cort Wesley said, no longer
hearing the hammering clatter of the rain hitting the
roof and windows.

"Something else. Famous young actor whose name
I won't mention paid us a visit to research a role. Came
with an honor guard of security accompanying him so
he could soak in as much of the place as possible. His
guard escorts left him and his private security entourage in a holding area to respond to a potential riot in
the yard and returned to find his protectors beaten to
hell and the actor stuffed in a broom closet crying like
a baby." Frankie Cakes took some deep breaths as if
to settle himself from the memory. "We found Jalbert
Thoms taking a nap in his bunk, cell door still open as
if he wanted us to know he'd done it. Goddamn, Cort

Wesley, you don't want this thing anywhere near your life."

Cort Wesley realized he'd been squeezing the cell phone Jones had given him so hard he'd actually bent the casing. "My intentions exactly."

"Wait, I'm not finished. You ever hear of Rubicon X-Ultra?"

"Mercenary outfit, as I recall."

"Plenty more than that, Cort Wesley. They're assassins for hire that fill their ranks with psychos like Thoms along with army types Sectioned Eight or dishonorabled out. Word is Thoms hooked up with them well before he began his stay in our hallowed halls. Makes me wonder if these X-Ultra boys had his back. See, the deputy warden in The Walls tried to nail Thoms for what he did to that movie actor and had his house burned down with his wife inside. But she'd been raped and stabbed to death first."

"Thanks, Frankie," he said, ending the call.

So much heat had flushed through Cort Wesley that sweat stuck his shirt to his chest and he felt drops of it rolling down his face. He didn't remember saying good-bye or laying the phone down on the room's night table. Outside the slowing rain had taken on the din of Fourth of July firecrackers, the brightening sky making it look like blood drops smacking the glass.

Cort Wesley found himself lifting his cell phone back up and pressing out Dylan's number, staring at the digits without pressing Call.

56

"Say that again?" Tepper urged, coming out of his chair behind his desk so fast he spilled over the contents of his Alamo ashtray on the blotter.

"Which part?" Caitlin asked him.

"Oh, I don't know, let's start with the Rangers taking on homegrown terrorists bent on blowing up the state."

"The homegrown terrorists, least the ones we know of, are dead. It's Anwar al-Awlaki himself we're facing now."

"Jesus H. Christ, Hurricane, you have genuinely reached category ten proportions on a scale of five this time."

"Makes you glad to have me back, doesn't it?"

Tepper shook his head, gnashing his teeth together as he felt through his pockets for his Marlboros without success until he checked the jacket he'd draped over his chair. His first deep drag seemed to calm him enough to flush the red from the lines on his face that looked like dry riverbeds carved out of the land.

"Jones wants to meet with you," Caitlin resumed.

"And I always thought he was a figment of your imagination."

"Yours too now, D.W."

Tepper looked at her through the cloud of smoke thickening between them. "And you figure what you learned from Doc Whatley pretty much lays the missing pieces out nice and neat."

"Some of them. Jones's missing terrorists disappeared

all right, into the identities of dead men like Alejandro Pena." Caitlin finally sat down. "Can I ask you a question?"

"Since when did you need permission?"

"Since my provisional reinstatement. This alert Whatley was talking about concerning men 'appearing' to be of Arab descent—did it cross your desk too?"

"Ranger, it crossed the desk of every law enforcement commander in the country from a police chief in Podunk to the public safety commissioner in New York City."

"You agree with its intent?"

Tepper shrugged. "Never gave it much thought, to tell you the truth."

"So it never occurred to you or Whatley, or the chief of police in Podunk or public safety commissioner in New York City, that we may be turning American-Arabs and ordinary peaceful Muslims into terrorists by treating them that way?"

Tepper gazed theatrically up toward the ceiling.

"What are you looking at, D.W.?"

"The high horse you rode in here on, Ranger. See, there was this thing called nine/eleven . . ."

"And from my high horse, I can see that American-Arabs and the American Muslim community in general had no more to do with that than you or me."

"Spare me, Hurricane. Just this once, could you please blow in a different direction?"

"How about toward Teo Braga?"

Tepper blew his next waft of smoke through his nose. "You know him sending that fruitcake was strictly to get a rise out of you, and I'd say you played right into his hands."

"Except I walked out alive, in case you're forgetting."

"Good thing too, since it allowed me to drink my morning coffee over the news someone's planning to start Armageddon here in Texas, and there's a dozen bodies in a Houston morgue with John Doe toe tags until this gets sorted out. Am I leaving anything out?"

"Only that Jones believes a terrorist the world thought dead is here pulling the strings."

"Oh yeah, how could I forget that?" Tepper pressed his cigarette out on his desk blotter, missing his cracked Alamo ashtray altogether.

"Whatley tell you about the rest of our conversation?"

"For God's sake, Hurricane, haven't I heard enough?"

Caitlin pushed her chair closer to his desk. "He told me about the trip you made with Earl and Jim to Austin to interview the fraternity brothers of those murdered pledges. Told me about my dad's interview with the expert on Jean Lafitte on his legendary lost treasure."

"There a point to you raising this?"

"Maybe it's not so legendary."

"You don't have enough on your plate in the present to go mining the past for more?"

"The *Mother Mary*'s remains were under that oil rig too, D.W. Just answer me this one question: what got my dad so hot and bothered about that trinket that looked like a crucifix you found in one of the dead boy's hands?"

"I have no idea what you're talking about."

"Don't lie to me."

"Ranger, you are trying my—"

"Whatley said the three of you headed to Louisiana from Austin. What'd you find there? What is it you're not telling me?"

Tepper's phone buzzed before he could respond, his eyes wide with surprise when he laid the receiver back on its cradle. "Well, it seems as if your friend Teo Braga just saved you a trip, Ranger. He's downstairs now."

57

SAN ANTONIO, THE PRESENT

"Who were they?" Sam Harrabi asked Anwar al-Awlaki, as their River Walk tour boat cruised the channel with shops and restaurants on either side. "Special Forces? A CIA assassin team?"

"The imam believes most of them were Mexicans."

"Mexicans?"

"That's what he said. He described one of them as a giant with hands the size of trash can lids. He said he may never sleep again with that man haunting his dreams."

"They weren't wearing masks?"

"Only the two Americans."

"This makes no sense."

Al-Awlaki actually found some comfort in that, since everything suggested the United States government hadn't been behind the raid, at least not the traditional authorities.

"Perhaps we should consider alternatives?" Harrabi suggested.

"Like what?"

"The timing, *sayyid,* only the timing."

Al-Awlaki kept silent, expressionless as he seemed to study the faces of the tourists strolling the River Walk. He looked placid, though his eyes were narrowed more from harshness than the glare of the sun.

"Like the timing of what happened to you, to your family, in Tennessee?" he asked suddenly. "What was the name of the town again?"

Harrabi hesitated. "Wolfsboro."

"And you have seen what happened there as punishment for your failings, your betrayal, for too long. You were serving Allah's purpose then, just as you are now. A means to an end. The path He chooses for us is often not straight. But in the end it takes us where we must be. Tell me about your path, my brother."

"I turned away from the one true God. I turned away from my people."

"But not for money, not riches."

Harrabi felt his insides quiver and spasm. "I fell in love."

"With an American."

"We raised a family," Harrabi nodded. "I was happy."

"Until those you trusted, those with whom you laid your faith, turned against you."

"After nine/eleven. I became their enemy, a man without friends. Looked down upon, shunned."

"So you turned back toward your own people who forgave your transgressons and forgave you."

"It brought me to Tennessee and a growing Muslim community in Wolfsboro where I only wanted to do good. Redeem myself for my indiscretions."

"And what happened as a result?"

Harrabi looked down. "You already know the answer to that."

"I want to hear you say it. I want to hear you confess out loud what happened."

"They murdered my sons," Harrabi said, swallowing hard.

"And what of your wife, the woman who accompanied you to Tennessee? How was she rewarded for her love and loyalty?"

"Please, *sayyid*."

"Say it."

"My wife witnessed the attack. She never recovered," Harrabi muttered, the words feeling like ground glass in his mouth.

"But she spoke to you, did she not? Gave you a message, a mission of your own."

In spite of himself, Harrabi nodded. "She told me to get back at those who murdered our children. To avenge them for her."

Al-Awlaki's gaze fixed on him tighter, flashing what looked like compassion. "Where is your wife now?"

"A facility in San Antonio. I had her moved here so we could be close."

"Then you should visit her, my brother," al-Awlaki said, as the tour boat snailed toward the dock. "I will accompany you. Now."

Harrabi stood at his wife Layla's bedside, staring down at her emaciated form, her once luxurious hair gone brittle, her beautiful eyes closed perhaps forever to reflect on the final terrible sight they recorded. But for Harrabi the feeding tube was the worst, because it signaled the loss of all hope. Of course the doctors told him his beautiful Layla might yet come back to him, but he knew she was gone for good.

"Look what they have done to you," al-Awlaki said, his warm grasp suddenly closing on the top of Harrabi's shoulder. But then Harrabi felt the cleric stiffen. "We have sacrificed so much. I had to die so I could live, my brother. The Americans had to think me dead so I could be free to bring them to their knees. There is no retreating from that. I have only my deeds, my work, to sustain me. But I feel a great freedom too, because what else can they take from me I have not already taken from myself? You can't kill a man who's already dead."

The cleric's gaze returned to Layla Harrabi's bedside. "A part of you is dead too, my brother. Look at the happiness they have stolen. Look at it and tell me our mission can be put off in any way." Al-Awlaki settled himself with a deep breath. "Tell me about that night that freed you as my death freed me. Tell me what happened."

"It hurts too much, *sayyid*."

"Share it with me so I can know your pain and help to take it away."

"Our numbers were already swelling in Wolfsboro by the time I arrived, so a bigger mosque was needed. Money was raised, land purchased, the proper permits acquired. I helped with the design myself, volunteered to do all the electrical schematic and engineering work."

"Your specialty," al-Awlaki nodded, "the very skills that drew us to you. Fate again."

"I'm thankful for that much."

"You were a good neighbor, a good American. You even served in the armed services where your expertise was demolitions. Tell me, my brother, how did it feel killing your own in the Gulf War?"

"It hurts now, *sayyid*. I've seen how wrong I was."

His eyes locked on the inert form that had once been his beautiful Layla. "I paid a terrible price for that when the people in Wolfsboro rose up against us," Harrabi said through the thick clog that had formed in his throat. He tried to swallow, but his mouth was too dry to manage the effort. "After their efforts failed in the proper chambers and courts, they sabotaged the heavy equipment at the work site. And when that failed to deter us, they blew up a dam and flooded our land."

"And what did you do?"

"We started over, believing this to be a test of our faith and looking forward to the rewards our new holy place would yield."

Al-Awlaki's hand tightened on Harrabi's shoulder. "But that never happened, did it?"

"No."

"Why, why my brother?"

Harrabi tried to swallow again but failed, his eyes moistening. "I was standing guard duty one night with my sons and my Layla."

"How old were your sons?"

"Fourteen and sixteen, *sayyid*."

Al-Awlaki reached out and touched the depression on Harrabi's skull. "That's where you got this, when trespassers assaulted you with a baseball bat."

"My boys both played baseball. They were stars."

"And when you regained consciousness, what did you find?"

Harrabi opened his mouth to speak, but no words emerged right away and when they finally did, it seemed to be in someone else's voice. "My sons were both lying there on the ground. Beaten to death. My beautiful Layla was cradling the head of one in her lap. His face was . . . gone."

"Close your eyes."

"*Sayyid?*"

Al-Awlaki eased a hand that smelled of lavender and lilacs over Harrabi's face and eased his eyes closed for him. "Picture your wife as she was before that awful night. Can you see her?"

Harrabi's throat was too clogged to respond, so he simply nodded.

"Now open your eyes."

Harrabi did, focusing again on the feeding tube that was keeping his once beautiful Layla alive.

"Look upon your wife now, symbol of not just your broken dreams but of the broken dreams of our people. We have the ability to break this nation's dreams as they broke yours. When struck by tragedy as you have been, it is in our nature to grieve and bemoan our fate. But these times demand we forge a new fate, that we make something of the tragedies that will haunt us forever. You and all the others who had their dreams broken were selected for this mission for a reason— not by me, but Allah Himself. I am merely His vessel, fulfilling the holy mission I've been charged with. There can be no alteration to our plans. Our mission has already been blessed. It will not fail. And when it succeeds, we will have the redemption we seek, and all we have sacrificed will be justified. You will have atoned for all your mistakes and misjudgments, and nothing can be allowed to get in the way of this opportunity Allah has provided." He waited for Harrabi to look at him before continuing. "Is the meeting with the American set?"

"Yes, *sayyid,* for this afternoon. How many others will be accompanying us?"

"None, my brother."

Harrabi couldn't hide his surprise.

"The American believes us to be nothing more than businessmen," al-Awlaki explained. "So that is what we must be."

58

SAN ANTONIO, THE PRESENT

They met in the conference room that was currently overrun with boxes of case files waiting to be transported to storage: Caitlin, D. W. Tepper, Teofilo Braga, and three of his lawyers who said nothing but glared a lot.

"You and the Rangers have my sincerest apologies, along with those of Braga Waste Management," Braga said to Caitlin and Tepper. "And I want you to know, it's crucial to understand, that I had no knowledge of Mr. Thoms's actions or intentions."

"But he was working for you, right?" Caitlin asked. "You did ask him to deliver that document to me."

Braga looked like a man baffled by the inability of others to see him properly. "Yes, I did, as part of BWM's Second Chance program through which parolees and ex-convicts are provided with an opportunity to reintegrate themselves into society."

"Well, sir," began Tepper, "I believe it's safe to say that Mr. Thoms squandered his. Ambushes and gunfights in a bar are no way to start a path to redemption."

"You have any idea how many men work for me?"

"Nope," Tepper responded. "How many of them are pedophiles?"

"I've never even met Jalbert Thoms. Mistakes happen. I believe we're all fortunate here no bystanders were hurt."

"What about the boy Thoms molested with his eyes?"

"I wasn't even aware of his employment with my company until your call alerted me to the fact. I've already turned over all our records and alerted the police and corrections departments that he is no longer in my employ."

Braga looked utterly unruffled to Caitlin, his skin powder dry and gaze resolute and unwavering. She knew he was lying, could feel it in her bones, but nothing in the man's tone or mannerisms gave him away. She had known plenty like him in her time, hardened criminals mostly. Men who constructed elaborate facades built on rationales meant to justify actions as reprehensible as they were immoral. In Caitlin's experience, such men grew calmer the deeper they dipped into cesspools of depravity, exceedingly comfortable in their own skin that might as well have been reptilian scales.

"I don't know what else I can do under the circumstances," Braga finished, the calmest she had seen him yet.

Caitlin eased her chair closer to the table, drawing flinches from the annoying screeches it made scratching across the floor. "How about this, Mr. Braga, how about you answer a few questions?" She could feel Captain Tepper tense across from her, as she finished.

"If I can, Ranger."

"I think you gave Jalbert Thoms this assignment yourself knowing exactly how things would turn out."

"That's not a question, Ranger."

"I think Thoms drove out to Shavano Park knowing full well I wasn't there just to scare the wits out of a couple of teenage boys."

"He may well have done that, but not on my orders."

"Then that's where we differ. I provoked you in our interview and this was your response. I understand you're not a man who likes getting pushed around, Mr. Braga. I get the fact that you've had to overcome a lot of obstacles and enemies to get where you are. But that doesn't give you license to intimidate or threaten others, sir. And bringing children, threatening them no less, into the mix crosses a line Rangers have been drawing since my great-great-grandfather rode in the days before the Civil War."

"Ranger—" Tepper started, but Braga cut him off.

"Are you finished?"

"You tell me, Mr. Braga."

Braga stared at Caitlin for a long moment, his eyes not budging or blinking. He snatched a pencil from a holder before him and began tapping it on the table. "You know the toughest job I ever had, Ranger? Breaking up sludge in one of the company's wastewater treatment facilities back in the days when I was still working for Alvin Jackson. You familiar with the process?"

"No, sir, I'm not."

"Well, what you basically do is separate the water out from sewage. The sludge is what you're left with, this awful stench-riddled gunk that permeates your skin and soaks through your pores. I went down into that tank for hours at a time, lugging a heavy high-pressured hose over my shoulder to blast away at the sludge collected under three feet of black water. Never seemed to get to the bottom since you can't see the bottom, and the whole time this smell like ammonia filled me up. It made me want to gag a thousand times, but I didn't give in no matter how light-headed or sick I got. Just kept blasting away with that hose, feeling the muck churning at my feet."

"I'm sure it looked good on your résumé, sir."

"You know what didn't? For every day you spend shoveling sludge, it takes a week to get the smell off you and a month to get rid of the queasy feeling in your stomach. Alvin Jackson didn't have to send me down into that sludge tank; he did it to see if I'd quit. And when I didn't until we'd liquefied every ounce of that black shit, he promoted me to foreman and entrusted me with the kind of responsibility I'd only dreamed of previously."

Caitlin looked at Braga today, dressed casually but fashionably in linen slacks and a crisply ironed shirt, and tried to picture him in overalls hefting that hose. "Mr. Jackson sounds like he made for a pretty decent mentor, sir."

Braga passed the pencil from one hand to the other. "He was that and much more, Ranger."

"Explains why you speak of him so highly."

"I owe him a debt I'll never be able to repay and he's never far from my thoughts. Without him taking me under his wing, I might be nothing now."

"Is that all?"

Braga regarded Caitlin suspiciously. "I'm not sure I know what you mean by that."

"You mentioned Mr. Jackson was from Louisiana, Cajun country I believe, in our first interview."

"That's right. Alvin had lost his parents by the time I met him, but his grandfather was still living."

"A witch, right? The gris-gris, you called it."

"More like voodoo and other Cajun magic, but I suppose witch is close enough," Braga said, seeming to relax slightly.

"Did you know Mr. Jackson did a stretch in Louisiana's Angola prison, Mr. Braga?"

The pencil stilled in his hand. He looked honestly surprised. "I did not, no."

"He beat and robbed a man who fired him, he believed unjustly. He did three years of a five-year stretch and moved to Texas when his probation was done."

"And why is this relevant to the matter before us today, Ranger?"

Caitlin made sure Braga could see her looking at him. The room's lighting was dull, as if someone had neglected to flip all the switches on, and the resulting shadows made it look like someone had poured Braga's eyes into his face. They kept shifting about, liquid pools of darkness.

"Well, sir, there's also the matter of the three union organizers who disappeared in these parts back in the early seventies. They were last seen at a sewage treatment facility managed by Alvin Jackson very similar to the one you're describing."

Teo Braga snapped the pencil he'd been holding into two, squeezing the twin halves in both his hands.

"Your mentor was a psychopath who believed violence was a legitimate way to respond to people who wronged, challenged, or opposed him. I thought that might sound familiar. Did you learn it from Mr. Jackson too?"

"That's enough," one of Braga's lawyers said, lurching to his feet. "We're done here."

But Braga kept his eyes locked with Caitlin's as he dropped the splintered pencil atop the table. "I don't know what else I can say to convince you I played no part in Mr. Thoms's actions of last night. And unless you can prove otherwise we're finished here."

The room went silent except for the stubborn buzzing of an overhead bulb about to fail. Braga held Caitlin's stare as if he were afraid what might happen if he broke it, something else she'd surprise him with once he looked away.

"We're not finished yet, Mr. Braga, not hardly. I shot and killed two men last night, two men who were trying to do the same to me."

Without realizing it, Caitlin had slid forward so she was almost nose-to-nose with Teo Braga, his lawyers too scared to intervene and D. W. Tepper too slow. One of the lawyers jostled the conference table while back-pedaling for the door and both halves of the pencil Braga had snapped clattered to the scuffed-up linoleum floor.

"I believe you sent your attack dog after me and the rest tumbled from there. I haven't seen the report yet, but my guess is the two men I capped were shooters Thoms met inside Huntsville. And if you had any knowledge of their continuing association, that makes you guilty of harboring a criminal."

Captain Tepper finally wedged himself between them and started to ease Caitlin away. "Let's go, Ranger."

"And if Jalbert Thoms comes anywhere near the Torres boys again," Caitlin called out to Braga as she went. "I'm gonna shoot both of you in the balls."

59

SAN ANTONIO, THE PRESENT

Tepper slammed his office door behind them and took his phone off the hook.

"What's that about?" Caitlin asked him.

Tepper's leathery face had gone red, his ears seeming to have straightened in anger like a Doberman's. "I figure the governor, maybe someone from the senate, or the president himself is gonna be calling any minute, and I want an excuse not to talk to them."

"Blame me."

"Nope, it's my fault for believing you could be part of this century for a change. What the hell was I thinking. . . ."

Caitlin started to sit down, then stood back up. "I didn't say anything they didn't know already and were prepared for."

Tepper felt about his cluttered desktop for his Alamo ashtray. "And what does that prove exactly?"

"You don't really think Thoms was the only violent offender Braga put to work as part of his Head Start program, do you?"

"Second Chance," Tepper corrected.

"Yeah, whatever. He's building an army in the tradition of his mentor Alvin Jackson."

"I've read Jackson's file too, Caitlin. He was nothing more than a grunt for the corporate boys Braga eventually bought out."

"That was gonna be my next question downstairs. How exactly he came by the money. The article in *Texas Monthly* was a little vague on that issue, along with everything else in Braga's history from a financial standpoint."

"Seems to satisfy the country club folk Braga keeps company with."

"Because they don't have reason to think otherwise. I do." Something changed in Caitlin's expression. "I never saw Dylan so scared before as when he described the way Thoms looked at him."

"Really taking this mothering thing seriously, aren't you, Hurricane?"

Caitlin squeezed her shoulders together. "Harder than a gunfight."

Tepper lit up a Marlboro despite not finding his ashtray. "I'll bet you threw it out," he said, continuing to look, "didn't you?"

Caitlin was about to respond when a knock fell on the suddenly open door.

"Hope I'm not interrupting," said Jones.

60

SAN ANTONIO, THE PRESENT

"I swear I must've died last night and went to hell," Tepper said, after introductions were exchanged.

"I'd like to hear about that meeting you had this morning with the medical examiner," Jones said, focusing only on Caitlin.

"You're out of your element, Jones. Surprised they let you beyond the Washington city limits without an ankle bracelet."

"The call I got from your boyfriend said

with everything else in Braga's history from a financial standpoint."

"Seems to satisfy the country club folk Braga keeps company with."

"Because they don't have reason to think otherwise. I do." Something changed in Caitlin's expression. "I never saw Dylan so scared before as when he described the way Thoms looked at him."

"Really taking this mothering thing seriously, aren't you, Hurricane?"

Caitlin squeezed her shoulders together. "Harder than a gunfight."

Tepper lit up a Marlboro despite not finding his ashtray. "I'll bet you threw it out," he said, continuing to look, "didn't you?"

Caitlin was about to respond when a knock fell on the suddenly open door.

"Hope I'm not interrupting," said Jones.

60

SAN ANTONIO, THE PRESENT

"I swear I must've died last night and went to hell," Tepper said, after introductions were exchanged.

"I'd like to hear about that meeting you had this morning with the medical examiner," Jones said, focusing only on Caitlin.

"You're out of your element, Jones. Surprised they let you beyond the Washington city limits without an ankle bracelet."

"The call I got from your boyfriend said you'd

found one of my terrorists who still has his fingerprints."

"Who exactly you work for again, Mr. Jones?" D. W.
Tepper asked him.

"Same man you do."

"The governor of Texas or commander of the Rangers?"

"Try the president of the United States. When all's
said and done, that's who we all work for."

Tepper looked toward Caitlin. "He always this evasive?"

"Today's actually one of his more plain speaking
days."

"I assume Ranger Strong has brought you up to
speed," Jones said, drawing closer to Tepper's desk.

"Found it!" he said, snatching his Alamo ashtray
from between two file folders just in time to flick a long
ash from his Marlboro. "Ranger Strong has indeed
brought me up to speed on this issue of a potential terrorist strike and the Rangers are at your disposal . . .
providing you tell me exactly whose disposal that is."

"Homeland Security."

"I'm afraid I need something more specific than
that."

"That's as specific as it gets in my business, Captain."

"I was talking about who your superior might be,
who can authorize what you're asking for on a piece
of government letterhead."

"Got a pen handy?"

"I must not be speaking plainly enough myself
here."

"You think I'm any different from your Ranger
over here?"

"No, and that's what scares the heck out of me."

The three of them went silent, running their eyes from one to another as if to gauge the intentions of each.

"Why don't you just get to the point, Mr. Smith?" Tepper asked him.

"It's Jones, Captain."

"And this be the same Jones, Smith, or whoever who helped out Hurricane here in Bahrain way back when. The same Jones who let her down at that gunfight in Juárez, so Colonel Paz had to bail her out. After that I hear you were generous enough to provide satellite recon of the Patriot Sun facility just to make sure she and Masters would go in with guns blazing. Oh, and you funded Colonel Paz's private army down in Mexico. So, tell me, have I left anything out?"

Jones's breathing had picked up and Caitlin could see red flushing into his face. But he didn't respond.

"Why that mosque, Jones?" Caitlin asked him. "How'd you know to have an eyeball on it?"

"Anwar al-Awlaki assembled these men specifically for this operation. His own personal A-team. Their presence in that mosque tripped our security program."

"Tripped?" Caitlin said, her torso canting forward.

"As in facial recognition technology, advanced software keyed into supercomputers capable of a billion computations a second."

"I think I get it now," Caitlin said nodding.

"Get what?" Jones asked her.

But instead of answering him, she took out her SIG-Sauer and laid it atop Tepper's desk not far from the Alamo ashtray in which his cigarette was smoldering. "If I don't hand this over, I might shoot this son of a bitch, Captain." She swung back toward Jones. "You told Cort Wesley you had a plant inside the cell who got himself killed."

"That's what I told him, yes."

"But it was a lie, wasn't it? You didn't have anybody inside anything. You made this cell because of their presence inside that mosque and nothing else. Because something somewhere set off a flag. Maybe the times they showed up, or the frequency. Maybe the way they cut their hair or forgot to zip their pants up."

"You got a problem with that, either of you?"

"How many other mosques you got eyeballs on, Jones?" Caitlin challenged.

"You don't have the security clearance to ask that question or hear the answer."

"I'm going to take that to mean quite a few."

Jones hesitated, uncharacteristically tentative all of a sudden. Caitlin realized the reddening of his face stood out all the more because his skin was dry and pale. His neck looked smaller and midsection a bit paunchier than what she remembered, evidence of too many hours inside and away from the gym.

"We're all friends here, Mr. Jones," Tepper said diplomatically. "If we're gonna sign on to this project of yours without that signature I was referring to, we need the whole picture."

Jones nodded as if someone was moving his head for him. "All."

"*All?*"

"Every mosque in the country, Captain. We got eyeballs on them all."

61

"You don't see that as a violation of civil rights?" Caitlin asked him, still not believing what Jones had admitted.

"I see it as a way to keep this country safe," he said stridently. "You want to find Muslim men who've potentially been radicalized, you don't look in synagogues or churches, you look in mosques."

"I want to make sure I got this right," Tepper said, coming out of his chair. "You got surveillance on every mosque in the entire U.S. of A.?"

"Along with Islamic Centers and whatever else they're being called these days. And if we didn't, we'd never have caught wind of this Texas plot."

"Where's the suspected perpetrators getting executed fit into that scenario?"

"I already explained that, Captain. Whatever al-Awlaki assembled them to do was done. He didn't need them anymore."

"Could be something else," Caitlin suggested.

"What's that?"

"Accidental death of that man in our morgue might've spooked your king terrorist. He wipes out those men you found in the basement of that mosque to keep anybody from drawing possible connections."

"I think we're both right, to varying degrees."

"The difference being I'm not a racist asshole like you."

Jones frowned at her. "Is that a fact, Ranger? Because history may dispute it. The early Texas Rangers were the ultimate profilers and the massacres of innocent Mexicans through the years are common knowledge. Almost got the Rangers disbanded for good around World War One, I'm told."

Tepper pressed out his cigarette in disgusted fashion, spraying ash across the contents of his desk blotter. "We learned from our mistakes, Mr. Jones, and you'd be wise to do the same."

"No can do, Captain. I have my orders. The whole damn thing is my operation at Homeland. They turned me into a desk jockey and gave me a whole host of new weapons to fight my war. You think I can't handle a shooting war anymore? Truth is I'm in one every day, only I'm firing off pictures, not bullets."

"Well, I imagine that's a bit safer anyway, Mr. Jones."

"I liked it better before when we were knocking down doors and renditioning targets."

"You mean suspects, don't you?" Caitlin asked him.

"Same thing. You know why I loved serving in Afghanistan? Because it was so goddamn backward. War gone primitive. You search a cave, the bad guys are either there or they're not. Not the case when a subject like al-Awlaki comes along who's not a run-of-the-mill towel head. He's American, which means he *knows* how we think, not just how he *thinks* we think. But he also knows this is his last stand."

"Your department ever look into what makes a homegrown terrorist?"

"That's somebody else's department, Hearts and Minds. I'm in Bodies and Bullets."

Tepper just shook his head. "You're a real piece of work, Mr. Jones. What Ranger Strong has told me over the years just doesn't do you justice. She might be a hurricane of category ten proportions, but you, sir,

you are an asteroid the size of Nevada, a genuine extinction event in khaki pants and a polo shirt."

"I think what my captain is saying," Caitlin picked up, "is that maybe your actions have helped spawn these homegrowns more than helping to catch them. You're turning people into terrorists to justify your own existence."

"Throw a stone into the air in one of these mosques, Ranger," Jones said, his expression close to a sneer, "and you're bound to hit someone who justifies my existence with no help from Homeland."

"Well, what I'm really saying," Tepper started, "is that this whole thing stinks to holy hell and I think it's a matter for the Department of Public Safety, the National Guard, the Lone Ranger, and the ghost of John Wayne. We are way out of our league and way past our authority here."

"Your authority is whatever Homeland wants to make it and Homeland is standing right here in front of you saying this is how we've got to play it. The last thing we need is every goddamn Tom, Dick, and Harriet chasing their own tails and making it impossible for us to operate in the arena as we define it."

"Do you ever stop to listen to yourself, Mr. Jones?" Tepper chided.

"Once we get firm intel on what al-Awlaki's up to, we'll call in the cavalry."

"And where's this intel supposed to come from?" Caitlin asked him.

"Starts at the coroner's office with that body. I'd appreciate you phoning the proper authorities to tell them I'm on my way over."

Tepper was already reaching for the phone. "Yeah, I'm sure they'll be thrilled to see you."

Jones slid out the door, leaving Caitlin and Tepper alone in the office.

"The fact that you're still here doesn't bode well for my acid reflux," he told her.

"Need you to authorize some evidence to be dug up from a past case."

Tepper rubbed his stomach. "Yup, I can feel it now. . . . Don't tell me, Ranger, Galveston Island again."

"Remember that broken cross my dad found in one of those dead frat boys' hands?"

Tepper stiffened a bit and reached for his ashtray as if forgetting he'd already pressed his Marlboro out. "Doc Whatley tell you something about that trip the Strongs and I made to Louisiana?"

"He told me to ask you."

"Tell you what, let's have supper later in Marble Falls. I'll see if I can get a hold of that cross in the meantime." Tepper saw the look on Caitlin's face and felt his turn dour and cautionary. "Trail's dead, Ranger. There's cold cases, then there's frozen ones."

"We'll see," Caitlin said, heading for the door.

62

ROUND ROCK, THE PRESENT

Teo Braga worked the controls for the big John Deere Waste Handler, a modified bulldozer built for the express purpose of handling waste materials. This one was the 850J model with an elongated curved blade perfect for pushing sludge. A lot had changed since he'd worked under Alvin Jackson back in a time when environmental concerns were normally an afterthought. The only thing that hadn't changed, in fact, was probably the stench of the sludge itself. Then as now an ammonia-like smell permeated the air surrounding storage lagoons comparable to the one he was now clearing.

Braga used the Waste Handler to push the lagoon's waist-high sludge toward the pumps that funneled it into his waiting tanker truck. And the more the day wore on, the more he was able to get away from the meeting at Texas Ranger Company D headquarters. Caitlin Strong had caught him off guard with her remarks about Alvin Jackson's criminal record, even more so about the disappearance of those union organizers who'd threatened to upset the delicate balance the company maintained between management and workers over working conditions and wages. He wondered if she suspected that they'd ended up in a sludge pile not unlike this one and that their bodies had ultimately been shoveled into black fifty-five-gallon drums to be dumped in landfills or at sea. Braga didn't know where those particular barrels had ended up exactly and didn't much care; he'd been manning the dozer that day, while Alvin Jackson himself supervised the process.

They both stunk to high heaven by the time it was over, three dozen identical black barrels sealed closed and stacked on the back of a massive flatbed for transport. Since there was no time to shower before they drove that flatbed to the disposal unit, they rode with the windows open as time slowed to a crawl.

"How'd you like to own this company, son?" Alvin Jackson had asked him on the way.

"In my dreams," a much younger Braga replied.

"I mean, what if there was a way? What if I could help you pull it off?"

"I don't think I understand, Mr. Jackson."

"I'm a black man, son, with a past that'll make folks raise their eyebrows. Me coming into such an ownership would make most look crossways and the rest look away altogether. See, I've done things I'm not proud of, but couldn't avoid neither. And the sudden procurement of the kind of funds necessary to enact the advancement that comes with ownership would no doubt raise flags I don't need flying over my life right now." He'd stopped and looked across the seat, carrying the stench of sludge even on his breath. "But a young man like you with education and a hard-luck story behind him would lower such flags."

"You have an investor or something, Mr. Jackson?" Braga had asked.

"Something," Jackson said, smiling broadly. "I been waiting for just this day and just this time. What you helped me with tonight, what you did on the company's behalf, has proven your loyalty and made me consider you for a gift I've found no one else worthy of bestowing it upon. And you do seem like a man well capable of taking a secret with him all the way to the grave. Am I right about that, son?"

"Mr. Jackson, we're hauling three bodies on that bed behind us. I think that should answer your question."

Jackson nodded. "Gonna take us a trip soon. We'll be gone a couple days. I'll tell you the story in the course of the drive back to where I was born and bred."

"You don't speak about your family very much," Braga noted. "When that subject comes around, we always speak of mine but never yours."

over as he approached. Having expected only the one he'd met previously, the presence of the second man threw him for a slight loop. The stranger was hardly intimidating—he looked almost too calm, too compliant. The kind of man Braga had learned to be leery of above all others.

"I don't believe we've met," Braga said to the stranger when he reached the two men, comfortable with Thoms riding his back.

The stranger extended his hand. "We are business partners by association."

Braga took the hand, finding the grip dry and flaccid. "One deal doesn't make us partners, especially when it leaves a Texas Ranger crawling up my ass."

The two men exchanged a glance, quick but not too quick to hide the concern it carried.

"Perhaps if you could be more specific," said the man with whom Braga had made the deal.

"Specific? Okay. The Rangers have video evidence of several of the barrels I contracted you to move in Gulf waters. And I don't believe that makes a very good case for you exercising the discretion I'm paying for."

"An oversight," said the stranger, rolling over the other man's words.

"Why am I talking to you?"

"Because we're associates, as I said."

"No, we're not," Braga said, finger thrust toward Harrabi. "You're his associate, not mine. I don't know you. You're not the one I paid to do this job for me."

The stranger remained emotionless, speaking with his eyes on the other. "But I pay him, which means you are now dealing with me."

"Let's take a drive. There's something I'd like to show you gentlemen."

* * *

Braga and Thoms rode in the cab of the tanker, now full to the brim with sludge pumped from the lagoon, the two men following in their SUV. They parked in the lot of his processing plant and Braga led them inside under Thoms's watchful eye.

The building was warehouse-sized, crammed with automated machinery connected by a labyrinthine network of pipes, baffles, exhaust vents, and hoses. In here the bitterly corrosive smell of super-heated lubricating oils mixed with that of the sludge, worsened all the more by the heat friction and the closed confines.

"You have to wear these," Braga said, handing each of his guests a hard hat and then fastening one atop his own head. "It's the law and we wouldn't want to break the law now, would we?"

The men complied, the one he knew clearly anxious while the stranger still showed no emotion whatsoever.

"Follow me," Braga told them.

"Why have you brought us here?" the stranger asked.

Braga continued on, ignoring him and stopping before the largest piece of equipment on the floor. "This is called a centrifuge," he explained, voice raised over the constant din of the machinery that churned twenty-four hours a day. "Separates solid from liquid. The water is treated at the adjoining facility, while the solids are pumped down to remove the solvents and allow for drying. The result is this," he said, reaching a slide that funneled dried sludge in pellet form into orange barrels. "Stores better with less toxicity while taking up much less space than it would have as solid waste."

"You still haven't answered my question," the stranger said.

"Which one of you am I working with?"

"Both of us, but today I am the one speaking."

Braga nodded in apparent concession. "You see anyone else in this building?"

"Just him," the stranger said, indicating Jalbert Thoms.

"That's because this plant is fully automated, requiring only regular maintenance to continue its tasks unabated. You understand the purpose of regular maintenance? To prevent anything from going wrong. The cost of dealing with a breakdown can be catastrophic. You're here because the business between us had a breakdown and it led back to me."

"In the person of this Texas Ranger," the stranger concluded.

Ignoring him again, Braga grabbed what looked like a small, handheld spade from its slot on the wall and moved to a rectangular connecting line that ran from the centrifuge to the pellet processor. He jimmied a catch bracket, opening the front side of the line to reveal moist, mudlike clumps of black sludge.

"This stuff can clog the line, gum up the whole process," Braga resumed, using his tool to clear all the sludge from the works, including the portions that had gobbed up behind the pistons and baffles. "Somebody does this every day. Today it's my turn. Takes several hours but potentially saves the company millions in the event a shutdown is required. You see what I'm getting at here?" Braga asked, scooping an even larger clump of sludge right at the stranger's feet.

"Preventative maintenance," said the stranger.

"I'm glad you got my point. That's what you failed to perform and now we have an expensive breakdown to deal with."

"Was that your point in summoning us here?"

"My point is that breakdowns, as I said before, are expensive to deal with and this one is going to cost you."

"So this is a renegotiation."

"No," Braga told him. "That implies you have a choice. You've moved half the barrels so far. You'll be moving the second half at half the price we agreed upon." Then, with his eyes on Jalbert Thoms, "Breakdowns cost." Braga took a rag from his pocket and began wiping the sludge dust from his face, succeeding only in creating grimy smears where it had collected in the greatest concentrations. "Are we clear on that?"

Anwar al-Awlaki watched him impassively, then picked up the tool Braga had discarded and mimicked his actions precisely in clearing the sludge from the line. "Perhaps our philosophies are closer in step than you think," he told Braga, swiping at the innards of the pipe through the open hatch. "I have experienced many such breakdowns in my time, but sometimes they are out of our control and cannot be avoided no matter how much maintenance is done. When that happens, one must take responsibility and accept its burden."

He pulled the curved tool out, tilting it so the sludge he'd cleared fell straight onto the tips of Braga's work boots. "That particular burden is ours and we will shoulder it. So, yes, we are clear."

Braga ignored the gesture, aware Jalbert Thoms had tensed noticeably by his side, his hand listing a bit closer to the cannon-sized pistol holstered under his jacket. "Burden," he repeated. "Is that what you call murdering two dozen oil rig workers?"

"I have no idea what you are speaking of," al-Awlaki said without hesitation.

Braga looked the man over. "You notice I didn't ask your name."

"Just as I didn't introduce myself."

"So we have ourselves an understanding. You don't tell me my business and I'll only tell you yours when it affects mine. I retained you to do a job and I'll see that you complete it without any further complications. Is that clear enough for you?"

"You mean, sir," al-Awlaki began quite calmly, "a complication like the one you're facing with this Texas Ranger?"

Braga swabbed his face with the rag again, this time succeeding in clearing away a hefty portion of the muck. "You just dispose of the rest of the barrels like you're supposed to and leave the Ranger to me."

64

SAN ANTONIO, THE PRESENT

Cort Wesley's rental car was parked in the shade of a flowering cottonwood tree across the street from Thomas C. Clark High School, when the door opened and Caitlin Strong climbed in.

"Been here long?" she asked him.

"Only all day."

"So I figured."

"Couldn't sleep last night. Kept closing my eyes and seeing Jalbert Thoms showing up on the premises."

"Captain Tepper asked the San Antonio police to station a cruiser outside Luke's middle school."

"But not here."

" 'Cause I knew you'd be here, since it was Dylan that Thoms picked out."

Cort Wesley turned away from the school building toward her across the front seat. "Can the Rangers really afford to be without you for any stretch of time? Thought they'd learned their lesson."

"I believe D. W. Tepper would tell you I haven't learned mine."

"What's that mean?"

"I honestly don't know. I guess I'm becoming more a pain in the ass than I'm worth."

"You're a Ranger through and through."

"Maybe that's the problem. I've got an old school attitude in a new school time and, I've gotta tell you, Captain Tepper has a point. I flew off the handle in back-to-back meetings today. My dad and granddad both preached that temper never comes into play for a Ranger. That's how he—"

"Or she . . ."

"—can walk into a simmering crowd and shut down whatever was coming. Because of their calm in the face of everyone else about to give in to the tendencies I felt firsthand twice today."

Cort Wesley flashed her a look. "And what do you attribute this to?"

Caitlin frowned at him. "I think you know."

"Do I now?"

"I owe you an apology, Cort Wesley."

"For what?"

"Will you stop asking me questions?"

"Not until I get a straight answer, Ranger. What is it you want to apologize for? No, let me make that a statement: apology accepted."

"You don't even know what I was going to say."

The sun had found a straight path through the shade, a swatch of the car's black fabric upholstery turning hot and pushing Cort Wesley sideways, closer to Caitlin. "You were going to say you were sorry for being critical of me for gunning down the drug dealer who killed Dylan's girlfriend. You were going to say now you finally understand how kids change you in ways you can't possibly get until you're responsible for them and they become your life. You were going to say you finally realized that maybe you really can't have it both ways, which is why you've always kept your distance no matter how close we seemed to get. But it's what you weren't going to say that's most important."

"What's that?"

"That you stepped in when I stepped out, and you didn't hesitate, not even for a second. You didn't change your priorities, Ranger," Cort Wesley said, holding her eyes with his as deeply as he ever had, "you just realized where they were all along."

"Rangering cost my mother her life and my father his happiness with another woman years later in Midland."

"So you learn anything from that?"

Caitlin's stare dug into him, vulnerable and relentless at the same time. "I never wanted to kill a man more than I wanted to kill Jalbert Thoms last night."

"He's just a peripheral player here."

"You know what I'm getting at. He pushed buttons in me I never even knew I had."

Cort Wesley reached over and cupped Caitlin's head in his hand, stroking her hair. "I like it this way."

"I think prison made you soft."

"Nope. I've been like this with you since the beginning. You're just noticing it now."

Caitlin eased her hand over his. "Maybe they got a pill or something I can take."

"An antidote to kids?"

"Something like that."

"Would you take it?" Cort Wesley felt her stiffen under his touch and decided to switch gears. "I'm moving back home."

Caitlin missed his touch as soon as it was gone. "I'm meeting Captain Tepper up in Marble Falls for dinner tonight. Why don't you pick up the boys and come along? Be a good way to break the ice now that you're back in the picture."

Cort Wesley shifted about uneasily. "I got butterflies in my stomach the size of monster trucks, Ranger."

"This isn't like the last time, Cort Wesley. They didn't even know you existed back then."

"And I don't know how long I'm gonna be around again now."

"Why?"

"Jones."

"You signed on for one job with him, and one job only."

"It's never only one with men like him. They're a different breed entirely, Ranger. They see the world a whole different way and everyone else is just a means to those ends. How do I know how long he's gonna hold this prison thing over my head?"

"I'll talk to him, if it comes to that."

Cort Wesley's face wrinkled in derision. "What good's that gonna do?"

"You want to trust me on this or not?"

"Do I have a choice?"

"No more of one than you do about joining Captain Tepper and me for supper tonight."

"Then I guess we'll be there," Cort Wesley said with a frown that couldn't quite hide the pleasure he felt at the prospect. He slid the windows up and started the engine to get the air-conditioning on and flush out the heat for a time. The rush of cold air blasted into his skin, drying the sweat collected there almost on contact. "You want to check with your captain first?"

"He can't be any madder at me than he is already, and it could be about to get worse."

"How's that, Ranger?"

"I'm about to tell him the last thing in the world he wants to hear."

"You wanna try it out on me first?"

Caitlin turned away, indicating she didn't. "It's too crazy to believe, Cort Wesley. Trust me on that."

65

SAN ANTONIO, THE PRESENT

Cort Wesley was standing outside his rental car when Dylan emerged at the end of the school day amid a rugby scrum of friends all pushing and jostling each other. Pretty much all of them were bigger than he was, but none of them was as good-looking, as attested to by the gaggle of smiling girls seeking him out for attention.

The sight sent a wash of pride through Cort Wesley that felt as tangible as blood flow, until he thought of Jalbert Thoms ogling Dylan and a fresh rush of heat rage pushed the pride out. He didn't realize his hands had clenched into fists until his son spotted him and froze, his teenage entourage continuing on without him.

Cort Wesley held his ground, his feet heavier than he'd ever felt them, as if his boots had morphed into plate steel. He saw Dylan coming toward him slowly, face squeezed tight as if the boy didn't believe the sight and needed to convince himself. Cort Wesley felt his legs go weak and spongy, tried to swallow down some air but found his throat too clogged with nerves to manage the effort.

Man, he'd walked into a potential kill zone two nights before without feeling anything close to this. . . .

Dylan jogged the last stretch to him, throwing himself into his father's big arms, Cort Wesley feeling the boy's tears against his own face.

"Let's go pick up your brother," he said, tossing an arm around Dylan's shoulder. "Hey, you wanna drive?"

The boy was a good driver, much better than Cort Wesley remembered. Slow and cautious, good with the mirrors and, most important, capable of ignoring his cell phone which rang and beeped nonstop.

"You mind if I throw that thing out the window?" Cort Wesley asked him.

"Be my guest," Dylan said, without producing it from his pocket. "Give me an excuse to get that new iPhone."

"I *what*?"

Dylan rolled his eyes. "Never mind." His gaze moved to his father, then back to the road. "You were hoping he'd show up at school, that guy from the other day, weren't you?"

"What do you think?"

"I think I'd never have known. I think he'd be stuffed in your trunk before anybody was the wiser."

"Not before I removed certain parts from his person."

Dylan's face wrinkled. "Dad, please."

"Sorry."

"Don't be. What I meant was I was hoping you'd save that for me. The man didn't seem real, more like a special effect inserted into a movie."

"Don't blame George Lucas or James Cameron for this freak show."

Dylan took a long moment before responding. "I missed you, Dad."

"I missed you too, more than you'll ever know."

A horn honked behind them and Dylan started the rental on through the intersection, checking both his left and right first.

"You never met your granddad," Cort Wesley resumed. "Mean son of a bitch if ever there was one. You know the first time he rode with me behind the wheel? When I was fifteen, him perched in the back of his truck to keep some stolen televisions from spilling off the top of the pile."

"Why don't we ever do fun stuff like that?"

Cort Wesley stared across the seat at his seventeen-year-old son, the long black hair that reminded him so much of the boy's mother framing his face.

"What are you looking at?" Dylan asked him.

"Don't know," Cort Wesley said, holding his stare with a smile. "That's what I'm trying to figure out."

PART SEVEN

Acts 1935, 44th Leg., p. 444, ch. 181, sec. 10.
Art. 4413(il). THE TEXAS RANGERS

(1) The Texas Ranger Force and its personnel, property, equipment, and records, now a part of the Adjutant General's Department of the State of Texas, are hereby transferred to and placed under the jurisdiction of the Department of Public Safety, and are hereby designated as the Texas Rangers, and as such, constitute the above mentioned division of the Department.

(2) The Texas Rangers shall consist of six (6) captains, one headquarters sergeant, and such number of privates as may be authorized by the Legislature, except in cases of emergency when the Commission, with the consent of the Governor, shall have authority to increase the force to meet extraordinary conditions.

(3) The Compensation of the officers shall be such as allowed by the Legislature.

(4) The officers shall be clothed with all the powers of peace officers, and shall aid in the execution of the laws.

66

"So when are Cort Wesley and his boys coming?" Captain Tepper asked, as a waitress set a thirty-two-ounce beer before him on the table at Opie's Barbecue in the center of Main Street in Marble Falls.

Caitlin checked her watch. "Any minute. Thought you might be upset I invited them."

Tepper shrugged her off. "The way you been pissing me off lately, company's just what's needed to keep me civil."

Caitlin watched him take a hefty sip from his beer, leaving a trail of foam on his lips that he swiped off with a sleeve. "You got any other habits sure to kill you I should know about, D.W.?"

Tepper took an even bigger sip. "Since Hurricane Caitlin climbed back in the saddle, booze ain't about drinking, it's about surviving." He watched her playing with her menu. "Try the chicken fried steak, Ranger. It's the best you'll ever eat. The brisket's seasoned with real black bark and the baby back ribs got this sweet, chewy crust. Prime rib's the safest choice if you're worried about your stomach."

"Thought we were eating at the Blue Bonnet Cafe, though."

"We were. Blue Bonnet might have the best pie in

the state of Texas, but Masters's boys'll enjoy this place more."

Tepper actually lived on a converted hog farm twenty miles south of Marble Falls with four houses on his property that were home to three of his five children. Although the hour commute to and from San Antonio had started to weigh on him, he still welcomed it for the time spent clearing his head after a day devoted to commanding Company D in San Antonio for the Texas Rangers. By the same token, he loved everything about Marble Falls. From its quaint period architecture that captured rural Texas in the shadow of the big cities nearby, to the traditional Main Street district laden with historic buildings, to old-fashioned traditions like a local art show in April to an annual soapbox competition down Main Street in just a few days' time. The competitors would be forced to negotiate the road's center island adorned with fresh plantings that added an even more rustic feel to the town's down-home Americana.

From the window aside Tepper's favorite table, they had a view of the world that seemed detached from that where Texas Rangers were required to keep or restore order. The police force was small, the crime rate practically nonexistent, and it was hard not to walk down the street without recognizing someone you knew. None of the buildings exceeded three stories, adorned with peaked roofs and the typical brown tones and hues in keeping with a Texas tradition that began with a need to disguise the ever-present dirt. Marble Falls was as clean a town as they came, though, reminding Caitlin of something lifted out of Disney World and planted right here in Texas.

Caitlin made a cursory check of the menu just to satisfy herself. "Chicken fried steak it is, D.W."

"Got an appetizer here for you." Tepper reached into his pocket and extracted a sealed evidence pouch frosted by the years. "I believe this is what you were looking for, Ranger."

Inside the pouch was what looked like a small crucifix with the topmost portion broken off. It was the size of a pendant, something someone might wear dangling from their neck.

"The boy you found this on," Caitlin said, holding the cross pendant through the pouch, "you recall if he was wearing a chain or something else it could have hung from?"

"This was thirty years ago, Ranger. I can barely remember my cell phone number and names of my grandkids."

"I know you, D.W. When it comes to cases, you might as well have the files imprinted on your brain."

"Well, I'm sure it's cataloged somewhere among the boy's effects but, no, by my recollection the victim we found holding the cross had no jewelry on him at all, not even a watch." He drank more of his beer, squinting from the sun pouring through the window flush with their table. "Where you going with this?"

"Humor me, Captain."

"You figure the cross belonged to someone else and it broke off in the struggle."

"Thought never crossed your mind, my dad's mind, or granddad's?"

"Since we didn't see any sign of a struggle, not really. And we dusted the cross for prints and came up only with the boy's, no second party's. And in a follow-up interview, I recall the boy's parents saying they believed he did have a crucifix that matched the general description. Confirmation present from his grandparents or something."

"But you didn't show them this," Caitlin followed, holding the cross through the plastic of the pouch.

"Never got the chance."

"What do you mean?"

"Another part of the story, the one that explains why you never heard anything about this particular tale before."

"And me thinking that was on account of the fact that you and the Strongs never solved it."

"Like I said, we never got the chance. It was out of our territory to begin with. But five college boys get themselves killed, who you figure the Rangers are going to send? Earl and Jim were the best they had and that's what they needed here, although that didn't help much with the final result. Wait," Tepper added suddenly, stopping his beer glass halfway to his mouth, "I just thought of something."

"What?"

"Goes back to the visit we made to Louisiana straight from the University of Texas in Austin. Struck me as strange at the time but I never really thought about it again until now."

Caitlin settled back in her chair, crossing her arms before her. "I'm listening, D.W."

67

LOUISIANA BAYOU, 1979

"Think I'm gonna be seasick again," Tepper said as the airboat skipped atop the bayou's black surface.

He and the Strongs had arrived at the St. Mary's Parish sheriff's station in the calm and relative cool of the late afternoon after the sun had sunk beneath the reach of the cypress trees that hung gracefully out over the water. The station was perched on the bank of a levee shaded by live oak trees, the leaves of which were still wet from a sudden and quick storm they must have just missed.

The parish sheriff was expecting them and one of his deputies already had an airboat fired up and ready to go, the roar of its propeller blade spinning inside a steel cage drowning out all other sound.

"Airboat?" Earl Strong asked him, shouting over the din.

"Only way to get where you're going. You want me to tag along?"

"Not as long as your deputy knows the way."

The sheriff, who had a collection of moles all over his face amid sun-darkened skin with the texture of bark, grinned. "It's Beaudoin Chansoir we're talking about, right? 'Cause he tends to move around a lot. But if you hurry, you can catch him at the bait shop he tends at the mouth of the bayou."

"Shit," D. W. Tepper said, leaning his head over the side of the airboat twenty minutes later. "What you call these hairy-looking things swimming on the surface?" he asked after puking on one of them.

"Nutria," said the deputy.

"What the hell's that?"

"Like a beaver, D.W.," Jim Strong answered.

"Everybody's a damn expert," Tepper said, lowering his head again into a shaft of sunlight riding the black water's surface like an upended column.

"We got foliage and wildlife here you won't find anywhere else in the world," the deputy added.

"And I believe I've now puked on most of it."

Earl and Jim Strong exchanged a grin, their faces wet with sweat from the humidity that seemed to bleed off the water. As they drew deeper into the bayou's reaches, deep enough to spot alligators basking on shore and predatory barred owls awaiting nightfall to begin swooping down on their prey, the airboat began cutting through a thin mist rising off the water's surface. What looked like lily pads floated atop it, drifting toward mangroves that stretched out from the shoreline to reach for whatever their grasp might bring them.

"Mist like this always rises after a storm," the deputy informed them. "Makes for great fishing, which gives you a better chance of finding Beaudoin Chansoir at his perch. If he's not there, you may have to wait until morning."

"You telling me you really don't know where he makes his home out here?" Jim Strong asked him.

"Ranger, out here at night his spread might as well be the size of a postage stamp."

They came to a break in the protective canopy formed by the overhanging trees, the mist disappearing to be replaced by the murky reflections of the nearby shoreline as they cruised past. The deputy had cut the airboat's speed, seeming to use the landscape to guide him to the spot where Beaudoin Chansoir set up his bait shop most days at the mouth of the bayou.

A rickety dock appeared in the narrowing distance, the deputy gliding the airboat toward it as a skiff with two black fishermen inside slid away into the shadows. Chansoir's bait shop was located just up from the shoreline on an even patch of land that sat on the bank of a twin waterway on its eastern side. Just a table really, with a flimsy and soaked tarpaulin strung over it and supported by wooden poles driven into the soft ground. Chansoir sat in a chair beneath the makeshift covering, smoking a corncob pipe near his bait and lures and seeming to pay their presence no heed at all.

The deputy slid the airboat to a halt against the dock and tied it down to a mooring that was cracked along the center. The Rangers had already climbed off by the time he finished, their weight pushing the floating dock dangerously close to the water's surface.

"Let me introduce you," the deputy said, moving past them up the small hill. "Mr. Chansoir?" he called as they drew closer.

"You ain't for sure customers, you," Chansoir greeted, pipe held in hand now. "Never seen nobody looked like them in these parts, no."

"These are Texas Rangers," the deputy told him. "They'd like to talk to you, Mr. Chansoir."

"Ain't mister. Beaudoin, just Beaudoin."

"Nice to make your acquaintance, Beaudoin," said Earl Strong, moving closer.

"Mister Chansoir to you on account of you being a stranger in mine eyes."

"You able to talk to us, Mr. Chansoir?" Earl corrected.

"You able to buy bait, I able to talk."

"Well," said Jim Strong, "that fine bait would spoil by the time we got home, but what about a few of these lures here?"

"Make 'em myself, each and every. Each dollar you spend gets you a minute of talk."

Jim laid a ten-dollar-bill down on the table, then changed his mind and replaced it with a twenty.

"Where's home?" Chansoir asked him, dropping the bill into a cigar box he held in his lap.

"Texas," Jim told him.

"You cowboys?"

"Texas Rangers."

Chansoir laughed heartily, showcasing a mouth nearly empty of teeth. His skin was taut but strangely smooth except for the areas around his eyes that were stitched with spiderweb-like patches of deep wrinkles. He squinted badly, even though what was left of the sun was at his back, his eyes watery and oozing something from both sides.

"No such thing as Rangers no more," Chansoir said when he finished laughing. "They all dead now, they. That'd make you dead too."

"Plenty would agree with you on my account anyway, sir," Earl told him.

"Beaudoin to you since you called me sir. How old you be, Dead Man?"

"Seventy-nine last time I checked, Beaudoin."

"Believe you got twenty years on me there, though I ain't be entirely sure." Chansoir's eyes moved to Jim Strong and then Tepper who still had a green tint to his skin. "You didn't come here to buy no lures, no."

"Nope," said Earl, "we come for information."

"Good thing I sell that too, me."

"You get a visit from some fraternity boys from the University of Texas a few days back?" Jim asked him.

"Don't know what a fraternity be. Don't know if they was boys or men. But they was here."

"They come looking for Jean Lafitte's lost treasure?" Earl picked up.

"No, Dead Man, they come looking for the map to take them to it."

"Which you gave them."

"Nope—sold 'em. Five hundred bucks, couple weeks' worth of bait and lure business. I like it when they's shows up, me. Every few months, tourists mostly, but those fraternity boys sometimes too. They's money all look the same to me, yeah."

"Could we see this map, Beaudoin?" Earl asked him.

"For five hundred you can, you. Then I draw it for you. I draw 'em out, one per time, from the memory of what my folks told me and their folks told them."

"Galveston?"

"The island? Nah, dat's all wrong. Treasure's here in this very land. Hidden good, it is. I draw the map from my memory but the land's different now than it be before. Dat why nobody ever find the treasure, 'cause where it really be ain't exactly where any map shows it is."

Earl, Jim, and Tepper exchanged confused glances, trying to make sense of what the old man was telling them.

"Mr. Chansoir," started Jim Strong, "those fraternity boys were found dead on Galveston Island, not here in the bayou. Are you sure you're not mistaken?"

The slits that held the old man's eyes opened wider, showing uncertainty and discomfort. All the wry playfulness was gone, though they continued to leak something that looked like gumbo down both cheeks. Earl Strong had recently caught his granddaughter Caitlin playing with bullets taken from the slots on his gun belt. The look on her face when he caught her was almost the same as Beaudoin Chansoir's until his eyes narrowed again, reducing the scope of the world.

"Know what I sold those boys, me. You wanna know what took 'em somewheres else, you have to ask 'em."

"They're dead, Beaudoin," Earl said. "Remember?"

From his expression, Chansoir clearly did. "Then I guess you's never gonna know, just like me. They come, they go. What happen after, I don't need to see but for more bills I try. Use the magic, me, but the magic costs."

Earl took off his Stetson and flapped it against his side. "So you didn't draw these boys a map of Lafitte's old Campeche base camp on Galveston Island."

"Listen better with your ears, Dead Man. There those things on the sides of your head there. Them boys came by skiff boat they musta rented. Lot more scraped and busted up than when they took it out I saw for sure, me."

The old man tapped his wrist to signal they'd spent all of Jim's money even though twenty minutes had clearly not passed. D. W. Tepper handed Chansoir a ten this time.

"What else?" he asked.

"Nothin'. That be all there is to tell, yeah. Here," he said, dropping the ten-dollar bill at Tepper's feet, "take your money back and get yourselves gone from here. Ain't gonna draw no map for you, no matter how much you's offers, me."

He rose fast from his chair, knees creaking, his half open shirt billowing in the wind.

"Dead Man," he said, addressing Earl, "you take your boys and do the get-go. You heard what I got to say and there ain't no more to be said."

68

MARBLE FALLS, THE PRESENT

"It was when he stood up," Tepper finished.

"What?"

"I saw something that didn't really register at the time. It wasn't much really, just a faded portion on the top part of his chest. Figured it was a scar or birthmark or something and didn't think any more about it. But the mark was about the same size as that cross in that pouch there."

"So if you're right, it could mean Chansoir gave the cross to whoever eventually murdered those college kids."

"Except we couldn't make any sense of the disconnect between those boys following a map of the Louisiana bayou to Galveston Island. And we never really got the chance to try."

"That's the second time you raised that issue, Captain."

"We didn't know it then, but our trip to the bayou was pretty much the end of things as far as the investigation was concerned."

"With you and the Strongs teamed up, I find that hard to believe."

"Subject for another day," Tepper said, his voice lower, clearly not interested in continuing the tale.

"You rule out any of the five frat boys being targeted personally?"

"Course. Nope, near as we can figure this was an utterly random crime, those boys being in the absolute worst place at the absolute worst time. We figure they surprised somebody who was up to no good in that clearing, but were never able to figure out exactly what kind of no good they were up to."

"You went back to Galveston, didn't you?"

"We did indeed, Ranger." Tepper drained a hefty portion of what remained of his beer. "I'm just starting to relax. That makes this the wrong time to go about telling you the rest. It ain't good. Let's leave things at that."

"I've got my own part of it to add," Caitlin said, holding the evidence pouch up to the light for both of them to see. "What if this isn't a cross at all, D.W.?"

"You're talking about the broken off piece we never found at the scene," Tepper responded, unable to disguise his interest.

"I believe there are two missing pieces. Did some Internet research when I couldn't sleep last night."

"Yeah, gunfights'll do that to you, Ranger. . . ."

"You wanna hear what I found out?"

"I don't know, do I?"

Caitlin pulled some pages she'd folded up from her pocket. All three had pictures of the same object but from different angles: a cross with a heart extending from the top and a second piece extending out of the bottom that featured a swirl design with what looked like a grid pattern running through it. She used fingers on both her hands to cover up the extensions on the page featuring a dead-on view.

"Look familiar?"

Tepper compared it in size and shape to the item contained in the old evidence pouch. "Looks like our cross, all right."

"According to what I found out, this pendant is called Erzulie veve."

"Who? *What?*"

"Erzulie is the voodoo loa, spirit force, of love in Haitian folklore later adopted by Cajuns like Beaudoin Chansoir. A veve is a loa's spirit symbol, and that's what we got here."

Tepper viewed the symbol, then the cross through the cloudy plastic, trying to superimpose both of them over the faded spot the old Cajun had on his chest. The proportions were just about perfect.

"Okay, Ranger, you have now succeeded in linking a Cajun bait salesman who could barely see to a crime scene maybe a thousand miles away."

"No, I haven't. I've only linked his voodoo charm to that crime scene, toted there by somebody else," Caitlin said, laying the evidence pouch and sheets of paper down on the table. "But say you're a Cajun who wants to escape into the modern world. You'd start by changing the name Chansoir to an English equivalent, like Jackson maybe."

"Whoa, whoa, whoa, am I hearing you right on this?" He fanned his face with the dinner menu. "You suggesting that Alvin *Jackson*, Teo Braga's boss when he started out in waste management, was involved in those murders?"

"Braga raised the Cajun magic connection himself.

I'm just connecting the dots. Whoever killed those boys also knew enough about Cajun lore to ravage the bodies the way that mythical creature would, Rougarou or whatever."

"All this over some legendary treasure that probably never existed?"

"I'm not saying Alvin Jackson or anybody else found it, D.W. I'm just saying they might have gone to Galveston Island looking."

Tepper worked his nicotine-stained fingertip in and out of the deepest furrows that look liked ditches dug on his cheeks and forehead. "Forgetting one thing, aren't you, Ranger? That old man drew maps that sent treasure hunters like those frat boys deeper into the bayou, not to Galveston Island."

Caitlin thought about that for a moment. "You said you got a rise out of Chansoir when you mentioned that fact to him."

"He looked kind of sick, almost as bad as me, and I'd been puking my guts out. But what does that have to do with anything?"

"Assume Lafitte buried whatever he took off the *Mother Mary* on Galveston Island instead of the bayou. Assume Chansoir drew out a map for his grandson Alvin directing him to where the real legend said the treasure was *actually* hidden. . . ."

"And then these frat boys come along almost right afterwards, and he draws them the identical map instead of the one that would've taken them deeper into the bayou." Tepper nodded, weighing Caitlin's assumption. "I like you better when you're thinking instead of shooting, Ranger. Except I don't know where you're going with this theory exactly."

Caitlin grabbed a warm roll wrapped in a linen napkin from a breadbasket before her. "I believe I've got a way to prove it, sir," she said, as a big Ford Expedition with blacked-out windows pulled into a no-parking zone across the street.

69

MARBLE FALLS, THE PRESENT

"And don't you think I didn't hear about those fights you got in," Cort Wesley said to Luke, broaching the subject for the first time since they'd driven north to Marble Falls to meet Caitlin and Captain Tepper for dinner.

Luke frowned so hard that the sides of his mouth seemed to disappear entirely. "I lost two of them."

"Well, that's something we gotta work on."

"Don't bother," Dylan said, giving up on trying to find a decent radio station. "He sucks."

"He's right. I do."

"Well," Cort Wesley started, as they cruised down Main Street looking for a space close to Obie's Barbecue, sliding under a banner strung across the road announcing a Soapbox Derby right here that weekend.

Luke leaned forward. "Hey, that could be fun."

Dylan shook his head, blowing the hair from his face through pursed lips. "It's gay."

"Now why you gotta use that word that way?" Cort Wesley said critically.

"What way? What *word*?"

Cort Wesley just shook his head and lined up his rental to parallel park adjacent to a black Ford Expedition with its nose against the curb.

"I think I see Caitlin inside the restaurant," Luke said, waving to get her attention.

Caitlin took a bite of her roll and chased it down with a gulp of water from a glass laden with shards of melting ice. "I think that's Cort Wesley's rental car parking across the street in front of that drugstore."

"You sound like a high school girl."

"Stop it."

Tepper grinned. "I say something wrong?"

Caitlin started to smile back but then stopped, her features freezing as she spotted something else outside. "Get your gun ready, Captain."

"We haven't even ordered yet, Ranger," he said, drawing his .45 as Caitlin showed her SIG over the table.

"Duck your heads!" Cort Wesley yelled at his boys, noticing the Expedition's back window sliding down in the midst of parallel parking.

"Huh?" from both his sons together.

"*Get down!*"

He jerked the car to a halt and jammed it into park only half in the space. He had his Glock in hand in the next moment, kicking the driver's door open just as the muzzle flashes erupted, bursting out of the Expedition's open rear window.

* * *

Caitlin and Tepper hit the floor together before they could get off a single shot, the staccato barrage of machine-gun fire blowing out Obie's plate-glass window overlooking Main Street. Shards of glass and bullets poured inward, the gunfire's sound drowned out by the screams of diners diving for cover everywhere.

"Jesus H. Christ," Tepper rasped, his voice sounding like someone had strained his words through steel wool.

Caitlin started crawling toward him. "You okay? You hit?"

"Hold your horses, Ranger. Just been a time since I been in a shooting war."

"How long?"

"Let you know if I live," Tepper told her, popping up even with the window's bottom and firing off shots toward the Expedition.

Cort Wesley hit the ground and rolled, poised and ready to fire from a prone position when the Expedition's four doors opened in a single motion and four figures clad in black from head to toe lurched out. He hit the Glock's trigger and kept pulling, focusing his fire on the two men on the vehicle's driver's side to which he had an unobstructed view. Last thing they would've been expecting which should have given him the advantage.

At least eight of his shots, four for each, were on target, knocking the gunmen off kilter while not seeming to slow them down at all.

Armor suits!

He'd heard of the suits but had never actually seen one in action, save for video footage of some bank robbery where the crooks shot up an entire police department while walking straight down the street. Cort Wesley seemed to remember they used automatic weapons to mow down cops, all the while with bags of money slung over their shoulders.

He popped a fresh magazine home, already twisting his angle to account for headshots instead. Only by then the two gunmen whose armor he'd hit were swinging his way, assault rifles ready to dance in their hands.

With only eight shots in his .45, Tepper had to reload before Caitlin. The pistol was a commemorative model issued just last year to celebrate the great Ranger tradition that had started with Samuel Walker's Colt, custom designed to shoot from horseback in 1881, and continued well into the next century with the Springfield Model 1911 .45. The brute force of the .45 slug was second to none, packing maybe twice the stopping power of Caitlin's nine-millimeter shells. But neither of their shots managed to do anything but ruffle the advancing gunmen's forward motion.

"Frigging Terminators," Tepper mumbled, jamming a fresh magazine into his .45. "We're gonna need goddamn ray guns or something."

More bullets peppered Opie's, raining stray glass downward. Caitlin held to her position long enough to see one of the gunmen twisting toward Cort Wesley, tip of his M-16 angling downward. She fired, not for him, but the side window glass immediately at his rear. Three shots that sent glass flying everywhere, distracting him long enough for Caitlin to risk standing all the way up and measuring off a shot straight into the center of his face.

She watched the hollow point shell erupt from the back of his helmeted skull dragging chunks of bone and flecks of brain matter with it. Impact whipsawed him sideways, slamming him into the second gunman on the driver's side in the very moment that man was sighting down on Cort Wesley.

Curled up half on the seat and half on the passenger side floor, Dylan reached up and popped open the glove compartment.

"Dylan!" Luke wailed from the backseat.

"Shut up!"

"*Dylan!*"

"Keep your head down!"

Dylan's groping fingers finally closed on the cold steel of a .40 caliber Glock where his dad always kept it no matter what vehicle he was driving. Dylan's hand was shaking, all of him was shaking, as he drew it to him, racking the slide as he pushed the door open and lurched out onto the street.

The two gunmen from the Expedition's passenger side fired twin nonstop barrages through the open space where Opie's plate-glass window used to be. Caitlin and Tepper hit the floor again, each soon to be down to their last magazine.

For some reason, Caitlin registered the sound of cooking grease sizzling. "Cover me!" she called to Tepper, already pulling herself across the glass-splattered floor.

"Bad idea, Ranger!"

"No good ones right now."

Cort Wesley had the man in his sights but his angle precluded the headshot he desperately needed. He tried two shots low, hoping to hit skin and bone beneath the armor suit. But the hollow thunks told him the Kevlar or ballistic nylon padding stretched all the way to the man's feet. The man opened up with a barrage that strummed against the rental's driver's side, digging divots from the steel. Pop up and Cort Wesley would be dead for sure. Stay down and it would just take longer.

Pop! Pop! Pop!

Caitlin doing the shooting, he figured, until the sound and the trajectory proved all wrong, and he glimpsed Dylan coming round the rental to catch the gunman totally by surprise. A couple of shots slammed into the armor like it was a man-sized cardboard target, Cort Wesley having the sense of mind to register his oldest son was shooting for the first time at flesh and blood.

Cort Wesley thought he heard a half dozen more shots, at least two of them smacking the armor with dull *whops*. But it held the man steady and stopped his assault long enough for Cort Wesley to bounce upward to one knee and empty his Glock for his face. Might have hit it once or eight times; he didn't know, since it only took one to put the man down in a burst of blood spray after slamming him into the door. The man's rifle strap ended up snaring on the mirror, leaving him suspended only halfway to the pavement.

Cort Wesley's eyes found Dylan, looking at the dead man instead of him, the .40 caliber shaking up a storm in his hand. All he could do was lunge to his feet, positioning himself to shield his son as Caitlin Strong emerged from Opie's to confront the remaining two shooters.

70

Marble Falls, the present

Caitlin dropped down behind a standing mailbox, never more gratified than now by the postal service's work ethic that had failed to collect today's accumulated mail, further safeguarding her from the barrage that burned her ears as it clanged against steel. Her hearing came in fits and starts now, silence in one breath and blistering volume in the next. The latter detected the heavy booms of Tepper's .45 offering resistance, buying time to . . .

To *what*?

For some reason, her mind flashed back to the gunfight inside the school all those months before. How she'd felt when she realized one of her bullets had found an innocent boy. There were still bystanders scurrying everywhere in the street, and she had to fight not to temper her instinct by not taking a shot when the first opening allowed. Confidence had never been an issue for her, not since she was a girl. But today, for the first time, she felt suddenly hesitant about firing, afraid of downing another innocent.

Caitlin figured maybe a minute at most had passed since the shooting had started with the spray that peppered Opie's window, but it felt like an hour. Times like these, her granddad had told her, were when the gunfight stopped and all-out war began. And she had to be ready to fight it on those terms. Think too much and she was dead; it was as simple as that.

With Tepper's fire at least slowing the gunmen's advance, Caitlin pushed herself prone and angled her

SIG in the small space between the mailbox's bottom and the sidewalk. She propped the tip upward on the other side, believing the armor suit to be weakest over the throat. If she got lucky, one of her hollow points might carve a path straight through it, leaving only the one gunman to contend with.

The shot was difficult, impossible almost, as she had to peek around the outside of the box to aim, her appearance greeted by a fresh barrage before Tepper's final bullets bought her a few extra moments. The street had gone briefly quiet, devoid even of screams when she fired five shots, glimpsing the nearer gunman twist in the direction a clean hit would have taken him.

But the brief sense of elation fled her when no blood spray accompanied the impact and she knew her latest shots had been mere distractions as her others had been.

"Damn!" she said out loud.

Both her dad and granddad had survived scrapes just as bad as this, except for the fact that nothing they, or she, had ever come up against before compared to the firepower and murderous intent these shooters displayed. They were professional hitters bred of military training, not run-of-the-mill cowboys like the friends Jalbert Thoms had brought along with him to the Red Stripe bar the night before. Caitlin had just decided upon an all-out frontal charge as her only remaining move, the suicidal nature of it not withstanding, when the explosive roar of an engine claimed the street.

Cort Wesley didn't say a word to his oldest son, too many thoughts cascading through his mind to manage the effort. Those thoughts came in splotches like still photographs passing before his eyes, all in a heart-beat's time.

The other two gunmen were advancing toward Caitlin.

He couldn't take them out with the bullets he had left.

He had no other weapon to go at them with.

Except he did.

Cort Wesley was on his feet in the midst of that final thought, surging toward the Expedition and hurdling inside through the open door with the man he'd shot in the face still attached to the mirror. The engine was already on, the vehicle shot to hell and smelling of grease and gasoline over the fresh leather interior. Cort Wesley hit the gas and jammed the Expedition into reverse in the same moment, following the rest of what transpired through the backup camera on a five-by-seven-inch screen high on the dashboard.

He saw the remaining two gunmen grow in shape.

He heard the clatter of the dead man dragging along the vehicle's side.

He watched one of the gunmen swinging as the Expedition surged over the central island and burst upon him.

He saw that gunman open up with a barrage drowned out by the roar of the engine.

He saw both gunmen swallowed up by the Expedition's charge, one heavy thump followed almost immediately by another.

His mind registered the two men clinging side by side to the Expedition's rear and kept the vehicle right on going toward the heavy wood frame structure at the entrance to Opie's Barbecue.

Impact against the building barely slowed the

Expedition at all, Cort Wesley with his foot pressed all the way down by that time, mashing the final two gunmen against the wall. He heard a crunching sound, followed by a squishing accompanied by a sensation not unlike stepping on a marshmallow, except he felt it from the driver's seat. The engine belched smoke and the stench of burned and seared tire rubber flooded the cab. He was aware of nothing else in the next moment, other than the absence of sound, which meant the absence of gunshots, and lunged from the vehicle past the dragged body to find Caitlin charging toward him with pistol raised.

Cort Wesley's gaze turned to the Expedition's rear, whatever was left of the two gunmen he'd plowed into pressed between the frame and the wood splintered at Opie's entrance. He reached in through the open door and switched off the vehicle's engine, Caitlin already at its rear with gun poised just in case.

"Man oh man," D. W. Tepper said, emerging stiff-legged from inside and shaking his head at the sight before bringing his eyes to rest on Cort Wesley. "Glad you made it, Mr. Masters."

71

SAN ANTONIO, THE PRESENT

Guillermo Paz stood outside the Islamic Center of San Antonio, gazing up at the lime-colored dome centered atop the flat roof of the one-story building he'd learned was also known as a *masjed*. The building was dwarfed in size and scope by a nearly completed replacement structure being erected further back that was more than three times its size. The new building looked to be formed of ridged white limestone and was bracketed in the front by a series of spiraling pillars.

Paz spotted a man in robes and skullcap kneeling on a prayer rug in a shadow cast by the limestone of the new *masjed*. He approached, his boots gliding silently across the grass as it gave way to rough gravel and stone. He stood back from the man he recognized as the head imam from a picture outside, ignored until the man noticed a second shadow fall over him.

"Oh," the imam said, after turning to find Paz's massive shape looming over him.

"Don't get up on my account, padre, please," Paz said.

But the imam rose anyway, dwarfed as much by Paz's shadow as he had been by that of the sprawling new structure.

"Hey, what should I call you? Padre doesn't seem to cut it."

"Imam will do. You can even call me Faisal."

"Faisal?"

"It's my first name," the imam smiled.

"You mind if I stick with padre?"

"That would be fine. You're Spanish then?"

"Venezuelan by birth, but my ancestors were Mayan warriors. Something I think you can relate to."

The imam cocked his head to the side, as if to look at Paz differently. His embroidered cap captured a thick mane of hair and his complexion was ruddy and marred by acne scars.

"I don't think I understand."

"Do Muslims believe in confession, padre?"

"Allah is so merciful that when someone commits a sin and asks for forgiveness He forgives. Should the person again repeat the same act and ask for forgiveness, He forgives until seventy times pass."

"What happens after seventy? Bad joke, I'm sorry. See, I've spent a lot of time confessing my sins these past few years. It's helped me reconcile who I am in the context of the world around me."

"That is the best one can hope to achieve through religion."

"I'm not really religious. But I've committed so many sins, my confessions were long overdue. What I've learned is that it comes down to context. That sinning isn't always a matter of right and wrong necessarily."

The imam regarded Paz suspiciously, his eyes darting one way and then the other perhaps in the hope someone else would approach. "And why do you come to me with this?"

"Because I want to understand."

"Understand what?"

"How your people can do the things they do, the jihadist wing I'm talking about. See, padre, there was a time when I was guilty of the very same kind of acts in service to my government and president. Now, in looking back at those years, I hate myself for what I did and my whole life ever since has been about that forgiveness I just asked you about."

The imam stiffened, defiance replacing fear and reservation in his expression. "So it's not help for yourself that you've come here seeking, is it?"

"I guess not."

"Because we are a peaceful people. These others you speak of, these jihadists, make up a very small percentage indeed. They act the way they do because they feel they have no other choice, that God has not given them one."

"You blaming God, padre?"

"Not me, them. Isn't that what you want, an explanation?"

Paz took a step closer to him, enough to make the imam shrink back his shoulders, flinching. "Some of your brothers—I'm sorry, *jihadists*—are planning something right here in Texas, something that's going to get a lot of people killed. People they don't know, who've done no harm to them. I had to leave my own country after I refused to murder the people of a village who'd accepted help from a foreign reformer to win hearts and minds. That made him a much bigger threat than commandos and Special Ops teams. But these jihadists don't care about hearts and minds. They prey on fear and seek to spread it like a plague."

The imam squeezed his eyes closed, his lips moving as if he were having a silent conversation with someone else. When he opened his eyes again, they were wide with hope, welcoming and respectful in their gaze.

"Tell me," he said to Paz, "have you ever read the Arab philosopher Edward Said? He wrote that 'So far as the United States seems to be concerned, it is only a slight overstatement to say that Muslims and Arabs are essentially seen as either oil suppliers or potential terrorists. Very little of the detail, the human density, the passion of Arab-Muslim life has entered the awareness of even those people whose profession it is to report the Arab world. What we have instead is a series of crude, essentialized caricatures of the Islamic world.'"

"Orientalism," Paz nodded, elaborating on the quote.

"I'm truly impressed. So do you believe that Said's words hold validity?"

"They don't justify violence against innocents, padre. They don't justify the war that's coming."

"Nor do they condone it. They only seek to explain it. And until we understand the cause, we can do nothing about the effects." The imam waited for Paz to respond, resuming when he didn't. "I'm sorry I couldn't satisfy your curiosity or supply the answers you seek."

"But you did. I came here hoping there was another way and you've given me no reason to believe there is. What you've justified is the purpose behind the presence of people like me in the world. I think the whole reason for me visiting confessionals was to find the answer to that question, and you're the first to actually supply it. Because this elusive cause you speak of is *un pedazo de mierda*."

The imam regarded Paz questioningly.

"A load of shit, padre, pardon my English, because if we figure out one cause, the people who murder innocent people to suit their ends will just find another. It was that way with the drug dealers I killed in Mexico and the so-called patriots I killed in a compound in Texas. And as for these people of yours who are plotting this Texas thing, I'm going to kill them too. So thank you for clarifying things for me."

While the imam stood there speechless in the setting sun, Paz's phone beeped with an incoming text message and he excused himself to check it.

"Sorry, padre, we'll have to finish this another time," he said, squeezing the phone so hard the plastic case actually cracked at the top and bottom of the frame. "Looks like that war I was telling you about got started early."

MARBLE FALLS, THE PRESENT

"Well," said Captain Tepper inside Opie's Barbecue, which had become the de facto command center for the investigation that would soon include every three-letter organization out of Washington, "only thing we know about the four shooters for sure is that none of them were Jalbert Thoms."

"He might as well have been number five," Cort Wesley told him. "Prison guard friend of mine who knew Thoms inside The Walls claimed he was tight with a mercenary group called Rubicon X-Ultra. This thing's got their stamp all over it."

"Well, that's something anyway."

Caitlin shook her head slowly. "I doubt it, sir, since we'll never find anything linking Thoms to X-Ultra. Hell, there's probably nothing that's going to link those four bodies to X-Ultra in the first place. Their fingerprints will likely lead us to empty folders or files we're not allowed to see."

"We've got DPS, ATF, and FBI converging on Marble Falls like Sherman's army on Atlanta. Maybe they can see what we can't."

Cort Wesley read the response to a text message he'd sent a few moments before. "Paz is on his way."

"Oh," Tepper scowled, "that makes me feel a whole lot better."

"Jones too, for sure," Caitlin added.

"Not quite," a voice said from the doorway. "He's already here."

MARBLE FALLS, THE PRESENT

"Rubicon X-Ultra?" Jones repeated.

"You claim you've never heard of them, I'll shoot you right here," Caitlin told him.

He scoffed at her remark. "Sure, I've heard of them, but I've never used them. Those psychos make Blackwater look like choirboys, typical of the whole private army cottage industry that's sprouted up. All of a sudden, the shit I wipe off my shoes gets drummed out of the military and straight into six-figure employment. The crazier, the better, and plenty in Homeland feared just this kind of profile would end up being retained by the likes of the Patriot Sun. Remember them, Ranger? That's exactly why I sent you in there."

"My recollection on the subject's a bit different, Jones."

"Sure," he smirked, stopping just short of a wink, "whatever you say."

"If the two of you are done rehashing the past," D. W. Tepper interrupted, "I'd like us to focus on the present. I just heard from Doc Whatley at the Medical Examiner's Office. Says he may have uncovered something that could crack this terrorist thing wide open. Says he needs another day or so to be sure, which gives us that long to figure out what to do about four stone killers dressed up like Robocops shooting up Texas streets. That was aimed at you, Mr. Jones," he added after a pause.

"This X-Ultra thing's no lead, if that's what you're thinking," Jones told him, gazing sidelong at Caitlin as he spoke. "There won't be anything connecting your gunmen to them and even if there was, they don't have an office, a Website, anything to publicly advertise or even acknowledge their existence."

"Sounds like a peculiar way of doing business, Mr. Jones."

"Not so much in the circles I move in, Captain. If you have a need for the services they provide, chances are you've heard of them through back channels or know somebody who has."

"You're wrong about one thing, Jones," Caitlin told him. "We've got a connection to these X-Ultra boys in the person of Jalbert Thoms."

"Just itching for another go at him, aren't you, Ranger?" Tepper asked her.

"He's just a small part of this, Captain. It's his boss I'm after, and if you want to tell me I'm off base or out of line or trigger happy or a menace to society, feel free."

Tepper nodded to himself, his narrowed expression seeming to push his eyes even further back in his head. "Have at it."

"Did I just hear you right?"

"Ranger, I believe we are in the eye of the hurricane here right now, and we'd best deal with it before the storm hits us head-on."

74

MARBLE FALLS, THE PRESENT

"We need to talk about this gun thing," Cort Wesley told Dylan, stammering through the words the whole way in a back corner of Opie's.

Cort Wesley expected any number of responses from his seventeen-year-old son, none of them including the slight smile he managed. "That the best you can do?"

"I missed your last birthday."

"Huh?"

"It just occurred to me that after missing the first fourteen, I promised I'd never miss another. I apologize for breaking that promise."

"It's not, like, you could help it. You were in that prison 'cause of me, 'cause of what you did to the asshole who ran down my girlfriend."

"That doesn't make it any easier for me. Worst thing is I didn't even know I'd missed it. Inside that prison dates have a way of slipping away from you. All the days are the same."

"How'd you survive exactly?" Dylan asked, while his younger brother remained fixed by the shattered window watching the night fall over the chaotic scene beyond.

"I had to hurt people," Cort Wesley said, quickly correcting himself. "No, not the way you think, son. Bare-knuckle fights staged in makeshift rings for the viewing entertainment of all. I lose one and I'd be a dead man."

"So you never lost."

"Nope. Thinking about you, your brother, and Caitlin just wouldn't allow it." His eyes sought out his son's that were dark and brooding just like his mother's. "And I imagine that's the way it was for you tonight when you went for that gun."

Dylan pursed his lips, started to blow out some breath but stopped. "I wasn't really thinking that far. I knew the gun was there and I knew I had to get it. I don't even remember shooting, just missing."

"It saved my life all the same."

"You back for good?"

"I believe so."

Dylan suddenly looked very young. "So you're not sure."

"Caitlin and I got some business to finish."

" 'Cause of tonight . . ."

"There was something else even before then and it was that something else that got me sprung from jail."

"She tell you what we found on that oil rig?"

"She told me she caught you smoking a joint. You want to tell me that's not true?"

"I'm seventeen, Dad. You wanna tell me you hadn't done worse when you were that age?"

"We weren't talking about me and I don't even want to get into what qualifies as worse. You share the joint with your brother?"

"Fuck, no!"

"And how'd you feel if you caught him doing the same thing?"

"I'd knock him upside his—"

Dylan stopped, realizing he'd made his dad's point for him even before catching the look on Cort Wesley's

face. He sighed deeply and let his expression dissolve
into a frown.

"Believe we're done here for now, son."

The boy started his hand forward. "Dap me, Dad."

"Come again?"

"Dap me. It's like, you know, shake."

Cort Wesley met his hand halfway with a resound-
ing slap.

"Daps," said Dylan. "One more thing," he added,
letting go of the grasp. "Who sent those men to kill
Caitlin tonight?"

"Can't say for sure," Cort Wesley told him, only half-
lying. "But they're gonna have a real bad time once we
catch them."

75

MARBLE FALLS, THE PRESENT

"Hold on a sec," Caitlin said, after spotting the black
truck flash its lights down Main Street, "got something I gotta take care of."

She left Cort Wesley and the boys halfway between
Opie's and Cort Wesley's rental car. It was after mid-
night, the clear night quickly darkening with storm
clouds. Heat lightning flashed in the sky with the por-
tent of an electrical storm that might or might not get
this far. The dead gunmen's machine gunning had
blown out the windows on both her SUV and Tepper's
truck, and she was more than happy to hitch a ride
with Cort Wesley and the boys back to San Antonio.

Both of them had been interrogated by the FBI, ATF, and Texas Department of Public Safety officials about their respective parts in the gunfight. They answered questions while Dylan and Luke watched Opie's big-screen bar television, always in sight to the point where Cort Wesley insisted on accompanying the boys to the men's room when necessary. The spray of bullets had left numerous bystanders wounded, mostly by flying glass, but miraculously only the four gunmen were dead. The officials' questions were repetitive and perfunctory, and they remained especially suspicious of Cort Wesley's presence until Jones pulled the agents aside and made some facts plain to them on behalf of Homeland Security.

Another silent burst of heat lightning blazed the sky to the west, illuminating the face of Guillermo Paz seated in the big truck's driver's seat. He was breathing hard and squeezing the wheel yet harder. He looked even more mountainous than usual, wearing a long-sleeve shirt that rode his arms tight enough for Caitlin to see the tight bands of muscle coiling on his forearms through the sleeves.

"I see the circus has come to town, Ranger," he greeted, gaze drifting down the street

"You shouldn't be here, Colonel. You're still a wanted man in Texas."

Paz let his gaze drift down the street again. Another flash of lightning pierced the sky, making his eyes look like twin flashbulbs. "Looks like the circus has other things on their mind tonight."

"There's nothing new on the terrorists."

"There will be, Ranger, and very soon. I saw it in a dream, the same way I saw this."

"This or what came before?"

"There were four men, gunmen, yes? In the dream I couldn't see their faces and they all looked the same, and bullets were bouncing off their skin."

Caitlin could only shake her head. "You really do amaze me, Colonel."

"Who were they?"

"It doesn't matter right now."

"You don't believe that any more than I do."

Caitlin moved closer to the window. "This isn't your fight."

Paz looked away, toward nothing in particular this time. "You saved my life, Ranger."

"I seem to recall it being the other way around, Colonel."

"You know what I mean, so I'll ask you not to tell me this isn't my fight."

Caitlin nodded. "Paramilitary group that calls itself Rubicon X-Ultra. I believe they were hired by a man I'm chasing down on another investigation. They're the ultimate ghosts. No address, no Website, strictly referral, friend-of-a-friend crap. Nobody has any idea how to find them, even Jones."

"I do," Paz said simply, turning back toward her.

76

Caitlin and Cort Wesley sat side by side again on the porch swing, both Dylan and Luke sleeping inside or at least trying to.

"Captain Tepper approved use of the Ranger plane for us tomorrow," Caitlin said, sipping from a mug of steaming coffee even though humidity held the night in its grasp as tightly as the day.

"So long as there's room for the boys on it."

"Plenty."

"Guess they'll be safer in the air than on the ground here."

"They'll be safer *anywhere* than on the ground here."

"Glad we're of the same mind on that, Ranger."

"When are we not, Cort Wesley?"

He looked at her face framed by the light mist rising from her black coffee. "There it is again."

"What?"

"The look you get whenever it comes down to guns."

"Mine didn't do us much good tonight."

Cort Wesley looked away, far into the night. "I almost wish I hadn't put that backup Glock in the glove compartment."

"So Dylan wouldn't have been able to use it."

"That's what I was thinking."

"And you'd likely be dead," Caitlin said. "Me too."

Cort Wesley looked back at her, his eyes full and sad. "We dragged both of them into our shit tonight,

Ranger, and I only wish it could be just as easy to drag them out. Dylan especially. Know what my biggest hope for him's been these past three years? That he keeps his gunplay to cardboard cutouts and never fires at a man. Guess I need to come up with a better wish."

"How about that he stays on just the track he's on: compassionate, smart, kind, and brave as hell."

"Don't forget hot, Ranger, or haven't you noticed how all the girls look at him."

"That fatherly pride talking?"

"Maybe a bit of jealousy."

"How do you think I look at you?" Caitlin slid away from him, nearly spilling her coffee in the process. A stiff breeze blew up, rattling the wind chimes Luke had hung from the porch eaves. "The truth is I got myself this coffee and was coming out here to tell you that I want to stay. The two of us together, under the same roof. No more disappearing or ranging to parts unknown."

"A happy couple."

"Well, not sure if I'd go that far, but I'm starting to think desk duty suits me just fine."

"No," Cort Wesley said simply.

"No what?"

"No, I don't want you moving in, because that's not who you are. *This* isn't who you are. You like coming around when the time suits you because it helps temper that gun of yours and remind you of why you do what you do. But you dial it down all the time that way and you'll hate yourself in the process because it's just not who you are."

"My granddad managed okay."

"He was eighty years old."

"Seventy-nine."

Cort Wesley started to speak, then stopped and grinned instead. "We're quite a pair, aren't we?"

"Amazing those boys in there are turning out as good as they are. Maybe we're not as bad at this parenting stuff as we think."

"You just made my point for me."

"What's that?"

"Figure it out," Cort Wesley said, easing himself closer to her on the swing, as he extended his hand. "Daps, Ranger."

PART EIGHT

"The versatility of the Texas Rangers is reflected in the diversity of the assignments in which they have engaged," the DPS reported to the legislature. "Running the gamut from cattle rustling and burglary to the investigation of bank robberies, they have encompassed the field of law enforcement in establishing and manning road-blocks, engaging in man hunts, seeking escaped prisoners, diving for drowning victims, searching for missing persons and lost children, and rendering reports on parole violators." Rangers also assisted the legislature's Crime Investigation Committee "in that body's successful efforts to ferret out crime interests within Texas."

Texas Department of Public Safety,
Department of Public Safety Biennial Report
Fiscal Years 1951–52, pp. 12–13
(As quoted from *Time of the Rangers* by Mike Cox)

77

"Look at the world, my brother," Anwar al-Awlaki said, standing stiff and still at an observation window at the Tower of the Americas, his hands like claws against the glass. "Look at the world that is about to change at our hands."

Sam Harrabi tried to, but everything beyond looked blurred to him, as if someone had drawn a sheer curtain before his eyes.

Built originally for the 1968 World's Fair, the Tower of the Americas remained to this day one of San Antonio's prime tourist attractions, featuring a revolving restaurant and newly renovated banquet hall, along with a view of the entire city. On the clearest of mornings, like this one, the view seemed to stretch beyond the horizon, and al-Awlaki imagined he could see the rest of a state that would soon be ravaged by his plans. And that was only the beginning. No part of the United States would remain unaffected, life in his cursed homeland changed irrevocably forever.

"You never considered your Arab heritage much while growing up, did you, my brother?"

"No, *sayyid*, I suppose I didn't."

"Quite the opposite, I'm told. You were more prone

to extol the virtues of America. You even wrote an award-winning essay on the subject."

"You read it?"

Al-Awlaki nodded. "Along with your high school graduation speech. Very impressive, but, as I'm sure you'll agree now, very wrong. You were laying the very foundation for the split from your people in favor of a country that ultimately betrayed you."

"I am grateful for the chance to avenge that betrayal, to grasp the heritage I had forsaken."

"You are fortunate God does not hold grudges, my brother. He brought me to you in the wake of the tragedy that has come to define you. The world truly works in mysterious ways. You and all your expertise were delivered on to me. As Allah wills, yes?"

"Indeed."

"And now we are about to bequeath on America what the Koran itself called a thousand years of pain."

Before al-Awlaki could continue a bird swerved at the last moment and hit the glass.

"You know what it is like to lose your way. But we cannot afford to lose *our* way now, my brother," he said, as feathers fluttered through the air seven hundred fifty feet up. "The price we pay for that is too great."

78

"Thanks for seeing me, Professor," Caitlin said, entering the apartment to the blast freeze of an air conditioner cranking out frigid air nonstop. She felt goose bumps prickle her flesh, even as her eyes glanced around at the various academic memorabilia displayed on shelves and hung on just about every wall.

Al Dahlberg, the University of Texas at Austin history professor interviewed by Jim Strong thirty years before, clearly retained his passion for his school. Just over eighty years old now, his studio apartment was situated in an assisted-living center specifically because it offered a view of the edge of the campus, including the infamous tower where a sniper gunned down sixteen people and wounded thirty-two more in 1966.

Captain Tepper had managed to wangle the lone Texas Ranger airplane, a twin engine Cessna, to transport Caitlin, Cort Wesley, and the boys to Austin. Cort Wesley adamantly refused to let her make the journey alone and, just as adamantly, insisted that after last night his sons not be let out of his sight unless he was sure they were safe. He took them to explore the campus while Caitlin spoke with Professor Dahlberg, who looked pretty much exactly as she had pictured him in the tale from 1979, albeit with thicker glasses and grayer, thinner hair.

"As I said on the phone, sir," Caitlin began, while Dahlberg closed the door behind her, "I believe my dad interviewed you way back in '79 about the murder of those fraternity boys on Galveston Island."

"I remember the incident well, Ranger. Terrible tragedy."

"And your talk with my father?"

The old man frowned. "Not as well, I'm afraid, the mind not being as sharp as it once was."

"I understand, sir."

"I've made tea. Would you like some?"

Caitlin told him she did, if nothing else to relieve the chill the cranked-up air conditioner was pushing through her bones. They sat at a table just beyond the galley kitchen in full view of an older, non-widescreen television.

"You gave my father a lot of information on Jean Lafitte and Jim Bowie, the two of them running slaves from the Campeche colony on Galveston and—"

"The *Mother Mary*!" Dahlberg interrupted excitedly. "Of course! I remember now. Jim Strong . . . That would make you *Caitlin* Strong. Of course! I've read all about you."

"Don't believe everything you read, sir."

"I'm a historian, Ranger. I understand the limits of words in recording deeds."

Caitlin watched Dahlberg pour brewed tea from a pot. It was dark and smelled strong. She added sugar and sipped from the steaming cup.

"I buy the Indian variety direct from an importer. It's the best I've ever tasted."

Dahlberg filled his own cup, both his hand and aim steady. Caitlin could tell by the way he held his eyes and moved them that his mind remained sharp and vital, perhaps even more so than he was letting on.

"The *Mother Mary*," he repeated, sitting back down and offering Caitlin a cookie from a plate laden with multiple varieties.

"You were kind enough to tell my father everything you knew about its legend; from the stranger on board, to the unidentified language spoken by the slaves the ship was carrying, to the appearance of Lafitte and Bowie on deck."

"And don't forget their theft of whatever that stranger had hidden on his person."

"I haven't, Professor. In fact, that's why I'm here."

Dahlberg bit into a cookie and sipped his tea, his eyes urging her on.

"I don't think you were entirely truthful with my father. Or, more accurately, you chose not to tell him all the truth."

Dahlberg showed no reaction. "An interesting conclusion, even for a Texas Ranger as celebrated as you."

"And I wouldn't insinuate such a thing if the whole truth wasn't vital to an investigation I'm currently involved in that may be connected to more murders, even more than happened from that tower you can see from your window there."

Dahlberg smiled slightly, the gesture looking sad and reflective. "Well, I'm past the time of being able to do anything about it anyway."

"About what, sir?"

"Jean Lafitte's lost treasure. When your father came to me, I was still entertaining the notion of tracking it down myself."

"And toward that end you left out certain parts of the story you'd figured out on your own."

Dahlberg tapped the table with both hands.

"Remarkable conclusion, Ranger. If you were my student, I'd give you an A."

"That language those slaves spoke, sir. I believe you knew it was likely Portuguese since this was right around the time the best of the slave traders figured out Brazil made for easy pickings with a lot less sail time to boot. So the way I figure it the *Mother Mary* picked up this Quentin Cusp, or whoever he really was, around the same time the ship picked up the slaves Lafitte and Bowie later stole."

Dahlberg smiled longer this time. "In point of fact, I believe Cusp had booked passage on the ship to take him to the United States. An unusual business had brought him to Brazil and he was returning to the United States in the hopes of expanding it considerably based on the samples he was hiding in a pouch on his person."

"Samples, sir?"

"That would become Jean Lafitte's lost treasure, Ranger: diamonds."

"Almost everyone believes large-scale diamond mining didn't begin until 1858 in South Africa," Dahlberg continued, almost dreamily, as Caitlin's teacup rattled back onto its saucer, "but nothing could be further from the truth. Diamonds were discovered by alluvial gold miners in Brazil in 1725, right about the time that Indian diamond sources were near exhaustion and European demand for the stones remained insatiable. Cusp was actually an employee of the Hearst family and, yes, the Hearsts were already involved in such endeavors as early as 1820 and before. They saw an opportunity to open the American market for diamonds on the European model and the contents of the pouch Cusp carried on his person were to be the means to begin that process."

"Until Lafitte and Bowie made off with them."

"Bowie traded in at least a portion of his, explaining his sudden purchase of huge tracts of land in Texas. But Lafitte died in a battle at sea in 1823, his share of the treasure lost forever."

"What if it's not?"

Dahlberg nearly spilled his tea. "Pardon me?"

"The fraternity president told my granddad about a Cajun, a kind of caretaker of the map that led to the lost treasure. Man named Beaudoin Chansoir. You've heard of him, haven't you, sir?"

Dahlberg nodded, almost reluctantly as if clinging to the last of his secrets. "His great-great-grandfather was a slave whose cooking skills led him to actually join Lafitte's pirate outfit, which he remained a part of until Lafitte burned the Campeche colony and sailed south in 1821, on the hunt for more diamonds many believe."

"You're saying he knew where the treasure, the diamonds, were hidden."

"And passed the information down through the generations. But this Chansoir and all that followed believed the treasure to be cursed, blaming it for Lafitte's death. So they resolved never to pursue it themselves and left it to others to scavenge the bayou for it."

"Except Lafitte didn't bury it in the bayou, Professor. He buried it on Galveston Island."

"No," Dahlberg stammered, "that's simply not the case. He abandoned his Campeche camp and burned it to the ground, just like I said."

"That's right, maybe to ensure no one would ever come looking for his treasure. Lafitte figured he'd be coming back and what better way to assure the diamonds would be waiting when he did? Beaudoin Chansoir wasn't about to give the true location up to anyone he didn't want to have it."

Dahlberg looked as if the very life had bled out of his face. "Those students killed on Galveston Island . . . are you saying they actually *found* the treasure, is that what you're saying?"

"No, sir, I don't believe so. But I do believe they got there around the same time somebody else may have."

Dahlberg's eyes widened, his lower lip trembling within an expression trapped suddenly in disappointment and dismay. "But how can you ever be sure when there's no one left alive who can tell you?"

"Actually, Professor, I believe there is."

"You can keep the shotgun seat," Caitlin told Dylan, as he started to climb out of the rental car they'd picked up at the airport.

"I'm a gentleman, Caitlin," he smiled, climbing into the back to sit next to his brother. "You should know that."

"I do indeed," she said, stepping into the car off the curb outside the assisted-living center where Cort Wesley had picked her up.

"So?" he asked

"Pretty much just the way I figured, only better."

"What now?"

Caitlin reread a text message she'd just received from D. W. Tepper. "Captain says we're supposed to meet up at the Medical Examiner's Office at seven o'clock this evening. Gives us plenty of time to make another stop on the way home." Caitlin pocketed her phone and cocked her gaze toward the backseat. "You boys ever been to the Louisiana bayou?"

79

HOUSTON, THE PRESENT

Guillermo Paz swung round in the desk chair when the office door opened; the man who entered was so drenched in the rays of the late-morning sun streaming through the glass that he had to squint and raise an arm to shield his eyes.

"Been a long time, Colonel," the man greeted, coming up just short of a smile.

"That it has, Payne." Paz continued to regard him casually. "You know, I never asked you what your first name was."

"That is my first name. The last is Battles."

"Payne Battles? That's a joke, right?"

Payne Battles wasn't laughing. "I notice my receptionist wasn't at her desk."

"Must be on break."

"Along with the two guards who weren't at the door?"

"What can I say, Mr. Battles? Good help, it's hard to find these days. Rest of your staff won't be interrupting us either. They're kind of indisposed too."

Battles glanced back toward the door and then, just as quickly, abandoned any thought about the possible flight it offered. "Is this business?"

"As in Venezuela's national interests?" Paz shook his head. "I don't share those anymore."

"So I heard."

"Of course you did. When I refused to kill all those villagers three years ago the assignment fell to X-Ultra, didn't it?"

Battles smirked, ever so slightly. "We do good work, Colonel. You know that better than anyone."

Paz rose, the chair rocking back and forth from the force of his bulk. "Done any in these parts lately?"

"Domestic? Not in our job description yet, but we're reconsidering based on the needs of local police forces with their numbers so depleted by budget cuts."

"You gonna cut them a break, Payne, maybe give them a reduced rate for machine-gunning parking violators and speeders?"

Battles started forward, further into the spill of the sun, refusing to shield his eyes any longer. "How'd you get in here exactly?"

"You mean because none of the building elevators stop on this floor. What number is it exactly?"

"If you're looking for work," Battles started, trying to sound like he was in charge.

"No, I've got plenty of work, more than I can handle."

Battles smirked, angling himself to move the sun from his eyes. "I've heard rumors about some of it. The drug cartels in Juárez for one. That what happens when somebody gets on your bad side?"

"You're about to find out."

"CIA developed this," Paz said, holding a vial up for Payne Battles to see from the desk chair to which he was now duct taped. "Liquid explosives. Kind of like a stable form of nitroglycerin. But here's the catch, Payne: it's meant to work *internally*. Heat sensitive to 98.6 degrees. Guess you can figure why," he said, circling around to the rear of the chair. "Back in Venezuela, before my transition, I tried it on victims through injection, drink, and dart. I prefer drink."

With that, Paz jerked Battles's head back, flicked off the top of the vial, and jammed it down the man's throat. Battles gagged and retched, but couldn't keep from swallowing the vial's thick and salty contents.

"You got about five minutes before it heats up. Don't worry, Payne, you won't be going alone. Your associates in the other offices here on the floor will be keeping you company."

Battles was still coughing, spittle and phlegm dripping from his mouth with portions congealing in both corners. His face wrinkled from the liquid's awful taste and he shuddered from the oozy sensation of it crawling its way down toward his stomach, a thin coating left in its wake.

"It hits those juices in the gut, the temperature starts rising," Paz told him. "You made a big mistake in Marble Falls last night. Your men went after someone important to me."

As if on cue, four explosions sounded in rapid succession, shaking the walls and rattling the windows like the percussion of a thunder strike. Paz thought he felt the glass at his back actually buckle a bit. Two more blasts followed almost immediately.

"See, Payne, just like I told you," Paz said, starting toward the door.

Battles's face had turned a dark shade of red, his

cheeks starting to purple as he struggled for breath, mouthing words without sound.

"You happen to meet God, Payne," Paz told him from the door, "give him my best."

80

SAN ANTONIO, THE PRESENT

Captain Tepper was smoking a Marlboro and making a show of checking his watch when Dylan and Luke beat Caitlin and Cort Wesley in a race to the front door of the building housing the Bexar County Medical Examiner's Office. "You boys get on inside, so I can shoot the adults here," he said.

Luke and Dylan slid past him, Luke turning back when they reached the door. "You shouldn't smoke, Captain."

"On second thought, why don't you stay out here so I can shoot you too." The boys disappeared inside and Tepper's eyes fixed on Caitlin. "Why do I get the feeling Hurricane Caitlin has reached category fifteen proportions?"

"Sorry we're late, Captain."

"Oh, I don't mind. It's the U.S. government and the state of Texas that mind. In case you forgot, we're facing a bit of a crisis, a crisis Doc Whatley says could be a whole lot worse than we ever imagined."

"He say why?"

Tepper stamped his cigarette out under his boot heel. "No, Ranger, he wanted to wait for you to get back from Louisiana. Find what you were looking for there?"

"I'll explain everything later."

"Except some trouble in Houston reported earlier today."

"Trouble?"

"Bunch of investment bankers got blown up by experimental liquid explosives somebody made them swallow."

"Market have a bad day?"

"You think this is funny?" Tepper said, leading the way down the hall now.

"I thought you were kidding."

"Nope. And I'm not kidding either about the fact that your friend Jones later informed me they weren't investment bankers at all. That was just a front for that Rubicon X-Ultra paramilitary outfit we went up against last night. Guess nobody'll be coming up against them again." Tepper stopped to settle his breathing. "You see your friend Paz, you tell him . . ."

"Tell him what, Captain?"

But instead of responding, Tepper circled his lips and blew out some breath in a half whistle. "Hear that, Ranger? Wind's picking up again."

"You may be looking at the first man in history to die three times," medical examiner Frank Dean Whatley told the assembled crowd over the corpse of the man who'd taken the identity of Alejandro Pena.

His body was laid out, covered by a sheet up to the neck, on a steel table in Whatley's lab just as it had been on Caitlin's last visit.

"Will somebody tell this man I'm not in the mood for riddles right now," said Jones.

Whatley smirked, his puckered cheeks bulging like balloons filling with air. "Then try this: I couldn't get some of those earlier symptoms I mentioned to the Ranger here out of my head, so I ran some additional tests on our friend here. And what I found, well, let me explain."

Whatley eased the sheet back, revealing a careful stitch job down the center of the dead man's abdomen, as good as anything a surgeon might do on a patient.

"Three things I want to point out to you," Whatley continued, directing their attention to that scar. "Now, I already reported that my initial exam revealed significant trauma to the inner wall of the abdomen consistent with chronic nausea and vomiting. Next thing I need to tell you is that this man's blood counts were remarkably low, indicating a truly pervasive infection. The white cells were particularly affected by the fact he also suffered from anemia and there's evidence of persistent bleeding, of his gums for example, due to low platelet counts."

As he spoke, Whatley ran a thick finger up and around the exterior of the corpse's abdominal wall, illustrating and enunciating each of his respective points. Then he lifted one of the corpse's arms that looked more like a doll's than a man's.

"Finally, I'd like you to take a look at his skin. You can see signs of intense reddening, blistering, and ulceration that is also present on his other arm, both legs, and scalp."

"I think I noticed it on his torso too," Caitlin noted.

"Very observant, Ranger," Whatley complimented,

twisting the arm around so Caitlin could view the other side. "So tell me what you make of this."

Caitlin studied an assortment of blotchy bumps and nodules. "Looks like a real bad case of acne or hives maybe."

"Specifically caused by damaged sebaceous or sweat glands. And what about this?" the medical examiner queried, directing her attention to a patchwork of skin that looked scraped raw.

"That's easy," Caitlin said, almost smiling. "I remember it from the days of traipsing through the woods to shoot with my granddad and coming home infested with poison ivy. That's what my skin looked like until the calamine lotion kicked in."

"Very good."

"You want to tell us what all this adds up to, Doc?" requested Tepper.

"Theoretically?"

Tepper started shaking his head. "Why can't anybody give me a straight answer anymore?"

Whatley eased the corpse's arm back down to the slab. "Well, the anecdotal data's pretty reliable on this particular subject, although this is the first time I've actually seen a case of it. Then again it's not what killed this man, but it would have eventually and before too much longer. I checked the case studies, almost all of which come from post–World War Two Japan and Russia in the late 1980s, and the findings are consistent."

"You keep me here guessing any longer, Doc," Tepper interrupted, "and I'm gonna put you on that slab myself."

Whatley covered the body back up. "This man was suffering from radiation poisoning, Captain."

81

"I don't believe his condition was due to prolonged exposure," Whatley continued, "like the kind exhibited occasionally by clumsy X-ray technicians or nuclear plant workers toiling in unsafe conditions mostly seen in foreign countries. It was much shorter term than that, but intense."

"How so?" Jones asked him.

"Well, a 'gray' or 'Gy' is a unit of radiation dose absorbed by matter. To gauge biological effects the dose is multiplied by a quality factor that is dependent on the type of ionizing radiation. Such measurement of biological effect is called 'dose equivalent' and is measured in 'sievert' or 'Sv.'"

"Doc, I know you're enjoying yourself here, but you have utterly lost me," said Tepper.

"Then let me put it this way. To exhibit the range and severity of the symptoms experienced by Alejandro Pena, or whoever he is, we're talking about an exposure level of twenty sieverts over approximately a one-month period. That's about a million times the normal annual dose of radiation deemed safe for a human being, which is point-zero-zero-five. If it had been the radiation that had killed him, as it would have before too much longer, I'd pinpoint his cause of death as acute radiation syndrome, or ARS."

"Any ideas on how he got it?"

Whatley shook his head, his balloon cheeks deflating. "Sorry, Ranger, that's where I draw a blank."

"What about exposure to uranium?" Jones asked him.

"As in the construction of a nuclear bomb?"

"That's what I was thinking, yeah."

"Then banish the thought. Overexposure to elements like uranium, plutonium, or other radioactively toxic materials presents entirely differently from this. No, this is more consistent with a containment problem at a nuclear plant. I've done plenty of reading on the mess they had in Japan after the earthquake and tsunami, so I'm familiar with the effects."

"So maybe we're talking nuclear *waste* here instead," Caitlin posed, feeling like she'd just swallowed an ice cube.

"That would be my thought, Ranger, exactly."

Caitlin turned toward Tepper, running her eyes over Jones and Cort Wesley briefly on the way.

"Don't even say it, Ranger, don't even say it," Tepper charged, waving a thin, nicotine-stained finger at her.

Caitlin swung toward Jones. "How good's your database on American-born Muslims?"

"I don't think you want to know."

"Then you'll want to run a check on those with engineering or construction experience, someone with the kind of skills that could have convinced Teo Braga that he could handle the disposal of a whole lot of barrels of radioactive waste." She turned back to Tepper. "That's where Braga fits into this, Captain. Al-Awlaki's people figured out what he was up to and offered up their services. Simply stated. I imagine, given the dangers involved, that there weren't a lot of others waiting in line for the job."

Caitlin noticed Jones stiffening, his gaze avoiding hers.

"Something wrong, Jones?"

"You really need to ask me that?"

"I can tell when you got something else on your mind. Why don't you tell us all what it is?"

Jones met her gaze and held it as he walked out of the room.

"What's his problem?" Tepper wondered.

"I don't even know where to start to answer that. But I do think it's time I took another run at Teofilo Braga."

Tepper scratched at his scalp. "Well, you better have something more sure than this to stick in his face, Hurricane."

"I believe I do now, Captain," Caitlin said, holding her gaze on Cort Wesley. "I believe I do."

"Hold up a sec there!" Tepper called to her just as she and Cort Wesley reached the lobby doors, Dylan and Luke back in tow.

Caitlin stopped and Tepper caught up huffing, so winded he had to lay his hands on his knees to steady himself. "You all right, D.W.?"

He straightened back up. "I promised to tell you the rest of the story about what happened when your dad, granddad, and I got back from the bayou."

"I believe it can wait, under the circumstances."

"I'm not so sure about that anymore, Ranger."

82

"Well, that's bullshit if I ever did hear it!" said Earl Strong upon being given the news.

"It's the way things are done these days, Dad," Jim explained, trying to console him.

"Then the way things are done these days is crap. Texas Rangers don't yield ground to nobody. What do these federals expect me to do, go home and take a nap? Hell, they don't even want to know what we found down in the bayou."

"On account of the fact that they don't care," said D. W. Tepper. "I already told you, there were some Mexican laborers on the island at the time of the killings they can connect to a ritualistic killing cult south of the border."

"The federals actually interview any of these ritualistic killers?"

Tepper shook his head. "They disappeared afterwards. FBI is basing their suspicions on that one fact alone. They issued all kinds of bulletins, to what good I don't know since if they're back in Mexico we can't touch them, ritual killers or not."

"I normally shoot men who bring me news that bad, D.W."

"You wanna do that to the messenger, go ahead."

Then Earl's gaze softened just enough. "Nah, I enjoy your company too much and it's gonna be fun watching you puke your guts out again."

"Huh?"

"You, me, and Jim are going back to Galveston Island."

Sheriff Plantaine again accompanied them to the crime scene that looked pristine compared to only two days before. The crime scene tape was gone, along with the cones and sawhorses the locals had set in place, and rain had washed the ground clean of both blood and whatever stray evidence might have remained.

"Okay," Tepper, even more white-faced than on their last visit, said to Earl and Jim Strong, "thanks to both the bridge and causeway still being impassable, we're here. Now what?"

Jim used an old kerchief to mop his brow. "The old man and I got a theory."

"Old man?" Earl raised.

"Eighty would seem to qualify there."

" 'Cept I'm seventy-nine. I'll accept the label next year."

"Anyway, *Ranger Earl* and I got to thinking that the key here is the map that brought those boys this far."

"On account of the fact that Chansoir drew it by accident when he meant to draw the one that normally sent treasure hunters deep into the bayou where no treasure was waiting for them," Tepper concluded.

Earl spoke before Jim had a chance to resume. "Our point being that maybe these frat boys surprised the first party he drew the same map for. Maybe surprised them in the process of not just searching for the treasure, but after they'd actually found it."

Tepper tried to process what he was hearing. "Wait a sec, are you boys saying Lafitte's lost treasure is *real*?"

This time Jim spoke first. "We're saying it's a possibility that would provide clear reason to murder five innocent fraternity pledges who happened to be at the wrong place at the wrong time."

Tepper felt his stomach starting to dance again and settled himself with a few deep breaths. "Well, it makes more sense than Mexican laborers who happened to be part of a killing cult."

"Yeah," said Earl, "I did some checking on that."

Both Jim and D.W. waited for him to continue.

"Turns out," he resumed, "all of the contractors currently on the island can account for all their workers." He looked toward Sheriff Plantaine, whose mouth had dropped and was about to respond in protest. "Also turns out the four you were referring to were off the island with permission and returned last night. So take these murdering Mexicans out of the picture and what we got is whoever got to the island ahead of those frat boys, following the identical map."

"How 'bout we see for ourselves where it led them?" Jim suggested.

Sheriff Plantaine hung to the side, as the Rangers stepped back to better view the clearing where the five college students had been murdered. Without the bodies to disturb it, the land looked pristine and unspoiled again, smelling of fresh leaves and drying soil.

"Wasn't much of a clearing back in Lafitte's time, I'd imagine," Earl said.

"A hundred sixty years of storms have played holy hell with the trees in these parts, reduced the coastline dramatically too," Jim noted. "And that college professor told me Lafitte burned the colony before leaving to boot."

"Even if he hadn't," started Tepper, "oaks and cottonwoods like these living that long would be a stretch."

Earl's gaze emptied, as he pictured the boys trudging along to the guidance of Beaudoin Chansoir's map. "I think one of the map's prime landmarks was that big tree there, since all the victims were killed within a few feet of it." He thought of something and swung toward the sheriff. "They had a name for this part of the island in times past, didn't they?"

Plantaine nodded. "Hollow Cove, Hollow Ridge, Hollow Beach—something like that."

"Named for the fact that many of the big oaks had hollowed themselves out, little more than dead standing bark, going down as far as the thickest roots."

"Like an underground tunnel," Jim followed.

"Not a bad place to hide some treasure where nobody would ever think of looking," his father said to the three of them. "Lafitte must've figured he'd be gone maybe a couple years at most. Problem we got is that hollow tree, wherever it was, must be long gone."

"Maybe it was already gone even back then," said Tepper.

"Come again, D.W.?"

But Tepper had already started toward the big oak tree and laid his back against it. "Lafitte settled Campeche here 'cause of a creek on the left for water from where I'm standing and the thick brush on the right for protection. Now the tree we're likely looking for would have been about halfway between the two and favoring the north."

"Why's that?"

"Considerably less sun, which would account for the tree being hollow or just dead roots."

"Well, there's nothing here now but brush and trees no older than the three of us," Jim commented.

"Those frat boys were killed close together, weren't they?" Earl asked, fingering his chin.

"Seemed to be, based on where the bodies lay when we found them," Sheriff Plantaine told him. "And there were no blood trails indicating otherwise. Course the rain would've washed them away by now, but . . ."

"Bunched up like they were following the trail together, nothing to see before them and nothing that spooked them in a way that would've made them run off to create more distance between 'em."

"What's your point, Earl?" Tepper asked.

"That whoever killed them wasn't in plain view when they got here."

"Could have been hiding."

"I suppose they could, Jim, but I'm thinking they were out of sight. Underground maybe while close enough to pounce quick."

"Behind them," Plantaine muttered, too deferential to speak the words loud.

"What was that?" Earl asked him.

"I said maybe we got this wrong. Maybe they walked right over the spot where that old hollow tree stood and didn't even know they had company underground."

"Or," picked up Jim, "that company had just found the treasure and were worried these boys had come here to rob them."

Earl nodded. "I like that. The killers would never believe it was coincidence. They'd figured they were followed and on a pitch black night never would've recognized those fraternity boys for what they were until it was too late."

"What was it the ME said was used to rip their insides out?" Jim asked. "Some kind of garden hoe or spade, something like that, wasn't it?"

"So the killers expected the tree to be gone, knew it was the ground they had to clear to find what was left of where the roots dug deep."

The four men walked about, kicking and smoothing at the ground with their boots instead of garden tools, searching for a patch of land that had grown over the opening left when the big hollowed-out oak finally keeled over and died due in large part to the island's soft, sandy soil bed.

"Whoa," Sheriff Plantaine said suddenly, "got a depression of some kind over here."

The Rangers gathered around the patch of earth he'd just stepped back from and knelt almost in unison. They swiped the surface brush, gravel, stones, and twigs aside gently, like a prospector sifting for gold, to make sure they didn't miss any potential evidence. First, one bit of empty blackness was revealed beneath the product of their toils, then another. Before too long, they'd cleared a space approximately equal to a large tree stump that had finally given up its hold on living death in one of the many storms that had ravaged Galveston Island. Beneath it, roots had dried out and died, becoming part of the earth again, to reveal a hole in the ground that went three feet down and swept to the south like a tunnel.

"Direction of the creek bed," Jim Strong noted. "That's the way the roots would have grown." Then he watched his father lowering his head into the hole. "Whatcha think you're doing?"

"Just hand me a penlight. D.W., I know you always carry yours on you."

"Why?" Tepper asked, producing it.

" 'Cause I think I spotted something down here."

The object Earl had spotted was a flashlight, but he hadn't brought any gloves along with him and elected to leave it just where it lay a good five feet underground.

"How fast can you get a crime scene unit out here?" he asked Plantaine as soon as he popped back up.

"An hour from the time I make the call from my cruiser."

"Tell them to go over this hole with a comb, a brush, or whatever it takes to find any hair, fiber, blood samples, broken fingernails, shoe impressions, or bad breath." Earl looked toward Jim and D.W. "Whoever went down that hole likely stayed there awhile, 'til they found whatever it was they was looking for."

Plantaine took off his hat and scratched his brow. "You saying somebody honest to God found Jean Lafitte's lost treasure?"

Earl's expression was grim and deadpan. "They wouldn't have bothered killing five innocent boys if they hadn't have found something."

The old Company D headquarters in San Antonio was abuzz with the Rangers' return, word spreading quickly they'd brought back evidence that might be the key to finding the true killers of the five students from the University of Texas at Austin.

The company captain, a husky man with a huge barrel chest named Bertrand Ash, closed the door to his office behind him, ignoring the flashlight contained in an evidence pouch Earl Strong had laid on his desk.

"You boys have caused me a heap of trouble," he said, addressing the three of them with hands planted so tight on the sill of his desk that his fingers reddened with trapped blood flow.

Earl, Jim, and D.W. exchanged an uneasy glance.

"I don't think I heard you right, Captain," Earl said.

"Oh, yes you did, Ranger. Federals are looking at those missing Mexicans for the murders and nothing we say or do's gonna change a goddamn thing."

Jim Strong thrust a finger toward the flashlight. "I don't think that belongs to any of those Mexicans unless they were searching for Jean Lafitte's lost treasure."

"That's the last thing I wanna hear about goddamn lost treasure!"

"What's going on here, Captain?" Tepper asked him.

"Why don't you tell me, D.W., being that you're the only Ranger of the three of you who understands the political realities of certain situations."

"What the hell does that mean?" Earl asked him.

"Tell him, D.W."

"I'll leave it to you, Captain."

"That's an order, Ranger," Bertrand Ash followed with his eyes locked on Earl.

The men continued to hold stares while Tepper began, his stomach still queasy from the boat ride back to the mainland hours before. "Sheriff Plantaine said it best our first trip over and what we saw with our own eyes said it even better. Lots of money in Galveston, lots of people with big Texas names investing in its future prosperity as a future resort island with marinas, hotels, golf courses, fancy beachfront condominiums. I need to go on?"

"Please do," Ash said, finally dragging his eyes off Earl.

"Five fraternity boys get themselves murdered by anything but crazed Mexicans long gone from the area could, no, *would* put a serious damper on those big Texas names getting a proper return on their investment. Hell, *any* return." Here Tepper looked squarely at Captain Ash, the anger building in him starting to push the color back into his face. "So the governor gets wind of things and makes the call to turn the whole thing over to the federals, knowing that a phone call or two will keep the case buttoned up under his thumb, as opposed to leaving it with us. Have I said about all there is to say on the matter, Captain?"

Ash hadn't budged, his big chest expanding with each heavy breath. "Pretty much."

"Well, screw that to hell!" roared Earl Strong, showing a side of his temper he seldom revealed, even when going up against Al Capone's boys in Sweetwater or ambushed by Mexican gunmen in the desert or facing a drugger army in the famed Battle of Juárez.

"Watch your tongue, Ranger."

"Watch my tongue? What the hell's going on here? We're *Texas Rangers*. We never look away or stand aside for nobody, least of all the federals or friggin' politicians."

"We're not," Ash told him. "The governor is."

"Since when do we listen to the governor?"

"Since a thing called the present ushered in something else called reality, Earl. How many years ago was it you cleaned up Sweetwater?"

"I don't know, near fifty give or take a few."

"You did your job."

"Exactly as ordered."

Ash finally pulled his palms off his desk with a squishy sound as if his flesh had started to stick to the wood. "Same thing here, Ranger. You do your job. Exactly as ordered."

Jim leaned in, trying to ease his father away and feeling heat radiating through every inch of his body, reminding him of his daughter, Caitlin, when she had a bad fever. "You telling me you got no problem with this, Captain?"

Ash frowned and shook his head. "Of course I've got a problem with it. What I don't have is a choice. And that means neither do any of you. God, in the person of the governor of our fine state, has spoken."

"Pompous ass," Earl muttered.

"God or the governor?"

"Whoever called us off. Whoever's not gonna let us find the killers of those five boys."

"Let it go, Earl," Ash said, softer, taking the tone of a man speaking to someone who'd defined the Texas Rangers for nearly half a century.

"You ever known me to let anything go, Bert?"

"You're eighty years old—"

"Seventy-nine."

"—with enough history to fill a dozen books and make people take off their hats when you pass. You don't need this shit anymore."

Earl ran a long, thin finger down one side of his face

and up the other. "I take my badge off now, this case'll haunt me 'til the day I die."

Ash's gaze grew warm, sneaking a look at the .45 on Earl's hip and thinking of the Colt previously holstered there that had made him a legend. "You got more important things to concern yourself with, like that beautiful granddaughter. Mark these words, Earl Strong, someday she's gonna be the first woman to ride with the Rangers, thanks to your teaching."

83

SAN ANTONIO, THE PRESENT

"Rest, I suppose," Tepper finished, "is history now."

Caitlin found herself transfixed, wishing there was more to the story and sorry it had come to an end. She had no idea how much time had passed, how long Cort Wesley and the boys had been waiting for her outside.

"And here you are, Hurricane Caitlin about to break her grandfather's last case wide open."

"What happened to the flashlight, Captain?"

Tepper shrugged his shoulders, pushing the pointy bones up against the seams of his shirt. "Federals took it. My guess it's at the bottom of a lake somewhere between here and Washington."

"Not that voodoo pendant, though."

"Nope, we'd already inventoried that, and Captain Ash conveniently forgot to make mention of it to the FBI."

"You think he knew this day would come?"

"I believe he hoped it would. Rangers and politics have never been a smooth mix, Caitlin. Our history more than bears that out. I don't believe your granddad putting men on the chain the way he did in Sweetwater would go over very well at all today."

"Well, sir, some of my methods haven't been too far off from that."

She'd meant for the remark to get a smile from Tepper but instead all she saw was a glum look that quickly turned sad. "And you've paid a price for that, haven't you?"

Caitlin gazed out the window toward Cort Wesley and the boys waiting patiently in his rental car. "Depends on your meaning, sir."

Tepper followed her gaze. "You know my meaning, Mom. I barely knew the woman you've been these last few months up until you found that oil rig. And, truth be told, I'm not sure which of you I like better, but I think we both know which one was happier."

"Seemed like that rig found *me*, Captain."

"I know."

"So maybe I don't have as much a choice as you think."

"Something I left out of the story," Tepper told her. "Old Earl didn't lay his badge down on Captain Ash's desk that day we got back from Galveston, but he may as well have. I'm starting to wonder if you're coming to a similar crossroads."

"I am a bit younger."

Tepper's gaze drifted through the entry glass where Dylan and Luke were still plainly in view. "Earl walked away 'cause he had you and he knew you needed him more than the Rangers. You get my point?"

Caitlin tried not to let Tepper see her swallow hard. "I'm going to pay Teo Braga a visit tomorrow, Captain."

"This have anything to do with whatever it was you found in the bayou?"

"Only everything," Caitlin told him.

84

SAN ANTONIO, THE PRESENT

The faces of the four men appeared in each corner of the laptop's screen, their heads bowed slightly in reverence.

"You hold the hand of God as we prepare the final stage of our holy mission. It comes tomorrow and you are its bearers, and for your service heaven will be at your feet and history will remember you as heroes forever." Al-Awlaki bowed his head to match theirs. "But let us now pray for the souls of our lost brothers, who were sacrificed to a greater purpose. Let us remember the pain they suffered and bore, a pain each of us share as one. I close my eyes and see a man whose wife was raped and murdered because she was a Muslim. I see a man who was falsely accused of terrorist activity and hasn't been able to get a job since. I see men who were turned down for jobs, denied mortgages, forced out of their communities—their lives disrupted for no other reason than their cultural heritage or their religion. And the only thing they all have in common, each and every one, in addition to their faith, is that they are Americans."

As al-Awlaki continued with head bowed, Harrabi's mind flashed back to that night in the Wolfsboro, Tennessee field where stake and strings traced the outline of the Islamic Center the local Muslim community had financed and obtained the permits for, all on a totally aboveboard basis. The air had smelled of gasoline and machine oil from the construction equipment that had been vandalized just the week before and would begin digging out the foundation tomorrow under a forecast for a perfect day. . . .

Harrabi was certain he caught the scent of manure in the crisp, cool air, even though this hadn't been an active farm for years. The neighboring ones were too far away to account for the scent, making him wonder if smells could have ghosts too, and he dozed off to sleep that night thinking of his new life filled with new hope.

With both his boys in high school now, Harrabi looked at their night of guard duty like a campout spent without electronic distraction, even more pleased when his wife, Layla, agreed to come with them. She'd always hated the outdoors, the bugs and the dirty air, and their boys made sure she remembered that while cooking dinner over an open fire. This area lacked even cell phone service, meaning he had his family to himself from dusk to dawn at least. Time to get reacquainted with them in a way their mutually divided schedules never seemed to allow anymore.

But the night had not gone nearly as well as he had hoped, with the boys growing quickly anxious and impatient over the lack of their phones and computers. They had finally sulked off to sleep and Harrabi vowed not to bother rousing them, intending to cover the entire night's guard duty himself until they emerged from their tent together right on time. . . .

"Like our departed brothers, you are Americans all who did everything right and have paid a terrible price for your loyalty. One of you was forced to bury his parents when they were run off the road and killed after being harassed at a restaurant. They stare at you when you board airplanes and they turn away in revulsion at the color of your skin and depth of your faith. You always looked at yourself as one of them, one of the many, until their actions left you with no choice but to turn away and seek the fair-minded response with which I have entrusted you."

Harrabi was sleeping with his beautiful Layla cradled against him, when he heard the thunk. It wasn't much of a sound, shouldn't even have been enough to awaken him. But he lurched upward in his sleeping bag as if it had been a thunderclap, later recalling the odd sensation that it had been the ghosts of his parents that drove him from his slumber. Sending him out into the night where his life would change forever.

"Is the fate we would visit upon them any worse than that which they have visited upon us? Another of you was shot through a living room window as he watched television. The daughter of yet another had bleach thrown in her face. And the ambulance refused to come into his neighborhood because of the perceived danger, and she lost her vision. Blind now, yet still able to see the terrible portrait this country has drawn of our people, my brothers."

The night was moonless, but clear and filled with stars. Harrabi stumbled from the tent with his eyes struggling to adjust to the thin light coupled with that from a flashlight rolling back and forth on the ground and capturing the unthinkable in its spill.

A big man dressed in black was standing over his downed oldest son, wheeling a baseball bat up and over his shoulder and bringing it down on the boy's skull to a sound like a bottle breaking on the floor.

"NOOOOOOOOOO!"

To this day, Harrabi wasn't sure if he screamed the word or just thought it. But the second and even bigger man holding his younger son's face in a pool of mud and fetid water looked up and abandoned the boy whose body continued to twitch, feet spasming. He came at Harrabi with a limp, dragging his left leg as if it were a dead weight behind him. Harrabi could have easily made a successful run for it, but in the haze of disbelief he hesitated, moving instinctively for his younger son and shoving the limping man from his path, hearing his own wails echo in the night.

"I was part of this country too once, remember, but I turned away and aside because I saw the hatred on their smug faces. Knew it was only a matter of time before they came for me as they came for others. And when they finally did, I used it to my advantage against them. Their politicians thrive on blaming us for their

problems, believing with utter absurdity we would en-
force sharia law on their soil when all we wanted was
to live in peace as the Americans we were."

*Harrabi's hands had closed on his son, feeling the
stiffness and rigidity of his body, death's hold already
ensnared, when the blow struck him. He felt himself
sliding downward in the air toward his son's side, his
head feeling soft as if it were all flesh, cartilage, and
muscle with no bone. As if somebody had stuffed it
full of cotton, while leaving him his presence of mind
and full grasp of the reality around him. So when the
man leaned over to retrieve the baseball bat impact
had stripped from him, Harrabi jabbed a thumb upward into the man's eye. He felt the edge drive home
and kept it going until it pierced the eyeball and
Harrabi thought he heard a pop.*

*The bigger assailant screamed and screamed. But
then the bat was in the limping man's grasp, lashing
down at Harrabi again. He couldn't stop it from hitting him, or maybe he didn't want to. Maybe he wanted
darkness to come and take all this away from him,
perhaps leave him with the fleeting and however brief
hope that this was just another dream he would soon
awaken from.*

*Light exploded in front of his eyes on impact and
the last thing Harrabi remembered was a watery
sound coming from his ears, as the light flashed to
darkness.*

*He awoke groggily, his head feeling split down the
middle, to the sight of Layla holding their youngest
son's head in her lap, stroking his hair with fingers
smeared in the boy's blood as she sang his favorite*

lullaby as a young boy, "Yalla Tnam." She had learned to sing it in Arabic so their sons would understand and never forget that part of their heritage, which made Harrabi love her even more.

Yalla tnam Rima
Yalla tnam Rima, yalla yijeeha elnoum

"But that is no longer an option now and tomorrow we embark on a new path that will avenge all the wrongs done onto you. And not just you, but all our people. And not just now, but for generations. Others before us have sought to make this kind of difference, this kind of impact. But they have all come up short. They have failed in the holy mission where we will succeed. Tomorrow we strike a blow on our enemy that will be felt until the end of times. . . ."

Harrabi dazedly listened to his beloved wife singing the rest of the lullaby to their dead son, continuing to stroke his hair.

May she grow loving to pray and to fast
Oh God make her healthier each day
May she go to sleep
and I will cook a delicious pigeon
Go pigeon bird, don't believe what I am saying,
I just say it so that Rima will sleep
Rima, Rima, beautiful rose of the prairies,
you have shining hair
The one who loves you shall kiss, and the one
    who hates you will go away

Harrabi's mind stopped there, jolted back to the present, because he realized the song's meaning and impact, why its melody haunted him every day of his life.

> *The one who loves you shall kiss, and the one*
> *who hates you will go away ...*

Only the haters had never gone away and the kisses of loved ones had not been enough to keep his sons safe and alive. He was helpless that night and had felt helpless every day since.

But not anymore.

Not after tomorrow.

"*Āmin*," Harrabi heard al-Awlaki say.

"Amen," he followed.

PART NINE

The average Ranger spent seventy-four hours and thirty minutes a week on the job, with no overtime pay. Even in remote parts of the state such as Sierra Blanca, Ranger J. S. Nance handled 166 criminal cases in 1956, including four homicides, two bank holdups, a kidnapping, several armed robberies, and sixty-eight burglaries. Ranger J. A. Sykes investigated eighty-one cases, logging 2,055 daylight working hours, 821 night hours, and 200 hours scouting the Rio Grande.

—Karl Detzer, "Texas Rangers Still Ride the Trail,"
Reader's Digest, September 1957, pp. 140–141
(As quoted in *Time of the Rangers* by Mike Cox)

85

Teofilo Braga was walking the line of BWM's recycling facility when he saw Caitlin Strong approaching, wearing her Ranger Stetson instead of a hardhat.

"I believe you're not allowed to have any contact with me," he said to her. "Or maybe you haven't been informed that my lawyers have filed papers."

"Oh, I've been informed, but I figured I'd drop by anyway." Caitlin gazed around the massive warehouse-sized building with machines that chopped, minced, flattened, separated, and ground their contents respectively. The smell reminded her of walking a beach in the wake of a storm, the corrosively bitter, salt-laced stench of dried seaweed and dead fish washed up on the shoreline. "Nice facility you've got here."

The hum and clack of the machines fighting for space on the cluttered floor expelled heat the exhaust fans could only partially flush out. The result was air baked in strange waves and currents, interrupted by cool shafts blowing outward from the huge, floor-mounted air-conditioning units. A network of catwalks were strung in a crisscrossing pattern above, permitting more convenient access to the largest machines and overhead magnets that separated out the metal from lighter papers and plastics.

The sorters were massive machines that looked like huge versions of trash compacting trucks with a giant feed slot through which materials were sucked in with the heavier materials, like glass and metal. Once separated from the lighter ones, they were sent via conveyor belt to an adjoining station. This particular MRF, or Materials Recovery Facility, handled both clean recyclates that had been separated from the rest of the garbage prior to transport as well as garbage and recyclates that were mixed. That made it unique in the industry in general and Texas in particular, adding considerably, Caitlin imagined, to Braga's profit margin.

The scant number of windows and overhanging catwalk three stories above made Caitlin feel as if she was inside some huge submarine. She smelled lubricant oil along with the coppery stench of machine metal operating at high temperatures.

Braga drew his cell phone from his pocket. He was dressed in overalls that bagged slightly over the clothes they must have been covering. Caitlin noticed the overalls were outfitted with the BWM devil logo on the lapel.

"Call your lawyers if you want, sir, but you may want to hear what I've got to say first."

Braga returned the phone to his overalls, seeming to relish the challenge of facing Caitlin head on. "They're bloodsuckers anyway, while you just spill it. That what brought you out here today, Ranger?"

Caitlin looked around her, ignoring him. "The original building that used to be here burned three years ago. Circumstances were deemed suspicious by the fire marshal, but nothing was ever proven."

"It's nice to see you're a true student of history."

"I believe you'd made an offer to buy the facility

but the original owners turned you down. Then the place caught fire and burned to the ground. Turned out those original owners were underinsured. You got this place for a song at a bankruptcy sale."

Braga held his ground, as if his feet were welded to the concrete floor. "You disappoint me, Ranger."

"Do I?"

"Yes, if dredging up the past is the best you can do."

"Actually, I'd like to go back a bit farther, sir. To Galveston Island. I'm here because I know you killed those five college boys in 1979."

86

LOUISIANA BAYOU, THE DAY BEFORE

The Cessna carrying Caitlin, Cort Wesley, and the boys landed in a private airfield just outside of New Orleans where a St. Mary's Parish sheriff's deputy was waiting to drive them out to the bayou. Having never seen the bayou up close, they actually were well inside it before they realized the outer reaches were formed of lavish flora rimmed by homes both new and old, some perfectly fit and others in terrible states of disrepair. Those homes, a few palatial in scope, bracketed the swampy water on both sides of the waterway, their shorelines shored up by a combination of live oak trees and wild, overgrown vegetation. The water itself looked brownish-black in stark comparison to the bright blue sky overhead, the sun shining down brightly enough on the shoreline homes to look like heavenly light.

Deeper into the bayou, just before they reached the boat that would take them the rest of the way, the homes became older with roofs formed of corrugated tin. The sunlight able to sneak through the thick canopy of tree branches reflected off these in blinding fashion.

The sheriff's deputy had led them down the dock onto a police boat moored there and, after they'd set out on the water, narrated the sights and scenery for the boys as if they were here on a school trip. The deputy's narration continued as the houses thinned to a smattering of buildings that looked out of place amid the world they shared with unspoiled flora. That is until the inlet narrowed and something that looked like a Halloween haunted house appeared on the banks of the bayou in a rare sun-drenched clearing just up ahead.

It had been manually cleared many years before, long since erasing any sense of human intervention in the form of stump patches or discolored ground suffering from the loss of trees. As a result the clearing looked like a geographical anomaly, an accident of nature that had allowed this rectangular building to be built upon raised concrete pillars that formed a crawlspace so water and wind might pass beneath it. The building, once home to a Cajun family that had grown rich thanks to their illegal alcohol production way back in Prohibition, looked as if it was listing to the side, shrouded more in darkness this late in the day.

"It's kind of an old folks home now," Caitlin heard the deputy say. "The rooms all converted to house men and women who've lived their whole lives on these waters. Somewhere in the area of a dozen residents, give or take. Beaudoin Chansoir's been here almost since the renovation was completed twenty years ago with state money to keep a historical landmark from sliding into the bayou. This place hasn't been evacuated in a single hurricane. The residents and staff all believe it's blessed."

Caitlin finally noticed that the nametag on the deputy's lapel identified him as PLANTAINE. "You have a relative ever serve as sheriff on Galveston Island? Folks called him Mugsy."

"Believe that would be my uncle," said the deputy.

"He worked a case with my father and grandfather more than thirty years ago," Caitlin told him. "Matter of fact, that's why we're here today."

The deputy led them up a stone walk rimmed by thick overgrowth on either side that, judging by the stray shavings, had just been trimmed. He used an old-fashioned knocker on a heavy wood door that was warped at the bottom, opened moments later by a black woman with thick gray hair and wearing an apron.

"Miss Bessie, these are those folks we told you about."

Miss Bessie regarded the four of them with a disapproving glance, not nearly as welcoming as her down-home appearance might have suggested. "You tell them that old man ain't made no sense since I come here?"

The deputy glanced at Caitlin and Cort Wesley. "They wanted to see for themselves."

Bessie frowned. "Man can't even say how old he is on account of he's got no birth certificate, but there are days he claims to remember the Civil War."

"This shouldn't take too long, ma'am," Caitlin told her.

"Heck, let it take as long as you like. He ain't gonna remember any of it after you leave anyway."

"We just need to show him a few things, pictures and the like."

"*Show* him? Pictures?" Miss Bessie shook her head, coming up just short of a laugh. "Well, good luck with that, 'cause old Beaudoin's been blind as a bat for a decade now."

Beaudoin Chansoir's room overlooked the thick foliage that sloped up the rear of the old home. He sat in a chair by the window with the sun on his face and old hands clutching the arms tightly as if afraid he might fall through the cushion. Both those hands were riddled with tremors, as was his lower lip that drooped a bit further with each breath.

The boys remained in the doorway, Caitlin and Cort Wesley approaching Beaudoin Chansoir alone.

"Mr. Chansoir?"

His head twisted toward her, as if on a piston instead of a neck. His eyes were mere slits held behind lids oozing thick pusslike fluid that left dried, scabby trails down his cheeks.

"Who you be?" the old man asked in a surprisingly strong voice, his bald scalp gray-toned in patches.

"My name is Caitlin Strong, sir. I'm a Texas Ranger."

"I never been to Texas, no. What you want with me, you?"

"I believe you met my father and grandfather a bunch of years back. They came to ask you some questions about some college boys who were murdered in Texas."

"Never been there."

"You drew these college boys a map to lead them to Jean Lafitte's lost treasure."

But Beaudoin Chansoir seemed not to hear her. His eyes had pried themselves open enough to view at least the shape of Cort Wesley through the gooey substance coating the lenses.

"Is that my grandson?" the old man asked, voice peppered with excitement. "You done brought Augustin with you?"

"I'm right here," Cort Wesley said, not moving.

"Where you been, boy?" Chansoir asked, one frail hand flailing at the air to feel for him. "You ain't come by in a lot of sunsets. I can tell it's that time when the heat pulls away from the glass, me."

Cort Wesley took the old man's hand. "I'm sorry about not coming around."

"You be in trouble again? You need me to hide you?"

"I'm fine. I've come about the treasure."

Chansoir twisted in his chair and blindly clamped his second hand atop Cort Wesley's. "Our secret, that. I drew you the map."

"You remember?"

"Sure, I do, me. You and that other boy. Remember you both."

Caitlin and Cort Wesley looked at each other.

"What trouble you got yourself into now, you?"

"I found the treasure," Cort Wesley said, without thinking.

"Course you did. Our secret. I remember."

"I told you about that night?"

"What night? I remember the day you was born like it was yesterday. Maybe it was for all I know."

"But you drew me that map. Sent me to that island called Galveston."

"Don't know what it be called, Augustin," Chansoir said, as Cort Wesley and Caitlin exchanged a glance at the name he'd repeated. "Only know where the treasure lay on it from my own granddad. He showed me exactly where it was and made me promise never to go looking. Said the treasure was cursed, that anybody finds it gonna be hurt on its account. Made me promise to keep the secret just like I done with you, passing on the map just as he did to me, yes."

"And the boy who was with me the day you passed it down. You remember him?"

Beaudoin Chansoir turned back to the sun as if his mind had shown him something he didn't like seeing. "He wasn't one of us, but you said he was family and should be treated as such. You got a family of your own now yourself, Augustin?"

Augustin Chansoir, Caitlin thought, comparing the name to Alvin Jackson.

Cort Wesley's eyes stayed on Caitlin briefly before moving to Luke and Dylan in the doorway. "I do, *Paw-Paw.*"

The old man smiled, displaying a mouth devoid of teeth. "You ain't called me that in the longest time."

"You remember that necklace you gave me?"

"Necklace?"

"From around your neck. Told me it was magic, that it would bring me luck."

Beaudoin Chansoir jerked a knobby, vein-riddled hand up to his chest, as if to feel for the missing voodoo charm. The hand dropped inside his shirt, touching the very spot where D. W. Tepper had noticed a discolored portion of skin consistent with the charm's size and shape. Chansoir's fingers held there, as his features relaxed.

"I'd already given one to you, boy. This other one that I was wearing, it was for your friend. On account of you calling him family and all, yes."

"The friend I brought with me," Cort Wesley said, looking back at Caitlin. "You remember his name, *PawPaw*?"

"Nope, can't say I do. Gave you the map too, I did, just like my *PawPaw* done with me. Made you promise me you'd never go back to Angola, you. Bad place. You come outta there with a smell like the devil on you. Rotten earth it be like. I remembers when you came back 'fore you moved away again." Chansoir reached out and grasped Cort Wesley's hand even harder. "You back for good this time?"

"I hope so."

"Gets lonely here, you know."

"I do."

"I can still make my lures, me. Earn my own keep, Augustin, something your dang father never did a day in his whole life."

Cort Wesley gently extricated himself from the old man's trembling grasp. "I've got to be going now for a time, *PawPaw*."

"But you'll be coming back."

"I will. Promise."

Beaudoin Chansoir returned his hands to the arms of his chair. "Remember to keep your promise, you. No more Angola, no more trouble. You got your own to take care of now."

87

"Look familiar?" Caitlin asked Braga, holding up the evidence pouch containing the voodoo pendant she'd managed to identify a few days before.

"I have absolutely no idea what you're talking about."

"So you weren't the young man Alvin Jackson brought with him to the bayou."

"I was not."

"And you're telling me you've never seen this before."

"Of course, I have," Braga said, gesturing toward the evidence pouch. "It belonged to Alvin Jackson."

"So if I told you this pendant was found in the hand of one of those dead college boys, you'd be suggesting he tore it off Alvin Jackson's neck in the struggle."

"You're the one doing all the suggesting here, Ranger. I owe more to Alvin Jackson than any man on earth; I cried harder at his funeral, after he passed of a heart attack, than my own father's. But we both know he had violent tendencies, don't we?"

"And what about you, Mr. Braga? Do you share some of those same tendencies?"

Braga stiffened and held Caitlin's stare as he responded. "I believe we all do. But there's a difference between that and being party to the murder of five college students." His eyes locked on the pendant again. "If Rangers found that at the crime scene, there's only one man it could have belonged to."

"Alvin Jackson?"

Braga nodded. "As much as it pains me to say that."

Caitlin took a deep breath, her expression empty of emotion. "I reread that article about you in *Texas Monthly*, sir. There was a picture of you with Alvin Jackson taken just after you bought the company in 1983. A pendant identical to what this one used to look like was dangling outside his shirt. Means it couldn't have been torn off his neck that night those boys were murdered on Galveston Island."

Braga looked at her the way he had at Covel Gardens, then again in the conference room at Company D headquarters: unruffled and almost amused by her insinuation. Unlike normal people, men like him, true sociopaths used to ignoring society's laws, grew increasingly placid the more they were confronted with the truth. Right now Braga looked bored, at least indifferent, as if the murders of five boys thirty years before were no different from crushing ants under his boot.

"You ever hear of Rubicon X-Ultra, Mr. Braga?" Caitlin asked him, continuing her assault.

"Did you bring another warrant with you, Ranger?"

"They're a paramilitary group that farm themselves out to the highest bidder."

"You didn't answer my question about the warrant."

"We're just making conversation here for the time being. Don't need a warrant for that, do I? Anyway, my captain and I came up against some of those psychos last night. I thought I'd ask since we've been able to link your employee Jalbert Thoms to them."

Caitlin thought she saw Braga stiffen ever so slightly. "Mr. Thoms is no longer in our employ, I already told you that. And I haven't seen him since the unfortunate incident at that bar."

"Which followed the unfortunate incident with a teenage boy I was responsible for at the time. Or did that slip your mind, Mr. Braga?"

"Show me a warrant or get out, Ranger," Braga said, raising his voice above a sorting machine that had just kicked into a higher gear as a fresh load of trash fed into it down the biggest conveyor belt Caitlin had ever seen.

"I don't have one, Mr. Braga. I thought you might like to cooperate of your own volition."

"And why would I do that?"

"Because you and Alvin Jackson, born Augustin Chansoir, followed his grandfather's map to Galveston Island where you managed to find Jean Lafitte's legendary treasure in the form of diamonds mined in Brazil. But Mr. Jackson's grandfather inadvertently drew the same map out for some college boys on a fraternity scavenger hunt and they had the misfortune of showing up that same night, just after you found the treasure."

Caitlin stopped, as if expecting Braga to comment, but he remained strangely silent, breathing like a snake through his mouth.

"I believe these diamonds provided the stake you needed to buy the company that evolved into Braga Waste Management," she continued. "I can put you away on all that for sure. But, on the other hand, we've got the body of a possible homegrown terrorist in the morgue who was suffering from a severe case of radiation poisoning that would've killed him if a car accident hadn't done the trick first."

Something changed in Braga's expression, no matter how hard he tried to hide it. It was subtle, just a slight shift of his eyes, a swelling in his throat as he swallowed hard.

"We've got firm intelligence that the cell this dead man was a part of is planning an attack based right here in Texas. We know it's gonna be bad and we know it's coming soon and now we know it almost surely involves radioactivity."

"I have no idea what any of this has to do with me, Ranger. You're wasting my time."

"Am I, sir? I believe you know about the serious problem of storing radioactive waste all across this country, and that the companies behind the power plants responsible pay exorbitant black market fees to anyone who'll take it off their hands and dump it any-where they can." Caitlin hesitated, just long enough. "Like the ocean, Mr. Braga, in barrels identical to the ones we found beneath the *Mariah*. And when the rig's ROV happened to find the remnants of a ship-wreck on the sea floor, they shut down operations, but not before the same ROV also spotted your barrels. The terrorists must've figured that would jeopardize their plans, so they killed the whole goddamn crew to keep the secret."

"You can't prove any of this."

"Just like I can't prove you've cornered the market on the illegal dumping of radioactive waste and made yourself tens of untraceable millions in the process." Braga started to speak, but Caitlin rolled right over his words. "This is much bigger than you, me, and whatever we got between us. I need you to tell me how many barrels we're talking about and where I can find them now."

Braga took a step backward into a spot on the floor

the big overhead lighting rigs reached only in shadows. The result was to cast him like a specter, more phantom than man, like something out of a horror movie. His sneer stuck out absurdly, the light sheen of sweat on his face looking like laminate brushed over his skin. He looked down, then up again—beyond Caitlin toward something that had clearly claimed his vision.

"You haven't really left me with any choice at all, Ranger."

Caitlin saw him nod ever so slightly toward the spot beyond her an instant before bullets clanged off the steel just over her head.

88

Up in a darkened corner of the network of catwalks, Cort Wesley heard the shots too. He pinned down their point of origin as a platform extension on some sort of mobile rig that looked like a cherry picker capable of reaching any point of the facility all the way up to the ceiling for maintenance.

"*Told ya he was up here!*" he heard Leroy Epps's voice blare in his mind. "*That freak show Thoms got a death wish for sure! I'd shoot him myself if I could still hold a gun!*"

Cort Wesley was already in motion by then, Glock palmed in his hand as he rushed across the catwalk toward the platform on which Jalbert Thoms was hiding. The platform was raised higher than the catwalk and Thoms had taken a shooting angle that hid him from this angle anyway.

More gunshots clacked off in rapid succession, clanging off steel with a hollow echo. On the floor below, Cort Wesley glimpsed Caitlin Strong lurch behind a beam for cover as Braga scampered away. Then she was returning fire, her shots missing badly but distracting Thoms from his approach.

Except that drawing closer still did not yield him even a glimpse of the gunman, much less a clear shot.

"What a cluster fuck, bubba," Leroy Epps said in his mind.

Braga had told Jalbert Thoms to wait for his signal. He knew that Caitlin Strong would be coming in the wake of the disastrous gunfight last night. She couldn't take a hint, didn't understand the price she'd ultimately pay for going up against true power.

Thoms didn't care about any of that. He'd lived his entire life giving into his most base urges and predilections. He never held back, whether it be with a boy he wanted for his own or a man he wanted dead. Whatever gene regulated such behaviors was clearly not in his DNA, and that had suited him just fine until Caitlin Strong had sent him scurrying out of that bar in which he'd intended to leave her dead. The look on Dylan Torres's face earlier that same day, the fear he'd inspired in the boy, was what he craved and was accustomed to. Not the suppressed rage and sense of purpose he saw on Caitlin Strong's in that bar. Thoms knew of her reputation and her prowess that made him long for this kill all the more, mandated by nothing more than his own remorseless intentions to take down a Texas Ranger who'd made her name with her gun.

It was the Old West all over again and he wouldn't stop until one of his bullets scrambled her brains.

Cort Wesley figured the pause in Thoms's firing meant he was exchanging a spent magazine for a fresh one. The available seconds were enough to bring him within shooting angle of the platform, but all he glimpsed was the far edge of the sound suppressor affixed to the end of an assault rifle barrel. Fire at that, in little more than frustration, and he'd succeed only in giving himself away to no good or realistically meaningful end.

"*He's gonna keep shooting 'til your gal is dead, bubba.*"

"Tell me something I don't know."

"*Gotta go up or down as opposed to sticking here. How's that?*"

"Just what I needed to hear," Cort Wesley thought, or maybe said, as he dashed along the catwalk for the nearest stairs.

Braga slinked further off, using the machinery for cover. Caitlin trained her SIG on him, not sure if she really intended to fire when a ricocheting bullet fired by Jalbert Thoms caught him in the leg and pulled the floor right out from under his feet. She scrabbled out after Braga, keeping low, the echoing din of Thoms's fire sounding in her ears.

"I oughtta let you bleed to death," Caitlin said, dragging Teofilo Braga behind as much cover as she could find.

"You can't win this," Braga said, grimacing in pain as Caitlin fastened her kerchief into a makeshift tourniquet on his leg. "You have no idea what you're up against. A thirty-year-old murder? I'll never spend a day in court, not a single day."

"It's you who's in the dark this time, sir. Hanging's still on the books for treason, you know."

"Treason?"

"You knowingly conspired with terrorists on the transfer of radioactive waste you've been stockpiling from nuclear plants all over the country. How much did those plants pay you, Mr. Braga, how much did it take for you to sell your country out?"

But Braga remained unmoved. "You still don't get it, do you?"

"Get what?"

"What's really going on here." Then he noticed her eyes veer suddenly toward the clamor of what sounded like boots rattling steel.

"What are you looking at?" Braga asked her.

"Justice, sir."

Jalbert Thoms felt a sense of utter calm seize him. It was the same feeling he got when ready to move on a boy he'd been keeping in his sights with just that moment in mind. This was no less of a game than that, and Thoms felt his heart slow to the utter certainty of his ultimate victory. Sooner or later the Ranger would show enough of herself for him to take her down. Patience just wasn't part of her vocabulary. So long as she had bullets to fire, she'd make a game of it, unable to accept defeat any more than he could. The modified M16/AR15 ArmaLite rifle wasn't the ideal sniper tool, but from this distance it suited his needs just fine and its scope made it seem as if Caitlin Strong was a finger-length away.

Sure he'd have to go on the run when this was done, but he'd always fancied himself an outlaw and he had the X-Ultra boys to help place him in a new country with plenty of work and plenty of long-haired fodder he could pretend were Dylan Torres when he took them for his own. In the right country, nobody would even know they were gone.

The mere thought of that sent Thoms's heart flut-tering in his chest, eye squeezed against his scope to ready his next shot when the platform rocked beneath him.

Cort Wesley knew if Thoms spotted him he'd be dodg-ing 5.56mm bullets in his rush to the truck cab con-trolling the overhead platform on which Thoms was perched. But he reached it without incurring a single shot, not realizing he'd been holding his breath the whole way until he eased the cab door closed behind him and sucked in air laced with thin trails of refuse from crushed and collected recyclables.

The machines' heavy din had camouflaged the sounds of his charge across the floor, staving off the fusillade of fire that would otherwise likely have blazed down upon him. And now Cort Wesley was free to rapidly familiarize himself with the controls in the cab, almost identical indeed to the cherry pickers he'd driven in summer construction jobs as a teenager before he'd started interning in burglary with his dad Boone Masters.

He jammed the truck into gear, feeling its tires whine against the concrete floor as he sought to put more distance between Caitlin and the psycho he saw himself tearing apart piece by piece, starting with his private parts. Beyond that he had formed no real plan, until the moment he turned the truck parallel with the massive trash separating machine that reminded him of something out of his son Luke's sci-fi video games.

Cort Wesley was half expecting some tentacled monster to leap out at him from within it, glimpsing sorting rakes that looked like robotic teeth belonging to a prehistoric shark. Then he heard the rattle of 5.56mm fire clanging against the cab roof, imagining he could feel the heat of Thoms's bullets struggling to find him.

"I don't scare easy, Ranger."

"You ever see the inside of a military prison? It's not pretty, but I imagine that's where you'll be staying for a time."

Caitlin watched Braga smile through the pain knifing through him. "You think that's the way the world works? You think this strong vengeance of yours is gonna end up putting me away? I almost feel bad for you."

"Save the gesture for somebody who needs it."

"Oh, you need it, all right; you just don't realize how much. You think I did this all on my own? I just said you had no idea what you were up against, but I guess you didn't hear me."

"Why don't you spell it out?"

Braga's next smile quickly dissolved into a grimace. "I'd rather let you find out on your own, have to wash the egg off your face when this whole thing blows up in it."

"You're protected? Is that what you're hinting at?"

"Figure it out yourself, Ranger."

"What I've figured out so far is that you're now an accessory to the attempted murder of a Texas Ranger. You wanna see how that plays out in a San Antonio courthouse?"

Braga managed another smile. "Your mind has this twisted around. I'm the one who's shot, remember? Whoever's doing the shooting is acting on their own."

Cort Wesley worked the controls to lurch the truck back and forth, hoping to preempt any further shooting by Jalbert Thoms, if not dump him off altogether.

Dump him off . . .

He thought it might have been Leroy Epps's words in his mind, or maybe they were his own thoughts this time. Either way, he jerked the truck into reverse, feeling a fresh spray of bullets slamming the roof, searching for a soft spot or an angle through the windshield that was pasty with refuse dust.

Then he heard the distinctive clack of Caitlin's SIG, echoing loud enough to rise over the clamor of the machines and conveyors powering the facility. Cort Wesley didn't think she'd be able to hit Thoms but her fire stopped his long enough for Cort Wesley to drive the truck forward now, picking up speed as the platform rocked above him.

"*Love that gal, bubba!*"

"Me too, champ."

At that he worked the truck's wheel and brake at the same time, tires squealing against concrete until its frame slammed into the separator machine's housing. Impact smacked his skull against the windshield, just as it jostled the platform forward too.

And Jalbert Thoms with it.

Cort Wesley was too dazed to see him fall straight into the separating machine's steel teeth, but not too dazed to hear Thoms's terrible screams over all other noise as a spray of blood lifted into the dirty air along with macerated bone and gristle. He thought he could still hear Thoms's high-pitched wails until a sucking sound like air from a spent balloon blew outward and the blood shower stopped.

Cort Wesley reached for the door latch, but his hand froze halfway there, starbursts pulsing before his eyes before darkness claimed him.

89

UVALDE, THE PRESENT

Caitlin and Braga heard the sound too, Braga looking at her smugly.

"There goes your one potential witness," he said.

"Man you claim was acting on his own."

"Because it's the truth."

Caitlin held his stare for a long moment. "So what's to say he didn't kill you too before we got him?"

Braga's eyes lost their confident gleam. He looked away, about, as if in search of some kind of exit.

"Those powerful friends of yours gonna fast rope

down from the ceiling or storm the building to rescue you? I don't think so, Mr. Braga, meaning there's nothing to stop me from mixing pieces of you with Thoms's. Make a nice follow-up in *Texas Monthly,* don't you think?"

"You," Braga started, stopping as if something had stolen his breath. He tried to hold Caitlin's gaze but couldn't, not liking the surety of the message it held. "What do you want?"

"To know what happened that night on Galveston for starters," Caitlin told him.

Braga swallowed hard, keeping his lips pinned closed. "What's it matter now?"

"It matters to me."

Braga looked away again, Caitlin certain he was done talking until he began to speak softly, his lips not seeming to move and his eyes fixed on the floor. "*Tu eres como un clavo caliente en el culo* ... And a pain in the ass like you will be dead before you can use any of this against me."

"Chance I'm willing to take, sir."

Braga twisted his gaze back on her defiantly, trying to find the customary bravado that had eluded him. "I didn't kill anyone. It was Alvin Jackson. We followed the map, the first real one his grandfather had ever drawn from memories of the stories passed down. I didn't believe for a minute the treasure was real. Alvin thought those kids had followed us out to the island to steal the treasure and went at them with a knife in one hand and the damn lawn tool we'd used to find the hollow in the other. I tried to stop him, Ranger, I did. And when I couldn't I tried to help those boys as best I could. Only one of them was still alive. I guess he must've been the one who tore off the pendant

Beaudoin Chansoir had given me. Didn't realize I'd lost it until we were back home."

"The FBI pinned the murders on Mexican workers so business on Galveston could go on as usual," Caitlin picked up. "You got lucky back then, Mr. Braga, but your luck has run out today."

"Really? How exactly do you intend to prove it? You know I'll deny this conversation ever took place."

Caitlin eased a smaller pouch containing half of a broken pencil from the front pocket of her jeans. "You've got quite a temper, Mr. Braga. In our office conference room, all you broke was this pencil, though I strongly suspect you've broken far more than that in your time over the years. We got your DNA sample off the other half of this pencil and, you know what?, it turned out to be a perfect match for the DNA on this charm here. That's how I intend to prove it, sir."

Caitlin looked into Braga's eyes, trying to judge his intentions, but his expression was utterly blank, devoid of reaction or emotion like a statue with its features left unfinished. She waited for him to notice the piece of paper she was holding.

"This is that DNA report, sir," she said, crumpling it into a tight ball. "You tell me what I need to know to stop these terrorists and what happened thirty years ago goes away."

"Just like that?"

Caitlin stuffed the crumpled page in her pocket. "Just like that. You have my word, the word of a Texas Ranger. How many barrels we talking about here?"

Braga nodded sullenly, no longer defiant, face wrenched tight against the pain. "Ten thousand."

The number registered like a kick to her gut. "Ten thousand? *Ten thousand barrels* of radioactive waste?"

Braga nodded again.

"Where can I find them? Where have you hid them?"

"They were stored in one of my unused underground refuse cells in Covel Gardens, but they're gone now."

"Gone where?"

"Loaded onto freight trains for transport all across the state, as of this morning."

"*Where?* Which yards?"

Caitlin listened to his answer, feeling herself go cold.

PART TEN

"People are always asking me what a Ranger is like. They mostly have a notion that he's a big-hatted, belted, and spurred fellow wading through a cloud of pistol smoke with a gun in each hand. You know what I tell them? I tell them the truth. The Texas Ranger is a family man, a good neighbor, humble, kindly, and conscientious. He's a man of integrity, fearless, and courageous. He's tough when the occasion demands, able to handle any situation, and never retreats. He sits tall in the saddle and casts a long shadow. I know, I raise 'em."

—From a 1963 interview with Colonel Homer Garrison conducted by Stan Redding
(as quoted in *Time of the Rangers* by Mike Cox)

90

"Course I heard you," Captain Tepper said, the cell phone transmission strangely clear and distinct. "I'm not totally deaf yet. Four freight trains covering the major population centers in the state that might not be so major anymore if we don't beat this. What else he tell you?"

"All four trains are scheduled to head up the rails at five o'clock tonight. That's how long we got to end this once and for all."

"How many of Braga's fingers you have to break to get that out of him?"

"None, but he's got a bullet in his leg courtesy of Jalbert Thoms before Cort Wesley dumped Thoms in a trash compactor. Braga needs an ambulance and I need you to get Jones on the line."

"I can't, Ranger. He's gone."

"Figures."

"Sounds like you're not as surprised as you should be."

"I'm just hoping I'm wrong."

Caitlin was surprised when Jones actually answered his phone, his voice, along with a mechanical hum, filling the car through the Bluetooth speaker.

"It's true, isn't it?" she snapped at him. "What Braga told me about someone holding his strings."

"Look, Ranger—"

"Don't bullshit me here, Jones."

"I had no idea where this was going. If I had . . ."

"There you go again."

"Listen to me, Ranger. You know what was at the top of the list in our most recent threat assessment? The nuclear waste materials stored on site at virtually all the country's nuclear plants now. Nobody wants the shit, so that's where it stays. Trouble being that's a recipe for an enterprising terrorist igniting the mother of all dirty bombs. So some contacts were made to get rid of it."

"You brought in Braga. Let him do your dirty work. Literally. And he jobbed it out to al-Awlaki's home-grown terrorists."

"We had to reduce the risk. Priority one."

"A million lives in Texas being Priority two, then."

"Hear that sound, Ranger?" he asked, speaking over the constant whirring din. "That's the sound of me flying out of the state on a government jet. As far as the world's concerned, I was never there."

"So you, Homeland Security, are just dumping this mess in our laps."

"What mess is that, Ranger? I think we must have a bad connection here. Sorry."

The mechanical hum and Jones's voice both vanished with a *click*.

"Son of a bitch," said Caitlin.

"Guess that leaves it to us," Cort Wesley told her, holding an emergency ice pack against his forehead.

* * *

Caitlin called Tepper to give him the news.

"Son of a bitch," he said.

"I seem to recall me saying exactly the same thing. This is Rangers all the way now, Captain."

"Suits me just fine. But I'll tell you this much: your friend Jones ever sets foot in this state again, even one of those armored suits won't be able to save him."

"You still got that bazooka in your basement, D.W.?"

Caitlin thought she heard him chuckle until a raspy cough swallowed it. "Know what, Hurricane? Looks like sometimes even a dangerous wind blows in the right direction."

Tepper called back twenty minutes later.

"These freight lines link the big cities and major population centers, all right," he reported. "The governor's ready to shut down every freight line in the state as soon as we give him the word we're ready to deploy."

"Make sure he doesn't shut them down a moment too early, D.W. If we spook al-Awlaki, he just might blow all ten thousand barrels as they stand. Until we know what his game is, we need to play this close."

"Young Roger's working up some casualty scenarios based on estimates. Says each one of those barrels is like a mini-dirty bomb about to be blown out into the air. Says the level of contamination multiplies geometrically with each blast as far as spread and size of the killing cloud goes—that's what he called it, a killing cloud—or, in this case, four of them."

Caitlin felt another cold blast of air surge through her, as if the air-conditioning had pierced her skin. "We're still three hours from San Antonio, D.W."

"Hopefully we'll have the cavalry ready to move by the time you get here."

She pushed the rental car's accelerator down even further. Cort Wesley looked across the seat and watched Caitlin remove the crumpled-up piece of paper she'd told Braga contained the DNA proof linking him to the Galveston Island murders from her pocket.

"Oh," she said, handing it to him. "Forgot to give you this."

"What is it?" Cort Wesley asked, starting to uncrumple it.

"Luke's progress report. He's getting all As."

91

SOUTH TEXAS, THE PRESENT

"It's worse than we thought," Tepper told Caitlin and Cort Wesley over the rental car's Bluetooth system thirty minutes later. "I'm gonna put Young Roger on to provide the particulars, which means I'm gonna have to listen to them over again and get even sicker at the prospects."

A pause followed, longer than it seemed.

"Can you hear me okay?" Young Roger's voice started.

"Just fine," Caitlin told him.

"First off, we've identified four separate freight trains loaded with these barrels."

"Tell them the worst part," she heard Captain Tepper say in the background.

"This isn't the kind of radioactive waste the Japanese were pumping into the ocean back when the earthquake and tsunami caused their disaster. That was just treated water. Dangerous, for sure, but nothing compared to the spent fuel rods contained in the barrels we're looking at here. We're talking about the purest and most dangerous form of radioactive material."

"Ten thousand barrels full of it."

"The freight lines that show Braga inventory about to be shipped slice through Dallas, Fort Worth, San Antonio, and Houston. I just finished the computations, determining that as much as fifty percent of the state's population lives within the exposure range of one of these rail lines at rush hour. Now, not all those lines you're looking at are going to be carrying the radioactive barrels and not all those people are going to be exposed, but I think you get the idea."

"Give them the casualty estimates," Tepper ordered in the background.

"Until we know the precise number of barrels and their locations, my estimates are rough. But I believe we're looking at up to three million people at risk of exposure with half that likely to receive a dosage of radiation in the moderate to high category. Of those, we're looking at a fifty percent casualty rate."

Caitlin didn't need a smart phone or calculator to run the numbers. "That's *seven hundred fifty thousand* people!"

"Roughly."

"And you're telling me all of them are going to die?"

"Not right away and some not at all. That number covers those at the most mortal risk."

Caitlin couldn't even conceive of a civil disaster of such proportions, imagining overloaded hospitals and three of the nation's most populous cities dissolving into panic. She'd seen scenarios run for biological and other terrorist attacks and none of what they portended was good. She glanced toward Cort Wesley who'd gone stiff and pale with beads of sweat forming over his lower lip.

"Tell me how we're playing this, D.W.," she said to Tepper.

"Rangers are taking lead on a unified state effort that would make Sam Houston himself proud. We're gonna take each and every one of these freight trains at the same time before the bad guys know what hit them. We're gonna shut down every inch of track in the state until such time that we check under every tie and train car for explosives. And once we've got all those barrels in hand, we're gonna truck them down to NASA in Houston and load 'em up on a ship bound for goddamn Mars."

"Good thing there's no intelligent life there," Caitlin noted.

"I'm starting to think it's not much different here," Tepper said. "How far out of town are you?"

"Another two hours, give or take."

"The four freights carrying Braga's barrels are all scheduled to roll at five o'clock, just like you said. We're planning simultaneous raids at all four depots for just before then. That should put you back in town right around show time at the Intermodal Terminal here. You got my permission to speed."

"We're already doing ninety, Captain."

"Make it an even hundred, Ranger."

92

SAN ANTONIO, THE PRESENT

"Five minutes, Ranger," Cort Wesley said from behind the wheel, having exchanged places with Caitlin, as they tore through the outskirts of the city.

"Gonna be close," she noted.

"So what else is new?"

A traffic light turned red just before him, and Cort Wesley sped through it anyway, honking his horn. They could see the signs for the San Antonio Intermodal Terminal, opened by Union Pacific Railroad just a few years before at Old Pearsall Road, near Interstate 35 and Loop 410. The new three-hundred-acre terminal normally processed containers carrying clothing, electronics, and household items that originated at West Coast ports via ship from the Pacific Rim. The containers were then loaded onto trains headed to San Antonio's facility where they were off-loaded onto either eighteen-wheelers or smaller Union Pacific freight trains for passage up through the state.

According to Young Roger, their target was a fifty-car Union Pacific freight train that was to twist its way through the city proper to New Braunsfels, San Marcos, and other intermediary points en route to Austin. But those intermediate stops were moot right now.

Because San Antonio itself was sure to be al-Awlaki's target, not more than ten minutes from departing the yard.

Cort Wesley joined the convoy of San Antonio PD,

Highway Patrol, and Ranger vehicles just before it
sped into the yard through the open gate manned by
Union Pacific personnel. Even above the sirens and
racing engine, Caitlin heard the sound of a helicopter
overhead before its distinct shape swooped low over
the scene. It looked like the one chopper operated by
the San Antonio police department, but she couldn't be
sure.

As planned, their entry took all but the most senior
yard officials on scene totally by surprise. The freight
train with its share of radioactive waste loaded onto
its many cars was just ready to roll when a Ranger
parked his extended cab pickup across the tracks directly before the cab. Meanwhile, the same SWAT
team Caitlin recognized from Thomas C. Clark High
School months before took up strategic positions
around the train, their body armor and ATAC helmets
making them look like Star Wars storm troopers. She
thought she spotted Captain Consuelo Alonzo and
D. W. Tepper rushing out of the yard's administrative
headquarters, as more police support personnel moved
to backup positions for the SWAT team and the Rangers prepared to approach the cab of the now stalled
train. All fifty freight cars it carried were closed, denying view of the deadly black drums contained inside.

Barren of shade, heat had been building all day in
the yard, reaching its apex here in the late afternoon
just as the temperatures began to cool and a stronger
breeze started lifting off the water nearby. Right now,
though, that breeze did nothing but fan the heat and
whip chalky rail dust and dirt into the air, swirling it
about in mini-funnel clouds.

As a little girl, Caitlin recalled her grandfather's
colorful tales of how he and other Rangers searched

covered train cars in search of a gang of murderous hobos who'd wreak havoc in small towns and then hop aboard the next freight to escape. Earl Strong had finally caught the bunch by pretending to be one of their own, snoozing in a car they had the misfortune to board. One of them approached with a pipe wrench raised overhead, intending to kill him for sport, when Earl shot the man straight through the hand with his .45. He jailed the other five, two after they were released from the hospital and three more whose mug shots revealed numerous wounds inflicted when they had the bad sense to not go quietly.

"I got one demand here," Caitlin heard Captain Alonzo roar when she burst from Cort Wesley's rental, her voice rising over all other sound. "She goes nowhere near that train."

Tepper followed her gaze all the way to Caitlin. "As the person in charge here, Ranger, how you think I should handle the good captain's request?"

"Looks like you got things well in hand here, sir. I'm happy to sit this one out."

"Done your part already anyway," Tepper said, aiming his next words at Alonzo, "since we'd never even be here to stop this if it wasn't for you. What's the time, Captain Alonzo?"

"Four-fifty, Captain Tepper."

"Then what do you say we commandeer this train?"

93

San Antonio, the present

Caitlin stood next to Cort Wesley, watching eight Rangers wielding shotguns and assault rifles approach the train cab from both sides and directly down the track. The yard dispatcher had already ordered the freight to stand down, but Tepper wasn't about to take any chances.

She thought it would be easy to simply watch this play out from the shade but felt a gnawing in her stomach as the other Rangers, led by Lieutenants Steve Berry and Jim Rollins, continued their approach.

"I think we should take the boys away on a trip," Cort Wesley said, his voice almost in a whisper. "Maybe Disney World or something."

Much to her own surprise, Caitlin found herself easily distracted by his suggestion. "I'd like that," she said, just as the freight train began to roll.

"Dispatch," yelled Tepper into his walkie-talkie, "this is Ranger One! What the hell is going on?"

"Engineer is ignoring our order to pull brake. Repeat, engineer is—"

"I heard you, goddamnit! And you're gonna be one engineer poorer for the effort!" Caitlin watched Tepper switch to another channel. "This is Ranger One, boys. You have the go."

And with that the Rangers and members of the SWAT team opened fire on the now moving train, pouring a nonstop fusillade toward the cab that blew out glass and pockmarked steel. But the freight rolled on, smashing through the extended pickup parked on the tracks and picking up speed as its fifty-car length wound out of the yard and toward the center of San Antonio.

"Too bad we can't shoot out the tires," Captain Tepper was saying.

But Caitlin's attention had already strayed to the police helicopter hovering overhead. "Get that down here!"

Tepper didn't hesitate, giving the appropriate order as Captain Alonzo drew up next to him.

"That's *my* chopper!" she barked in response.

"Not today, ma'am."

"I'll thank you not to call me that."

"What?" Tepper asked her, the lowering chopper's roar beginning to drown out all other sounds.

"Ma'am. It's 'captain,' just like you."

"Okay, *Captain*. Now I'd appreciate you standing down so the Rangers can save some lives here."

Spoken as Caitlin and Cort Wesley moved out into the dust and debris spray of the descending chopper's rotor wash.

"No, no way!" Alonzo roared. "Those two are not authorized to board any police vehicle, no matter who's in charge!"

Tepper stuck a Marlboro Light in his mouth. "Well *Captain,* unless you got someone on your team capable of dropping out of a helicopter onto a freight train moving at forty miles per hour, I'd suggest you let us run the show."

* * *

The police chopper with Caitlin and Cort Wesley on board quickly drew even with the freight, holding position in the air a few cars behind its cab.

"If the cars were wired, I figure whoever's driving that thing would've blown them already," Cort Wesley said into his headset.

"Too much security in the yard to wire the cars," Caitlin followed. "They must have wired the track somewhere down the line."

"Driver's on a suicide mission, Ranger."

"That surprise you?"

Cort Wesley stripped off his headset. "It's time we stopped him."

Caitlin helped Cort Wesley out the chopper's open side door, and he lowered himself onto its landing pod. His weight and the stiff wind buckled the chopper, dragging it over to the right on an angle so steep he thought it might go down. But the pilot quickly compensated, leaving Cort Wesley dangling with his feet ten feet over a freight car two back from the cab.

"I don't stop him this way, you're gonna have to find another!" he yelled up to Caitlin.

"We'll grab his attention in the meantime!"

Caitlin held on to him with her eyes, her face angled outside the door so the last of the day's hot air hit her like a blast from a steam oven. Then she watched as Cort Wesley looked down one last time to measure his drop and opened his hand, plunging to the freight car directly beneath them.

* * *

Cort Wesley tucked his legs at just the right time, landing upon the car with his feet perfectly balanced. The harsh wind that came with traveling at forty miles per hour atop a train nearly knocked him to the tracks below. But Cort Wesley regained his balance by overcompensating in the other direction and then held fast to his footing as he started across the top of this freight car for the next.

"Get us up in front of it!" Caitlin ordered the police chopper pilot.

She knew freight cars offered no passage to the engine cab, which meant Cort Wesley would have to find a way to breach it from the outside. All well and good, except for the fact that newer engines like this were built to preclude precisely this eventuality. The locks and doors were reinforced and the engineer drove the train from what was essentially an armored cubicle. Even shooting him might prove no use at all since he'd likely tied his hand somehow to the throttle to make sure the freight would keep going even if he were killed. She wasn't sure about that, but didn't dare take the chance so long as Cort Wesley offered a better alternative.

The chopper dropped nose first directly before the window of the cab shattered by the Rangers' fusillade back in the yard. Caitlin figured they were a few miles at most from the point of a potential blast's optimal deadly effects where the track bed was likely rigged with powerful explosives. They'd be planted underground, invisible from any angle and wired not just to derail the train but blow up its deadly contents.

"You read me, Ranger?" she heard Tepper call over her discarded headset.

"Right here, Captain," she said, fitting it back into place. "We're in front of the cab now. Cort Wesley's almost there from above."

"Houston, Dallas, and Austin confirm their trains in hand and under control. Engineers all under arrest."

"You tell them we'll be joining them shortly."

Cort Wesley used a ladder to climb down the frontmost freight car onto the steel connector between it and the cab, confronting all at once the enormity of the task remaining before him. No way he could gain access to the cab without announcing his presence, just as there was no doubt the engineer would be armed in anticipation of precisely that eventuality.

He again considered alternate means to bring the train to a halt. Derailing it, even if he could manage that, was hardly an option given that it could produce the very result he was desperately trying to avoid. Which left, which left . . .

Which left *what*?

If he could reach the engine itself . . .

But even if he could, how could he cut or shoot through tempered steel to bring a ten-thousand-horsepower behemoth with all kinds of redundant backup systems to a halt? The answer was simple: he couldn't.

But the engine was the key. Stop it and the contents of the fifty freight cars it was pulling would be rendered effectively harmless. Or . . .

Or . . .

Cort Wesley realized what he had to do in that moment.

Caitlin knew they were running out of time, even before she heard the cop sniper riding next to the pilot speak in her headset.

"One mile before the train hits San Antonio center, Ranger. What's the play?"

Caitlin figured that gave Cort Wesley a minute, maybe ninety seconds tops. He was nowhere in sight now, only the engineer in view as a dim speck propped low in the cab. She wasn't sure the sniper could hit him in these conditions with the best system on Earth.

"Get ready on your rifle," she said anyway, figuring that might be the only chance they had.

Cort Wesley studied the coupling attachment assembly connecting the engine to the long line of cars pulled behind it. The device was the most modern available, constructed to give on even the sharpest turns and cornering, while also built to detach much easier than older models to avoid a whipsaw effect in the event of a derailment. But that made Cort Wesley's task to accomplish that very thing manually no easier since sabotage had been figured into the same equation.

No other choice he could see, though, and angled himself toward the ladder.

"Three quarters of a mile, Ranger," the pilot was saying. "If we're gonna take that shot, it better be now!"

Caitlin moved up closer to the San Antonio police sniper. "You heard the man."

"Doesn't change the fact that I don't have a shot. Engineer's still ducked low beneath the controls."

"Then shoot them. Shoot the hell out of them."

The sniper opened fire, his shots coming in quick bursts that sent sparks flying throughout the cab. Caitlin thought she could see wisps of smoke trailing them, hoping that meant they'd hit something vital. But the freight continued to barrel along, Cort Wesley still nowhere to be seen.

Cort Wesley first tried stamping down with both feet to dislodge the back fifty cars from the engine. When this produced no result whatsoever, he steadied his thinking enough to recall the time his father stole an entire train car with Cort Wesley by his side, along with a brakeman serving as the inside man on the job. Of course, that car had been part of a train parked in a yard, but the principle should be the same, meaning that the coupling was most vulnerable to detachment when the assembly was stretched taut. He recalled how he and his father had absurdly planted their shoulders against the car frame while the brakeman simply knocked out the bolt.

But this train's connections were hydraulic, filled with a thick noxious fluid that flowed like blood, leaks to be feared above all else.

Of course!

Cort Wesley cursed himself for not having thought of this before, hoping there was still time as he eased the Glock from his belt and aimed it down at the jockeying hydraulic line that created the tight connection between cars. He fired five times, enough to send jets of the black fluid spewing from the hose, weakening it enough so that the hose snapped under a bit of weight Cort Wesley laid upon it with his boot. More hydraulic fluid belched outward, eliminating any give in the coupling.

He stepped down upon it, angled so he could cant his body forward with his hands holding fast to the rungs of the ladder of the lead car. Then he started bouncing up and down, nothing happening at all until the coupling popped free in a single thrust that left him holding fast to the engine still barreling along.

He started swaying his body from side to side, picking up enough momentum to carry him clear of the tracks when he let go, hitting the track shoulder hard and rolling down an embankment as the engine thundered on all by itself.

He did it! Caitlin realized, the engine racing under the helicopter almost even with San Antonio center. *Cort Wesley did it!*

"Now get us out of here!" she called to the pilot.

He gave the throttle all it would take, soaring over the slowing assemblage of cars Cort Wesley had detached, as the engine rumbled on. It had just banked into a slight turn between industrial buildings not more than a mile down wind from the famed Alamo when the track beneath it erupted in a fiery blast that coughed the engine fifty feet into the air. Next came a domino-like burst of secondary explosions of equal magnitude rippling backward along the track bed. Through the resulting curtain of smoke and fire, Caitlin glimpsed the engine twist in the air and plunge back to the ground nose first in flaming husks of mangled steel.

Cort Wesley waved, signaling he was okay when the chopper flew over him. The roar of sirens blazed fast down the streets adjoining the tracks and he moved out to meet them, as the cars holding the barrels of promised death ground slowly to a halt a good quarter mile from the line of flames and mangled track bed.

"Four for four, Ranger!" Tepper said, hugging Caitlin after she'd bounded off the police chopper. "Looks like you saved the goddamn world again!"

"It was Cort Wesley alone this time, Captain," she told him.

"SAPD just picked him up. Soon as he gets back here, first round's on me."

"Better hold on that, Captain," said Young Roger, approaching with BlackBerry clutched in hand. "We've got a problem."

"Son, your brains are determined to be the death of me. Are those four freight trains secure or not?"

"They are, sir, along with five thousand fifty-five-gallon steel drums. I got the final manifests right here."

Caitlin felt her stomach sink. "But Braga said . . ."

The look on both Young Roger's and Tepper's faces told her she didn't have to finish the thought.

"Right," said Young Roger. "At least five thousand of those barrels filled with radioactive waste are still unaccounted for."

94

The sun was sinking toward the horizon when the helicopter landed on the helipad of the abandoned *Mariah*. Sam Harrabi climbed out, keeping his head ducked low like he saw in the movies, to find Anwar al-Awlaki waiting, a grim but resolute look stretched over his features. The cleric embraced him tightly, while a number of men Harrabi had never seen before hung back in the shadows. He could see others, similarly unfamiliar, patrolling the decks, as if on guard duty.

"The news is bad, my brother," al-Awlaki reported. "The trains were stopped, five thousand of the blessed barrels recovered."

"But how could . . ." Harrabi left his question unfinished and al-Awlaki didn't seem to be of a mind to answer it anyway.

"It's a blessing we planned our strike from two fronts, my brother," al-Awlaki said instead. The cleric smelled of sweet talcum powder and Harrabi noticed he had started growing his beard back. "Now the attack we launch from these waters grows more vital. Our presence here assures we will yet have something to celebrate for all of eternity."

"Yet you take a great risk by returning to this rig, *sayyid.*"

"Perhaps, but I choose to see the unfortunate circumstances that brought us here in the first place as a sign from God. It's the last place they'd ever think to look for us and high tide is just past dawn. Plenty of time to enjoy the interlude ahead of the chaos that is coming."

As the group's chief engineer, much of the operation's responsibility had fallen into Harrabi's hands. Every time his resolve started to weaken, he'd sit at his beautiful Layla's bedside and recall how blessed their life together had been before that night in Wolfsboro, Tennessee. Harrabi could only hope the pain this part of the plan promised to spread would somehow mitigate his own.

"Now," al-Awlaki continued, steering him toward the command center, "let us prepare to do right by your wife and sons. Let us prepare to make history."

95

SAN ANTONIO, THE PRESENT

"Go back to where this all started," Caitlin said finally, trying to make sense of what Young Roger had just told them.

"That oil rig," said Tepper

"Specifically those barrels Young Roger spotted on the video feed, Captain. They were there in one portion of the feed, gone in a later one."

"That much I already know."

"We can pretty much figure that finding those barrels was the reason why all those workers were murdered, and that al-Awlaki's terrorists were responsible."

"Point made," Tepper said, drawing closer to her. "Where you going with this?"

"The rig workers were murdered because al-Awlaki couldn't risk them alerting the Coast Guard or anybody else about what they'd found, couldn't take the chance those barrels would be pulled up and maybe set the stage for the rest of the five thousand or so to be uncovered too."

Tepper took off his Stetson and ran a hand through his hair that was flattened on the sides. "Hurricane Caitlin blew right by me this time."

"The plan wasn't just to blow Braga's radioactive waste after it was loaded onto those freight trains," she told them all. "The plan was to also ignite half the barrels in the waters of the Gulf."

"Oh boy," muttered Young Roger.

"You got something to say, son?" Tepper prodded.

Young Roger cleared his throat. "I don't think you're gonna like it very much, Captain."

"Son, I'm the last Texas Ranger to actually be hit by an Indian's arrow with the scar to prove it. If I can handle pulling that head out and stitching myself up, I think I can handle just about anything."

Young Roger nodded, his face twisted tight in what looked like pain as well. "Our problems aren't going to end in the Gulf, sir. What we're really talking about here are five thousand separate dirty bombs. Now, high explosives inflict damage with rapidly expanding, superheated gas. Dirty bombs use that gas expansion as a means of propelling radioactive material over a wide area as a destructive force in its own right. When the explosive goes off, the radioactive material spreads in a sort of dust cloud carried by the wind that reaches a wider area than the explosion itself."

"No wind underwater," Tepper pointed out.

"No, water has currents instead. And igniting that many barrels around high tide would maximize the wash of the deadly toxins inland to eventually soak through into the ecosystem, poisoning the ground and drinking water. Not a piece of fish, shrimp, or oyster would remain unaffected."

"I'm getting indigestion just listening to this, son."

"It gets worse, Captain. The infected waters would follow the currents toward Florida and then up the East Coast of the country, tracing the same lines as migrating fish."

"Any chance you're wrong about this?"

"Yes, sir; it could be even worse," Young Roger said, jogging his BlackBerry to its calculator function.

96

NORTHERN GULF STREAM, THE PRESENT

Harrabi had personally devised specially constructed shaped charges to work underwater. The real challenge lay in devising an equally sure means to transmit the remote detonation signal over such a wide area up to seven hundred feet below the water's surface. The energy of standard radio signals would be weakened and rendered ultimately ineffectual by the seawater. And infrared signals would be either swiftly absorbed or diffused by mud and other debris.

The solution Harrabi came up with was acoustic transmission using a digital processing system. This particular level of expertise, he supposed, was what had drawn al-Awlaki to him in the first place, fate playing the ultimate hand. Another member of the team, tragically oppressed just as he had been, had created a diode and chip encased in a waterproof plastic shield capable of receiving the acoustic signals as much as a thousand feet below the surface. It had vibrating sensors programmed to the specific wave pattern that would trigger the charge with the simple internal element akin to touching two wires together. The broadcast devices themselves were scattered strategically throughout the target area in buoys that were exact replicas of ones deployed by the Coast Guard.

It had been a long and painstaking process that required direct contact with the barrels and, thus, their toxic contents. Precautions only went so far and mistakes were inevitable in the arduous toil and labor that would have cost one of his team members their life had a car accident not done the job first.

Harrabi had expected he would've felt better about this moment. Instead, all he felt was empty, his great victory of vengeance lost in the fact that it would do nothing about the sadness filling his soul. It wouldn't bring his boys back, make his beautiful Layla whole again, or even improve his people's plight. But Harrabi was no longer a big enough thinker to care about any of that. He knew only that America would never recover from what he was about to unleash upon her, just as he never had. That might not have been enough, but it was something, all he had.

"We are heroes in the eyes of God, my brother," al-Awlaki said, continuing to lead him toward the *Mariah*'s elevated command center.

A trio of the great man's guards fell into step behind them amid the machinery squeezed and cluttered everywhere. Harrabi stopped to tie his shoe, crouching down and knotting his lace as al-Awlaki's biggest bodyguard ground to a halt over him dragging a lame leg.

Something cold gripped Harrabi's insides. His fingers shook and he retied his shoe again, his mind flashing back to the night that had changed him forever.

The man who had brought the baseball bat down on his oldest son's skull . . .

That man had walked with a limp.

The big man he was looking at now walked with a limp.

Harrabi closed his eyes, trying to recall more of the man's face as he'd glimpsed it in the darkness. The face looked the same, the hair looked the same, the eyes looked the same.

Because it was *the same man*! Sent that night not by locals intent on stopping a mosque in their town of Wolfsboro, Tennessee, not by fate at all . . .

But by the great Anwar al-Awlaki himself.

97

SAN ANTONIO, THE PRESENT

"You got something more to say or not?" Tepper asked Young Roger.

Young Roger looked up from calculations he'd been working out on his BlackBerry. "Well, think of it this way. Ten parts per million is considered safe when it comes to radioactivity. We're looking at something on the level of a hundred million times worse than that."

"Remind me never to hire anyone as smart as you again."

Young Roger grabbed a half-full bottle of water off the hood of one of the still warm SUVs parked in the freight yard. Then he picked up a handful of gravel from the ground at his feet.

"Make believe this is the Gulf," he said, holding the bottle up for them to see. "This would represent a safe level of contamination."

With that, Young Roger dropped a pinch of gravel dust into the water, swirling it around until it quickly dissolved.

"Now here's the equivalent of what we'd be facing if five thousand barrels of radioactive waste were released."

And here he sifted the remaining gravel dust in his hand into the bottle. He shook up the resulting contents, turning the water dark and gritty, though a large portion of the gravel dust remained undissolved on the bottom.

"The toxicity level," Young Roger finished, "would be virtually immeasurable."

"What's that mean exactly?" Caitlin asked.

"First off, there are actually differing opinions on the dangers of using the oceans as a toxic waste dump. Best example I can cite is the nearly fifty thousand drums of low-level radioactive waste dropped in the Gulf of the Farallones National Marine Sanctuary off San Francisco between 1946 and 1970. There are also huge dump sites in the Barents and Kara Seas used for decades by the former Soviet Union. In the case of those and the Farallones, there's virtually no empirical data to suggest any danger to marine or human life, even though the drums have long been leaking."

"Got a feeling there's a 'but' coming here," said Tepper.

"And that 'but,'" Young Roger continued, "is introducing the explosive element, since now you're not just talking about slow seepage but the release of 275,000 gallons of the most toxic of all nuclear waste *all at once*. Because the waste itself is much heavier than water, if just dumped—poured out—it would sink to the bottom. Plenty of damage, yes, but nothing on the order of what will happen when blowing up those drums softens the material's molecular composition so it ends up mixing with and dissolving into the water. And that's not all."

"Oh, shit," was all Tepper could say as he fumbled for a cigarette.

"In addition to the inevitable spread up the East Coast, we'd be looking at the toxins coming ashore not just with the currents but also in the rain."

"Rain?"

"Let me put it this way. Even a storm well short of hurricane proportions anytime for the next several days, weeks maybe, would dose residents stretching hundreds of miles inland with radiation equivalent to a few thousand chest X-rays. The run-off could also poison every ounce of drinking water in the same radius up the entire eastern seaboard."

"What about a storm *not* short of a hurricane?" Caitlin posed.

"More water whipped up would mean added toxicity and a deeper spread. Let me put it this way," Young Roger said, repeating himself. "Chernobyl and the recent nuclear disaster in Japan were both sevens on a seven-point scale of radiation spread and intensity."

"And where would this fall?" Tepper asked him.

"A ten."

"And even if we had a way to stop them, we've got no idea where they're at."

"I think I do," said Caitlin.

98

NORTHERN GULF STREAM, THE PRESENT

Harrabi felt numb, al-Awlaki's words no longer reaching him in the cramped confines of the bridge. He had been betrayed.

Again.

First by his own friends and neighbors, who had turned on him. And now by this man, who saw in him nothing more than a potential stooge with the expertise required to do his bidding. His former friends and neighbors had chased him back to the world he had forsaken where he became fodder for the very extremists he'd spent much of his life renouncing.

The whole tragedy had been a setup, Harrabi's sons murdered, his wife reduced to a vegetative state, his entire life destroyed so he could be enlisted, manipulated, to make al-Awlaki's murderous cause his own. The cleric had seized upon his weakness, taken advantage of his great vulnerability

A lie, all of it, every bit!

He thought of the other Arab-Americans and American Muslims who'd joined him in the cause. All victims of terrible tragedies apparently driven by hatred and racism when, in fact, they were victims instead of one man's singular purpose and vision. Anwar al-Awlaki had caused their pain so he could use it to his own purpose.

"You did not answer my question, my brother," al-Awlaki was saying, his voice suddenly tinged with suspicion.

"I'm sorry, *sayyid*," Harrabi told him. "I was swept away by the scope of all this, the fate we are visiting on our enemies in spite of the failure of the plan's initial phase."

That seemed to satisfy the cleric. "I was asking about the precise timing, the heavenly moment when Allah himself will smile on us from heaven."

"High tide is six-fifteen, ten minutes before dawn," Harrabi told him, recalling his earlier calculations. "To achieve the desired effects we will detonate the drums at six A.M. precisely."

But he wouldn't, he couldn't, not for this man, this fraud who had killed innocents and would kill tens of thousands more to serve his own cause. Anwar al-Awlaki, the man he so revered, who had lent meaning to his life when all else had failed and offered him redemption, was about nothing more than glory, self-gratification, and hatred. He served no higher power, only himself and his own twisted ambitions.

And in that moment, as if on cue, a lightning bolt lit up the sky, accompanied by a roar of thunder that shook all on the bridge except al-Awlaki who smiled tightly.

"A pleasant omen for the fires we are about to bring," the cleric said. He was standing before a bank of controls and monitoring gauges below the windows where Harrabi had set up his transmitter. Besides those con-

trols, a few filing cabinets and the operations installation manager's desk made up the command center's
sole contents. The walls were adorned with framed
photographs of other offshore rigs, mostly of the deepwater variety, captured to make them look almost ro-
mantic when framed against the horizon they seemed
to dwarf. "Tonight we change the world forever."

Harrabi looked over at al-Awlaki, sick to his stomach again, then closed his eyes to the sight of his sons,
happy and smiling. Playing baseball, taking driving lessons, the junior prom. Things that would now never
happen because of the cause and man he found himself
serving.

> *Go pigeon bird, don't believe what I am saying,*
> *I just say it so that Rima will sleep*

And now Harrabi saw the true meaning of the lullaby, the fact that *he* was the pigeon his wife, Layla,
had been singing about.

99

SAN ANTONIO, THE PRESENT

"Makes perfect sense," Caitlin said, after explaining
her theory. "It's where this began last week and where
al-Awlaki will want to end it."

"You damn Strongs are so spooky when it comes to
these damn feelings, I swear you're in touch with different planes of existence," Tepper said, shaking his
head.

"You ever know my dad or granddad to be wrong?"

"Not when it mattered most, which certainly applies here."

"I feel it too," Cort Wesley said, breathing hard from the sprint from the police car that had just dropped him off.

Tepper finally lit his cigarette. "You got that look," he said, before he turned to Cort Wesley. "You too. Problem is we got no way to figure out whether this theory's on the mark without getting on board that rig."

Caitlin took a step closer to Tepper. "Guess that leaves us with only one option."

"It does indeed," added Cort Wesley.

"Gonna take more than the two of you to get this done," Tepper told them both. "Gonna take a small army that's done this kind of thing before."

"Then it's a good thing we've got one," said Caitlin.

"Captain," Young Roger said suddenly, looking up from his BlackBerry.

"What is it now, son?"

Young Roger's face was ashen. "A storm, sir, a big one."

100

NORTHERN GULF STREAM, THE PRESENT

The Zodiac raft bucked the swirling waves, riding them like a roller coaster, its outboard engine steered by Cort Wesley while Caitlin sat up front. Paz and his six former Zeta Mexican Special Forces commandos were clustered tightly in the middle, checking weap-

ons currently sealed in waterproof pouches to shield
them from the elements as long as possible.

The tropical storm making its way through the Gulf
already seemed even stronger than forecast and still
building. Cort Wesley held his face to the pounding
rain and wind, as if trying to gauge their ferocity.

"Remember what you told me that Roger guy said
about wind and rain, Ranger?"

Caitlin looked at the black world swirling around
her, the sheets of rain like curtains drawn over the Gulf.
"They blow those barrels anytime soon and we're
looking at a world of hurt," she said back to him, as a
fresh blast of lightning illuminated the white-capped
seas.

A chopper pilot who'd flown combat missions in both
Iraq and Afghanistan had ferried them to Baffin Bay
through the first of the storm where a Coast Guard
patrol boat was waiting in port. The *Largo* was part
of a new generation of Sentinel class patrol boats that
were easily the most advanced for their time of any
the Coast Guard had enjoyed since being conceived
by Alexander Hamilton in 1790. The *Largo*'s captain
and his exec asked no questions as Paz and his Zetas
trailed Caitlin and Cort Wesley aboard, perhaps pretending not to notice them or the weapons they were
carrying. The patrol boat would get them as close to
the *Mariah* as possible, after which they'd board the
Zodiac to cover the remaining distance, hoping the
raft would be able to overcome the winds and waves.

Caitlin's thoughts aboard the Zodiac churned crazily,
focusing mostly on the boat trips her dad and granddad
had made to Galveston Island. The Strongs and D. W.

Tepper had gone to Galveston on the trail of killers who turned out to be Alvin Jackson and Teofilo Braga. It all, every bit of it, seemed fated to connect with the terrorist attack they were facing today. Only by investigating Braga had she learned the truth and been given at least a chance to save who knew how many lives.

"Let's go to work," Cort Wesley said as the shape of the *Mariah* appeared in the next flash of lightning.

"If this don't beat all," Leroy Epps said, as Cort Wesley steered the Zodiac the last stretch to the oil rig.

Cort Wesley was glad to see Leroy seated there next to him in the raft's stern, as soaked to the gills as a live person.

"You and the Ranger guns going again," Epps continued.

"Just me this time, champ."

"Not from where I'm sitting, bubba."

"Can't risk leaving my boys alone. That means one of us stays with the ship and it's not gonna be me."

"You sound rattled."

"I don't like the feeling I got about this, not one bit."

"Go back to what you said before."

"What's that?"

"About not wanting to leave your boys alone. The Ranger's made herself right at home, ain't she?"

"Her own mom died young. I wonder if that's part of it."

"Like, what, some kind of second chance?"

"Don't know, champ. It just feels like this is something she needs or, maybe, just deserves."

"Even though it be against her nature?"

"I'm not convinced of that. She gave up her guns for a time."

"*But they chased her back down, bubba, didn't they?*"

"What's your point, champ?"

"*Believe I was wrong about the nature being hers alone. Believe the picture may be bigger than that. You'd think from where I sit now I'd be able to see different. Truth is the view's clearer but no more complete.*" The whites of Epps's milky eyes seemed to shine in the night. "*Wish I could tell ya how this all turns out, bubba, but the truth is tomorrow's like a corner I can't see around.*"

"You and me both," Cort Wesley told the ghost of Leroy Epps.

IOI

NORTHERN GULF STREAM, THE PRESENT

Paz managed to hold the Zodiac steady against one of the *Mariah*'s legs long enough for Caitlin to tie it down just short of the ladder lifting upward into the storm-soaked night. The torrents of rain had grown so thick that the deck of the *Mariah*, just sixty feet up, was virtually invisible, creating the impression that the ladder climbed literally toward nowhere.

"What time is high tide?" Cort Wesley shouted toward Caitlin.

"Twenty minutes from now!"

"Means we gotta get a move on!"

Paz took the lead up the ladder, followed by his Zeta

commandos, Caitlin holding fast to the rope tie at the mooring leg's base. She fought the Zodiac's sway, feeling herself mashed against the cold steel each time a powerful swell carved its way under the *Mariah*'s deck six stories up. The rig itself seemed to be listing one way and then the other, Caitlin unsure whether it was a storm-fostered illusion or the way it had been constructed to avoid being toppled in heavy winds. The final Zeta reached up for the ladder and started to climb, and Caitlin felt Cort Wesley's breath against the back of her neck.

"Don't even think about following us up there, Ranger."

"You say that again I might shoot you myself, Cort Wesley."

"We lose this raft, we got no exit strategy."

She turned as much as she could to face him without giving him her hold on the rig's mooring leg. "That what this is about, an exit strategy?"

He kissed her hard on the lips, the force of the swirling winds seeming to hold their faces together.

"Check your radio," Cort Wesley said, reaching up for the ladder.

Caitlin moved her wrist-mounted microphone. "Test one, two."

"Three, four," Cort Wesley followed, before disappearing into the night and the storm.

102

"Sixteen minutes," al-Awlaki said, eyes glued to his watch.

Beyond the bridge, the deck of the *Mariah* was lost in a blur of storm-driven rain and wind. The torrents pounded the bridge windows with such blinding ferocity that they might as well have been a curtain drawn over the glass.

"We'll never be able to chopper out in this," Harrabi said from the control panel. "We're trapped."

Al-Awlaki smiled, calmer than Harrabi had seen him yet. "This storm is a blessing from God, my brother, one that I have prepared for accordingly. Rest assured that my planning has taken the good fortune He has bestowed upon us into consideration."

If Harrabi had a weapon, any weapon, he might have launched himself on al-Awlaki, murderer of his children, then and there. But he didn't want it to end that way; he wanted it to end with al-Awlaki's realizing the explosions would never come, that he had failed, that his ultimate fate had been denied him. Harrabi wanted to see the look on his face in that precise moment of understanding and the sense of futility that accompanied it.

"Twelve minutes," the cleric said and Harrabi opened his eyes, wondering where the time had gone. Were the minutes speeding up?

Then, through the sheets of rain pounding the windows, flashes flared in the empty darkness beyond, like torches lighting a way toward hope.

* * *

Water splashed a few yards away on the rig's deck,
Cort Wesley sliding forward to the support extension
of the mooring leg for cover. A guard, likely alerted by
what looked like shifting shapes in the storm, approached with submachine gun leveled before him.

Cort Wesley lurched upward, wielding a knife. Blade
starting forward, finding the man's chest and heart in
the same moment.

"*Man's gotta do what a man's gotta do, bubba,*"
he heard Leroy Epps say in his head. "*Let's get a
move on.*"

Caitlin was holding on for dear life, every inch of her
body so soaked that she had the sense she was drowning even above the surface, on the verge of being swept
away by the storm. Her gun had become an afterthought and she hated being stuck here holding the
Zodiac in place with the battle likely under way now
above her. Just sixty feet in the distance, but she'd
never felt farther away from Cort Wesley, even when
he was in Cereso prison.

She was fighting to clear the stinging seawater from
her eyes when a dark shape reared up before her, rolling through the last of the waves directly in line with
the raft. Caitlin recognized it as some kind of launch,
or small cabin cruiser, having braved the storm to ferry
al-Awlaki's team out of here once their deadly mission
was complete. She knew it was going to hit the Zodiac, glimpsed the pilot working the wheel frantically
behind a single windshield wiper deflecting the rain
from his viewing angle as best it could. The launch

was slowing, but not fast enough. Caitlin leaped up and grabbed hold of the ladder at the last, feeling the launch crash into the Zodiac with enough force to knock one of her hands from its slippery hold. The launch compressed the raft's rubber, bleeding the air from it.

Caitlin dangled, legs kicking the air. The pilot and a second man in the bridge she hadn't noticed before spotted her, shouting at each other as the shock and clear meaning of her presence along with the raft's struck them. They each seemed to be reaching for something, one coming up with what looked like a shotgun when Caitlin managed to strip her dark jacket aside enough to tear her pistol free.

Swaying from the ladder in the storm-drenched night, she emptied the magazine through the boat's windshield. The men disappeared behind the shattered glass now pierced by the rain as well, and the launch suddenly surged on. It turned sideways, as if one of the now dead men had jammed the wheel, being sucked away by the storm until a huge wave pushed it broadside. The launch slammed into the support leg just beneath her and clung there, the force of the storm seeming to hold it in place.

Caitlin holstered her pistol and looked at the launch. She could go back down and take refuge on it, but its precarious perch made her think going up was actually safer. Then she added her second hand to the ladder and began to climb.

103

Cort Wesley had no idea of the opposition's number or placement. They seemed to be everywhere and nowhere, scurrying about in panic, recognizable from their lack of proper storm gear in stark contrast to Paz and his similarly dark-clad Zetas who moved as one with the storm.

He angled for the rig's elevated bridge while Paz's team swept inward from the outsides of the deck, herding their victims into an increasingly concentrated killing zone. He'd fought by Paz's side four times now, continuing to marvel at his warrior-like skills and disciplined sensibility. The man was an odds changer all by himself, a human killing machine like none Cort Wesley had ever encountered before.

But the bridge was Cort Wesley's to take, and he took up position behind an exhaust baffle and sighted in toward the command center glass, before which stood a single figure.

The series of flashes had brought al-Awlaki right up to the window, face squeezed against it with hands cupped over his eyes to better see out onto the deck. When he finally pulled back again, a ring of misty condensation had formed in line with his mouth that was now agape in panic.

"Someone's out there," Harrabi heard him mutter.

Motion flashed amid a burst of lightning in the storm

beyond, at least one shape angling for the elevated bridge from below. The big man with the limp barreled into al-Awlaki and took him to the floor an instant before the glass exploded behind a barrage of automatic fire, shards showering in all direction ahead of the storm following them. The cleric's other two guards offered return fire until a fresh barrage blew them backward, past Harrabi who found himself hugging the floor in the next instant.

"How? *How?*" al-Awlaki screamed over the howling winds that had invaded the bridge. Then his bulging, furious eyes fixed on Harrabi. "Do it! Do it *now!*"

Harrabi remained prone, motionless, strangely calm. "No."

"Trigger the blasts!"

"No."

"Coward!"

Harrabi moved his gaze to the big man, then back to al-Awlaki. "Cowards kill innocent boys with baseball bats."

Al-Awlaki's mouth dropped.

"Their coffins were closed because of what you did to their faces!" Harrabi raged on, thinking of his wife, who'd given up her world for his, only to pay a terrible price for her love.

"That was God's work!"

"No, it was *yours* and now you pay!" Harrabi screamed, as wind gusts pushed more of the storm in upon them. "Because God does not murder children . . . or women."

"You speak of your wife, an *American*? I did you a favor by ridding her from your life and turning you toward the light!"

"The light . . . Is that what you call my cursed life now? It was you who cursed me! Not God, not fate—*you* to serve your own ends."

"I gave you the chance to rejoin your people, to make amends for indiscretions that are sins in the eyes of Allah! You can still have your redemption, my brother," al-Awlaki continued, a sense of calm returning to his voice. "Send the signal. Trigger the blasts. Make the Americans pay for all they have done to our people."

But Harrabi held his ground stubbornly. "I'd rather make you pay, for what you've done to me."

Cort Wesley thought he'd hit at least one person in the command center, maybe two, but couldn't be sure. He sliced forward, darting into the open long enough to better his angle. Waiting for a firm target or at least motion before opening fire into the command center again.

Caitlin continued to climb, the wind and torrents of rain lashing her like strikes from a bullwhip. The force of the storm had jarred some of the ladder's support truss loose, which made her ascent that much more perilous. She'd never had a particular fear of heights and glancing down now revealed only blackness that gave up nothing discernible after ten feet. But her stomach felt fluttery and a sudden wave of dizziness left her holding hard to the ladder with both hands, eyes squeezed closed.

She peeled them open enough to see the next rung, stretching a hand up to it. The deck of the *Mariah* was close now, not more than fifteen feet away, but that fifteen feet in her dazed vision might as well have been forever, and a dread fear that she wasn't going to make it filled her. But she pushed herself on regardless, try- ing to visualize each motion as one in itself. Her legs grew heavy, almost impossible to budge, leaving the arduous task almost exclusively to her arms, which strained under the pressure. Her hands were wet with nervous sweat as well as seawater and the rungs grew more slippery with each grasp.

Caitlin felt her breath settle when the deck came within reach, just as the truss broke from its bracket. She reached out, groping at the air, realizing the rig was starting to slip away. Her feet slid off the ladder and she kicked with them, as if dog paddling like a child, hoping to swim through the air and force the ladder back against the deck mount.

The swirling wind buffeted Caitlin before a sudden gust helped drive her back close enough to the *Mariah* to latch a hand onto the raised deck sill an instant before the ladder broke off altogether, plummeting toward the sea. Caitlin managed to jerk her second hand over the sill as well, her feet flailing to find pur- chase on something, anything, to help in the effort.

With no other choice, she resolved to dig her palms into the sill edge, feeling steel slice into her flesh. The pain sent starbursts before her eyes but provided the grasp she needed to lift herself up in agonizingly slow fashion. She heard herself scream over the howling of the wind that sounded like crazed laughter. The rain hammered her, the wind fighting her final hoist with renewed effort, as Caitlin felt herself tumble to the cold wet deck.

* * *

"You're a fake, a fraud!" Harrabi continued, his rage bubbling over.

"I was serving God! Everything I did was to serve Him. I made the world believe I was dead to serve Him!" The cleric's eyes bled fury and hate, his coarse short hair drenched in rainwater that ran down his face. "The death of your sons, what happened to your wife, was His bidding, not mine. I am only his vessel, as are you. Know that as you bring hope to our world."

"No, *your* world," Harrabi shot back at al-Awlaki. "A world of blood, pain, and needless suffering wrought by you to justify your own existence. How many lives did you take, did you destroy, to set your plan in place? All for naught now because you are the traitor. Traitor to everything Islam should stand for."

"This coming from a man who turned away from it, who shunned his own people and his own world."

"It was never my world."

"Trigger the blasts! It is your duty!"

Harrabi didn't move, didn't speak. Al-Awlaki popped up into the spray of rain, greeted instantly by a hail of fire rendered silent by the storm's banshee-like roar whipping around the deck. He swept across the bridge in a crouch, seeming to dodge the bullets, and captured Harrabi by the throat in a surprisingly strong grasp.

"Perform your duty to God or die here and now! And when you die, you will go to hell."

"I'm already there," Harrabi said, as al-Awlaki started to choke him.

"Did you get him, bubba?" Leroy Epps asked.

"I don't know," Cort Wesley told him, jamming a

fresh magazine into his submachine gun. "Angle's all wrong. I can't see a goddamn thing."

"Bad sight angle means bad shooting."

Around Cort Wesley, Paz's Zeta commandos closed on the final terrorists their sweep had pinned down in a tight cluster of storage containers. Cort Wesley thought he heard words screamed in Arabic struggling to be heard over the storm's wail, perhaps asking for mercy or trying to surrender. But the Zetas didn't play by such rules. They knew only one way and taking prisoners wasn't part of it. Soft, quick pops split the night, confirming his assumption.

"We're running out of time, bubba!" Leroy Epps shouted at him.

"Tell me something I don't know!" Cort Wesley tried to find his ghostly specter through the storm. "Don't suppose you can cover me, champ."

"Sorry, not in my job description."

"Didn't think so," Cort Wesley said, and took a deep breath before spinning out for the bridge.

104

NORTHERN GULF STREAM, THE PRESENT

Harrabi was ready to die, until he thought of the man squeezing the life out of him, the same man who had ordered the deaths of his sons.

He would die soon enough. But not now.

And with that thought he pulled himself free of al-Awlaki's grasp and unleashed a flurry of blows, the rage and sadness spilling out of him. In that moment he realized how he had nothing to live for and found renewed purpose in killing the man who had destroyed everything he loved. His life had ended that night in a sodden field in Wolfsboro, Tennessee, all that followed nothing but a charade, a fake existence he had fallen into. The purpose al-Awlaki's mission had provided had been a fraud too, but killing the cleric was anything but. Killing him was about reclaiming his life, and he could feel the blood flowing through his veins for the first time since that terrible night, as he continued to find the cleric's flesh with his fists.

Then Harrabi felt a sudden rush of warmth running out of him, turning his insides as cold as his flesh. There was pain, dim and vague, near his spine and he felt himself sliding down the air for the floor, hitting it to the sight of the big man with the limp steadying his pistol on him again. But a fresh barrage of gunfire poured through the storm and turned the big man who'd murdered his oldest son into a marionette, twisting him about the floor before cutting the strings and letting him crumple.

Harrabi felt only tired, nothing else. He wanted to grab al-Awlaki as the cleric crawled past him, but his arms wouldn't obey. He was still trying when al-Awlaki stripped a hand grenade from the big man's ammo vest.

Harrabi watched him crawl toward the shattered window and then fixed his eyes on the big man's pistol that had skittered to a halt just a few feet from him. He knew he was dying. He felt it without regret or fear, comfortable in the certainty he'd soon be with his sons. That thought helped him find the strength to pull himself toward the pistol, as al-Awlaki hurled the grenade into the night.

The blast rattled the deck beyond Cort Wesley, sending a curtain of flame and shrapnel to mix with the pounding rain. The percussion alone was enough to tear his feet out from under him, while he was spared the deadly spread.

He found his muscles spongy and unresponsive to his commands. He realized he'd lost his submachine gun, then remembered it was slung from his shoulder and thus pinned beneath him. But the night was too cold and he was too tired to reach for it, nonetheless finding the will to push up to his knees, ready to move for the bridge when a shape stepped out over him.

Al-Awlaki spun back toward the control board, the time he needed to trigger the blast that would change the world his now. He had watched Harrabi rig the device, thought he knew the way to trigger it. Then he heard a grunt and turned to see a pistol trembling in Harrabi's hand.

"Shoot me and you shoot God," the cleric said, standing there reverently as if in prayer.

"I'm not going to shoot you. I'm not a killer. You taught me that much," Harrabi told him and emptied the rest of the magazine into the transmitter that would've sent the acoustic signal across the Gulf to blow the barrels had al-Awlaki managed to trigger it. Sparks leaped everywhere, trailed by smoke and the noxious stench of burned wires.

"*Noooooooooooooo!*"

The cleric's desperate scream pierced his eardrums through the howling of the storm, the most glorious sound Harrabi had ever heard. He saw a pistol flash in the cleric's hand, fire blazing toward him from its barrel. Harrabi closed his eyes to sleep, dream, and meet his sons again.

Paz helped Cort Wesley to his feet, smelling like air scorched by flames.

"The Ranger's on board," he said.

"*What?* You saw her?"

"I don't need to see her, outlaw."

Cort Wesley felt Paz drag him on, slowly recovering his own footing.

"My men are sweeping the deck in search of more terrorists. I saw a few jump off into the sea."

"Let's find Caitlin."

Caitlin moved about the deck, searching for Paz or Cort Wesley. She thought she'd heard gunfire and then a blast, more piercing and concentrated than thunder, ignited a bright flash not far from the raised structure she recognized as the bridge from her first visit to the rig. That thought made her remember the emergency life pods and rafts, like the one used by the engineer that had drifted straight to the fishing boat she'd chartered at Baffin Bay.

How long ago had that been?

It felt like years but was barely a week. Caitlin had no idea how the evacuation procedures actually worked, only that she better learn them fast before the now hurricane-force storm toppled the *Mariah* into the sea.

The temperature was climbing, the warmth recharging her while making her torn palms hurt more. She thought she could hear continued sporadic gunfire above the storm, the flashes looking curiously like D. W. Tepper's match strokes before lighting a Marlboro. She took a wide route around the rig deck, recalling the location of the life pods and rafts from her initial visit to the rig. No way anyone was getting off on the helicopter she'd spotted perched on the helipad that hung out over the sea.

Caitlin had just formed that thought when a gust of wind blew the Sikorsky onto its side and then into the sea.

Al-Awlaki watched the helicopter fall into the sea but wasted no time bemoaning its loss. He knew God was behind him and his holy mission, knew God would guide him from this hell even as he wondered to what purpose he had come here. His failure must have been ordained, a test he needed to pass in order to fulfill an even greater plan God had in store for him. Hadn't the Jewish God laid similar tests at the feet of Moses, Abraham, and Isaac? Al-Awlaki would learn from their lessons and someday, a day very soon, he would be blessed with the true vision of the end of days it was his duty to bring.

Everything, all his planning and preparation, all his sacrifice, had fallen apart on this rig in the face of an assault from forces sent from hell as a final test to see if he was truly worthy to battle the demons on Earth. He should never have expected a mission this holy, this wondrous, to be a mere act of strategic planning. He had been meant to fail to prepare him for something bigger and better.

Al-Awlaki looped around a series of outlying structures that looked like portable storage containers, coming face-to-face with a number of flattened orange rafts hanging from hydraulic emergency lifts that would launch them to the sea once inflated. The process to manage that task was surprisingly simple, as it had to be for a man in the midst of panic to handle the effort. But al-Awlaki felt no such rush, only contentment and surety that fate had delivered him this far and had grand plans for him ahead. He moved to the nearest emergency raft and studied the rigging. He pulled a cord that inflated the raft and automatically activated the launching system, the storm no longer seeming so fearsome.

Until a flash of lightning illuminated the dark figure of a phantom silhouetted before him.

105

NORTHERN GULF STREAM, THE PRESENT

It was *a woman,* al-Awlaki realized, edging closer to the raft now lying horizontal, close enough to board. Her hair was twisted into a wild tangle, her face pale and her frame silhouetted against the pounding storm as if the rain slanted to avoid her. Something dark dripped from both her hands, one of which held a pistol aimed straight for him.

* * *

"I'm a Texas Ranger!" Caitlin announced, holding her ground as the wind howled, strong enough to buckle her knees. She felt like Dorothy in *The Wizard of Oz,* about to be lifted up and out into the sky. "Stay where you are or I'll shoot you where you stand!"

Caitlin had studied dozens of photographs of the cleric Anwar al-Awlaki, one of which pictured him while in college at Colorado State University twenty years ago before becoming radicalized. That shot, showing him with close-cropped hair with the texture of a Brillo pad, resembled the man before her too closely to be coincidence.

"You're going to put your hands in the air *now!*" she said loud enough for her words to rise over the storm.

The man didn't move, didn't raise his hands. "What are *you?*"

"Already told you that."

"Another test, is that it?"

Caitlin raised her gun further.

"You're Him, aren't you? Coming to me in guise to find whether I'm worthy or not."

"Don't move!"

But al-Awlaki's eyes caught fire, seeming to glow in the blackness between them. "No, I see it now! You are *Iblīs!*"

"I said, don't—"

"*Šaytān!*" al-Awlaki bellowed, twisting to reveal a pistol wedged in his belt.

His right hand went for it, even as he thrust himself backward over the lip of the escape raft. A sputtering whirring sound told Caitlin the hydraulic system had been activated to launch it. She opened fire in the moment al-Awlaki's pistol cleared his belt, pulled the trigger and just kept pulling.

Pop! Pop! Pop! Pop!

The sounds might have been whippets of thunder or the thin echoes of her gunshots. Either way, the air burst from the escape raft in a rippling wheeze, its flattened remnants and passenger sent hurtling downward into the storm-ravaged air before disappearing into the dark depths of the sea.

Caitlin had just reached the edge to look down in search of him, when Paz swung round a corner supporting Cort Wesley. Both of them joined her gaze, having glimpsed the raft's plunge as well.

"It was al-Awlaki," she told them both. "I sent him to hell for sure this time."

EPILOGUE

In the spring of 2008, the Rangers became involved in a headline-grabbing case somewhat reminiscent of the Branch Davidian standoff fifteen years earlier. Once again, it involved a splinter religious group with a fortresslike house of worship standing prominently on private property. . . .

When the Rangers got ready to enter the four-story temple, a group of fifty-seven men ringed it, holding hands. Their leader told Captain Caver they intended to offer "passive resistance."

"Define 'passive resistance,'" the captain said.

The man replied that the men would continue to stand around the temple but once the Rangers approached they would not physically resist. Instead, he said, they would kneel and begin praying.

"That's a damn good idea," Caver told the man.

Still concerned about an attempt at violent resistance, Caver had his own plan. The Rangers let the men stand around the temple all day long before finally approaching it later in the day. If the men had any fight in them, the West Texas heat had sucked it out of them.

—Mike Cox, *Time of the Rangers*

"Never thought I'd be setting foot on this thing again," D. W. Tepper said moments after he'd arrived at the rig on a Coast Guard cutter.

The storm had blown out shortly after dawn, its residue being a crystal blue sky and oppressively humid air smelling of sea salt and musty foliage churned up by the winds on shore. Guillermo Paz and his men were gone by the time the first Coast Guard patrol boats and cutters converged on the scene. Caitlin couldn't comprehend how he'd managed it until she recalled the launch al-Awlaki and his men would've used to escape had things turned out differently. The launch that had snared on the rig's mooring leg after she disabled it, long gone now with Paz having appropriated the craft.

Tepper gazed around him, face wrinkling at the sight of the bodies of al-Awlaki's men lying where Paz and his commandos had gunned them down. "Let's see if we can get this sorted out."

It took several hours to even approach that point. All the terrorists had been killed, although the circumstances surrounding the deaths of the four found inside the bridge seemed muddled and contradictory, to be figured out later.

"Good news," Tepper told Caitlin and Cort Wesley, "is that the Coast Guard is in the process of locating each and every one of those five thousand barrels. How they bring 'em up's a different story, but they'll get it done, you can bank on that."

"What's the bad news?" Caitlin asked him.

"Waters are too deep to bother looking for al-Awlaki's body."

"It's there, Captain. I'm not worried."

Tepper took his hat off, exposing his pale skin to the sun. "Winning sure feels good, I'll tell ya. Guess there's still a place for gunfighters like you in this world after all, Ranger."

"It means a lot to hear you say that," Caitlin told him, her now bandaged hands still throbbing.

Tepper felt about an empty ledge behind him. "Thought I set my bottle of root beer down here," he said, frowning. "Matter of fact, I know I did." He continued, still mystified by the bottle's absence. "Anyway, what we do know is that you managed to solve the case your dad, granddad, and me couldn't. Teo Braga's no better than the garbage he disposes of. Soon as he recovers from that gunshot wound, we'll arrest the son of a bitch as an accessory to whatever you want to call this."

"It won't stick, Captain. You know that as well as me."

"But it'll feel good to make him uncomfortable for a time," Tepper said with a wink. "I'll tell you this much, he and Jones are a goddamn match made in heaven."

"Or hell," Caitlin told him.

* * * *

She and Cort Wesley stood near the edge of the *Mariah* not far from where Anwar al-Awlaki had dropped sixty feet to the sea.

"I'd like to pick up our conversation," Caitlin said to Cort Wesley.

"Which part?"

"The one about you not wanting me around anymore."

Cort Wesley eased his arm around Caitlin's shoulder and drew her in close. "I don't recall saying anything of the kind."

"I think I'm done looking for fights I don't need. I think that's finally been burned out of me."

"Earl or Jim Strong ever face a similar transition?"

"My granddad after the Galveston Island fiasco when he was near eighty and my dad after his heart started to give out. What?" Caitlin added, when Cort Wesley continued to look at her without responding. "What?"

"I believe you know."

She gave up on that train of thought. "Like you're any different. Like Dylan's not exactly the same and even Luke more than you think."

"I believe a point is coming here."

"We're the Addams Family of Texas, Cort Wesley. A genuine freak show. All that's missing is the old, dark mansion."

Cort Wesley started to smile. Then his expression went distant and dreamy as he tightened his grasp on her. "Moments like this got me through Cereso. Picturing them's how I won all those fights."

"You forgetting the boys?"

"Not once. Never. You still up for that vacation?

Guns, cell phones, video games, and teenage girls all left behind."

"Well, I've never been to Disney World," Caitlin said, feeling the rigid band of muscle that extended from the bottom of his rib cage across his abdomen.

For a moment, Cort Wesley thought he spotted Leroy Epps casting him a wink from a nearby stanchion he was leaning against. Then he moved his gaze toward the deep blue waters before them, empty and strangely calm for as far as the eye could see.

"Actually, I was thinking about a fishing trip instead," he said, joining Caitlin in a smile and then a kiss.

Turning away from the Gulf, he noticed Leroy Epps was gone, an empty bottle of root beer left on the rig's grated deck where his ghost had been standing. He watched Caitlin retrieve it, shaking her head as she poured out the last few drops.

"I believe Captain Tepper may finally be losing it, Cort Wesley."

He took the bottle from her, certain he could smell the talcum powder with which old Leroy regularly doused himself. "Losing something's not a problem, Ranger, when you know how to get it back."

"Amen to that," Caitlin said, kissing him again as a laughing gull swooped toward the choppy waters below and plucked a grunion from the surface.

Turn the page for a preview of

STRONG
RAIN
FALLING

·

Jon Land

Available in August 2013
from Tom Doherty Associates

A FORGE BOOK

I

PROVIDENCE, RHODE ISLAND

Caitlin Strong was waiting downstairs in a grassy park bisected by concrete walkways when Dylan Torres emerged from the building. The boy fit in surprisingly well with the Brown University college students he slid between in approaching her, his long black hair bouncing just past his shoulders and attracting the attention of more than one passing coed.

"How'd it go?" Caitlin asked, rising from the bench that felt like a sauna in the sun.

Dylan shrugged and blew some stray hair from his face with his breath. "Size could be an issue."

"For playing football at this level, I expect so."

"Coach Estes didn't rule it out. He just said there were no more first-year slots left in the program."

"First year?"

"Freshman, Caitlin."

"How'd you leave it?" she asked, feeling dwarfed by the athletic buildings that housed playing courts, training facilities, a swimming pool, full gym, and the offices of the school's coaches. The buildings enclosed the parklike setting on three sides, leaving the street side to be rimmed by an eight-foot wall of carefully layered stone. Playing fields took up the rear of the complex beyond the buildings and, while waiting for Dylan, Caitlin heard the clang of aluminum bats hitting baseballs and thunks of what sounded like soccer balls being kicked about. Funny how living in a place the size of Texas made her antsy within an area where so much was squeezed so close.

"Well, short of me growing another four inches and putting on maybe twenty pounds of muscle, it's gonna be an uphill battle," Dylan said, looking down. "That is, if I even get into this place. That's an uphill battle too."

She reached out and touched his shoulder. "This coming from a kid who's bested serial killers, kidnappers, and last year a human monster who bled venom instead of blood."

Dylan started to shrug, but smiled instead. "Helps that you and my dad were there to gun them all down."

"Well, I don't believe we'll be shooting Coach Estes, and my point was if anybody can handle an uphill battle or two, it's you."

Dylan lapsed into silence, leaving Caitlin to think of the restaurant they'd eaten at the night before, where the waitress had complimented her on having such a good-looking son. She'd felt her insides turn to mush when the boy smiled and went right on studying the menu, not bothering to correct the woman. He was three quarters through a fifth year at San Antonio's St. Anthony Catholic High School, in range of finishing the year with straight A's. Though the school didn't formally offer such a program, Caitlin's captain, D. W. Tepper, had convinced them to make an exception on behalf of the Texas Rangers by slightly altering their Senior Connection program to fit the needs of a boy whose grades hadn't anywhere near matched his potential yet.

Not that it was an easy fit. The school's pristine campus in historic Monte Vista just north of downtown San Antonio was populated by boys and girls in staid, prescribed uniforms that made Dylan cringe. Blazers instead of shapeless shirts worn out at the waist, khakis instead of jeans gone from sagging to, more recently, what they called skinny, and hard leather dress shoes instead of the boots Caitlin had bought him for his birthday a few years back. But the undermanned football team had recruited him early on, Dylan donning a uniform for the first time since his brief stint in the Pop Warner Football League as a young boy, when his mother was still alive and the father he'd yet to meet was in prison. This past fall at St. Anthony's he'd taken to the sport again like a natural, playing running back and sifting through the tiniest holes in the defensive line to amass vast chunks of yardage. Dylan ended up being named Second Team All TAPPS District 2-5A, attracting the attention of several small colleges, though none on the level of Brown University, a perennial contender for the Ivy League crown.

Caitlin found those Friday nights, sitting with Cort Wesley Masters and his younger son Luke in stands ripe with the first soft bite of fall, strangely comforting. Given that she'd never had much use for such things in her own teenage years, the experience left her feeling as if she'd been transported back in time, with a chance to relive her own youth through a boy who was as close to a son as she'd ever have. Left her recalling her own high school days smelling of gun oil instead of perfume. She'd been awkward then, gawky after growing tall fast. Still a few years short of forty, Caitlin had never added to that five-foot-seven-inch frame, although the present found her filled out and firm from regular workouts and jogging. She wore her wavy black hair more fashionably styled, but kept it the very same length she always had, perhaps in a misguided attempt to slow time if not stop it altogether.

Gazing at Dylan now, she recalled the headmaster of his school, a cousin of Caitlin's own high school principal, coming up to her after the victorious opening home game.

"The school owes you a great bit of gratitude, Ranger."

"Well, sir, I'll bet Dylan'll do even better next week."

The headmaster gestured toward the newly installed lights. "I meant gratitude to the Rangers arranging for the variance that allowed us to go forward with the installation. That's the only reason we're able to be here tonight."

She'd nodded, smiling to herself at how Captain Tepper had managed to arrange Dylan's admission. "Our pleasure, sir."

Now, months later, on the campus of an Ivy League school in Providence, Rhode Island, Dylan looked down at the grass and then up again, something furtive lurking in his suddenly narrowed eyes. The sun sneaking through a nearby tree dappled his face and further hid what he was about to share.

"I got invited to a frat party."

"Say that again."

"I got invited to a party at this frat called D-Phi."

"D *what*?"

"Short for Delta Phi. Like the Greek letters."

"I know they're Greek letters, son, just like I know what goes on at these kind of parties given that I've been called to break them up on more than one occasion."

"You're the one who made me start thinking about college."

"Doesn't mean I got you thinking about doing shots and playing beer pong."

"Beirut."

Caitlin looked at him as if he were speaking a foreign language.

"They call it Beirut here, not beer pong," Dylan continued. "And it's important I get a notion of what campus life is like. You told me that too."

"I did?"

"Uh-huh."

"I let you go to this party, you promise you won't drink?"

Dylan rolled his head from side to side. "I promise I won't drink *much*."

"What's that mean?"

"That I'll be just fine when you come pick me up in the morning to get to the airport."

"Pick you up," Caitlin repeated, her gaze narrowing.

"I'm staying with this kid from Texas who plays on the team. Coach set it up."

"Coach Estes?"

"Yup. Why?"

Caitlin slapped an arm around the boy's shoulder and steered him toward the street. "Because I may rethink my decision about shooting him."

"I told him you were a Texas Ranger," Dylan said, as they approached a pair of workmen stringing a tape measure outside the athletic complex's hockey rink.

"What'd he think about that?" Caitlin said, finding

her gaze drawn to the two men she noticed had no tools and were wearing scuffed shoes instead of work boots.

"He said he liked gals with guns."

They continued along the walkway that curved around the parklike grounds, banking left at a small lot where Caitlin had parked her rental. She worked the remote to unlock the doors and watched Dylan ease around to the passenger side, while she turned back toward the hockey rink and the two workmen she couldn't shake from her mind.

But they were gone.

2

PROVIDENCE, RHODE ISLAND

"What's this WaterFire thing?" Dylan asked, spooning up the last of his ice cream while Caitlin sipped her nightly post-dinner coffee.

"Like a tradition here. Comes highly recommended."

"You don't want me going to that frat party."

"The thought had crossed my mind, but I'm guessing the WaterFire'll be done 'fore your party even gets started."

Dylan held the spoon in his hand and then licked at it.

"How's the ice cream?"

"It's gelato."

"What's the difference?"

"None, I guess.

They had chosen to eat at a restaurant called Paragon, again on the recommendation of Coach Estes, a fashionably loud, lit, and reasonably priced bistro-like restaurant on the student-dominated Thayer Street, not far from the university's bookstore. Dylan ordered a pizza while Caitlin ruminated over the menu choices before eventually opting for what she always did: a steak. You can take the gal out of Texas, she thought to herself, but you can't take Texas out of the gal.

"I hear this WaterFire is something special," Caitlin said, when she saw him checking his watch.

"Yeah? Who told you that?"

"Coach Estes. What do you say we head downtown and check it out?"

They walked through the comfortable cool of the early-evening darkness, a welcome respite from the sweltering spring heat wave that had struck Texas just before they'd left. Caitlin wanted to talk, but Dylan wouldn't look up from his iPhone, banging out text after text.

They strolled up a slight hill and then down a steeper one, joining the thick flow of people heading for the sounds of the nighttime festival known as WaterFire. The air was crisp and laced with the pungent aroma of wood smoke drifting up from Providence's downtown area, where the masses of milling people were headed. The scents grew stronger while the harmonic strains of music sharpened the closer they drew to an area bridged by walkways crisscrossing a river that ran the entire length of the modest office buildings and residential towers that dominated the city's skyline. A performance area had been roped off at the foot of the hill, currently occupied by a group of white-faced mimes. An array of pushcarts offering various grilled meats as well as snacks and sweets were lined up nearby, most with hefty lines before them.

The tightest clusters of festival patrons moved in both directions down a walkway at the river's edge. Caitlin realized the strange and haunting strains of music had their origins down here as well, and moved to join the flow. The black water shimmered like glass, an eerie glow emanating from its surface. Boaters and canoeists paddled leisurely by. A water taxi packed with seated patrons sipping wine slid past, followed by what looked like a gondola straight from Venice.

But it was the source of the orange glow reflecting off the water's surface that claimed Caitlin's attention. She could now identify the pungent scent of wood smoke as that of pine and cedar, hearing the familiar crackle of flames as she and Dylan reached a promenade that ran directly alongside the river.

"Caitlin?" Dylan prodded, touching her shoulder.

She jerked to her right, stiffening, the boy's hand like a hot iron against her shirt.

"Uh-oh," the boy said. "You got that look."

"Just don't like crowds," Caitlin managed, casting her gaze about. "That's all."

A lie, because she felt something wasn't right, out of rhythm somehow. Her stomach had already tightened and now she could feel the bands of muscle in her neck and shoulders knotting up as well.

"Yeah?" Dylan followed before she forced a smile. "And, like, I'm supposed to believe that?"

Before them, a line of bonfires that seemed to rise

out of the water curved along the expanse of the Providence Riverwalk. The source of these bonfires, Caitlin saw now, were nearly a hundred steel braziers of flaming wood moored to the water's surface and stoked by black-shirted workers in a square, pontoonlike boat, including one who performed an elaborate fire dance in between tending the flames.

The twisting line of braziers seemed to stretch forever into the night. Caitlin and Dylan, amid the crowd, continued to follow their bright glow, keeping the knee-high retaining wall on their right. More kiosks selling hot dogs, grilled meats to be stuffed in pockets, kabobs, beverages, and souvenirs had been set up on streets and sidewalks above the Riverwalk. The sights and sounds left her homesick for Texas, the sweet smell of wood smoke reminding her of the scent of barbecue and grilled food wafting over the famed San Antonio River Walk.

Caitlin was imagining that smell when she felt *something*, not much and not even identifiable at first, yet enough to make her neck hairs stand up. A ripple in the crowd, she realized an instant later, followed almost immediately by more of a buckling indicative of someone forcing their way through it. Instinct twisted Caitlin in the direction of the ripple's origin and the flames' glow caught a face that was familiar to her.

Because it belonged to one of the workman she'd glimpsed outside the hockey rink back at Brown University. And the second workman stood directly alongside him, hands pulling their jackets back enough to reveal the dark glint of the pistols wedged into their belts.